# SHELL GAME

# SHELL GAME

### INSPIRED BY ACTUAL EVENTS

## JOSEPH BADAL

SUSPENSE PUBLISHING

SHELL GAME
by
Joseph Badal

DIGITAL EDITION
* * * * *
PUBLISHED BY:
Suspense Publishing

Joseph Badal
Copyright © 2012 Joseph Badal

PUBLISHING HISTORY:
Suspense Publishing, Paperback and Digital Copy, June 2012

ISBN: 0615654843
ISBN-13: 978-0615654843

This is a work of fiction. Names, characters, places, brands, media, and incidents are either the product of the author's imagination or are used fictitiously. The author acknowledges the trademarked status and trademark owners of various products referenced in this work of fiction, which have been used without permission. The publication/use of these trademarks

BOOKS BY JOSEPH BADAL

The Pythagorean Solution
Evil Deeds (Bob Danforth Series, #1)
Terror Cell (Bob Danforth Series, #2)
The Nostradamus Secret (Bob Danforth Series #3)

# DEDICATION

" Shell Game" is dedicated to my son, Robert, who has been a great source of pride to me in all his endeavors and accomplishments.

# ACKNOWLEDGEMENTS

My gratitude and thanks go to my friend, Byron Matthews, a serious student of the recent financial markets meltdown, who cajoled me to write this story and who suggested a number of changes that improved the content and flow of the book.

My thanks, as always, to my agent, Maureen Walters, Curtis-Brown, Ltd., who has given freely of her advice and support.

I appreciate the help provided by my friend, Lewis Campbell, who reviewed the manuscript for legal accuracy. He made a real difference.

Many thanks to John & Shannon Raab for their assistance and encouragement.

I want to acknowledge the bankers and business owners who suffer from arbitrary rules set down by Federal regulators who were asleep at the switch when capital markets were operating out of control, and who now have over-reacted and are taking past errors out on community banks and their clients all over the United States.

Finally, I want to thank my many readers for their support and encouragement. You stimulate me to continue writing. Your feedback makes a difference.

"Banking has never seemed so dirty as it does in "Shell Game," the pulse-pounding new thriller from Joseph Badal. The author brings a lifetime of business experience to this tale, which shows how banking regulations can ruin lives and how a villain can manipulate such rules for his own gain. Don't miss it!"

—Steve Brewer, author of "Lost Vegas"

"Yes, He Can! Once again Joseph Badal has proved himself a thriller author above the ordinary cut. Some may think it impossible to write a convincing (and exciting) novel about the recent bank implosions and real estate market collapse, but Joe has both the chops in investment banking and the narrative skill of a polished suspense author to pull off this difficult feat.

"It's a high dive for anyone to try, but Joe Badal scores a "10" with this judge."

—Rob Kresge, author of the Warbonnet historical mysteries and former CIA senior analyst

"Another tightly plotted, deftly executed page turner from a master of suspense and international intrigue. Joseph Badal writes timely stories with authority and compassion. Highly recommended."

—Sheldon Siegel, *New York Times* bestselling author of "Perfect Alibi"

# AUTHOR'S HISTORICAL NOTE

"Shell Game" is inspired by actual events that occurred in the United States economy and were the results of a long-term series of actions. Although not a complete list, the following are some of the more important macro-economic, micro-economic, and political events and actions which led to the capital markets crisis that began in 2007, affecting the U.S. and global economies, and precipitating a housing crisis, high unemployment, and a stock market crash:

In 1975, The U.S. Congress passed the Community Reinvestment Act, which, in part, forced banks to make loans to weak borrowers.

Between 1991 and 2008, the Government Service Enterprises, the Federal National Mortgage Association ("Fannie Mae") and the Federal Home Loan Mortgage Corporation ("Freddie Mac"), became rabidly political, making huge political campaign contributions, compromising Congressional oversight of these entities.

Between 1991 and 2008, Congress authorized expanding Fannie Mae and Freddie Mac, which gave them the ability to do greater lending volume with lower lending standards. This allowed the GSEs to make sub-prime loans.

In 1995, the U.S. Congress ruled that 42% of all Fannie Mae and Freddie Mac loans must go to low-income borrowers.

Between 1995 and 1999, the Federal Reserve prepared the economic ground for another boom/bust cycle by expanding the U.S. money supply and thereby reducing interest rates.

In 2000, Congress ruled that 50% of all Fannie Mae and Freddie Mac loans must go to low-income borrowers.

In 2003, the Federal Reserve lowered the Federal Funds interest rate to 1% and left it at that extremely low level for one year.

In 2003, Fannie Mae and Freddie Mac bought $82 billion of sub-prime loans.

In 2004, the Housing & Urban Development Agency ruled that by 2007 56% of all loans it guaranteed should be for low-income borrowers.

Between 2003 and 2008, the U.S. Congress ignored repeated warnings about a housing bubble.

When it became apparent in 2007 that the above events and actions had created an unhealthy excess in the housing market and in the economy in general, the U.S. Congress and the U.S. Treasury took little or no action to mitigate the problem.

From 2008 to 2012, Congress and the U.S. President scapegoated the issue by blaming Wall Street and the banking community.

There is no question greed played a huge part in creating recent economic problems. Participants in that greed included borrowers, lenders, investors, rating agencies, Wall Street investment banking firms, politicians, and others. The housing bubble was not just a banker-generated or a Wall Street-generated event. Without the excess perpetrated by Congress, U.S. Presidents, and the Federal Reserve, the housing bubble wouldn't have occurred and the economy would not have been as badly damaged as it was.

Every American is painfully aware of the economic recession that began in 2007/2008. What most Americans are not aware of is that the heavy-handed actions of Federal bank examiners exacerbated the situation, restricting community banks from making commercial real estate loans, mandating that banks raise capital at a time when capital was not readily available, taking over banks all over the country and selling them to investors, and forcing banks to pay bloated FDIC insurance premiums three years in advance. These regulatory actions made the real estate market even weaker, driving down valuations and rents and raising vacancy rates.

I labeled the capital markets crash that began in August 2007 as a "1929 event," and used that language in August 2007 when I communicated my fears about the future impact of the crash with members of Congress and with U.S. Treasury officials. My warnings were ignored.

Time has proved my warnings correct, but I gain no satisfaction from this. I can only wish the brain trusts in Washington, D.C. and on Wall Street have learned something from past and current events. I am not hopeful.

# 1989

## PROLOGUE

Katherine Winter had had it made. Not that she was arrogant or over-confident about it. That's just the way things were. Tall, blonde, athletic, and beautiful in a patrician, Grace Kelly way, she looked at least five years younger than her thirty-seven years. She was married to Frank Winter, the love of her life, and had two bright, healthy children: Thirteen-year-old Edward and eight-year-old Carrie.

The family had a comfortable life, living in a five-bedroom home on a two-acre lot in Chestnut Hill, a high-end community on the northwest side of Philadelphia. The children attended private schools in the area. They summered in Cape May, New Jersey, where the family owned a vacation home, and took annual ski trips to Taos, New Mexico.

Frank Winter was president and majority shareholder of First Savings Bank, chairing the board of the local country club while Katherine oversaw the board of Carrie's school and served as a director of several popular charitable organizations.

Katherine's vision for the future was all "up" and no "down." Until forty-year-old Frank had dropped dead from a massive coronary episode in 1988.

Frank had been Katherine's first and only love, her hero. They'd met at the expensive Villanova University, which Frank, the third son of a western Pennsylvanian coal miner, attended on a football scholarship, and Katherine, the orphan child of Irish immigrants killed in a car wreck, attended on an academic scholarship.

Losing Frank was a numbing nightmare to Katherine. But she sublimated her grief as she tried to comfort her son and daughter. She saw their sorrow in the strain on their faces, in the lost look in their eyes. Edward no longer met people's gazes, preferring to stare at the floor, slightly hunching his shoulders. Carrie alternated between crying and retreating into an emotionless, silent shell. For the five days between their father's death and his funeral, the children retreated into a dark universe Katherine couldn't penetrate.

On the day of the funeral, Frank's absence stabbed at Katherine. The children's silence and obvious grief were weights immersing her in an ink-dark gelatinous pool from which there was no escape. Her son was catatonic. At least Carrie, when she cried, showed her grief.

The family walked from the limousine to the gravesite. While Carrie lagged behind, Katherine wrapped her arm around Edward's teenage shoulders, hoping to feel something other than the rigidity that had defined him for the last five days. Twenty steps from the car, Edward suddenly stopped and turned to face her. Katherine searched his face, waiting for him to speak.

"Mom, I'll take care of you and Carrie," he said, a seriousness in his voice she had never heard before. "I don't want you to worry about a thing."

This was the last thing she imagined her son telling her, and it was the last thing she wanted to hear.

Two days later, on Monday morning, Katherine met with Paul Sanders, the family attorney. Professionally, she had dealt minimally with Paul; Frank had handled their business affairs and her contacts with the lawyer had been primarily social. Paul was a distinguished, professorial-looking Philadelphia lawyer from the Main Line. He was of medium height and trim, and she couldn't remember a time when she had seen him wearing anything but a blue pinstripe suit. Katherine had always vaguely liked the man, but thought he was nerdy and perhaps too obsessed with the law.

"I'm so sorry about your loss, Katherine," Paul told her. "I can't believe he's gone. Frank and I used to talk nearly every day. I feel a void I can't seem to fill."

"Thank you, Paul. I know you and Frank were close. He thought the world of you."

"He was my best friend."

"Mine, too,"

Paul nodded and sighed. "Well, shall we take care of business?"

Katherine nodded back.

Paul pulled out a chair in front of his desk for Katherine, then walked around to the other side and sat down. He cleared his throat and opened a file on his desk.

"Frank accumulated significant assets—real estate primarily." He paused and cleared his throat again, looking at Katherine uncomfortably. "Unfortunately, nearly everything is mortgaged.

With the recent downturn in real estate values due to the Tax Reform Act passed two years ago and the recent acceleration in interest rates, there isn't much equity left."

"What does that mean, Paul?" Katherine asked, feeling suddenly flushed. She shifted in her seat.

"It means Frank borrowed to get into real estate deals with a promoter. He even took out mortgages on your Cape May place and your residence here in Philadelphia. In the current market environment, any sale of these properties would yield almost nothing after paying closing costs.

"Our home, too? She paused, taking his silence as her answer. "How's that possible?"

Paul didn't look her in the eyes. "You signed all the loan documents, Katherine."

"I didn't know what I was signing. Frank managed these things."

"I know"

"What about the bank accounts?" she asked.

"Well, of course there is *some* cash." He riffled through the file and clarified: "$23,000 and change in a checking account, and $188,000 in Frank's retirement account."

"At least there's the bank stock," Katherine said. "We—"

Paul interrupted. "He used the bank stock to collateralize the real estate debt. The dividends from the stock have covered part of the losses from the real estate holdings over the last couple of years. Half his salary was being used for the same purpose. He even borrowed against his life insurance policies to support the real estate deals. So, there's little you can expect to get from those policies. With Frank gone, without his salary, the banks he borrowed from have started to protect themselves. They want to know how you're going to keep the loans current."

"How can I make those payments? I have no income of my own."

"If you can't make the payments, the banks will foreclose on the real estate and the bank stock, which will involve a protracted, expensive legal process."

Katherine covered her face with her hands. She sat silently for several seconds, then dropped her hands and stared blankly at Paul. "What does this mean?"

"I've had appraisal reviews done on all the real estate: Apartment houses, warehouses, one office building. I asked a realtor to write up a market analysis on your home here and the Cape May place. The only property that has any real equity is your primary residence. Trying to hold on to any of the properties will make your financial situation worse. Because of the economy, the commercial properties have a lot of vacancies, meaning the rents don't cover the expenses. With no other income, you have no way to cover the mortgage payments and other expenses. The upshot is you can pull about $25,000 from your home, the $23,000 in the checking account, $27,000 from the insurance policies, and the $188,000 from Frank's retirement account. That's $263,000 in total. There will be taxes and expenses to pay on that, income and probate. You might have $200,000 after all is said and done."

Katherine steeled herself for her next question. "What about all the real estate loans you referred to?"

"I've contacted the lenders. They seemed amenable to taking title to the properties and writing off the loans against them if they can avoid going through the foreclosure process. It's called taking deeds in lieu of foreclosure. This will avoid legal fees and months, if not years, of aggravation and legal wrangling."

"Does this mean I'll lose all of the real estate, including our homes?"

"That's exactly what it means." Paul hesitated a moment and added, "Frank wasn't stupid, Katherine. He made excellent investments that, in the long run, would have paid off. With his job, he kept the payments current. He just got whipsawed in the current real estate cycle." Frank rubbed his temples and then added, "When those idiots in Congress passed the 1986 Tax Reform Act, they ruined the commercial real estate market."

"You mentioned a promoter a minute ago."

"Yeah, the guy who put Frank into all of these real estate deals. Fellow named Gerald Folsom."

An electric jolt ripped through Katherine. Gerald Folsom. She hadn't thought about that bastard in at least fifteen years, and now she learns it was Folsom who had put Frank into the real estate deals that had ruined them. Katherine felt disoriented and nauseated. It wasn't possible. Frank had never mentioned Folsom to her. But Frank had never brought business matters home.

"What's wrong, Katherine?" Paul asked.

"I . . . nothing." She brushed away a tear and said, "Paul, I won't pretend to understand any of this, but still . . . .. How could I not have had a clue about any of this? How could I have been so unaware? Frank had to be under tremendous stress."

"Don't beat yourself up. How could you have known if Frank didn't share his problems with you?"

Katherine stood, took in a big breath and let it rattle out slowly. She tucked her handbag under her left arm and shook Paul's hand. "I appreciate what you have done. Please make the arrangements with the lenders. I'll sign the . . . what did you call them?"

"Deeds in lieu of foreclosure."

"I'll sign the deeds in lieu of foreclosure. Please act on the house first. I don't want to live there any longer than necessary. Too many memories."

"I'll take care of everything."

Katherine released Paul's hand and forced a smile. "I know you will, Paul."

He hustled to reach the office door before her. In a quiet voice, he said, "You know he thought he'd live forever. All he ever thought about was doing the right thing for you and the children. The investments were intended to make your futures secure."

"Thanks, Paul."

Katherine left the office and walked stiffly to her car. Leaning against the car door, the events of the last week broke through her mental dam: Frank's death, her children's terrible withdrawal and heartbreak, and the realization their life style was about to change in dramatic fashion. And a thought pierced her brain like a red-hot spike: What if all that had happened had been because of what happened between her and Gerald Folsom fifteen years ago? Tears pushed through the cracks. What was she going to do? How was she going to tell her son and daughter they had just lost their home? How was she going to live with the guilt?


Paul had looked out his window and watched Katherine Winter in her car. She could have been crying but he couldn't be certain. He thought about going outside to comfort her. He badly wanted to hold her in his arms and tell her that everything would be fine, that he would see to it. But what could he say to her that would make a difference? That would be appropriate? Sorry, Frank Winter had screwed up? Sure Frank was intelligent, but he was also naïve. Too naïve to be a successful investor. The man knew how to lend and provide great service to his bank customers; he should have stuck to that. He was too trusting. Especially in the case of doing business with Gerald Folsom.

There was nothing Paul could legally pin on Folsom, but the man always seemed to come out ahead of his partners in any deal. That was the scuttlebutt, anyway. When Frank came to him with Folsom's prospectuses, Paul told him to walk away. Frank was putting up all the equity; Folsom was getting a significant percent of the deals in return for sweat equity and managing the properties. But Frank ignored his advice. And, to make matters worse, Frank had borrowed much of the equity he'd invested.

Paul reflected on how quickly the banks had indicated they would consider taking over the properties. He'd expected a bigger battle. None of the bankers even hesitated in offering to write off the loans if Katherine signed the properties over to them. He scratched his head and wondered if there was something sinister behind their decisions. Even the banks holding Frank's First Savings Bank stock were quick to strike a deal in return for Katherine signing away her interest in the stock. Normally, the stock would have had significant equity over and above the loans against the shares. But First Savings Bank's loan portfolio had deteriorated with the real estate depression brought on by the Tax Reform Act of 1986, so its stock value had declined as well.

Paul told himself he would have to look into all of this at some point. Maybe after things were settled for Katherine and her children.

# THURSDAY
# JULY 14, 2011

# CHAPTER ONE

Katherine Winter looked up at the dais and felt warmth of pride in her son course through her. Twenty-two years had passed since her husband had died, and her son had not wasted one minute on self-pity, nor used his father's death as an excuse for not giving his best.

Edward attended Central High School, finishing at the top of his class. Then he attended the University of Pennsylvania on a full scholarship, and received his MBA from Harvard Business School, again on a full ride. And he'd always held down a job, even while in school, to cover his out of pocket expenses. Carrie too, had soared, earning her own scholarship. The money Katherine had put aside for their educations had not been needed.

After graduate school, Edward joined the U.S. Army, went to Infantry School at Fort Benning, Georgia, and graduated first in his officer candidate class. His three-year hitch was almost up when Islamic extremists crashed airplanes into the World Trade Center towers and the Pentagon on September 11th. He extended his tour for one year and was assigned to Iraq, where he earned two Purple Hearts, a Silver Star, a Bronze Star, and a Meritorious Service Medal.

The night Edward returned to Philadelphia and civilian life from Iraq, Katherine disclosed to her children she had $425,000, half for each of them. She'd invested the money from Frank's insurance wisely. But neither of them wanted the money. Katherine was adamant, however. "Just tell me when you want it and it's yours," she told them.

Two months later, Edward and Carrie came to her with a proposal. The family of one of Edward's Harvard classmates owned a chain of fast food restaurants named Hot N' Chili, specializing in Mexican food in the New Mexico style. Edward's friend, Peter Mora, had worked in the company's Santa Fe headquarters since he'd graduated from Harvard and was now in charge of national franchising. Mora had contacted Edward with a proposal to take over the franchise rights for all of Pennsylvania, along with two restaurants that were floundering. He made them a sweetheart deal, waiving the franchise fees in return for them assuming two $250,000 delinquent loans at a local bank covering the costs of the two existing restaurant locations.

Carrie partnered with Edward in the restaurant investment, and both of them agreed to take the money from Katherine only if she joined them as a one-third partner. That was in January 2002.

Carrie worked in the business for two years, but then decided it wasn't what she wanted. The business was just starting to take off when she announced she was going to join the Army. She went to Officer Candidate School, graduated with her commission as a Second Lieutenant, and was recruited by Special Forces, being promoted to First Lieutenant within the year. She had quickly earned her green beret, jump wings, and a reputation as a rising star. After a year of language training in Arabic, she was assigned to Iraq in an intelligence role. Although women were not permitted to serve in Special Operations assignments, she came as close to being a Special Ops officer as a woman could.

A noise brought Katherine abruptly back to the present. Someone had tapped the microphone on the dais. She refocused on the day's event and Edward's recognition for his achievements with Winter Enterprises. Now nine years since forming the company, they owned twenty-four restaurants in and around Philadelphia. The business grossed over $58,000,000 annually and employed four hundred people. Katherine's dividends from the business enabled her to move from the tiny bungalow in Germantown to a new three-bedroom home on five acres on Philadelphia's Main Line. Edward and his wife, Betsy, owned their own home in Chestnut Hill. Betsy was pregnant and due in less than four weeks. Carrie was still happily single at twenty-nine years of age and running around the world doing God-knows-what for the Army.

Katherine smiled at Betsy, seated to her left, and then turned to the right to smile at Paul Sanders. Paul had bloomed into a dear friend since Frank died and he now handled Edward's legal affairs.

"Quite a ride, Kat," Paul said. "Frank would be proud of all of you."

# FRIDAY
# JULY 15, 2011

# CHAPTER TWO

Edward Winter was still riding an emotional high from the Chamber of Commerce luncheon yesterday when he arrived for his appointment with Stanley Burns, his account officer and Senior Credit Officer at Broad Street National Bank. He stopped outside the bank entrance and buttoned his suit jacket. He'd worn his banker's outfit for the appointment today: Blue pinstripe suit, red power tie, and black Ferragamo tasseled loafers. Shifting his black leather briefcase to his left hand, he walked confidently through the entrance to the elevator at the back of the lobby, then rode up one floor to the mezzanine to stop at Burns' secretary's desk on the edge of the bank's executive level. The building dated back to the 1920s and looked like what Edward always thought banks should look like: Marble floors and counters, brass teller cages, and lots of heavy mahogany furniture. He smirked to himself. Considering the amount of interest he paid to the bank on his loans, the least the bank could do was create a plush environment for the customers.

"Hello, Helen. How are you today? Is Mr. Burns treating you well?" This was a standard part of the banter between Edward and Helen. He always told her she could come work for him if she wasn't being treated well.

"Everything's fine, Mr. Winter," the woman said in a monotone, dry voice. "I'll tell Mr. Burns you're here."

Edward was surprised at Helen. She must be having a particularly bad day, he thought. Helen returned a few seconds later.

"You can go in now, Mr. Winter," she said, an apologetic look on her face.

Edward walked past Helen's desk into Stanley Burns' office. Burns stood and greeted him, then ushered him into his usual chair. "Please sit down, Edward," Burns said, closing the office door and seating himself opposite Edward.

"You look beat, Stan," Edward said.

Burns shrugged. "The economy's impacting a lot of our clients."

Edward passed Burns a financial report his Chief Financial Officer, Nick Scarfatti, had prepared for the second quarter ending June 30. "Thank God our business hasn't been impacted." He didn't want to gloat, especially when so many other businesses were suffering, but Edward was more than pleased with the condition of Winter Enterprises, Inc. "You will see in those reports that our sales are up. We're requesting an increase in our credit to finance the acquisition of seven new sites and the construction of new restaurant buildings in Pittsburg. We've already identified the managers for all seven of those stores. We—"

Burns held up a hand, stopping him. "Before you get too far along with this, I need to tell you there are a lot of changes going on around here. We're . . . I'm sorry to tell you, we will not be able to finance any more of your sites."

Edward felt as though he'd been punched in the gut. "What are you talking about? Our financial condition has never been better."

"We just can't extend you any more credit. That's it. Plain and simple."

Edward tried to calm his anger. "Stan, do I recall correctly that you begged me to move my business to Broad Street National three years ago and told me at that time your bank had a statutory loan limit of $40 million to any one customer? We currently owe you $20 million, secured by at least $50 million worth of real estate. We've never been late a day on any of our loan payments, and we keep several million dollars in deposits with you. So what the hell's going on?"

"It's a different environment out there, Edward. We can't do what we used to do. It's just that simple."

"You keep saying that, Stan. But it's not simple. We've got a huge growth opportunity here. We're growing market share as our competition is falling by the wayside, closing locations, or going out of business entirely. There's never been a market more conducive to growth, and now you're telling me you don't want to be our financing partner anymore?" Edward stood and looked down at Burns fiercely. "This is a hell of a shot out of left field, Stan. I've already signed purchase agreements, put down forfeitable earnest money deposits on lots in Pittsburgh, and signed employment contracts with the seven store managers based on your past assurances of financing support." He turned to leave the office when Burns' tired voice halted him.

"Edward, please sit down. I haven't told you everything."

He whipped back around. "What more could there be?"

"The bank's under a great deal of pressure. The Federal bank regulators ordered us to reduce our exposure to commercial real estate. You're one of our largest commercial real estate borrowers, so the loan committee has instructed me to reduce our commitment to your company specifically."

Edward, still standing, glared malevolently at Burns. "You've already explained that to me."

"No. You misunderstand. We want you to pay off all of your loans as soon as possible."

Edward laughed bitterly. "What are you smoking, Stan? The bank is making a lot of money off my business. You probably don't have a better client than Winter Enterprises. We've got a large amount of equity in the real estate you've financed and we pay our bills on time. Is this a joke?"

Burns' face had turned beet red. "This is no joke. I can't tell you how badly I feel about this. I'm just following orders."

"We have a loan commitment from the bank. We signed a master note with a twenty-year maturity on it, backed by all twenty-four of our restaurant properties."

"That's true, Edward, but the bank has the right to call that note at the end of each five-year anniversary of the note. The first five-year anniversary is July 29 of this year. We will need you to make other arrangements so you can pay us off entirely by no later than that date."

"That's two weeks from now. Impossible."

"Nevertheless, that's the way it's got to be."

"I want to talk to Sol Levin."

Burns sighed. "That won't do you any good."

"I'll be the judge of that," Edward said.

"The regulators ordered our board of directors to terminate Mr. Levin this morning. He's no longer the president of the bank."

# CHAPTER THREE

Edward was as angry as he could remember ever being. He didn't quite understand the machinations behind the bank's actions, but he sure as hell understood the implications. Now he had to go through the painful process of establishing another banking relationship in two weeks, putting together a massive loan application package and then schmoozing some new banker who knew nothing of his business and escorting the new banker to some or all twenty-four of his restaurant locations. By the time he reached his dark-blue Corvette parked in the bank parking lot, he'd calmed down enough to plot out a course of action. It would take a lot of time and effort to get together the package, but there had to be at least half a dozen banks in the area big enough to handle Winter Enterprise's business and which would salivate at the opportunity.

After driving out of downturn and getting on the Schuylkill Expressway back to his office in Mt. Airy, Edward called Nick Scarfatti, his CFO, on his cell phone to ask him to clear his schedule that afternoon.

"What's up?" Nick asked.

"Broad Street National Bank just dumped us as a client. I'll explain when I get there." He paused for a second and added, "You should call Paul Sanders; have him come in about three this afternoon. And you'll need to start working on a finance package."

Edward signed off and slammed his palm against the steering wheel, knowing the poor position he'd put Nick in. Nick Scarfatti was scheduled to go to Hawaii at the end of the week for a two-week, well-deserved vacation, but there was no way Nick could be out of the office at this time. "Damn bankers," he growled, hitting the steering wheel again for good measure.

Edward was back in his office by noon. He called Nick Scarfatti into his office. As usual, Nick looked as though he'd stepped off a page from *Gentlemen's Quarterly*. His blue pinstriped suit showed no wrinkles, his white shirt was starched, and his red power tie was perfectly knotted. His black wingtip shoes were spit-shined and his hair and mustache were perfectly cut in a conservative style. He was dressed like a stereotypical Wall Street banker. Luckily for Edward and Winter Enterprises, Nick was as conscientious about preparing accurate financial reports as he was fastidious about his personal appearance.

"I hate to do this to you, Nick, but I need you here until we resolve this financing issue."

"I figured that already," Nick said with a wry grin. "My wife's going to kill me."

"I'm sorry, Nick. We're on the ropes here. Stan Burns only gave us until the end of this month to pay off our loans at the bank."

Nick waved a hand. "Annie'll understand. Eventually. I'll get started on a presentation for the banks. Which banker are you going to call first?"

"Probably Van Snowden over at Curtis Bank & Trust. He's been after me for years to take some of our business over there."

"He's a good banker, Eddie. I think Curtis Bank & Trust would treat us right."

Edward shook his head. "I just don't get it. Broad Street was kissing our butts a couple years ago. Now they, in effect, kicked those same butts out into the street."

Nick started to leave, but Edward stopped him. "Nick, don't argue here, but the company's going to pay for a trip to Hawaii for you and your family. Hopefully soon, right after we get past this hiccup. It's the least we can do."

Nick smiled, genuinely this time, at Edward. "That will take some of the heat off me when I talk to Annie. Thanks." He hesitated a second and then said, "Can I convince you to call Annie and tell her about postponing our trip?"

"I'd sooner go back to Iraq."

"Chicken."

Edward laughed. "You got that right. When do you think you'll have an updated financing package?"

"It's Wednesday. Make an appointment with Van Snowden for Monday."

"I'll do it. Thanks."

As Nick left the office, Katherine walked in.

"So, what happened at the bank?" she asked as she took a seat on the couch. "Nick told me right after you called him that they want us to pay off our loans."

"Mom, I don't have a clue. There's something really wrong at Broad Street Bank. Burns told me the regulators ordered the directors to fire their president. Sol Levin's been at the bank for twenty-five or thirty years. Wanting us to move our business can't have anything to do with us; it's got to be an internal problem at the bank. Our business is very profitable and we've always complied with the requirements of the loan agreement."

"Maybe Paul will know something; he's usually got his ear to the ground."

"He'll be here this afternoon," Edward said, nodding.

"I pulled all the bank loan files for him to review," Katherine said. "Maybe there's something in there that will give us more time."

"Good idea," Edward said, "but don't count on it. Burns wouldn't have pulled the plug on us unless he'd done his homework."

"You seem pretty calm about this."

"I am really angry at the way Burns treated me. But I'm not worried. With our history and financial position, every bank in the area should be begging us for our business. This is just a little bump in the road, albeit a painful bump." He grimaced and added, "I had to ask Nick to postpone his vacation."

"That's terrible. He's put off taking a family vacation for three years now. I don't envy—"

Nick Scarfatti entered the office quickly, without knocking, and turned on the television in the corner. "Sorry to interrupt, but I thought you'd want to see this."

The screen showed a close up of a reporter holding a microphone. The sign on the building behind her read Broad Street National Bank. " . . . but, according to a press release issued by the bank's board of directors, Broad Street National Bank is in excellent financial condition, citing that the termination of Sol Levin, the bank's long-term president, was due to deterioration in the bank's commercial real estate loan portfolio. Broad Street is one of Philadelphia's larger independent financial institutions and one of its largest commercial real estate lenders. We called the local office of the Federal Deposit Insurance Corporation to see if they had anything to add to the bank's press release, but they declined to comment. As Eye Witness News has reported over the last two years, the Federal Deposit Insurance Corporation has taken over more than two hundred banks in the United States. We will keep our viewers informed of any further developments. This is Linda Reynolds, Eye Witness News."

Nick turned off the television with the remote and gave Edward an open-armed gesture. "Very strange."

"There's more to this than 'deterioration in the bank's commercial real estate loan portfolio," Katherine offered. "That stupid reporter will probably start a run on the bank as a result of her spurious little statement about the FDIC."

"I think replacing Broad Street will work out for us," Edward said. "It sounds like they've got big problems."

After Nick and Katherine left his office, Edward pulled up Sol Levin's cell number from his BlackBerry and called him.

"Hello?" a woman answered.

"Patsy, it's Edward Winter. I just heard the news about Sol and wanted to say how sorry I am."

"Thanks, Edward," Patsy Levin said. "Let me get Sol for you."

Edward second-guessed his decision to call Sol as he waited. As bad as his problems were with the bank, Levin's appeared infinitely worse.

"Hey, Eddie," Levin said, his normal basso voice resonating over the telephone. "I appreciate the call."

"I don't know what to say or do, Sol. But if there's any way I can be of assistance, I hope you'll call me."

"Patsy and I are going to our place in the Poconos for a couple weeks. When we get back, I'll call you. Maybe we can get together for a drink."

"I'll look forward to it, Sol."

Levin didn't respond for a moment and Edward wasn't sure what else to say. He was about to say goodbye when Levin said, "I'm not the only one with problems, Eddie. Before I left my office today, I found out about the edict the bank examiners had brought down on the bank. They're forcing Broad Street Bank to slash its exposure to commercial real estate loans. That means companies like yours are going to be run out of the bank."

"I know, Sol. Stan Burns broke the news to me today."

After another quiet pause, Levin said, "Things are changing, Edward. I suspect the Feds are going to take over the bank. If they do, they'll wipe out our shareholders and bring in a new owner. Don't trust the Feds or any new owner of the bank; don't tell them anything more than you absolutely have to. You have no friends at the government or at the investor the Feds bring in to take over the bank."

# CHAPTER FOUR

Gerald Folsom, at sixty-two, had accumulated wealth beyond even his voracious appetite for it. He had been a scrapper since he was a kid growing up in the Germantown section of Philadelphia. His parents couldn't afford to join the "white flight" to the suburbs, so Gerald learned to fight or get along with the black kids in the neighborhood. Those he fought learned to respect him; those he got along with found out he was a straight up kind of guy. None of them understood that Gerald didn't care about any of them. He had his sights set on a different element of Philadelphia society.

Folsom began thinking about the future after graduating from high school in 1966 and beginning work as a waiter at a restaurant in Chestnut Hill. The difference between the residents on "The Hill" and the people in Germantown, despite being only a few miles apart, was like the difference between a developed country and a third world backwater swamp. He fantasized about the rich girls he served in the restaurant. He conjured up the scent of their perfume, envisioned the creamy-white texture of their skin under their sweaters, bending as close to them as possible when he served their meals and bussed their dishes. He admired their confidence and the way they talked, but it ate at him that he had to wait on these girls instead of throwing them on the floor and screwing their brains out. He could tell from the way some of them eyed him that they liked his dark good looks, and he suspected one or two were intrigued with him in the same way they might find a wild, dangerous animal in a cage intriguing. But he soon came to the realization that, without money, he'd never have a prayer connecting with girls like these. Maybe if he had gone to college, that would have helped, but he'd never had the patience for school work. Money. That was the thing. . That much he knew for sure. He had no doubt about where he wanted to go; the question was how to get there.

One Saturday, he overheard a customer talking about a commission he'd just made on the sale of an office building: $58,000. The guy didn't own the building; all he did was sell it. It was that day in 1967 that Gerald Folsom found his direction. He began reading everything he could find about real estate: How it was bought and sold, how it was appraised. He studied for the real estate licensing exam, even though he couldn't take the test until he was twenty-one. He began attending open houses to learn what buyers wanted and to meet real estate agents. He grilled agents about the business, and when they ran out of answers, he found others. He was a few days past his nineteenth birthday when the owner of a real estate agency stopped by an open house and was so impressed with the young man that he offered him a job doing maintenance work on his properties. Two years later, in 1969, Gerald earned his real estate license and began assisting other agents in the company with their listings.

In the first year after receiving his license, Gerald made four times what he'd made at the restaurant in any one year. But he was frustrated by the fact that most residential buyers and sellers weren't comfortable doing business with someone his age. He was stuck backing up the more senior agents, sitting their open houses on weekends and doing grunt work, for a small portion of the sales commissions. Then one day, while sitting an open house, a couple walked in and everything changed.

"I want to confirm that the mortgage on this place is an FHA loan," the man said.

"That's correct, sir," Gerald responded. "It's a $31,000 balance with a six percent interest rate. The asking price is $35,000, so you'd need four grand to put down, plus closing costs."

The man laughed. "I was born at night, but I wasn't born *last night*. The owner of this place is out of work. He's late on his mortgage payments. He needs out from under the mortgage bad. So, that's what we're prepared to do for him -- save his financial ass. We'll assume the mortgage. He can cover the closing costs out of *his* pocket."

"Well, I can always present your offer," Gerald said, suppressing an urge to laugh at the guy's arrogance. "There's no guarantee he'll accept it."

"How much you wanna bet he'll kiss your feet when he sees our offer?"

Gerald just shrugged and wrote up the offer; sure it was a waste of everyone's time.

When the seller saw the offer, he didn't kiss Gerald's feet, but he looked like he might hug him.

"Damn, I was afraid we'd never sell the house in this awful market," the seller said. "With the economy down and interest rates going up, I thought we'd have to declare bankruptcy."

"You realize you're going to have to write a check at the closing table to cover closing costs?" Gerald asked.

"Yeah, I understand. But it's better than ruining our credit."

When Gerald called the buyer to let him know he'd made a deal, the man said, "No shit, Sherlock. It's like stealing candy from a baby."

What an asshole, Gerald thought. But he was captivated. "You sound like you've done this before."

"Twenty-three purchases in less than six months."

"Holy . . ." Gerald couldn't complete his phrase.

"You heard right," the man said. "Twenty-three houses at an average price of $33,000, with an average interest rate of five and three quarters percent, and no money down. As long as the FHA allows buyers to assume mortgages without having to qualify financially, I'm going to buy these places hand over fist."

"What're you doing with them?"

"What do you think I'm doing with them? I'm renting them out. People got to have a place to live. Most families would rather rent a house than an apartment, any day. Hell, I've rented some houses back to the people I bought them from. Even gave them an option to buy the places back down the road when they get back on their feet. At a profit, of course." He chuckled at that. "I'll hold the houses for seven to ten years and then sell them for at least twice what I paid for them. Mark my words. With the federal government spending money on Vietnam and the Great Society, inflation's going to be the name of the game. Meanwhile, the schmucks who rent the houses pay down the mortgages."

"You looking to buy more of these FHA deals?"

"Is the Pope Catholic, boy? Damn straight. Call me if you find any more."

Gerald wound up selling thirty houses to Warren Tatum, who he began calling The FHA King. Tatum was thrilled with Gerald, who was thrilled with the sales commissions, which he didn't have to share. And for every house Gerald sold to Tatum, he bought one for himself.

Then Gerald took the next step. He introduced himself to real estate lenders at local banks and savings & loans and convinced a couple of them, based on his success selling so many FHA properties, to list their foreclosed real estate properties with him. Gerald put together real estate limited partnerships that made low-ball offers on the best ones. He acted as the general partner of the partnerships, while investors – the limited partners – put up cash to cover upfront expenses, repairs, and operating costs until the places were rented. As general partner, Gerald made all the decisions and had full control over the properties. The banks were happy to dump real estate they'd taken through foreclosure from borrowers who fell behind on their payments, treating whatever money they got from Gerald as found money, having already written the loans off their books. In return for finding the deals and managing the properties, Gerald took a ten percent ownership interest without putting up any cash, and a six percent management fee. In just a few years, he went from having no net worth and making five grand a year as a waiter in a restaurant, to having a $2 million net worth and an annual income of $200,000.

Gerald Folsom had come a long way from those early days, but he still loved reflecting on those days, thinking about his journey from having nothing to being super wealthy. Now here he sat, attorney in tow, at a table with a bunch of federal government bureaucrats who were about to turn over to him the goose that would lay golden eggs. He briefly met Donald Matson's gaze and almost imperceptibly tipped his head at the man. Gerald knew if Matson was a woman, he'd sleep with her to get what he wanted, even though he was an ugly man, with a flat, large-nostrilled nose, beady black eyes, clumps of hair growing out of his ears, and what appeared to be bits of food imbedded in his bushy, untrimmed mustache. God, Gerald thought, Matson would be one god-awful looking woman.

But looks aside, Matson had been a patron saint for Gerald. He'd first met him when Matson was a functionary at the Federal Housing Administration, during Gerald's "FHA phase." Matson wanted to meet the sales agent who was disposing of so many FHA properties, turning delinquent mortgage loans into good assets, and their friendship grew over the years. That friendship had paid off for Gerald when Matson took a job with the Resolution Trust Corporation. The RTC was a federally-created organization established to dispose of the assets of financial institutions the federal government took over after the 1986 Tax Reform Act had helped destroy the commercial real estate market. Matson's first big gift to his friend Gerald Folsom came in 1988 when he brought Gerald in to take over some of the assets of Wyndmoor Savings & Loan.

Wyndmoor Savings & Loan had aggressively loaned to real estate investors and developers, and when the real estate market crashed, many of their loans were in jeopardy. One of Wyndmoor's borrowers was Frank Winter, Edward Winter's father. The loan was secured by real estate and the elder Winter's controlling interest in First Savings Bank. When Frank Winter died in 1988, however, his estate couldn't keep current on the loan payments. When the RTC began liquidating Wyndmoor's assets, including its loan to Frank Winter, Donald Matson devised a way to assist the federal government and to help his friend, Gerald Folsom at the same time.

Matson structured a deal whereby Folsom bought Winter's loans for fifty cents on the dollar, getting one hundred percent ownership of all of the real estate collateral and Winter's bank stock securing the loan. Like a shark cruising for prey, Folsom voraciously took over all of Frank Winter's loans at other banks, as well. Folsom knew where all of these loans were housed; after all, he'd sold the real estate deals to Winter in the first place. On the day Folsom became control stockholder of Winter's First Savings Bank, Donald Matson was given the key to a safety deposit box at that bank that just happened to hold $100,000 in cash.

# CHAPTER FIVE

Edward slapped the file closed on his desk and looked at Katherine and Nick. "Well, that does it. We've got three appointments next week: Van Snowden at Curtis Bank & Trust on Monday morning, Victoria Watts at Pennsylvania Industrial Bank on Monday afternoon, and Ernest Deakyne at Philadelphia Savings & Trust on Tuesday morning."

"Good idea going with three banks instead of just one," Nick said. "The market's in turmoil right now. Better to be safe. I'll have the loan presentations, including updated financials, finished by tomorrow morning. For all intents and purposes, they're already done, but I want to review everything one more time. I'll drop them off at your house by 2 p.m."

"Don't bother. I'll be here. Paul Sanders is coming in at 9 in the morning to go over whatever legal options we might have with Broad Street Bank. You and I can go over the loan presentation whenever you're finished tomorrow. And you'll need to clear your schedule for Monday and Tuesday. You should come along when I meet with the bankers." Edward looked at Katherine. "Maybe you should join us."

Katherine shook her head. "Our restaurant employees make deposits every night into Broad Street branches. They surely have heard the news about the bank. Some of them might wonder if the bank's problems could cause trouble for them. I'm going to spend the next few days touring all of our locations, talking to the managers and employees. Keeping things calm."

"You were supposed to be retired. Just sitting on the board of directors."

"So, what's your point?" Katherine asked, arching an eyebrow at her son.

"Nothing," Edward said. "Thanks for your help. Going to the restaurants is a good idea." Edward looked at his watch. "Well, it's 6:15. It's been a long week. I'm going to go have dinner with Betsy. I'll be back here after. Nick, maybe you should spend some time with Annie and the kids."

Nick smiled. "She's still angry about postponing the vacation. She understands. But that doesn't change the fact she's working me over. I think I'll order a pizza and stay right here."

Edward opened his mouth to apologize again for the price Nick was paying for the company's problems, but before he could, a knock sounded on his door. "Come in," he called.

Edward's assistant came in. "Mr. Scarfatti has visitors." She stepped aside and Annie Scarfatti stood in the doorway, holding a warming tray. Her two sons stood beside her holding paper bags.

"I figured you all would be working late tonight. The least we could do was make sure you had a decent meal."

Edward, Katherine, and Nick stood. "This is great," Edward said, "but I was going home for a couple hours.

"No, you're not," a voice said. Edward's wife, Betsy, stepped around Annie and her boys. "I figured you'd drive over an hour to eat with me and then come back here. I thought I'd save you the drive." She put on a stern face and added, "Besides, this bank problem affects all of us. Focus your attention on that."

"Let's set this stuff out in the conference room," Annie said. "I'm starving."

The Winters and the Scarfattis had barely sat down to eat when one of the Scarfatti boys, Johnny, discovered the large screen television. "Can I turn on the TV?" he asked.

"You bet," Edward said, picking up the remote control and turning on the TV. The screen came to life on one of the local news programs. Edward was about to hand the remote over to Johnny when the news anchor announced that a bulletin had just come across his desk.

"Federal regulators shuttered Broad Street National Bank at 5 p.m. this evening, making it the ninety-sixth bank to fail this year. This year's pace of bank closures is ahead of each of the last two years.

"The eighteen-branch Broad Street National Bank had $22.6 billion in assets. The Federal Deposit Insurance Corporation said the bank's failure would cost its insurance fund $3.1 billion.

"The FDIC sold all of Broad Street Bank's deposits and most of its assets, including its loans, to Folsom Financial Corporation, a Philadelphia-based investment firm that currently owns First

Savings Bank, Centurion Bank & Trust, and numerous other entities, including significant real estate holdings. Folsom Financial is owned by Gerald Folsom."

Edward looked around at the others in the room and noticed his mother had gone pale.

"What's the matter, Mom?" he asked.

She responded with a dismissive wave of her hand. "Nothing, son."

Edward looked back at the television and listened to the anchorman.

"The seventy-year-old Broad Street National Bank's capital base deteriorated precipitously over the last twelve months, according to the FDIC. The less capital a bank has, the weaker the bank is.

"Broad Street National Bank's closure is not good news for the Philadelphia area. It has been a big supporter of local businesses and a generous contributor to local charities. The bank has almost eight hundred employees."

Edward handed the remote to Johnny Scarfatti and turned to Nick. "That explains things pretty well, doesn't it?"

"Yeah." Nick looked worried.

"What's wrong?" Annie asked.

Nick momentarily shook his head, seemingly gathering his thoughts. He waved a finger at Edward, still appearing to collect himself. "When you talk to Paul tomorrow, you should ask about what happens now to our loans at Broad Street National Bank. That news guy said most of the bank's assets had been sold to Folsom Financial. What rights does Folsom now have regarding our loans? What about our deposits? We had almost $3 million in our accounts in Broad Street as of the close of business on Thursday. We—" Nick stopped and, after a few seconds, said, "Our receipts on weekends run about $600 thousand. We need to tell our managers to hold the receipts. No deposit drops in Broad Street National Bank over this weekend. We should have our armored car company deliver the receipts to us here. We'll put them in our vault."

"Why?" Katherine asked, her brow knitted and her eyes narrowed.

"I've heard too many horror stories about bank takeovers. I don't know Folsom Financial, but they could ..."

"What?" Edward demanded.

"Let's wait until we meet with Paul tomorrow, Eddie."


Katherine left the meeting and walked outside. She felt as though a massive hand gripped and squeezed her lungs. She reached to turn the key in the ignition but paused to think about Gerald Folsom's role in all of this. It made no sense. First, Frank had gotten into business with Folsom. Coincidence? Maybe. Now, the man owned the bank that held the loan on their business and that bank was playing very rough with her son. Another coincidence? Unlikely.

She reflected on the last time she'd seen Folsom, before she and Frank had married, while Frank was overseas with the Army. She and two girlfriends had been out to dinner, celebrating Katherine's engagement to Frank. They had moved to a club after leaving the restaurant. That's where Folsom had homed in on them like a heat seeking missile on a target. Katherine's girlfriends were single and weren't averse to Folsom's attention. He was tall, blue-eyed, and well-built, with jet-black hair and a roguish reputation. But Folsom was only interested in Katherine.

She ignored Folsom's sexual banter for a short while and then called it a night. She went outside to her car and reached to open the car door, when someone grabbed her by the shoulder and spun her around, pinning her to the car. Folsom!

"I wondered how long it would take you to dump your loser friends," he said.

She'd gawked at him as though he were an alien from another planet. "Get lost," she'd said.

He yanked her to him and shoved his mouth onto hers. She struggled, driving her knee into his crotch. Folsom cried out and dropped to the ground as though he'd been poleaxed.

"You bitch!" he groaned.

Katherine opened her car door and drove off, thinking she'd seen and heard the last of Gerald Folsom.

But Folsom had begun calling her, stalking her. She found threatening notes on several occasions; her car tires were slashed twice. After weeks of harassment, she filed a restraining order against the man. Katherine never heard from Folsom again, and there was no more vandalism. She never told Frank. She felt there was no point after Folsom seemed to drop off the face of the earth. But now, after all these years, Folsom had resurfaced.

# CHAPTER SIX

"How's the transition going?" Gerald Folsom demanded over his cell phone.

Folsom's Chief Financial Officer, Sanford Cunningham, blew out a loud stream of air that whistled in his boss' ear. Cunningham had worked for Folsom for twelve years, handling three bank transactions for Folsom Financial Corporation in that time. A man of medium height and weight, with a brush cut, acne-pitted skin, and cold-blue penetrating eyes, he was Folsom's bulldog. "These takeovers are always dicey," Cunningham said, "but from my experience, it couldn't be better."

"Be specific," Folsom ordered.

"Boss, this bank is a bird's nest on the ground. You'll remember July 15, 2011, as the day your net worth grew dramatically. As we determined during our due diligence, the loan portfolio is in great shape. The Feds took it over because they determined that the collateral is below the loan balance on a large number of the bank's commercial real estate loans. And they're assuming real estate values will continue to decline, so the loans will only be further under water as time goes on. Hell, the regulators are presuming that every city in the country will be another Las Vegas or Phoenix, with their real estate values plummeting. But most of Broad Street's borrowers are as good as gold, never missing a payment. So, even though the regulators made the bank write down the loans based on their estimated real estate value, the bank's loan delinquency rate is almost non-existent. Its president knew what he was doing when it came to lending."

"Any problems with the bank's IT systems?"

"No, they're all updated and functioning, so the transition to our systems should be seamless."

"What about the deposits?"

"As you know, we paid two point four percent for all of the deposits. Hell, if we do nothing else, we can invest the deposits in Treasuries and make money with zero risk. We'll send a notice to all depositors next Friday advising them we're going to reduce the rates we're paying on CDs to one point two percent. That will save about $17 million in annual interest expense. Then we'll bump up fees on checking accounts and reduce the interest paid on those accounts. That should generate another $37 million in fees and interest savings."

"We'll see a mini-run on the bank when those letters go out," Folsom said, not really worried. "Especially the retired customers. They'll cash in their CDs and take their money to some other bank that's paying a little more interest."

"We've got plenty of liquidity even if that happens. And there's always the Federal Reserve. We can borrow overnight Fed Funds at near zero and lend it out at four and a half to five percent."

Folsom chuckled.

Cunningham continued, "Our lawyers will start calling the owners of the real estate where our branches are located. We'll renegotiate the leases. Probably cut the rent in half. That'll save $60 million over the next ten years."

"That's one of the things I'll never understand," Folsom interjected. "How can the federal government take over a bank and then pass on the right to the new owners to renegotiate all of the bank's contracts? Leases, Certificates of Deposit, vendor contracts. They screw the original owners of the bank, the depositors, and the bankers' vendors. What a cluster fuck!"

"I assume you're not complaining about how the system works," Cunningham said with a laugh.

"Sanford, my boy, just the opposite," Folsom answered. "God bless my Uncle Sam." Then he added, "When can you get me a summary of the loan portfolio?"

"I'll email it to you on Monday afternoon. Loan amounts, interest rates, loan-to-value ratios, collateral descriptions, delinquencies, and borrower information."

"That's where the big bucks are hiding, Sanford. We buy the bank's deposits at a slight premium and buy the loans from the FDIC that we want and tell them to keep the stuff we don't want. And, according to the loss-share arrangement we have with the FDIC, if we experience any losses on any of the loans we buy, they'll cover eighty percent of those losses."

Folsom smiled. "And the losses are calculated against the actual loan balances, not against the discounted price we pay for the loans. It's heads I win, tails you lose."

"I did a quick and dirty analysis of the commercial loan portfolio," Cunningham said. "The current appraisals in the bank's files show that, as a result of the economic downturn, the commercial real estate backing up the bank loans is now worth only eighty-five percent of what it was when the loans were originally closed. So, for example, a million dollar property is now appraised at $850,000. That's in line with what we have seen in value depreciation across this market. But the Feds made Broad Street Bank write down their loans to an average of seventy-five percent of current loan balance. And the original loans, on average, were advanced at an average of only sixty percent of original appraised value. Therefore, if Broad Street loaned a borrower $600,000 against a million dollar property, the Feds now declare that the loan is worth only seventy-five percent of $600,000, or $450,000. Even though the collateral behind the loan is valued at $850,000. These loans are solid. And if a loan does go bad, we can always sell the property—the collateral —and pocket a profit."

"Sandy, what I'm really interested in knowing are which real estate loans mature in the short term."

"Just like with the other banks we bought," Cunningham said. "I've already anticipated that. You'll have that information Monday."

# SATURDAY
# JULY 16, 2011

# CHAPTER SEVEN

Attorney Paul Sanders arrived at Winter Enterprises' offices at 9 a.m. sharp on Saturday. He was still the distinguished-looking man he'd been two decades earlier. Still slim and elegant, but grayer, with thinning hair. Even on a Saturday, he wore a suit and tie. Nick met him in the lobby and led him to Edward's office where Katherine was just leaving to tour the restaurant locations.

Dressed in khaki slacks and a lime-green polo shirt, Katherine looked model-perfect. As usual, Paul couldn't take his eyes off her. That too, hadn't changed.

Edward felt bad for Paul. It had always been obvious to him how the lawyer felt about his mother, and just as obvious was her lack of interest. "Call me if there are any problems at any of the restaurants," Edward said to his mother.

After Katherine left, the men sat down. "I assume you've reviewed all the loan documents, Paul," Edward said. "Do we have any options?"

Paul shrugged. "A few. Your loan's anniversary date is at the end of July. The 29th to be exact. The bank has the right to demand payment in full as of that date. But the bank has new ownership. Maybe they'll want to extend the loan, which would take all the pressure off you to find alternative financing. But ..."

"But *what*?" Nick pressed.

"I wouldn't count on getting any relief from the new owner."

"Why do you say that?" Edward asked.

Paul visibly swallowed. His face reddened. "I need to tell you something I should have shared with your mother twenty-two years ago." Paul couldn't seem to go on.

"What is it, Paul?" Edward asked.

"Could I have some water?"

Edward went to the mini refrigerator and pulled out a bottle of water. He gave it to Paul and watched him open the bottle and take a drink nervously. He waited until the lawyer put the bottle down on the edge of his desk and then asked, "What happened twenty-two years ago that has anything to do with the new ownership at Broad Street Bank?"

"Folsom Financial Corporation is owned by Gerald Folsom, the same man who put your father into a bunch of real estate deals back in the '80s. Your father and I had a lot of conversations about those deals. He was under huge stress because of the loans he'd taken out. I am convinced that stress caused the heart attack that killed him."

"Did Folsom cheat my father?" Edward asked.

Paul shrugged. "I have no way of proving that. I do have my suspicions. But I found out after Frank died that Folsom took advantage of the situation. He bought your dad's loans from the Resolution Trust Corporation at a deep discount after the federal government took over the bank where one of the loans was housed. He did the same with other of your dad's loans at a couple banks. They were anxious to dump paper that looked bad. This gave Folsom control over the collateral behind the loans. By assuming loans whose balances had been deeply discounted, Folsom wound up owning one hundred percent of the real estate backing up those loans. He also captured your father's eighty-five percent stock interest in First Savings Bank. Did he cheat Frank? As far as I know, not legally. But he sure didn't deal ethically."

"What's the Resolution Trust Corporation?" Edward asked.

"An organization formed by the Feds to dispose of the assets of banks appropriated by the federal government. A vast number of banks and savings and loans were taken over by the federal government. In so doing, the Feds then not only had these financial institutions on their hands, but they had all of their assets: Billions and billions of dollars in loans backed by even more billions in collateral behind those loans. They started dumping those loans on the market and selling the collateral at deep discounts. I knew a fellow who bought a pool of $100 million in unsecured notes from the Feds for $5 million. He wound up collecting $58 million from the borrowers on those notes. Not a bad return on $5 million. Most borrowers were perfectly willing to repay their loans. But, once the RTC took over banks, the borrowers often couldn't find anyone to talk to about how to make their payments.

"Dumping real estate properties on the market at deep discounts only exacerbated the drop in value in the commercial real estate market that began with the passage of the Tax Reform Act of 1986. It took ten years for the real estate market to return to any sort of normality."

"Sounds insane," Edward said.

"Or corrupt," Nick added.

"Could be both," Paul said. "Frank didn't live to see the worst of the effects of the tax act, but in 1988, he was already predicting a disaster, and a federal conspiracy. Whether he was correct or not about the conspiracy, the results were the same. The beneficiaries of the Tax Reform Act of 1986 were the super wealthy of the world, the only ones with the cash resources to buy up the discounted assets the RTC put up for sale. The losers were the middle class who couldn't refinance their properties because of reduced property values or who lost their buildings, for example, when the real estate recession infected the rest of the economy and businesses failed and the property owners lost their tenants."

In the funereal lull now overhanging the office, Paul added, "And history is repeating itself. Bear with me, because this is a bit technical, but it's vital you understand why the banks are acting irrationally. The politicians in Washington, D.C., encouraged Fannie Mae and Freddie Mac to buy sub-prime loans because those politicans wanted to encourage universal home ownership, regardless of whether homebuyers could actually afford to buy. Then the Federal Reserve flooded the market with cheap money, keeping interest rates low to encourage borrowing on a monumental scale. Banks joined the party, making loans on the ridiculous assumption that property values would keep rising forever. Consumers were also part of the feeding frenzy, buying houses they couldn't afford because they, too, thought property values would go up and up. But then property values stopped going up. Some of those sub-prime borrowers stopped paying their mortgage payments. When loan delinquencies started to rise and property values dropped, the capital markets froze."

Paul sighed and took another drink of water, fiddling with the plastic cap. "The same thing is happening to you that happened to a lot of those borrowers. The quality of your, or anyone's, credit is apparently irrelevant to the Federal regulators because the financial markets are so damaged. Then, the same federal government that started the problem in the first place now rides in and *solves* the problem. It creates TARP, TALF, stimulus programs, and myriad other programs, funneling money into the big banks and securities firms. Then they impose new lending and capital rules on banks, all banks, whether they took TARP funds or not. I can't speak intelligently about how the rules have impacted the banks, or Broad Street National Bank specifically, but I can tell you, whether you call it the Resolution Trust Corporation, or the Federal Reserve, or the U.S. Treasury, the Feds are ultimately behind your problem today. They've disrupted the normal workings of the capital markets. And I will not be surprised to learn Gerald Folsom acquired Broad Street National Bank at a price much lower than the real value of the bank."

"If armed people invaded a bank and stole all of the bank's assets, you'd call that bank robbery," Nick said. "What do you call it when your own government takes over a bank and hands the bank's assets over to a guy like Folsom?"

Paul spread his hands in a frustrated gesture, saying nothing.

"Nick and I are going to meet with several bankers next week," Edward said. "With our financial situation, we should be able to refinance our loans somewhere."

"You should meet with whoever's now calling the shots at Broad Street Bank, as well," Paul suggested. "At least you might be able to learn something about what's going on down there."

# CHAPTER EIGHT

Gerald Folsom knew the transition from Broad Street National Bank to the FDIC and then to Folsom Financial Corporation would effectively take place over the weekend. Folsom had already ordered his people to begin the process of "problem" loan disposition as soon as possible. That included getting rid of loans, even if they were paying as agreed, especially those with short-term maturity dates. The Feds had made it clear they wanted the bank to reduce its exposure to commercial real estate loans. Folsom rubbed his hands together. Disposing of those loans was where the big bucks would be made.

He was absolutely gleeful. Money had that effect on him. It had only cost him $1 million in a "gift" to Donald Matson to take over Broad Street National Bank. $1 million to make hundreds of millions of dollars. Folsom knew Matson could have recommended any of a hundred different investors, including other banks, interested in buying Broad Street from the Feds. The "gift" had assured Folsom of being the winning bidder. He wasn't just gleeful, he was horny. Money did that to him, as well. He glanced at the photograph on the credenza in his office. It was taken on his third honeymoon. Three marriages over twenty years, with five-year-gaps between them. It crossed his mind that each of his wives was a replica of the others. They were all about the same age when he married them. All blonde and blue-eyed, all daughters of blue-blood Philadelphia families that had fallen on tough times. They were all more than happy to marry their daughters off to someone with real wealth and Folsom was excited to marry women who reminded him of the girls he used to wait on in the Chestnut Hill restaurant.

He rubbed his crotch as he looked at the photograph. Wendy looked so innocent. As had all his wives. Folsom knew it was his fault his previous two marriages had ended in divorces involving large financial settlements. But the money he gave his wives was mutually understood to be hush money. If the word got out he was a serial abuser, no woman would have anything to do with him and his business reputation would be damaged. No more deals from the FDIC. He shivered involuntarily at the thought of what he did to his wives. He enjoyed what he did to women. He just hated what it cost him when the women had had enough and came to the conclusion he would never stop.

Folsom knew Wendy was fast coming to that same conclusion. But he couldn't help himself. It felt so damned good when he humiliated women like those who used to look down on him. But the women he married weren't uneducated. They had connections and options. They would only put up with the mistreatment for so long.

He decided to go home to Wendy. He was in the mood to

celebrate. Might as well pull out all the stops tonight. He might not get another chance with her. First he'd call Sanford Cunningham at the bank; see how things had progressed since they'd talked earlier. Cunningham would tell him how much money he was going to make and that would just heighten his sexual desire.

After making the call to Cunningham, Folsom packed up his brief case and walked out to his black Mercedes, muttering, "Wendy, I've got something for you."

# SUNDAY
# JULY 17, 2011

# CHAPTER NINE

Katherine Winter didn't sleep well on Saturday night. She'd called Paul Saunders after she made the circuit of restaurant locations. She wanted to know how the meeting with Edward and Nick had gone. Paul gave her a play-by-play.

"Paul, I want to know how Gerald Folsom wound up with Frank's bank stock twenty-two years ago."

"Why now, Katherine? After all these years?"

"That should be obvious, Paul. Folsom's now in a position to ruin my son."

Paul explained the deals Folsom made with the government to take over Frank's loans and the collateral against those loans.

"When did you learn about this?" she'd demanded. "About what Folsom did?"

"Shortly after Frank died," Paul told her.

"And you kept this information to yourself all these years?"

"Listen, Katherine, I—"

Katherine had hung up on Paul before she said something she might regret.

Her thoughts now ranged from concern for Edward's future to visceral anger at Gerald Folsom.

She knew her children were resilient and could bounce back from even the worst experience – she'd observed that after they'd lost their father. But she suspected that losing a company he'd built from scratch and watching his employees walk away without jobs in a bad economy would be terribly difficult on Edward.

Her anger and hatred toward Folsom radiated off of her. Paul Sanders alluded to Folsom contributing to Frank's death through the stress his deals had put on Frank. That was an awful thing to contemplate. And she felt even worse about being so unaware of the pressure Frank had been under. She'd lived a privileged existence and never even suspected her husband was in financial difficulty. Now Folsom, the man who had harassed her before she and Frank married, contributed to Frank's financial ruin, profited from Frank's death, was now a threat to her son's business.

Katherine got out of bed at 4 a.m., went to the kitchen, and made herself a cup of tea. A thread of a thought tickled at her brain. She first tried to discard the idea but then embraced it and fleshed it out. She criticized herself for being naïve and stupid for even thinking about something this crazy. But her motherly instincts nurtured the thought.

After ping-ponging the idea in her brain for three hours, she came to the conclusion she had nothing to lose. She showered, put on her make-up, and dressed. Then she called Paul and told him her plan.

"Katherine, are you nuts? This is about the most inappropriate thing you could do. What in God's name do you think you're going to accomplish?"

She maintained her calm and said, "Paul, I didn't call you for your advice or opinion. I figured you could find out where he lives. If you can't do that, I'll find it some other way. You know I will. So, why make it difficult for me? Besides, you owe me. You should have told me long ago about Folsom's role in Frank's financial troubles. "

"I'm not trying to create difficulties; I'm trying to protect you."

Katherine paused and said, "I know that, Paul. But I've thought about this and I'm going to do it, with or without your help."

"Wait until tomorrow. You can talk to him at his office. Then you—"

"Goodbye, Paul," Katherine said, about to hang up. But before she could replace the receiver, Paul shouted, "Stay there! I don't have the information you want, but I can probably get it if you give me an hour. Okay?"

"Okay."

Paul called back in fifty minutes. "I have it, but I'm not going to give it to you unless I go with you. I'll pick you up in fifteen minutes." Paul slammed down his phone leaving Katherine gawking at the dead line.

The ride from Katherine's home to Philadelphia's Villanova area took fifteen minutes. It took another fifteen minutes to find Gerald Folsom's home. Paul was quiet during most of the drive, other than periodically muttering under his breath. When he pulled up to the curb in front of Folsom's address, a multi-acre, wrought-iron-fenced estate with a three-hundred-yard paved driveway bordered by cyprus trees, Paul parked the car and shifted in his seat.

"Now, tell me what you think you're going to accomplish."

Katherine was beginning to question that herself. What felt like a good idea at home now, in front of Folsom's house, seemed ridiculous. "I want to talk to the man. Tell him I know what he did to Frank years ago and that he has the opportunity to make amends by dealing with my children in a fair manner. I—"

Paul blurted a laugh. "Katherine, Gerald Folsom is not a nice man. I doubt you can reason with someone like him. And look at this place. It's a fortress. How do you propose getting past the gate?"

Katherine threw open her door and said, "I'll ring the bell." She got out of the car and began walking across a twenty-foot-wide strip of grass toward a huge stone column anchoring the right side of the fifteen-foot-high entry gate. She was still fifty feet away from the column when the gate suddenly began to open. Moments later a huge black Mercedes with tinted windows roared down the driveway, sped through the gateway and swerved left onto the street in front of the property. In five seconds, the car disappeared around a curve.

Paul got out of his car and shouted at Katherine, "I think that was Folsom."

"Are you sure?"

He hesitated. "No."

"We've come this far," Katherine said. "I'm not turning around now. Let's go up to the house and see if he's there."

A smile on his face, Paul pointed at the gate that was now closing. "I think we're too late. You'll have to ring the bell."

Katherine turned and ran toward the diminishing opening, making it in just before the gate clanged shut. Paul walked over and shook his head. "Now what?"

Katherine eyed the column and a small shack hidden behind it. She spied a one-foot-square metal door. She turned the handle on the door and found an electrical panel with a green and red button. She pushed the green button and the gate immediately began to slide open. She met Paul's gaze and snapped her fingers. "Nothing to it, Paul."

"Aw, jeez, what have I gotten myself into?" He walked back to his car and drove through the gate, stopping to let Katherine get in the passenger seat before proceeding toward an immense residence that was more castle than house. It was a four-story stone structure with a pitched gray slate roof and huge dormers. The driveway branched to the right toward a five car garage, and to the left to the front entrance. A stone fountain sat in the middle of the circular drive that was at least fifty yards across.

"You realize this is trespassing," Paul said.

Katherine didn't respond, waiting for Paul to stop by the front entrance. She got out of the car, walked up to the front door, and pressed the doorbell. She waited for thirty long seconds but got no response. She tried the bell again, with the same result.

Paul got out of his car. "He's gone, Katherine. Let's get out of here."

Ignoring Paul, Katherine lifted an enormous metal knocker in the center of the door and let it drop. The noise it made was loud enough to wake the dead, she thought. It also caused the door to move an inch. She turned around and said to Paul, "The door's not locked." She turned back to the door and pushed against it.

"Don't go in there, Katherine," Paul yelled, as he ran after her. By the time he reached the door, she was already inside, standing in the center of an entry half the size of a basketball court. A five-tier chandelier hung overhead; curved stairways rose to the next floor from each side of the entry.

"Hello, is anyone home?" Katherine shouted.

Paul grabbed her arm and groaned, "This is nuts. We can't be in here."

She shook off his hand and said, "Did you hear that?"

"Hear what? I didn't hear anything but my beating heart."

"Quiet, Paul. Listen."

They stood in the center of that massive area and listened. A few seconds passed before a sound drifted down from somewhere above the first floor.

"You hear it now, Paul?"

He nodded. "Sounds like it's coming from upstairs." He moved toward the bottom of the left staircase and waited. This time the sound came louder. Moaning and then sobbing.

No longer hesitant, Paul moved up the stairs as quickly as his out-of-shape legs would allow. By the time he reached the next floor, Katherine sprinted past him. They fast-walked down the corridor to the left toward an ornate double door. Paul pulled Katherine back before she could grip the door handle and stepped in front of her. He pushed down on the handle and slowly opened the door. Katherine moved around Paul and stepped into the room. A tall, young blonde wearing a silk robe that draped her shoulders bent before a vanity table, her hands on the table supporting her, looking into a mirror. She was sobbing terribly. She had apparently not heard them enter.

"Miss," Paul said.

The young woman whipped around and shrieked. "Who are you? What are you doing here?"

Paul had barely moved into the room, when his breath caught in his chest. The woman's robe was open and she wore nothing beneath it. Not only was her face marked with red and purple bruises, but her chest, stomach, and thighs were also badly bruised.

A pained grimace swept her features. A high-pitched screech that turned into a scream filled the room. The woman clutched her robe around her and shouted, "Get out!"

Katherine put up her hands, palms out. "I'm sorry. We came to speak to Mr. Folsom. The door was open and we heard someone moaning and ran up here to help."

The woman wiped the sleeve of her robe across her eyes. "Get out!"

"You look hurt, Miss. We can help."

"Get out or I'll call the police." She started crying.

Paul walked forward, taking a business card out of his shirt pocket and placing it on the vanity. "If you need help, call me." Then he turned and walked from the room.

Katherine backed out after Paul, turned in the hallway and followed him downstairs. They made their way back to the car and drove away, heading back to Katherine's place.

"Did you see the bruises on her face, on her body?" Katherine asked once the house was out of sight.

"Yeah. She looked awful."

"Folsom?" she asked.

"I guess?" Paul answered.

"The sonofabitch!"

"Still think you can reason with the man?"

# CHAPTER TEN

Gerald Folsom sucked on a cut knuckle on his right hand. Probably shouldn't have hit her so hard, he thought. He'd gotten carried away. The more she cried and pleaded, the more he was aroused, which only made him beat her more. But he'd almost knocked her out. He wanted his women awake and begging, fear showing on their faces, not unconscious. Otherwise, it just wasn't any fun.

He wondered briefly about the car he had passed after he left. A man and a woman. Older couple. Probably just taking pictures of his mansion. It happened all the time. People thought it was a friggin' tourist site. He put the couple out of his mind. He had more important things to dwell on. Sanford Cunningham was due at Folsom's offices at 10 a.m. to brief him on progress on the transition of ownership of Broad Street National Bank.

Folsom hated the damned banking business. Too many employees, too many branches, too many customers, too much regulatory oversight. And then there was all that bullshit about

CRA. Banks had to adhere to Community Reinvestment Act rules and regulations that essentially required lending institutions to "give back to the community" by making loans to disadvantaged borrowers, among other requirements. "Fuck CRA," Folsom muttered. He'd made a lot of money off the Feds, but they were all a bunch of bureaucratic pantywaists who were concerned about two things only: Their jobs and their retirements. These assholes had been asleep at the switch while loans were being made to anyone who could fog a mirror. Now they were covering their asses by demonizing the bankers and taking over perfectly good lending institutions. Good for him; bad for the bankers; bad for bank shareholders; bad for the taxpayers.

The Feds had "encouraged" him to buy Broad Street National Bank by threatening to not sell him any more loan pools. He'd been buying loan pools from the Feds at huge discounts, making tens of millions of dollars on each pool. Buy a $100 million pool at twenty cents on the dollar, or $20 million. Then strong arm the borrowers to pay up or forfeit their collateral. Even if he only collected $40 million from the pool, he'd doubled his money. The Feds were smart enough to realize how good the deals were they'd given him. Now they wanted him to come to their assistance. So, he'd forked over the bucks to buy this bank so the Feds wouldn't have to come in and close it down, scaring the crap out of the average citizen and the politicians in Washington, and depleting the FDIC insurance fund. The last thing the FDIC wanted was another Indy Mac fiasco —panicked depositors lined up to get their money.

Well, he'd collect whatever loans he could, liquidate the collateral on those he couldn't collect, and then liquidate the bank or sell the franchise to some big financial institution that wanted a branch footprint in Philadelphia—one of the big nine banks who were in bed with the Feds. Too big to fail, my ass, he thought.

He pressed the telephone button on his steering wheel and engaged his Bluetooth device, speed dialing Donald Matson's cell phone number.

"Hello," Matson answered in a hushed voice.

"It's Gerald," Folsom said. "Where are you?"

"In church. Hold on while I go outside."

"Church, my aching butt," Folsom groaned. "Probably begging God's forgiveness for taking bribes to fuck over unsuspecting bankers and dumbshit taxpayers."

"What was that?" Matson asked.

"Nothing," Folsom said. "Probably the radio. What are your employees telling you about the Broad Street Bank transition?"

"Everything's going great. Cunningham's a real pro. He's done this at least a dozen times now, right?"

"Three times since working for me; probably nine or ten times before that."

"So far, so good," Matson said. "The transition is seamless."

"Good. I just wanted to make sure my friends with Uncle Sugar are happy. You check the safety deposit box?"

"Yeah, thanks."

"I had to use a bigger box this time. The small ones couldn't hold that much money."

"Jeez, Gerald. Someone could be listening to this call."

"What? The National Reconnaissance Office is using a billion dollar satellite to track your conversations while rag head terrorists blow up people all over the Middle East, and retarded assholes from Africa stuff explosives in their underwear. I don't think so.

Go back to church. Put a large contribution in the offering plate in thanks for your new found wealth. But do it in cash and don't write it off your tax return. Wouldn't want Uncle Sugar to question how someone making a hundred-fifty grand a year can afford to be so generous. Oh, and give me a call when the FDIC has another loan pool for sale. I'm awash in cash."

Folsom punched the disconnect button without waiting for an answer and turned on his CD player. He cranked up the volume and pounded the steering wheel to the beat of Foreigner singing *Urgent*.

# CHAPTER ELEVEN

Edward and Nick met again at the company's offices on Sunday. They'd reviewed the loan package they were taking to Curtis Bank & Trust the next morning. The meeting was too important to take casually.

"I'll provide an overview of the company," Edward said. "Franchise situation, where we want to expand to, number of branches, that sort of thing. I'll rehearse that part of the presentation again this afternoon. You'll handle the financial statements and the three-year projections you prepared. Then I'll go into detail about our present relationship with Broad Street National Bank, our loan arrangements with them, and what we need from Curtis Bank."

"Who's going to be at the meeting besides Van Snowden from Curtis Bank?" Nick asked.

"Van told me he'd have his chief credit and chief operating officers with him."

"I'll make six copies of the presentation. That will give them an extra copy to send to their credit department for analysis."

"And we'll need copies for the meetings at Pennsylvania Industrial Bank and Philadelphia Savings & Trust. You might as well make all the copies at once."

"You feeling okay about things?"

"Yeah, Nick. Of course, I don't like the uncertainty, but if we can't get financing, with our financial situation, who the hell can?"

Nick nodded. "How's Katherine holding up?"

"Better than me. Most people see her as this quiet, gentile little lady. They have no idea how tough she is. I ought to call her just to say hello. Betsy and I usually take her to brunch after church on Sundays. Obviously, we didn't do that today."

"By the way, the staff did a hell of a job diverting the weekend receipts here. We've got $558 thousand and change in cash, credit card receipts, and checks sitting in the vault. We'll clear the credit card receipts and checks through whichever bank we move our accounts to."

"Good. That, plus the $3 million in Broad Street Bank should sweeten the deal for Curtis Bank." Edward leaned back in his chair and stared at the ceiling for a moment before looking back at Nick. "Katherine tells me a few of our restaurant managers were concerned about Broad Street Bank. They know what's going on in the financial markets and are smart enough to realize we could be impacted. I'd sure like to close a deal with another bank before rumors start scaring our people."

"Like you said, if we can't get financed, who can?"

Edward put on a brave smile. "Oh, that makes me feel so much better." He laughed, although it felt strained. "I'll pick you up at your home at 7:30 in the morning. That will give us enough time to get downtown, even with rush hour."


After Nick left his office, Edward called his mother at home. She answered on the first ring, sounding out of breath.

"You okay, Mom?"

"Fine, fine. What's up?"

"Sorry about brunch. I have to get ready for the meetings with the bankers tomorrow."

"Son, I understand. Besides, Paul and I went out for a while."

"You and Paul. That's interesting."

Katherine chuckled. "Don't read anything into it. We had some business to discuss. Remember, we're old friends."

"You know he's nuts about you," Edward said, a mischievous lilt in his voice, thinking how Paul had wasted years waiting for Katherine to give him one bit of encouragement.

"Now, do you have anything else you want to discuss other than my social life?"

"No. Just checking in."

"Call me after you meet with the banks."

"You can count on it. Wish me luck."

"You don't need luck. You've got everything going for you."

# MONDAY
# JULY 18, 2011

# CHAPTER TWELVE

Curtis Bank & Trust's headquarters occupied the first six floors of an eighteen-story concrete and glass structure on Walnut Street, a couple blocks west of Broad Street. Like most downtown Philadelphia banks, it presented a solid, conservative image. Van Snowden's office was on the first floor. Edward and Nick arrived ten minutes early, were shown to a conference room and offered coffee and water by Snowden's assistant. They accepted bottles of water and took two of three seats on one side of a rectangular, dark mahogany table. Snowden entered the room a couple minutes later, with a man and woman in tow. Snowden was a six-foot-two, fair-skinned blond with an erect posture that spoke to his military background. He wore a tan suit, light-blue shirt, and yellow tie. Edward knew he had graduated from Penn and gone on to Yale for an MBA. He looked the part of a Philadelphia banker.

Snowden introduced Chief Lending Officer, Daniel Blake, and Chief Operating Officer, Veronica Stangler. Blake was a bantam rooster type, with a confident air and a sour look to go along with his blue suit, red power tie, and starched white shirt. He seemed to like being the senior credit guy in a bank, where successful business people came in, hat in hand, to ask him for money. Edward thought he'd have to set the guy straight — after they negotiated a deal with the bank. Stangler was a dark-haired, olive- complected woman of medium height, who appeared to be warm and competent in her light-gray suit, off-white blouse, and wire glasses. Edward liked her right off.

The bankers took seats across the table from Edward and Nick.

"What can Curtis Bank & Trust do for Winter Enterprises?" Snowden asked.

"Thanks for seeing us," Edward responded. "Van, you and I have had several conversations over the past few years about your interest in moving Winter Enterprises' business to your bank. As you know, we've been with Broad Street National for a while now. They've taken good care of us, so we had no reason to move our business. Obviously, with the FDIC taking over Broad Street and selling it to Folsom Financial, the situation there is up in the air."

Snowden laughed, "That's an understatement." Stangler laughed along with Snowden; Blake's sour look didn't change. Edward smiled politely.

"Anyway, we feel that now would be a good time to seriously discuss your interest in Winter Enterprises' business."

Snowden grinned. "We're pleased you've elected to give us this opportunity. I see you have a presentation with you," he said, pointing at the stack of packages on the table in front of Nick. "Why don't you go ahead and start?"

It took Edward and Nick a little over an hour to complete their presentation, during which the bankers interrupted them a half-dozen times to clarify points. They then segued into what they needed Curtis Bank to do for them.

"We have a $20 million master note at Broad Street National, secured by $50 million in real estate, all of which are our restaurant properties. We want to roll the balance of that note into a $30 million master loan facility that will allow us to finance another seven locations over the next twenty-four months or so. We'll pay down the loan over five years, and will finance future expansion with internal cash flow. We'll secure the loan, regardless of the balance, with all of our real estate properties. I think—"

Snowden suddenly stood and looked at Edward. "I'm going to suggest Nick finish the presentation for Dan and Veronica. Edward, I think you and I ought to continue this discussion in my office."

Nick looked confused. Edward shot him a calming smile and rose from his chair. He didn't know what was happening, but he figured Snowden wouldn't have interrupted him unless there was a good reason. He and Snowden had a friendly relationship that spanned a dozen years, so he wasn't particularly upset by the interruption. He followed the bank president out of the conference room into an office at the far end of the floor.

Snowden's office was large: Twenty by thirty feet, Edward guessed. A red and blue Persian carpet lay on the wood floor. A large desk sat at the end of the room, beneath a bank of windows overlooking Walnut Street. Snowden pointed to a plush leather chair on one side of a coffee table and took the opposite chair himself.

"I apologize for breaking up the meeting that way, but I decided wasting any more of your time would be unfair to you."

Edward took a deep breath and let it out slowly. "Wasting my time?"

"What I'm about to tell you can't leave this room; I'm not quite ready to quit banking and I'd be out on my ear if the regulators learned I'd talked to you. But you need to understand the current banking environment. Okay?"

"Okay."

Snowden exhaled loudly. "I was just a young banker in the early '90s, but I remember what the regulators and the Resolution Trust Corporation did to the banks and to their business clients. As bad as things were back then, it is even worse today. Bear with me; this is going to take a little time. But what I'm telling you is a roundabout way of turning you down for your loan."

Edward's face turned hot. "No disrespect, Van, but making me suffer through a long-winded story, where I already know the ending, is the height of patronization. I—"

Snowden stopped Edward. "I understand, but this is for your own good. If you don't understand the present banking environment, you'll be going into battle unarmed."

Edward met Snowden's gaze and, after a second, nodded and said, "I apologize. Please go ahead."

"First of all, the regulators have issued cease & desist orders and regulatory letters to us, and to banks all across the country, ordering us to not make any more commercial real estate loans. That's why we can't even consider your loan request. The regulators believe that commercial real estate values are going to deteriorate and that any exposure to commercial real estate is too much. Earlier this year, Elizabeth Warren, the chairperson of the TARP Congressional Oversight Panel, said, and I'm paraphrasing, 'We now have 2,988 banks with dangerous concentrations in commercial real estate lending.' She also said that by the end of this year, about half of all commercial real estate mortgages will be underwater. What effect do you think comments like her's have had and will continue to have on the way the regulators treat banks?"

Without waiting for a reply, he continued, "We have a loan delinquency rate of less than two percent, but the examiners don't seem to care. To make matters worse, they ordered us to raise our core capital ratio.

"To put things in perspective, the current written guidelines for a well-capitalized bank are set at a six percent core capital ratio and a ten percent risk-based capital ratio. Before the market meltdown, the ratios used to be five percent and eight percent. The standards are relative to the relationship between the bank's capital and its assets. This sounds complicated, and I'll admit, is a bit convoluted. Loans are treated differently than securities, for example.

"But anyway, the changing standards are creating a vicious cycle. As community banks reduce their investments in commercial real estate loans, as the regulators demand, the less income the banks generate, meaning lower earnings and thus more difficulty in building additional capital.

"Our ratios are eight percent and twelve percent, significantly above the guidelines. But the regulators have now ordered us to raise our ratios to ten percent and thirteen percent. Why? I don't have a clue. Our examiner, when I asked her about this, in effect, told me it was none of my business how she made the decision."

"Couldn't you appeal?" Edward interjected.

"To whom?"

"Her boss?"

"Been there, done that. The guy was frothing at the mouth over me questioning one of his examiners."

"Then how about our Congressional delegation?"

"Those gutless wonders are less than worthless. Ever since the Keating Five back in 1987 got into trouble, not one of those guys would stick his neck out to intervene on behalf of a banker in a pissing match with a regulator. Besides, they're demonizing bankers. Haven't you heard? The Great Recession is our fault."

"What was the Keating Five?"

Snowden smiled at Edward. "Sorry. You were probably still in elementary school in 1987. The Keating Five was named for Charles Keating, Chairman of Lincoln Savings & Loan Association. Five U.S. Senators were accused of intervening in 1987 on behalf of Keating's bank, the target of a regulatory investigation by the Federal Home Loan Bank Board. I don't think the Senators ever thought they were doing anything wrong; they were just trying to get the regulators to back off a constituent they thought was being unfairly attacked.

"But politicians have a long memory when it comes to political liability and no one wants to be accused of interfering in the regulator's witch hunt against the big, bad bankers. The press, the President, Congress—they're all demonizing the bankers."

"It sounds like things have gone too far the other way," Edward said.

"It doesn't seem to matter. When it comes to the regulators, this isn't a democracy. As Sol Levin told me, 'I went to bed in America and woke up in the USSR.'"

"What happened at Broad Street National is unconscionable. It's a crime. The federal government stole that bank from its rightful owners, which included thousands of individual shareholders in Pennsylvania. Sure, the bank had some real estate loan problems, but nothing warranting the Feds going in and taking it over. I've talked with some of their people; I won't tell you who, but I have absolute confidence in the people I've talked to.

"One told me he discovered a major error in the calculations the OCC examiners used to determine the bank's loan loss reserve. When he brought it to the examiner's attention, the guy told him that it didn't make any difference. That they'd just change one of the other parameters so they'd come up with the same result. In other words, these Gestapo agents came into a bank with a predetermined mindset and then forced the numbers to fit that predetermination.

"Community banks like Broad Street and our bank here didn't get us into this economic mess. It was the politicians, Fannie Mae and Freddie Mac, and the largest financial institutions that undermined the system. The FDIC, the Office of the Comptroller of the Currency, the Office of Thrift Supervision didn't enforce regulations on the big banks; now, they're taking it out on the community banks while the bastards at the big institutions get bailed out."

"So there's nothing you can do?" Edward asked.

"I am ashamed to tell you I can't stand up to these people. They are in absolute control and I don't know why. But I do have an opinion. I think the politicians screwed things up so badly with the pressure they put on banks and on Fannie and Freddie to make subprime loans, and the regulators were so unaware that they are now all in the same bed covering one another's asses. They've made the bankers the fall guys, which is the same thing the politicians did during the Great Depression and again after the 1986 Tax Reform

Act."

"And the customer is screwed," Edward said.

Snowden nodded. "We can't win this game, Eddie. Just look at what New York Attorney General, Andrew Cuomo, did to Bank of America. He's just another politician to claim bankers are the villains who created the capital markets meltdown and the recession. Sure, the big banks contributed to the problem, but in 1999, who was it, as HUD Secretary, that established new affordable housing targets requiring Freddie and Fannie to buy $2.4 trillion in 'affordable' mortgages? Andrew Cuomo! Fannie and Freddie invested in subprime loans that will weigh on all of us for years. Huge losses there. And the tax payer has to cover those."

"My attorney told me about some of this a few days ago," Edward said. "But how can lending to good companies just stop? Didn't I read a little while back that the regulators are working to ensure the availability of credit to sound small business borrowers?"

"You did. It's bullshit. The politicians caused the problem, demonized the banks, and now they're very softly questioning the regulators for going too far in the other direction. And as long as there's money to be made by friends of the politicians and of the regulators, nothing's going to change. Sol Levin gets gored and Gerald Folsom gets the bank handed to him on a silver platter. That bastard Folsom must be sleeping with someone at one of the regulatory agencies. It seems like he turns up every time there's a sweet deal available."

"What's in all of this for people like Folsom?"

"A damn fortune. The regulators wipe out a bank's ownership, hand over the bank to one of their buddies who injects capital into the bank in return for a discounted purchase price of the bank's assets and a loss-share arrangement with the FDIC. The Feds share in any loan losses the new owner might incur. So Folsom is brought in to take over Broad Street at a sweetheart price, starts selling off bank assets at a premium to the discounted price he paid, gets indemnified by the Feds against a substantial share of any losses, and ends up with a bank franchise that has residual value when all is said and done."

"Unbelievable!" Edward exclaimed. "And who covers the cost of these bailouts? The taxpayers?"

"Indirectly, but yes. The Feds require banks to replenish the deposit insurance fund through higher premiums. In 2008, our annual premium was $300,000. In 2009, the agency forced us to pay $9 million in premiums for two years in advance. That means $9 million less in capital, and then we get criticized for not having enough capital. It also means $90 million less in lending capacity, assuming we can leverage capital 10 to 1. So, our earnings are impacted. How do we compensate? We raise our fees and interest rates on loans and lower our interest rates on savings and CD accounts. Who pays? It's always the consumer."

"If the Feds are spending all this money to take over banks and subsidize new owners, why don't they just do the same deal for the old bank owners and allow it to stay in business?"

Snowden's features hardened. Edward could see his question had struck a nerve.

"You're a smart guy, Edward. I wish we could handle your banking needs. You're the kind of client we normally want. I can't answer you with any specificity. But I have my opinions, for what they're worth. I've probably said enough on that subject already."

"When's this going to end?" Edward asked, feeling sick to his stomach. "*Is* it going to end?"

"Oh, sure, it'll end, but it'll take a few years, at least. The regulators will write down commercial real estate loans despite the strength of the borrowers. They're setting arbitrary values on collateral, regardless of appraisal values, deteriorating lending institutions' capital accounts. Then the regulators criticize the banks for being undercapitalized and take over every bank they feel like taking over. They bring in a Gerald Folsom who liquidates the bank's loan portfolio and forecloses when borrowers can't pay off their loan balances. After foreclosure, the bank dumps a ton of commercial and residential real estate on the market, depressing property values even further. The sharks ultimately come in and scoop up that real estate at fire-sale prices. Then, when the economy starts to improve, rents will rise and property values will increase, and the sharks will have made out like bandits. But that's an eight to ten-year cycle."

"It sounds like a shell game," Edward said.

"The ultimate shell game."

"How can you be so sure about the recovery time?"

"Two reasons. First, because it happened before. Someone once said that history is not one damned thing after another; it's the same damned thing over and over. It took ten years for real estate markets to recover after the '86 Act; it'll probably take at least as long this time. Economic and financial dislocations like this are dream killers. They destroy people's savings and investments, small businesses, and millions of jobs."

"Based on your description of things, it sounds to me as though the federal government is the real dream killer."

"You could say that," Snowden agreed. "It's the macro killer. But guys like Gerald Folsom, in a much smaller, but more personal, vicious way, murder people's dreams as well."

"You said two reasons."

"Yeah. In February of this year, the Congressional Oversight Panel of TARP issued a report about commercial real estate. It wasn't encouraging. Commercial real estate debt totals $3.4 trillion in the United States. Banks hold forty-five percent of that total, or about $1.5 trillion. According to the panel, smaller banks had commercial real estate portfolios equal to one point six times their total risk-based capital. By the third quarter of 2006, that had increased to three point two times. Because the typical commercial real estate loan has about a 20-year maturity and a 5-year call, there is real concern, especially in an environment like today's, where real estate values have declined so much, that when the 5-year call period is up on many of these loans, the value of the real estate will be below the loan amount. The bank and the borrower will find themselves underwater. Just like they did with residential properties."

"Fortunately, that's not our situation," Edward said, half-hoping Snowden might find a way to still finance the company's debt.

"Yes, but what if you can't find a bank to refinance your loans? What if every bank in the country has the same problem we do? If you can't refinance your loan balance when your loan matures, what do you think is going to happen?"

"The bank will place us in default on our loan," Edward said, feeling sick.

"I know none of this is fair, to you or to the banking community," Snowden said. "But it's the situation we have to live with. The regulators are forcing banks to shrink their balance sheets at a time when the country needs banks to stimulate the economy."

"So what do we do?"

"Try a couple other banks; maybe you'll get lucky. But I wouldn't count on it, because your financing needs are real estate-based. Commercial real estate loans have been branded by the regulators as toxic, regardless of the quality of the borrower or the current status of the loan. Your best bet is to work out a deal with Broad Street National."

# CHAPTER THIRTEEN

Katherine stopped at the post office on her way to the Winter Enterprises' headquarters building. She opened her box, hoping there would be a letter from Carrie. She hadn't heard from her daughter in over a month and had a difficult time not letting her imagination run away with itself with visions of her daughter lying in a pool of blood or in the hands of some Islamic terrorist group.

She rifled through the stack of mail and nearly shouted for joy when she saw an envelope with Carrie's handwriting. She rushed out to her car, throwing the rest of the mail on the front passenger seat and slicing open the letter.

*Dear Mom: I'm sorry I haven't written more often, but it's not really practical. Even if I wrote a letter, there would be no way to mail it.*

Katherine felt a pain in her chest. My God, she thought, what sort of hellhole is my daughter in? She continued reading.

*The good news is that my assignment is complete. I am being*

*treated for some intestinal bug you can't avoid where I was and I'll
be released in about a week from the Army hospital in Riyadh, Saudi
Arabia. I'll be on the first plane back to the real world. I should be
home when Betsy's baby arrives.*

*I've got a thirty-day leave scheduled, before I report for duty at
the Pentagon. Believe it or not, I'm coming home for that leave, and
then I'll be at the Puzzle Palace for at least twenty-four months. Think
about weekends in Cape May. I can already taste the linguini and
clams at Cucina Rosa.*

*Anyway, that's all for now. I feel rumbling going on in my nether
regions, which means I'll have to make a run to the john any moment
now. No need to worry. A bit of antibiotic and lots of fluids and I'll
be as good as new in a couple days.*

*Please hug Eddie and Betsy for me and give them my love.*

*Love, Carrie*

Katherine knew her daughter well enough to know she was
downplaying her illness, but couldn't help but feel relieved that
Carrie was back in civilization, so to speak. She couldn't wait to tell
Edward his sister would be home soon. Then Katherine came down
from her high, thinking about how Carrie's homecoming would be
in the midst of the crisis with the bank. It wouldn't be much of a
leave for her, with her mother and brother tied up with problems
at the company. But at least she'd be safe.

# CHAPTER FOURTEEN

Edward felt beat up as he and Nick walked out of Pennsylvania Industrial Bank's main office on City Line Avenue at 5 p.m. The bank's president, Victoria Watts, had been courteous and quite evidently embarrassed by the bank's present circumstances. She was nowhere near as candid as Van Snowden, but Edward could fill in the blanks. She did mention they had been required to raise their core capital and risk-based capital ratios, and they were not considering any new commercial real estate loans for the foreseeable future. She also told them U.S. banks had posted their biggest drop in lending since 1942.

"You know, I've got a thought," Edward said after he pulled out of the bank parking lot. "Let's call Ernest Deakyne at Philadelphia Savings & Trust and ask him if he has an interest in financing our real estate. If not, we won't waste his time or ours by keeping our appointment tomorrow."

"Good idea," Nick said. "I'm getting the impression these

bankers would be thrilled to have our business, as long as we don't ask for any credit."

Edward laughed. "I shouldn't see any humor in this, but I'm beginning to feel like Alice in the looking glass. Surreal." He handed his Blackberry to Nick. "Pull up Deakyne's number. Let's call him right now."

Nick found the banker's name and scrolled down to his office number. He listened to the car's Bluetooth system dial the number.

"Philadelphia Savings & Trust," a woman said. "Mr. Deakyne's office."

"Hello, this is Edward Winter of Winter Enterprises. I have an appointment with Mr. Deakyne tomorrow and need to talk with him for a minute."

"Yes, Mr. Winter. This is Jeanne, Mr. Deakyne's assistant. I made the appointment for you. Can you hold a second?"

Edward and Nick listened to the canned music on the bank's telephone system for about thirty seconds before Deakyne came on the line. "Ernest Deakyne."

"Hello, Mr. Deakyne. Edward Winter calling."

"Mr. Winter, good to hear from you. Are we still on for tomorrow?"

"That's what I'm calling about. By the way, I have you on speaker in my car. Our CFO, Nick Scarfatti, is here with me."

"Hi Mr. Scarfatti," Deakyne said. "What can I do for you?"

"We've been reading and hearing a lot about banks not wanting to make commercial real estate loans because of pressure from banking regulators. Our financing needs are heavily real estate oriented. We wanted to make sure this wouldn't be a problem for you. We didn't want to waste your time."

Deakyne paused, as though gathering his thoughts. Edward expected to hear that there was no point in visiting with them the next day. "I very much appreciate your courtesy in calling me, but, unlike most of the banks in our area, we don't have a big exposure to commercial real estate. When other banks were participating in the real estate boom, we took the conservative route. As a result, we have money to lend and feel that real estate values have pretty much hit bottom. We would be pleased to consider your loan request."

Edward and Nick looked at one another with expressions of ecstatic shock. "That's good to hear, Mr. Deakyne. We'll be there at 10 in the morning."

"Looking forward to seeing you, gentlemen."

Edward took his phone back from Nick, terminating the call and giving Nick a high five with his right hand. "Just when you think there's no hope, opportunity raises its beautiful head."

"I'm not deviating from my current negative mindset until you sign loan papers and I see the payoff confirmation from Broad Street Bank," Nick said, although Edward could hear relief in his voice.

"Kiljoy."

"Realist. After what we heard today, I didn't think there was a bank in America that could help us."

Edward looked at the dashboard clock and said, "4 o'clock. Even though I'm tempted to stop at McNally's Tavern and get one drink short of plastered, I'm going to the office. You want me to drop you off at your house first?"

"No, I've got a couple hours of work to do too. I'll need a ride home later."

"Just let me know when you're ready to leave. By the way, we ought to process the checks and credit card receipts in the vault.

We can't hold onto them forever. Even if we find another bank, it will take weeks to get the legal work completed."

"Already taken care of. We opened an account at Third Community Bank, that little bank down the street from the office. The branch manager nearly had a heart attack. A $600,000 deposit of checks and credit card payments is a lot of paper for a little bank."

"They shouldn't get too attached to that money. We're going to move it as soon as we find a new lender."

# CHAPTER FIFTEEN

Gerald Folsom entered the board room at Broad Street National Bank and sat at the head of the table. This was the first meeting he'd attended at the bank since the Feds took it over at 5 p.m. the previous Friday. Now that his CFO, Sanford Cunningham, had wrapped his hands around the high-level stuff – the computer systems, the loan and investment portfolios – he was ready to be briefed. Cunningham was already seated on Folsom's right; Eli Black, the bank's acting president, to Folsom's left. Others in the room were Stanley Burns, Chief Credit Officer, seated next to Black; Sarah Long, Chief Operating Officer, seated next to Cunningham; Alexi Chenko, IT Department manager, seated next to Burns; and Frances Dougherty, the Chief Investment Officer, seated next to Long.

Folsom pounded the file in front of him and barked, "Let's do this." He looked at his watch. "It's 3 o'clock. I want to be on the road by no later than 4."

Used to Folsom's management style, Cunningham looked around the room and wanted to laugh at the surprised looks on the others' faces, but knew that wouldn't be appropriate. Instead he jumped right into the agenda. "Ms. Dougherty, please brief us on your area."

Frances Dougherty was a fifty-eight-year-old woman who started at the bank right out of high school, working her way up from teller to Senior Vice President of Investments. She managed the investment portfolio, which included the bank's investments in Treasury bonds and bills, other securities, overnight funds invested with the Federal Reserve, among others. She also set interest rates on the bank's certificates of deposit and money market and savings accounts.

"As of close of business yesterday," she said, "we had $53.2 million in Treasuries, $36.0 million in mortgage-backed securities, and $112.0 million in municipal bonds in the bank's portfolio. In addition—"

"What's the average yield on the portfolio?" Folsom demanded.

Dougherty referred to a sheet of paper and answered, "three point one percent on the federal government bonds, five point eight percent on the MBS, and two point four percent on the Muni's. The weighted average yield is almost three point two percent. And keep in mind the Muni's are tax-exempt, so the actual after-tax yield is even greater."

"You're okay with that performance?" Folsom asked.

Dougherty's face reddened. She seemed confused for a moment. "I'd say that's pretty good performance considering the economic climate and the bank's aversion to taking too much risk."

"And on a mark-to-market basis, what's the current value of the portfolio?" Folsom pushed.

"The Treasuries and Muni's are in a profit position of 101.2, or slightly more than $167 million."

"And the MBS?"

"The mortgage-backed securities are marked at eighty-three percent of par. We've lost $6.1 million on that part of the portfolio."

"Jesus Christ! What idiot put us in mortgage bonds?" Folsom suddenly looked rabid.

Dougherty's lips compressed. She straightened her back and stuck out her chin a bit. "I am the head of the Investment Committee. I am responsible for our investment policy. I—"

Eli Black cleared his throat, interrupting. "Our investment decisions are made by committee. Frances executes our strategy. Despite the drop in the mark-to-market valuation of the MBS, the performance of that part of the portfolio is exceptional. Delinquencies are less than two percent, despite what has been going on in the residential real estate markets. And as the economy improves so will the value of these securities."

Folsom glared malevolently at Black. "Nice speech, Mr. Black. That kind of attitude caused the Feds to bring me in to salvage this sinking ship."

"I believe that's a mischaracterization of this bank, Mr. Folsom. Broad Street National has continued to be profitable, despite the economy, and the regulators' action in taking over this institution was without justification."

Folsom leaned back in his chair and roared with laughter. The others in the room sat as though frozen in place. Cunningham let slip a sly smile.

"You don't seem happy about the ownership change, Mr. Black.

In fact, you look downright displeased. The last thing I want is unhappy employees." He turned to Cunningham. "Sandy, escort Mr. Black down to his office, give him five minutes to collect his personal things, and then toss his unhappy ass out on the street."

Black jumped out of his chair and stormed out of the room without a word. Cunningham followed him out.

"Anyone else want to defend the bank's investment strategy or portfolio?" Folsom asked, an edge of malice to his voice.

Frances Dougherty lowered her head as the others stared at one another silently . No one made eye contact with Folsom.

"Ms. Dougherty," Folsom said.

She raised her head slightly and looked in Folsom's direction.

"What's the size of the CD portfolio and its average interest cost?"

Dougherty referred to another sheet of paper. "$479 million at an average cost of slightly less than three point five percent."

"Are you aware that when the FDIC takes over a bank it has the power to renegotiate all contracts, including CD contracts?"

She slowly nodded.

"Good. Mr. Cunningham will provide you with a letter tomorrow that I want mailed to every CD depositor on Thursday, reducing the rate we pay on all CDs. I want our average cost on CDs to be one point two percent."

Frances Dougherty looked frightened, but she mustered the courage to respond. "There will be a run on the bank. We have a large number of customers who are retired, who depend on their monthly interest payments. They'll cash in their accounts and take them elsewhere."

"Fuck them!" Folsom barked. "That's exactly what I expect and want to happen. The last thing I want around here is a bunch of retiree depositors sucking off this bank's teat." He paused and stared at Dougherty. "You have a problem with that?"

She shook her head and mouthed, "No, sir."

"Good." Folsom turned to Stanley Burns. "Okay Burns, let's hear about the loan portfolio."

Stanley Burns was a forty-nine-year-old who had started his banking career with Bank of America and been recruited by Broad Street National in 2005. The driving force behind the growth of Broad Street National Bank's commercial loan portfolio, he was a dynamic, sales-oriented lender who had a great way with customers. At the moment, though, he was not feeling good about his role in that growth. He hoped his weariness didn't show as he slouched in his chair, appearing as though he was trying to hide behind the table in front of him. At six feet four inches tall and two hundred twenty pounds, that wasn't easy. He hesitated during his presentation when Sanford Cunningham nonchalantly returned and took his seat.

"Something wrong, Burns?" Folsom asked.

Burns swallowed, shook his head, and continued to summarize the yield on the loan portfolio, the delinquent loans, those that were under-collateralized, and those maturing in the next six months. He estimated any losses the bank might take. After twenty-five tense minutes, Burns finished.

After a beat, Folsom began. "I want a few pieces of information, Mr. Burns," he said. "And I want them by the end of business tomorrow.

"First, I want specifics on the delinquent loans that are underwater. What's the estimated fire-sale value of collateral securing underwater loans? If we have personal guarantees on any of these loans, what's the chance of collecting on those guarantees? Are we holding other collateral in addition to the real estate on any of these underwater borrowers?"

Burns took notes at a frenetic pace.

"Second," Folsom continued without waiting for a response, "I want a list of all loans maturing in the next six months and the value of the underlying collateral and the fire-sale value of that collateral. Also, the amount of deposits these borrowers have in the bank. And, finally, I want a write-up on the businesses these borrowers own—profitability, stuff like that—and whether our loans are on owner-occupied real estate. Got it?"

"Yes, sir."

"Give that information to Mr. Cunningham tomorrow," Folsom said. Folsom stood and, in turn, derisively met the gaze of each of the bankers. "The rest of you can give your presentations to Mr. Cunningham. Understand something, ladies and gentlemen. If you want to keep your jobs here, you have one objective: To make money. I don't give a shit about the Community Reinvestment Act, or charitable contributions, or fucking retirees who depend on interest payments. I care about making money." He then added, "One of you will replace Eli Black as president of this bank on Friday. We'll see who wants that position most."

Folsom wagged a finger at Cunningham, wheeled around, and walked out, waiting for Cunningham to join him outside the room.

"The list of loans you sent me this morning. There was one to a company named Winter Enterprises. Tell me about it."

"I don't know a lot yet, except the company has fast food joints all over the city. The principal shareholder is Edward Winter. Why?"

"Find out if Edward Winter is related to a guy who was president of a bank over twenty years ago. A guy named Frank Winter."

Cunningham shrugged, unconcerned with Folsom's strange request. "I'll let you know."

# CHAPTER SIXTEEN

Folsom felt as though he'd popped six Viagra pills. The bank meeting he'd just left had given him a sexual high almost as good as kicking the shit out of Wendy. Even though mousey Francis Dougherty wasn't his type—too old, too heavy, too plain—the fear in her eyes stirred feelings in his groin. As he drove home, he pictured his bruised and battered wife and contemplated the pleasure she would give him.

Wendy Folsom stumbled as she moved slowly around her bedroom, still dressed in nothing but her bathrobe. She'd tried to put on panties, a blouse, and a skirt, but her body couldn't bend to accomplish it. Every movement hurt like nothing she had ever experienced before.

She was embarrassed that during the first year of her marriage, she had actually enjoyed Gerald's aggressive approach to sex. It was something new and exciting. But over the last year, he had become even more aggressive, slapping her with more force than usual, putting his hands around her neck and cutting off her breath during orgasm. It heightened the intensity of her orgasms, but it frightened her as well. But Saturday night, into Sunday morning, had been a different thing altogether. The only part that had anything to do with sex was Gerald penetrating her. Everything else was assault and battery, plain and simple. And she had never seen him so excited.

There was no doubt in Wendy's mind that her husband had stepped up to another level of violence, and she knew she would not suffer another such beating. She'd already had enough of his narcissism, his ego and his arrogance. Add in the violence and she was through.

She finished putting a few things in an overnight bag, including all of her jewelry and what little cash she had, and lugged it downstairs with a great deal of difficulty. She went through the kitchen, into the garage, and hoisted the bag into the trunk of her Infiniti SUV. On the way back to her bedroom, Wendy paused in the kitchen and poured herself a glass of orange juice. She hadn't had anything to eat or drink, except water, since Saturday evening, knowing her stomach wouldn't keep anything down. She sipped half the glass before her stomach began to cramp.

The climb back upstairs was slow and painful. She took one step at a time, resting on each tread but by the time she reached the top, she was exhausted. As badly as she wanted to dress and get out of the house, she couldn't muster the energy. Just a few minutes of rest, she told herself as she slowly sat on her bed. Groaning as she laid her head on her pillow, she closed her eyes. A fuzzy feeling invaded her head and she tried to force herself to stay awake. She knew what was happening. The heavy-duty pain killers and the muscle relaxers she'd taken were having an effect. Just a few minutes of rest, she told herself.

Gerald Folsom arrived home at 6:30 p.m. "Wendy, I'm home," he called out in a taunting voice. No answer. He called out again, with the same result. He climbed the stairs to his bedroom and tossed his suit jacket over a clothes tree. He stripped off his tie and shirt and dropped them on the floor.

"Wendy, where the hell are you?" he shouted. Still no response.

Folsom crossed through the bathroom between his and his wife's bedrooms and spied Wendy asleep on her bed, lying on her side with her back to him. She was still wearing the bathrobe she'd had on when he left that morning, the same thing she'd had on since Sunday morning. He prodded her shoulder with his fingertips. She groaned but didn't wake up.

He opened her robe and was briefly shocked at the extent of the yellow and black bruises and red and black hemorrhages on her body. He hadn't realized he'd beaten her so badly. The damage surprised him; it didn't make him feel shame or regret. In fact, the thought of screwing her battered body made him more excited, imagining the pain his weight on her would cause, and other ways to increase her pain. He poked her again, with no response.

"Shit!" he barked. "Bitch!" Fucking was no fun if she wasn't aware of it.

He shed the rest of his clothes and put on an exercise outfit before going outside and jogging around the interior perimeter of his property. After forty-five minutes, he returned to his room, showered, and dressed in khakis, a short-sleeved polo shirt, and deck shoes. He decided to go out to eat, hoping Wendy would be conscious by the time he returned. The thought of her being awake, her body bruised, gave him an erection.

# CHAPTER SEVENTEEN

Katherine hadn't made any plans for dinner; it was too late to start cooking something, and she didn't feel like going out by herself. Then the thought struck her that she had not treated Paul Sanders very well yesterday. She'd used him, put him at risk, and then hadn't thanked him for going to Folsom's house with her even though he had gone with her to protect her. "Aw, crap," she said, feeling guilty.

She went to her telephone, called Paul's number, and waited for him to answer, all the while wondering about what she was doing.

"Hello?" Paul answered.

"Paul, it's Katherine."

"Oh, hi. Is something wrong?"

"Well, yes, Paul. Something's wrong. I—"

"What is it, Katherine. Do you need me to come over there?" Paul sounded immediately urgent.

"Whoa, Paul. Let me finish. What's wrong is that I feel bad about the way I handled things yesterday and want to make amends.

Would you be willing to have dinner with me tonight? My treat."

"Are we going to break into anyone's house after dinner? Will I need to bring a flashlight and wear dark clothing?"

"Do you want to have dinner with me or not?" Katherine asked, beginning to get peeved at Paul's teasing.

Paul laughed. "Of course I accept your invitation. I'll pick you up in, say, a half-hour."

"Good," she said, and hung up, surprising herself with how much she was looking forward to dinner with Paul.


Edward, trying to restore some semblance of normality back into their home life, had a quiet dinner at home with Betsy. He knew his stress had infected Betsy: She usually was tired from the pregnancy, but had looked utterly exhausted the last few days.

"What time's your appointment at the bank tomorrow?" Betsy asked.

"Ten o'clock. I'm pretty encouraged. I had a nice conversation with the president of Philadelphia Bank & Trust this afternoon. His bank doesn't seem to be in the same situation as most others."

"That's good," Betsy said, somewhat absent-mindedly.

Edward stood and walked to the other end of the dining table and kissed Betsy's cheek. "Don't worry about anything; this is just one more bump in the road. That's what business is all about. Just think, I could have a job at one of the banks. What a nightmare that would be."

Betsy chuckled, brightening a bit, but Edward could tell she was still troubled. "We've got almost $4 million dollars in two banks, our real estate equity is around $30 million dollars—even in this market—and we own our home free and clear. What are you worried about?"

Betsy took his hand and lifted herself from her chair. She moved into his arms and buried her cheek into his chest. "I don't care about the money. I just don't want to see you lose what you've worked so hard building up. I don't know how something like that would affect you."

He hugged her tighter and said, "That isn't going to happen, honey," not disclosing that he had wondered the same thing a dozen times during the past few days.

Katherine and Paul got through both dinner and dessert without once mentioning the episode at Gerald Folsom's house. Katherine had been afraid they would talk about nothing else, which would only have embarrassed her further. But Paul had been a gentleman, as usual, and, instead regaled her with stories about humorous legal cases he'd handled, keeping her laughing through much of the dinner. Then somehow they'd segued to American literature.

"How do you find time to read so much?" she asked him.

"I don't sleep. If I get five hours a night it's a lot. I just finished reading Carl Sandburg's *Lincoln* last night."

"Any good?" she asked.

He smiled and said, "Well, let's put it this way. Edmund Wilson said, 'In my opinion Carl Sandburg is the worst that has happened to Lincoln since Booth shot him.' "

"Ouch! That's pretty rough."

"Pretty accurate, too."

They both chuckled, then the conversation lulled. Katherine

finally filled it. "What do you think is going to happen with this Tea Party movement?"

Paul showed a mischievous smile. "John Adams, in a letter to Abigail, wrote, 'I must not write a word to you about politics, because you are a woman.' "

Katherine hadn't realized that Paul was such a tease. She smiled back and said, "And Abigail once wrote to John, 'Men of sense in all ages abhor those customs which treat us only as vassals of your sex.' "

"Touché," Paul responded. "To answer your question about the Tea Party, I think it's causing people to focus on just how mad they are at all politicians. The citizenry is anxious to send a message to the political class that they're fed up with over-spending, over-taxation, and over-regulation. I think we're going to see incumbents of both parties get swept out of office, just like what happened in 2010."

"Of course, we could be in worse trouble if Congress gets taken over by a bunch of freshmen legislators dependent on the bureaucrats and their own staffers," Katherine said.

"Damned if we do and damned if we don't."

"Adlai Stevenson," Katherine said.

Paul stared at Katherine. "I'm going to have to be on my toes when I'm with you."

She smiled.

# CHAPTER EIGHTEEN

Folsom downed two scotch and waters before dinner and polished off most of a bottle of cabernet sauvignon with his rare steak and baked potato, feeling no pain as he got into his Mercedes and drove home. Images of Wendy lying in her bed, naked under her snow-white silk robe, intruded on his alcohol-fueled thoughts. His mind reeled with the possibilities of what the rest of his evening would be like, but derailed when an errant thought penetrated his mind.

What if he'd killed her? That question floated around in his head for a minute or two. He remembered how shocked he'd been when he saw how badly bruised Wendy was. The idea scared him and excited him at the same time. He'd never killed anybody. What would it feel like? What if he killed his wife? What would he do with the body? What sort of story could he come up with?

He shook his head as though to clear it of these strange ideas and questions, but they wouldn't dissipate. He knew he'd leaped to another level, like surging through a time warp membrane into a strange and unknown land. Murder! Another dimension altogether.

The drive home took him twenty minutes. By the time he entered the house through the garage, he was jacked up on alcohol, adrenaline, and testosterone. He climbed the stairs to the second level, picturing what his naked wife looked like, sprawled on the bed, robe open. He disrobed on his way to her room, dropping his clothes on the floor as he went, completely naked when he got to her bedside.

Wendy had shifted and was now lying on her back, spread-eagled on the side of the bed, the corners of her robe caught between her thighs.

Folsom thumped the side of her head with his middle finger. "You awake?"

Wendy groaned.

He shook her. "Wake up!" he shouted.

She rolled on her side toward him, groaning as she moved.

Enough of this crap, Folsom thought. He grabbed a handful of her robe and ripped it from under her, leaving it bunched under her head. He rubbed a palm over her stomach, pressing down firmly against her tight but bruised muscles.

The pain from Folsom's touch must have finally penetrated Wendy's brain. She sprang awake and cried out, "Jesus!"

"Jesus ain't gonna help you here, sweetie," he said, rubbing harder.

"No! Not tonight. I hurt so bad. Ple-e-e-aze."

"Especially tonight, Wendy. Especially tonight," he murmured

Folsom mounted her and quickly satisfied himself. He knew, and he knew she knew, that the worst was yet to come. He took her face in one hand and squeezed her cheeks, his fingers compressing the swollen areas around her eyes, until she screamed with pain.

"That's my girl," Folsom said. "You never disappoint me."

He moved his hand down to her left breast and squeezed the nipple until her screams came in a long, high-pitched sequence. He started to move down her body so he could put his mouth on her breast when a shrill ringing broke into his reverie.

"What the hell!" Folsom spat, knowing it was his cell phone. Very few people had the number, so it must be important, especially at this late hour. "Sonofabitch!"

He climbed off Wendy and slapped her face. "Don't move," he roared. "I'll be right back."

He went in search of his cell phone, which was in a pocket of the pants he'd dropped somewhere in his bedroom. In a corner of the room, he saw the light blinking through the fabric of his pants. Snatching them off the floor, he rummaged in the pocket, grabbing the phone, and jerking it free. He looked at the display and recognized the number: Donald Matson's. He pressed the TALK button.

"This better be good, Matson. You're interrupting something very important."

"I've got problems, Gerald. Bad problems."

Oh, Jeez, what a pussy, Folsom thought. "Your wife find you in bed with the babysitter?"

"This isn't funny," Matson cried. "The FDIC performed an audit of the safety deposit box owners at Broad Street National Bank. It was just a standard audit, looking for anything suspicious. You know, names of politicians or of organized crime members. But they found the box in my name. Someone from the agency's Inspector General's office just served me with an order to disclose the contents of the box when the bank opens tomorrow. They want to inventory the contents."

"So? You're a citizen. You're allowed to have a safety deposit box."

"They thought it was strange I had a box in downtown Philadelphia, when my office and home are on the northwest side of town."

"I still don't get it."

"The $1 million in cash you gave me is in there."

"You fuckin' idiot. You left the money in the box? In my bank?!"

"Where else was I going to put it? It's not like I can invest it in a mutual fund."

A sudden thought hit Folsom. "Don't tell me you've still got the safety deposit boxes at the other banks I've taken over, with the cash still sitting in them."

"Well, I've taken out some of the money. Gifts for the family, private school tuition. Stuff like that. But I can't buy boats or sports cars without raising questions."

"Matson, do you realize once the Feds find the cash in your box in Broad Street National Bank, they'll probably put two and two together and check boxes at all the banks you put me into? How are you going to explain millions of dollars sitting in a half-dozen banks?" What Folsom didn't add was that there was no doubt in his mind once the Feds started interrogating Matson, he'd spill everything he knew, including how Gerald Folsom had paid him off. They were both going to jail.

Matson began crying. "Oh God, Jerry. What am I going to do?"

Folsom considered the options and then snapped, "Pull yourself together. What else do you have in that box?"

"Nothing. Just the money."

"Okay, here's what you do. Pull together your car titles, mortgage documents and deeds, any insurance policies you've got at home. Take them down to the bank and I'll meet you there in an hour. And don't forget your safety deposit box key."

Folsom terminated the call and started to dress. "What a dickhead!" he growled. As he was putting on his socks and shoes, he called Sanford Cunningham.

"Hello?"

"Sanford, I need your help. That stupid twerp, Donald Matson, just got an order from his agency to disclose the contents of his safety deposit box at Broad Street Bank when the bank opens tomorrow at nine o'clock."

"Something in the box that shouldn't be there?"

"You could say that. But that's something you don't need to know. Can we get into the safety deposit box vault tonight?"

"Sure. I've got the combination to the room lock and the keys to the vault."

"It's not on a timer?"

"No, not like the main vault. If it were, we wouldn't be able to get in until 7:30 in the morning."

"Thank God for small favors. I'll pick you up. Matson is going to meet us at the bank at 11."

Folsom checked on Wendy, who was lying in a fetal position. He bent over and grabbed a handful of her hair. "Passed out again, huh? I'm sorry I had to break up our little love-making session. I know how much you enjoy them. But I'll be back in a few hours."

He walked out of the room laughing.

# CHAPTER NINETEEN

Wendy had closed her eyes as soon as Gerald returned to her bedroom, realizing from the phone conversation she'd overheard he had to go out. She forced herself not to flinch or moan when he grabbed her hair, and barely took a breath until he left the room. After she heard his car leave the garage and pass under her window, she gathered her strength and sat up, letting her feet rest on the carpeted floor. She took a deep breath, held it, and pushed off the bed, grunting as she stood, her head fuzzy from the sudden movement. Grasping the edge of the bedside table, she steadied herself until the dizziness passed.

Her robe was hanging to one side. She pulled it closed around her and in so doing felt something stiff in the left pocket: A business card. It took her a few seconds to remember where it came from. That man who had been in her bedroom. When was it? Yesterday? Last week? Why had he been here? She couldn't get her head straight around the memory. The card said the man was an attorney. She palmed it and shuffled to her walk-in closet.

After shucking off the robe and dropping it to the floor, she reached in a drawer for a bra, but decided there was no way she would be able to contort her body enough to put it on. She struggled into a pair of underpants and then put on a sweat shirt and a wrap-around skirt. The thought of putting on heels or lace-up shoes was intimidating. Instead, she selected a pair of sandals, dropped them to the carpeted floor, and slid her feet into them.

She knew Gerald kept a large amount of money in a safe in his bedroom, but she didn't know the combination. But there was also cash in his sock drawer. She stumbled out of the closet, through the bathroom, to his bedroom's top dresser drawer. She came up with a money clip filled with $100 bills and stuck it in her skirt pocket, along with the lawyer's business card. Leaving the upstairs, her heart stopped when she made it to the entry: Gerald's Mercedes was coming back up the driveway.

"Oh God! Oh God!" Wendy cried. She panicked, indecisive. Was he going to put his car in the garage? That's where her car was. She knew she needed to move, but she couldn't decide where to go. Then it hit her that Gerald had just left the house a few minutes ago. He'd probably forgotten something. Maybe his wallet. If she was correct, he wouldn't go into the garage; he'd come through the front door. She walked like a nonagenarian, every muscle aching, to the kitchen, and then to the garage. She stepped down into the garage and climbed behind the wheel of her Infiniti SUV. The pain from pulling herself into the high-profile vehicle slammed her brain like a jack hammer.

She sat and waited, hoping Gerald would turn around and drive away again. She thought about being free and safe. About being away from her monster of a husband. Then a wave of staggering fear washed over her. What if he goes into my bedroom and I'm not there? He'll look for me. She imagined the repercussions. Frozen in place, she realized her life was over if he went upstairs. She suddenly no longer cared about living, not if it meant living with Gerald. She waited for Gerald to come looking for her. The minutes ticked by on the dashboard clock—one, two . . . seven, eight. She heard a noise. Thinking it was the door from the kitchen to the garage, she steeled herself. For the violence. But he didn't enter the garage. Then she heard the roar of the Mercedes and the scattering of driveway pebbles as Gerald drove away.

Her chest hurt from holding her breath for extended periods of time. She breathed out slowly, waited two minutes, and then pressed the button on the garage door opener on her visor. She backed out of the garage, closed the door behind her, turned the car around and drove down to the gate. After the gate opened automatically, she drove away, with no idea where to go.

# CHAPTER TWENTY

Katherine noticed the wait staff at the restaurant was hovering near their table. She glanced around the dining room and was shocked to see she and Paul were the last two diners.

"Gosh, what time is it?" she asked Paul.

He looked at his watch. "Nearly midnight."

"What! I can't believe it. You'd better get me home before I turn into a pumpkin."

Katherine waved at their waiter. "Check please," she told him. The young man smiled as though he were a kid on Christmas morning and immediately presented the check.

"I guess I'd better leave him a larger tip than usual," she said to Paul. For some reason she found that funny and laughed. Paul started laughing with her. By the time she'd put cash on the table to cover the tab and the tip, and they moved toward the door, they were both laughing uncontrollably.

Outside in the parking lot, Paul took her arm and steered her to the passenger side of his car. He leaned close to her and whispered, "You had too much to drink tonight."

She looked at him askance and said, "Was it H.L. Mencken who said 'I've made it a rule never to drink by daylight and never to refuse a drink after dark?'"

"Ah, a quote and a challenge," Paul said. He released Katherine's arm and stopped to look up at the moon.

"What are you doing?" she asked.

"Searching for inspiration."

"I can't wait to hear this," she said, giggling.

"Ah, I have it," he said. "'We, cold water girls and boys, Freely renounce the treacherous joys Of brandy, whiskey, rum, and gin; The serpent's lure to death and sin.'"

"Where in the name of all that's holy did you come up with that?"

A frown showed on Paul's face. He seemed to think about her question and then said, "I really don't have a clue."

Katherine stared at him and then again broke out in peals of laughter. She kissed him on the cheek and said, "You're a surprise, Paul. I'm glad I called you."

"I'm glad, too," he said. "We should—" His cell phone interrupted him.

"Who could that be at this hour?" Katherine asked.

"I have no idea, but I hope it's a client I can charge twice my normal rate for annoying me. Hello?" he said.

"Mr. Sanders," a woman said. "I need your help. I—" Then the woman began sobbing. Paul could barely make out her words between sobs. "I don't know what to do. I have no place to go."

"Miss," Paul said, "I can't begin to help you if you don't tell me who you are."

A slight pause. Then, "Wendy Folsom. Gerald Folsom's wife."

# TUESDAY
# JULY 19, 2011

# CHAPTER TWENTY-ONE

By 1 a.m. on Tuesday morning, Gerald Folsom and Sanford Cunningham had accomplished their mission. They'd pulled the cash out of Donald Matson's safety deposit box and stuffed it in a backpack Matson had brought with him. They'd replaced the cash with Matson's personal papers and then closed the safety deposit box and vault, reset the alarm, and locked the bank lobby doors behind them.

In the bank parking lot, Folsom grabbed Matson's arm and squeezed the bicep until he yelped. He yanked Matson off to the side, away from Cunningham, and rasped, "You take that money someplace right now and hide it. And tomorrow you close out all the other safety deposit boxes you have and hide all the cash. Then figure out what you're going to do with it. Maybe, over a period of time, buy gold coins and gem stones. I don't give a shit. But don't ever jeopardize me again. You got it?"

Matson nodded, got into his car, and drove away in a hurry.

Folsom and Cunningham got into Folsom's Mercedes and headed towards Cunningham's neighborhood. Folsom didn't know what to say. Tonight's experience with Matson had unnerved him.

Cunningham eventually broke the silence. "By the way, I checked on Edward Winter as you requested."

Folsom jerked a glance at Cunningham. "What d'ya find?"

"Edward is the son of Frank and Katherine Winter. Frank was president of First—"

"I know who he was. Tell me about Katherine."

"She's on the board of Winter Enterprises. Besides Edward, she has a daughter named Carrie, an officer in the U.S. Army."

"I'll have special instructions for you about the Winter Enterprises' loan," Folsom said after a moment's pause.

Cunningham didn't respond for a minute and then said, "As a finance guy, I understand assets and liabilities. That FDIC guy, Matson, has been an asset up to now. I would say he just became a liability."

"I was thinking the same thing."

"What are you going to do about it?"

"I'll figure it out in the morning," Folsom said. "But, tonight, after I drop you off, I've got other business to take care of."

"It's late."

Folsom laughed. "It's never too late for this kind of business."


It was a few minutes before 2 a.m. when Folsom pulled into his garage. He was confused momentarily by the absence of his wife's vehicle. Then his confusion turned to rage. He ran into the house and stormed up the stairs. He searched her bedroom and then ran through every room on all four floors of the house. In the condition she was in, he hadn't thought it possible she could even negotiate the stairs, let alone drive away.

His rage now elevating to inferno level, Folsom went to his bar on the first level and poured himself a double shot of scotch over ice. He carried the glass into his home office and tried to figure out where the fuck Wendy had gone. Once he figured that out, he'd drag her back here and kick the shit out of her. Again.

Then a thought came to him. He grabbed for a telephone and called Sanford Cunningham's cell phone.

"Hello?" Cunningham answered, sounding groggy with sleep.

"Sanford, I want a hold put on all of Winter Enterprises' deposit accounts first thing in the morning."

"Why, what's up?"

"Just do it," Folsom shouted, and hung up the phone.


Paul had barely got Wendy Folsom's location and vehicle description from her when the woman went completely silent. He and Katherine found her car in a McDonalds's parking lot in Sharon Hill. She was slouched behind the wheel, her head against the window; her doors locked. Paul knocked on the window for half-a-minute before he roused her. He helped the disoriented and frightened woman move from the driver's seat to the passenger seat and then got behind the wheel and followed Katherine, driving his car, to her house. He had wanted to take Wendy back to his place, but Katherine persuaded him that if the woman needed help dressing or needed minor medical attention, she would be better off staying with another woman.

"You should see a doctor," Paul said.

"No, please. I know I look awful, but it's just bruises. Nothing's broken; I'm sure of that."

"What are you afraid of?"

"I need to hide for a few days. Do some thinking."

"Tonight, I'll go along with your wishes. But if you're not better tomorrow, I'm taking you to a hospital."

The drive to Katherine's house was slow and deliberate as Paul attempted to miss the potholes in Philadelphia's decrepit streets. Even so, every bump generated a groan from his wounded passenger. When they arrived, they half-walked, half-carried Wendy into the house and put her in Katherine's guest bed before moving to the kitchen. Paul sat down at the kitchen table, while Katherine made coffee.

"I'm exhausted," Paul said, his elbows on the table, head in his hands.

"Hell of a day," she agreed. "What have we gotten ourselves into?"

Paul dropped his hands and looked over at Katherine. "You know, we should call the police. At a minimum, Gerald Folsom should be charged with assault and battery. By the looks of that young woman, I could make a case for attempted murder."

"I think we should wait until we can talk to her, when she's alert. She needs to make the decision about bringing the police into this."

"Makes sense. But I'm going to think about what criminal lawyer should represent her. There's an old saying that goes, 'Three Philadelphia lawyers are a match for the Devil.' Against a man like Gerald Folsom, she's going to need at least one of those lawyers."

Katherine placed a cup of coffee in front of Paul and sat down across from him. "Finish your coffee—it's decaf—and then go home and get some sleep. We're both going to need a lot of stamina over the next few days."

# CHAPTER TWENTY-TWO

Despite the tenor and substance of yesterday's conversation with Ernest Deakyne, President of Philadelphia Savings & Trust, Edward was apprehensive in Deakyne's waiting area. He and Nick were as prepared as they could be, and he knew that their presentation had no weaknesses: Strong finances, experienced management and employees, a solid business plan. But he had learned over the past week that that meant nothing compared to the environment in the industry caused by the federal regulators, and that environment was, at best, damaged and, at worst, corrupt.

A voice brought him out of his thoughts. "Good morning, gentlemen. Thank you for coming in to see me."

Edward and Nick stood and shook hands with Deakyne, a short, completely bald, nattily dressed man. Deakyne was no more than five feet, seven inches tall and couldn't have weighed more than one hundred and forty pounds. He wore a light-weight gray suit, white shirt, and off-yellow bow tie.

"Let's go into my conference room," Deakyne said, leading the way into a room with a table that sat six. He directed them to chairs on one side of the table and sat down opposite them. "Coffee, tea, water?"

"Your assistant was very kind," Edward answered. "She offered us something to drink, but we're fine. Thank you."

"Okay, then let's get started. I should tell you we're quite excited about the opportunity to have Winter Enterprises as a client of our bank."

I like this guy more by the minute, Edward thought. "I hope we can work out an arrangement."

Edward spent twenty-five minutes giving Deakyne an overview of the Hot N' Chili franchise business, the history of Winter Enterprises, and the company's plans for expansion. Then he turned things over to Nick who went over the company's financial statements. By the time they had completed the presentation, an hour had passed. Edward was feeling positive and enthusiastic.

But Deakyne appeared to be suddenly uncomfortable. "I had no idea," he said, "that your firm was as large as it is. You said your loan balance at Broad Street National is $20 million against a loan commitment of $30 million. We couldn't come close to matching that number."

Edward fought hard to keep from showing how devastated he felt. "In other words, your loan limit to any one borrower is less than $30 million?"

"Less than $20 million, actually. Our statutory loan limit is $11 million. We couldn't lend Winter Enterprises more than that. This would leave $9 million of your loan at Broad Street unfunded. And would do nothing to support your expansion plans. I am so sorry, gentlemen. This is not how I wanted this meeting to turn out. "

Edward and Nick sat in silence, stunned. Deakyne moved his chair back from the table, started to rise.

"Can you give us another minute?" Edward asked.

Deakyne lowered himself back into his chair. "Of course. I would love to find a resolution in this matter."

"If I understand correctly, your bank could finance $11 million of our debt."

"That's correct."

"So, if we were able to divide our lending facilities between $11 million at your bank and $9 million at Broad Street, would that work for you?"

Deakyne considered Edward's suggestion and then responded. "I think that would work. Of course, this would be subject to a favorable review of your financial information and new appraisals on the real estate with which you would secure our loan. And then there are the deposit accounts at Broad Street. We would want a fair proportion of those deposits put in our bank."

"Maybe we can make this work after all," Edward said. He stood and reached across the table and offered Deakyne his hand. The banker stood and shook Edward's hand and then Nick's.

In the car driving back to their offices, Edward called Stanley Burns at Broad Street National Bank. He waited on hold for three minutes before a woman finally came on the line to inform him Stanley Burns was in a meeting and would have to call him back.

After Edward terminated the call, he said, "You know, Nick, every time I used to call Burns, he'd get on the phone in a matter of seconds. Even when he was in a meeting he'd take my calls."

"I guess he's got other priorities. Like keeping his job."

"By the way, when we were meeting the other day, when Annie and the kids came to the office, you started to say something about our deposits at Broad Street National. You said you wanted to look into something. What was on your mind?"

"I checked the Right of Setoff clause in our loan documents. That's where the bank can apply any money we have on deposit against our loan balance."

"That's fair," Edward said. "They should be able to do just that if we were delinquent on our loan, which we're not."

"True. But the language in that clause goes way beyond just delinquency. They can dip into our accounts if they believe the value of the collateral on a loan has deteriorated, or if they anticipate a borrower will not be able to pay off an obligation on schedule. Theoretically, both of these caveats apply to us. The value of our real estate has deteriorated and we're having a hell of a time finding financing to pay off Broad Street."

"They could take our deposits even if the net collateral value of our real estate is still $30 million over the loan amount?"

"Hell, Eddie, I don't know. I'm not a lawyer, but the language in that clause just talks about deterioration in collateral value. It says nothing about whether the collateral value is below the loan amount. Our real estate was worth $62 million five years ago when we took out the loan; now it's worth $50 million. That is deterioration."

"I think you should wire transfer our balances from Broad Street National to that little bank where you deposited last weekend's receipts. No point in risking $3 million. Most of that money is already committed to covering the costs of the land purchases in Pittsburgh. If we don't perform on those purchase contracts, we'll lose our earnest money deposits and get our asses sued by the sellers. Plus, we've already paid the franchise fees for two new sites."

Nick pulled his cell phone from his pocket and dialed the bank's Treasury Department number from memory. He asked for Mary Jane Wolitsky, his usual contact.

"Mary Jane, It's Nick Scarfatti. How are you today?"

"Okay, Nick. Things are changing around here, but I've still got my job."

"Hang in there, Mary Jane. Your customers wouldn't know what to do without you. Listen, I need to order a wire."

"Sure, Nick. How much and to where?"

Nick knew the company had $2.967 million and change in its accounts. The vast majority of the money the company deposited to its checking account was swept from that account to a money market account on a daily basis. The last deposits made to the checking account were made the previous Thursday. They always maintained a balance of $100 thousand in the checking account, so there was now at least $2.867 million in the money market account, not including accrued interest over the last few days.

"Move $2.8 million from the money market account to the following account." He gave her the name of the bank where the wired funds needed to go, the bank's routing number, and the account number.

"I don't think I can do that, Nick," Mary Jane said.

"Why not?"

"A hold has been put on your account in the amount of $2.75 million."

"By whom?" Nick demanded. "Who ordered that hold?"

"Mr. Cunningham did."

"And who the hell is Mr. Cunningham?"

"He's Lucifer's errand boy, Nick," She said in a whisper.

"And who's Lucifer?"

"Gerald Folsom. The new owner of the bank."

# CHAPTER TWENTY-THREE

The only way Gerald Folsom was able to fall asleep was by sedating himself with alcohol. He woke up at 11 a.m. on Tuesday morning feeling heavy-headed and fuzzy-mouthed and when he stood up, a wave of nausea overwhelmed him, driving him to the bathroom to throw up in the toilet. Wiping off his mouth with the back of his hand, he ripped off the clothes he'd worn to the bank late last night, showered, and shaved. By noon, he was beginning to feel half-human again.

He put on a pot of coffee and tried to eat a couple pieces of toast. But they only roiled his stomach further. He thought maybe a drink would help, but when he picked up the scotch bottle, his stomach began to heave.

"What the fuck is going on?" he said aloud. "First Donald Matson, then Wendy, and now my damned stomach."

Folsom knew he had lived a charmed life for decades; nothing ever went wrong. Now things seemed to be falling apart. He had to get back in control. What had Cunningham said to him last night? Something about assets and liabilities. That's what he should do. Eliminate his liabilities. But his head still wasn't clear enough to focus on what to do.

Wendy had no idea where she was. The room was unfamiliar, but from the color of the drapes and the bedding she could tell it was a woman's room. She felt an overwhelming need to relieve her bladder. Rolling over to the edge of the bed, a spasm of horrendous pain stabbed her back and she cried out, shifting back onto her right side. Her cry devolved into a moan as she lay there, not knowing what to do.

Suddenly the door opened and a woman entered, asking, "You okay, dear?"

"I need to . . . use the bathroom. I can't seem to get up."

The woman helped Wendy to a sitting position. "Come on, let's get you up." She took Wendy's arm and helped her to her feet, Wendy groaning as she leaned against the woman. They shuffled together to the bathroom. "Call me when you're done," the woman said.

When Wendy finished, she called out, "Ma'am, I need your help."

The woman returned and pulled Wendy off the john.

"You want to change your clothes?" the woman asked. "Get cleaned up?"

"I feel awful," Wendy said. "A bath would be wonderful, but I don't think I can get into and out of a tub. Maybe a shower."

"Okay. We brought your bag in from your car last night; I'll lay out fresh clothes."

"Who are you? Where am I?"

"My name is Katherine Winter. I'm a friend of Paul Sanders, who you called last night. This is my home."

"I remember calling Mr. Sanders, but that's about all."

"Do you remember how you got your injuries?"

"I'd rather not talk about it."

"Okay. Go ahead and get cleaned up," Katherine said. "I'll make something to eat."

With effort, Wendy removed her sweatshirt and then dropped her skirt and underwear on the bathroom floor. She turned toward the shower and flinched at movement to her left -- it was her reflection in a full-length mirror. Her breath caught when she stared at the damage Gerald had done to her. Her body looked as though it had been tattooed with black, red, and yellow ink and her face was swollen and cut along her cheek bones. She leaned against the bathroom wall and sobbed, full of shame and sadness.

But, as suddenly as the shame and sadness had overcome her, rampaging anger overwhelmed her. "The bastard!" she muttered. "The sick bastard!" She came to a sudden conclusion she sensed would change her life. Wendy wrapped a towel gently around her torso and opened the bathroom door. She shuffled across the bedroom to the door to the hall and called out, "Mrs. Winter."

Katherine came down the hall. "Yes, dear."

"Do you have a camera?"

"Of course. Why?"

"I want you to take some pictures."

# CHAPTER TWENTY-FOUR

It was 3 p.m. before Stanley Burns returned Edward's call. Edward called Nick on the intercom and asked him to come into his office, leaving Burns on hold until Nick arrived.

"I'm sorry it took so long, but we've been in meetings with the FDIC since early this morning." Burns said.

Edward didn't feel like exchanging pleasantries with Burns, but knew it wasn't in his best interest to antagonize the man. "It must be difficult dealing with new ownership and the regulators at the same time," he said.

"You have no idea. Anyway, you called. Is there something I can do?"

"Yes, a couple things. I learned earlier today someone put a hold on our bank account. We can't access our funds."

"I'm sorry, Edward, but that decision was made by the new owner and his representative. Of course, we'll release the funds in your accounts as soon as you pay off your loan. Have you made any progress finding alternative financing?"

Edward tried to force a cork into the bottle of his anger, with only limited success. "So, you just appropriated my money without even notifying me?"

"It's been done on every one of our commercial real estate borrower's accounts. The Feds are in agreement with the bank's decision."

"But that doesn't address my point. Why no courtesy call? No discussion? Do you have any idea the position you've put us in?"

Burns lowered his voice. "I'm really sorry, Edward, but I have no authority around here anymore."

"So, who do I need to talk to? Who has authority?"

Burns hesitated before he answered. "Ownership does not want to interface with bank customers."

The cork slipped a bit more out of the bottle. "Oh, is that what we're doing? *Interfacing*? Well, I want to *interface* with someone who can make a decision about my loan and my deposit accounts. I've got a bank interested in taking over $11 million of our debt as long as Broad Street keeps the balance of $9 million and releases its lien on fifty-five percent of our real estate. That would still give your bank a forty percent loan to value ratio on the remaining $9 million balance, the same as it is now."

"I don't—"

"And you need to remove the hold on our bank accounts immediately. Tying up our cash is going to force us to violate contracts we've already executed for our new restaurant locations."

"I'll have to look into this, Edward. I'll try to get back to you tomorrow."

"Tomorrow won't do," Edward shouted, the cork popping all the way out. "I want to know by five o'clock this evening what time my lawyer and I can come into the bank tomorrow. If I don't hear back from you by 5 p.m., my lawyer and I are going to go see the editor of *The Philadelphia Journal*. I'm sure the paper and the public will be interested in knowing how Broad Street National Bank, the bank's owner, and the FDIC are undermining perfectly good businesses in the Philadelphia area."

"I'll call you back today," Burns said and hung up.

"Jeez, where did that come from?" Nick asked.

"Where did what come from?" Edward snapped.

"You pushed Burns pretty hard."

"You know, I empathize with Stanley Burns' predicament, but this is our future we're talking about here and I'm tired of being jerked around by these assholes. Call Paul Sanders and ask him to clear his schedule for tomorrow. I don't want to go into a meeting with the bankers without legal counsel."

"What if they tell you to shove it? What if they call your bluff?"

"I wasn't bluffing, Nick. What the Feds and their cronies are doing is wrong. If they're treating bank customers across the country the way they're treating us, then it's no wonder the economy is in the toilet. Let's see if they can stand the light of day illuminating the situation."

"I understand your feelings," Nick said, "but you're playing chicken with all of our futures."

"We'll see about that," Edward said. "Besides, what choice do I have? Please make that call to Paul. I have another call to make. And close the door on your way out."

After Nick left, Edward reflected on his conversations with the banker and with Nick. He didn't regret for an instant what he had said to Burns, but he now wished he hadn't included Nick on the call. Nick had a wife and two children, and obviously thought he was playing Russian roulette with the company's future. Edward knew if the company went out of business, Nick would have a difficult time finding another job in the present economic recession.

But Edward was more concerned about the futures of all of his employees, and he wasn't going to allow the bank and the Feds to take down the company he'd built from scratch, and take down his employees with it. He called a number from memory.

"Peter Mora."

"Peter, it's Eddie."

"Hey, Eddie; *que pasa?*"

"Malo, mi amigo. Muy malo."

"What's going on?"

"You got time to talk?"

"Of course."

"Well, hang onto your hat, because it' ain't good."

Edward related the story starting with the meeting he'd had at Broad Street National Bank the previous week, when Stanley Burns had told him the bank wasn't going to renew his loan when it matured on July 29. It took almost thirty minutes to fill in all that had happened since.

"I know that was a lot of detail, but I wanted to warn you what might be coming down the road. If I can't refinance my loan, the bank will be in position to foreclose on all of the collateral they hold. That would mean the restaurants and the franchise rights as well."

"I wish I could tell you I'm shocked, but I've heard this same story over and over again these past three months. Franchisees have been foreclosed on all over the country because the banks wouldn't renew maturing loans. It's a bloody disaster."

"What's happening with those franchises?" Edward asked.

"The marginal ones, we just tell the banks to enjoy the fast food restaurant business. They usually come back to us and offer to release their lien on a franchise right in return for some nominal price. It's worth our while to pay a few dollars to get rid of the bank and then we'll resell the franchises to stronger investors when the timing's right. The stronger locations, we fight a little harder on those. By the way, how much do you owe the bank?"

"$20 million against current appraised real estate of $50 million."

"Jeez, Eddie. Normally, I could go to our banks and handle the refinancing for you. But the Federal regulators have forced them to cut back on commercial real estate exposure."

"I know, but I'm not about to give up. Let me know if someone from Broad Street National Bank calls you about the franchise rights."

"Oh, you can count on that. I won't make it easy for them."

"Thanks Peter."

"De nada. Vaya con Dios."

# CHAPTER TWENTY-FIVE

Edward dragged himself home at 10:30. He had agonized about how to save his business, but no realistic ideas had come to him. There just wasn't enough time to raise $20 million, especially in this financial environment.

Betsy met him at the door, kissed his cheek, and took his briefcase from his hand. "I've got dinner waiting for you," she said.

"I had a burger at my desk. I think I'll just watch the news for a while, try to decompress, and go to bed."

She gave him a sad look. "I wish there was something I could do."

He hugged her and told her somehow things would work out, but he didn't believe his own hollow words.

After Betsy went upstairs, Edward retrieved a large tumbler from the bar before cracking open a new bottle of Johnny Walker Red. He filled the glass with ice and took it and the bottle to the den and placed them on the coffee table. Picking up the television remote, he was about to turn on the set, but hesitated and then hurled the remote across the room into a plush chair. "Sonofabitch!" he said, in a subdued voice so Betsy wouldn't hear him.

He poured three inches of scotch into the glass and took a healthy pull straight from the bottle. Resting his head against the back of the couch, he closed his eyes and allowed his suppressed anger to build. Since meeting with Stanley Burns at Broad Street National Bank a couple days ago, he'd wanted to shove his fist through a wall—or, better yet, to punch out a banker, or a Federal regulator, or a politician. Then he thought about Gerald Folsom. Folsom. He would be the ideal target.

Despite his usual optimism, Edward now faced the very real possibility of losing the company he'd built from scratch. All of the effort he had put in would be for nothing. And with his personal failure would go his mother's and sister's investments in the company.

Beneath Edward's anger was fear. This wasn't like fighting in Iraq. In fact, he told himself, he would rather be back in Iraq than confronting the evil he was now dealing with.

"Bastards!" he growled. "Evil bastards!"

"What is it, Eddie?" Betsy asked.

He hadn't heard her come downstairs. She came to the couch and sat next to him. He knew she didn't like to see him drink; she'd grown up in a home with an alcoholic father. But she didn't say anything.

Edward set down the bottle and took Betsy's hand. "I don't know what to do," he said.

She rested her head against his shoulder. "Things will work out; you'll see."

Edward wanted to be strong for Betsy, but his overwhelming sense of defeat and fear quickly turned to bitter outrage and hatred.

"They're stealing my business, Betsy, and there's not a damn thing I can do about it. The unfairness, the injustice of it all is more than I can stand. The government, the regulators, the politicians, Wall Street. Take your pick. I'm just a pissant they can step on." He coughed a scornful laugh. "The bastards took over General Motors and Chrysler; they took over the banking system. Why am I even surprised?"

Betsy sat up and looked at him. "You'll figure it out. You always do. That's what attracted me to you when we first met. Your self-confidence."

For an instant, Betsy's words rubbed him the wrong way. He wanted her pity, not her stupid assurance. He almost yelled at her to leave him alone, when she added, "Win or lose, you can't give up. You do that and you'll never be able to live with yourself." She kissed him on the cheek and stood. "I'll be waiting for you upstairs."

Edward watched his wife leave the room. His stomach churned with acid, swamping his mouth with a sour taste. He was ashamed of the self-pity he had been basking in. Betsy was right. He couldn't give up. He may not win this battle, but he'd go down fighting . . . fighting every enemy he could in the process.

He stood and took the scotch bottle to the bar. He went upstairs to tell Betsy how much he loved her.

# WEDNESDAY
# JULY 20, 2011

# CHAPTER TWENTY-SIX

Folsom hadn't been back in his old neighborhood in years. His parents died still living in Germantown. He wanted to move them out of the area, but by the time he could afford to do that, his father was dead of lung cancer and his mother institutionalized with Alzheimer's. Until today, he'd had no desire or need to visit here. But things had changed.

He cruised down Germantown Avenue, passing Washington Lane, continuing on for another two miles. Many of the active storefronts of his youth were now boarded up, but street corners were still gathering spots for unemployed young black men. At Claremont Street, he made a right turn and drove down a block to Frankie's Pool Hall, a joint that hadn't changed since Folsom hung out there over forty years earlier. Parking the Mercedes in the four-car lot next to Frankie's, he walked to the front entrance and pushed through the door.

"You lost, man?"

Folsom stopped and wheeled around. He glared at a twenty-something black man slouched against the wall to the right of the door and growled, "Do I know you?"

The man's eyes widened, obviously surprised by Folsom's reaction. He pushed off the wall and straightened up. "Nah, you don't know me. What you doin' here?"

Folsom jutted his chin forward, shortening the distance between the two of them. "None of your fuckin' business," he rasped. "Back off or I'll embarrass you in front of all your brothers in here."

The younger man seemed to be considering his options. Without even turning around, Folsom knew that every eye in Frankie's was on them. He'd whispered his challenge so the guy would have the option of backing down.

"Tell you what," Folsom added, again in a whisper, "I'm going to put an arm around your shoulder and we're going to walk over to the bar with big smiles on our faces. Then I'm gonna buy you a beer like we're old buddies. How do you feel about that?"

"I could use a beer," the man said.

Folsom laughed, put his arm around the man and walked with him to the bar. He ordered two beers and asked the bartender if Frankie Jones still owned the place.

"Frankie's been dead some ten years," the bartender answered. "I'm his son. This is my place now."

Folsom turned to look at the young man next to him. "Why don't you take that beer over to one of the tables?"

The guy clapped Folsom on the back. "Sure, man," he said and walked away.

"You handled that well," the bartender commented. "I was about to pull out the baseball bat."

"I dealt with punks like that when I still lived in this neighborhood."

"You knew my dad?"

"I loved your dad," Folsom said. "He used to let me do odd jobs around here when I was twelve, thirteen years old. Taught me how to fight."

The bartender nodded. "Yeah, he was like that. My name's Tyrese. Somethin' I can do for you?"

"Used to be a guy named Toothpick hung around here. He's probably sixty by now."

The bartender smiled. "Bad guy, that Toothpick. Was short and skinny. Lot of guys underestimated him 'cause of his size."

"He still around?"

"Ain't so skinny no more. But he's still around. How 'bout I call him for you?"

Folsom smiled. "Appreciate it."

"I'd need some change for the phone call," Tyrese said.

Folsom kept his expression blank, but he was laughing inside. Nothing changes, he thought. "What's the cost of a call today?"

"Hundred bucks," Tyrese said.

"Damn inflation," Folsom said, peeling off a bill from the wad in his pocket.

Tyrese palmed the bill and shook his head. "Ain't it a bitch?"

The barman picked up a telephone receiver from the corner of the bar and punched in a number. He cupped a hand over the mouthpiece and talked to someone for about fifteen seconds. After he hung up he said to Folsom, "Why don't you take a seat over there? You won't have to wait long."

Folsom suffered curious or threatening looks from the pool hall's patrons, but no one challenged him. He sipped his beer and checked email on his BlackBerry. Only one message of consequence: Some customer of Broad Street National Bank was demanding a meeting with someone who could make a decision about his loan. Normally, Folsom would not have been bothered with stuff like this. But this customer was threatening to go to the media and Folsom didn't want that kind of attention. Even though the deals between the Feds and investors in banks were legal, they could be perceived as unfair by the average citizen. He didn't want a bunch of goody-goodies questioning the six different bank deals he'd done with the Feds over the past twenty-two years. And God forbid the deals he'd made on the loan pools he'd bought from the Feds at huge discounts became public knowledge. All thanks to his old friend Donald Matson.

He heard the door to the pool hall open and saw two black men in suits and ties enter. One of the men stopped by the door and looked around like a Secret Service agent guarding a President. The other, a short, hugely obese man, waddled over to Tyrese, who tipped his head in Folsom's direction. The man moved toward Folsom and said, "I hear you're looking for me." The man tilted his head to the side and squinted at Folsom. "You ain't no cop, and you sure as hell don't live around here, so what do you want?"

"Jesus, Toothpick, what the hell happened to you?" Folsom said. "You look like Jabba the Hut."

The man's face suddenly contorted in anger. He reached inside the pocket of the light-weight topcoat he wore despite the summer heat.

Folsom chuckled. "You wouldn't shoot an old friend would

you?"

His hand still in his coat pocket, Toothpick glared at Folsom and said, "No old friend be callin' me Jabba the Hut."

"You used to call me a lot worse than that. Like white trash, punk ass, shit-for-brains fucker."

Toothpick stared harder at Folsom. "You sort of look familiar."

Folsom smiled; Toothpick had moved his hand from his coat. "It's Jerry, man. Jerry Folsom."

Toothpick's mouth opened and his eyes bulged. "Sumbitch! You be lookin' uptown. Last time I saw you, you was waitin' tables, or sumthin' up on the Hill."

"Long time ago. A lot has changed."

Toothpick raised two fingers at Tyrese. "Whiskey, brother." Then he sat down on a cane chair across from Folsom, somehow not crushing it. After Tyrese delivered two whiskey shots and walked away, Toothpick downed his drink and raised the glass at Tyrese for another one before he had even gotten back to the bar.

"You always was crazy," Toothpick said. "Guys used to try to kick your ass just to make their bones. Word got around you could be knocked down but you wouldn't stay down."

"Tyrese's father taught me that. Can't show any weakness."

"Got that right."

Tyrese dropped off another whiskey shot, which Toothpick greedily downed.

"But you ain't visitin' for old time sake. So what you here for?"

"I have a need for someone with special skills, skills you used to have."

Toothpick met Folsom's gaze. "I used to have all kinds of skills. But like you say, time has changed things. Jabba can't do what he used to." He smirked at Folsom. "Jabba the Hut, my ass. You a crazy mother."

"So I wasted my time coming down here?" Folsom asked.

"Depends. You said you needed someone with special skills. I said I *used* to have them; maybe I can provide someone with those skills. Maybe you should be a little more specific."

"I have a couple problems that need to go away."

"That always means people problems. People problems aren't easy to fix. Lots of risks. Can cost a lot."

"How much is a lot?"

"We talkin' high-profile people?"

"Nah. A low-level federal government bureaucrat and a nobody woman."

"Ain't no such thing as a nobody woman. Especially if it's a bitch married to a guy with people problems."

Toothpick had always been quick on the uptake. "How much?"

Toothpick showed a huge white-toothed smile. "Special price for an old friend. Ten grand each."

"Tell you what," Folsom said. "I'll add another ten grand bonus if you take care of business within a week."

"Ten up front; the balance after your problems go away."

"Agreed. Let's go outside and finalize our business," Folsom said.

Toothpick struggled to his feet and moved toward the door, saying to Folsom behind him, "Don't forget to pay for the drinks." He walked outside laughing as though he'd told the funniest joke in the world.

# CHAPTER TWENTY-SEVEN

Katherine forced herself to remain composed while she photographed Wendy Folsom's injuries. Wendy, standing in only her panties in the middle of Katherine's bright living room, showed no emotion while the pictures of her body were snapped. The young woman's stoicism and determination gave Katherine the strength to do the job, as badly as she felt like crying.

After they were done, Wendy went into her bedroom to get dressed while Katherine went to her computer and downloaded the photographs. She then ran off two sets of copies on her printer and packed them into two large envelopes. By the time she returned to the kitchen, Wendy was seated at the table drinking a glass of water.

"Now what?" Katherine asked.

"Would you call Mr. Sanders and ask him if he will go to the police with me?"

"Of course. You know Paul Sanders is not a criminal attorney, but he can find one for you."

"I don't want another attorney. I want Mr. Sanders."

Katherine shrugged and went to the kitchen telephone. She dialed Paul's number and got his receptionist. "Mr. Sanders, please. This is Katherine Winter."

"Hello, Ms. Winter. Mr. Sanders has an appointment outside the office. In fact, he's meeting with Mr. Winter and some people at Broad Street National Bank. Can I take a message?"

"Please." Katherine left her home and cell numbers. "Tell him it's important."

Katherine explained to Wendy they'd have to wait for Paul to call back. "How about having some lunch while we wait?"

"Sounds good. I'm getting my appetite back. Now I just have to get my life back."

Katherine smiled. "That's what we're going to do, Wendy."


Folsom reviewed in his mind the actions he'd taken with Toothpick Jefferson. He'd opened his jacket and told him to take the envelope out of his inside pocket. That envelope contained the $10,000 in cash he'd packed while wearing rubber gloves. He'd guessed the hoodlum would want some money up front. The dollar amount was a good estimate. Also inside that envelope was a typed note with two names on it: Donald Matson and Wendy Folsom. He had typed Matson's office and home addresses below the man's name. It embarrassed him to not know where Wendy was hiding. He promised to get that information to Toothpick as soon as possible.

# CHAPTER TWENTY-EIGHT

Paul, Nick, and Edward got out of Nick's Lincoln Town Car in the Broad Street National Bank's parking lot and walked into the building. They skirted the lobby to the elevator and went up to the executive level, where Stanley Burns' assistant met and escorted them to a conference room where Burns was already waiting. He stood but didn't offer his hand to any of them, and he wouldn't make eye contact.

"You said we would be meeting with Mr. Cunningham," Edward said.

"Yes, yes, he'll be here any moment." Burns looked at his watch, even though a large clock hung on the wall in front of him. "Let's sit down. Can I get you something to drink?"

"No, thank you," Edward said. When Burns looked at Paul and Nick, they shook their heads.

Edward sat between Paul and Nick on one side of the table. Burns sat opposite them. After ten minutes, thinking the bank was playing games with him, Edward was just about to get up and leave, when a man entered the room and introduced himself as Sanford Cunningham.

"Sorry to keep you waiting, gentlemen. Let's get started. I only have thirty minutes."

Angry at being kept waiting, and at now being told the meeting would be over in thirty minutes, regardless, Edward started to stand, but Paul put a hand on his arm.

"Mr. Cunningham, I am Winter Enterprises' corporate counsel. I assume Mr. Burns briefed you on his conversation with Mr. Winter yesterday."

"He did," Cunningham said.

"Do you understand the implications of our meeting today?"

Cunningham had so far showed zero emotion. "Of course. Your client has threatened the bank with going to the media if we don't renew his loan and give him access to his deposit account."

"That's not quite accurate, Mr. Cunningham," Paul said. "Mr. Winter said he was prepared to go to the media if someone in a position of authority here did not agree to meet with him today."

Cunningham waved a hand as though to diminish the importance of the distinction Paul had made.

"But let's focus on what's going on," Paul continued. "In Winter Enterprises, you have a client that has met all of its obligations to the bank, has provided an abundance of collateral for its $20 million loan, even with the drop in commercial real estate values, and has maintained an average deposit balance of over $2.5 million for the last five years. Now, you refuse to extend your loan and have put a hold on almost $3 million of Winter Enterprises' money, jeopardizing the company's health and even its survival. I might be able to understand your actions, if my client had financial problems or presented a risk of loss to the bank, but that is not the case. So I have one question for you. Depending on your answer, we might not even take thirty minutes of your *valuable* time." Paul paused and stared at Cunningham.

"What's your question?"

"What is the bank's real motivation here?"

"I don't understand," Cunningham said.

"Sure you do, Mr. Cunningham. You understand me perfectly. I called a colleague at the Federal Deposit Insurance Corporation and she assured me the agency has not told any bank in this country to not renew a commercial real estate loan to a solid borrower. She did admit the agency has ordered banks to reduce their exposure to commercial real estate, but that can be accomplished by not making loans to new customers, by letting loans pay down in the normal course of business, and/or by raising additional capital. So, why would you want to drive away a borrower that has maintained a highly profitable relationship with your bank?"

Cunningham's cool demeanor seemed to melt just a bit. "We're under a great deal of pressure here. We are doing what we have to do."

"I see. And what happens on July 29, one week from now, when your loan to Winter Enterprises matures and the company can't pay it off?"

"The bank has rights. We will obviously consider exercising those rights."

"And what about my client's request of you to reduce his loan with Broad Street to $9 million, to release enough collateral to allow him to refinance $11 million at another lending institution, and to remove the hold you've put on his deposit accounts?"

"We have considered your client's request and have regrettably come to the conclusion we are unable to agree to his request."

Paul stood and looked at Edward and then at Nick. "We're done here," he said. He gazed across the table at Cunningham. "You'll be hearing from us. The next time we talk, you'd better have legal counsel."

"Before you go, there is one thing more I want to discuss with you and your client," Cunningham said, the steely look back in his eyes.

Paul didn't say a word.

Cunningham filled the silence, "Our loan agreement with Winter Enterprises specifically requires your client to deposit all company sales receipts in Broad Street National Bank. Winter Enterprises hasn't made a single deposit to their accounts here since July 15."

Paul gave Cunningham a bland look and said, "I can't imagine what has happened. Of course we'll look into that." Without waiting for a response, he walked from the room with Edward and Nick following.

In the parking lot, they stopped beside Nick's car. "Well, that didn't accomplish anything," Nick said.

"On the contrary," Paul said. "I now know who has some decision-making authority. I know for sure that they are going to play hardball, that they must think you were bluffing about going to the media, and that they have an ulterior motive in this matter."

"How do you know that?" Edward demanded.

"When you talked to Stanley Burns yesterday, you made a perfectly reasonable offer to reduce their loan down to $9 million, secured by over $20 million in real estate. Cunningham acknowledged that Burns had made him aware of your conversation, so he was familiar with your request. My conversation with my contact at the FDIC leads me to believe, despite the heavy-handed treatment the agency is employing with banks, they would not force Broad Street National to turn down an offer as reasonable as yours."

"What's the ulterior motive?"

"That we need to determine."

"So, where does this leave us," Edward asked, "besides up a creek without a paddle?"

"Well, not where we'd like to be, but we do have a few options. I don't want to get your hopes up, but this is war. You've spent how much on advertising over the past eight years?"

"Easily $10 million," Nick answered. "About half with *The Philadelphia Journal* and the rest with a dozen neighborhood newspapers and half a dozen different area television and radio stations."

"Good," Paul said. "That money won't buy you a guarantee of editorial content, but it should at least open doors for you. Call your media contacts and make appointments. See if you can generate interest about what's happening to the banks and the effects on the Philadelphia economy. Don't make it all about Winter Enterprises."

"What about our money sitting in Third Community Bank?" Edward asked.

"Just keep depositing your receipts there. I'm going to ignore Mr. Cunningham's comment about those monies. What are they going to do, call your loan? They've already done that. When is your next loan payment due at the bank?"

"Not until July 29, when we're supposed to pay off the entire balance," Nick answered. "Why?"

"I just don't want you to make any payments to the bank out of your Third Community Bank account. I don't want Cunningham to know where your other accounts are."

"What are you going to do?" Edward asked Paul.

"I'm going to call my contact at the FDIC and ask her a few more questions."

"What kind of questions?" Nick asked.

"I don't know yet. I'm sure something will come to me."

# CHAPTER TWENTY-NINE

When Paul Sanders called his office to check for messages, his receptionist told him Katherine Winter had called. He decided he'd wait until Nick and Edward dropped him off to return her call. Assuming Katherine had called about Wendy Folsom, he didn't feel it was his right to disclose to Edward what Katherine was doing.

As soon as Paul was dropped off at his office, he called Katherine's home number.

"Can you come here?" she asked.

"What's going on?"

"Wendy wants to go to the police. She had me take pictures of her injuries and she's going to press charges against her husband."

"That's good news," Paul said. "But why do you need me? She needs a criminal attorney."

"She won't hear of it. She wants you to represent her."

"Oh man. I'm not the best thing for her, and I'm tied up trying to help Edward save his company."

"Maybe if you talk to her you can convince her to accept another lawyer."

"All right, but I'm bringing a friend."

Paul and a criminal attorney named Sylvia Young arrived at Katherine's home an hour later. As Paul introduced Sylvia to Katherine and Wendy, he could tell from Wendy's body language and sour expression she was not happy about Sylvia being there.

"We're not just filing a complaint with the police," Paul said. "You need to understand your lawyer will have to do much more than that—filing a restraining order, making motions to the court, and responding to those made by your husband's legal team—and you will need someone who knows the inner workings of the criminal courts system."

"I want you involved," Wendy said.

"I'll be there for you, Wendy. But Sylvia needs to take the lead on this."

Paul, Sylvia and Katherine studied Wendy, who finally nodded in agreement.

"Great," Paul said. "Now I'm going to return to my office and Sylvia is going to take a statement from you."

Katherine walked out with Paul. "How did the meeting go at the bank?" she asked.

"The bank's being uncooperative. So, Edward's going to talk with the media and I'll dig and see if I can discover why the bank seems to want to put him out of business."

Katherine dropped her gaze toward the pavement instead of responding.

"What is it, Katherine?" Paul asked.

"I think I know why the bank is coming down hard on the company."

"What are you talking about?"

"Folsom. I had a confrontation with him after Frank and I got engaged. I was out with a couple girlfriends celebrating my engagement and Folsom tried to pick me up in a bar. He followed me out to my car and grabbed me."

"What happened?" Paul asked.

"I kneed him in the balls."

Paul laughed.

"It's not funny," Katherine snapped. "He started harassing me and didn't stop until I got a restraining order against him."

"Katherine, don't take this the wrong way, but I would be very surprised if something that occurred over two decades ago is the motivation behind the bank's treatment of Winter Enterprises. Besides, the bank is treating a lot of its customers in the same manner; I doubt that the mothers of all of those companies' presidents kicked Folsom in the balls, even if they wish they could."

Katherine couldn't help herself. She glared at Paul. "This isn't funny."

"I'm sorry, I didn't mean to make light of the situation. It's just that Folsom would have to be a sociopath to hold a grudge for that many years."

Katherine pointed back toward the house where Wendy Folsom and Sylvia Young were talking. "There's a doubt in your mind about Folsom being a sociopath? Or a psychopath?"

Paul rubbed a couple fingers across his lower lip and shook his head. Before he could respond, Katherine said, "Paul, I know you'll do everything you can to help Edward. I can't stand the thought of Gerald Folsom robbing my children now like he did twenty-two years ago. But don't ever forget that sonofabitch is a sociopath at the very least."

# CHAPTER THIRTY

"What happened at the meeting with Winter?" Folsom asked Sanford Cunningham.

"Just what you expected."

"They going to be able to pay off the loan?"

"I doubt it," Cunningham said. "They want us to agree to release some of our collateral in return for reducing our loan down to $9 million. They have a commitment from another bank to finance $11 million of our loan. Oh, and they want us to remove the hold we put on their deposits."

"What did you tell them?"

"Exactly what you told me to say. No."

"Perfect."

"Jerry, I've been a loyal supporter of yours for twelve years, so keep that in mind when I say this: There's something different about this guy. Winter's a combat vet. If he goes to the press with this, that's going to help his cause. Maybe we'd be okay if he couldn't pay down any of the loan, but the fact that he's prepared to reduce it by more than half won't make us look good.

"Before you take the chance of having those bastards in the media start looking into your holdings, think about whether how you got your wealth will stand the light of day."

"Everything I've built I did on the up and up," Folsom said.

"You're forgetting who you're talking to, Jerry."

"You with me or against me, Sandy?"

"Come on, Jerry. You know better than that."

"Then just do what I tell you to do. I know the Winter family. They don't have a clue how to fight, especially against a guy like me. They see the best in people, think people will always be fair. They're a fuckin' bunch of patsies."

"Whatever you say, Boss."

Folsom was excited about his plan for Winter Enterprises and the thought of taking down two generations of a Chestnut Hill family. He didn't have anything personal against Edward Winter, just like he had had nothing personal against the father, Frank. But people with wealth who went through life acting as though everything was hearts and flowers? He couldn't stand them. Frank Winter had been so naïve, and bringing him down with the help of the politicians in Washington, even if those assholes didn't know what they unleashed on the economy with the 1986 Tax Reform Act, had given Folsom an almost sensual pleasure. Especially after Frank Winter's bitch-of-a-wife had treated him like dirt in that parking lot so many years ago.

But thinking about the pleasure from Frank Winter's fall so

many years ago caused him to segue to the pleasure he'd gotten from Wendy. He'd miss that girl. He chuckled. At least with *this* wife there'd be no divorce settlement. Not if Toothpick Jefferson came through.

Donald Matson was sweating as though he was in a steam room. Between the ninety degree temperature and one hundred percent humidity, and the tension of rushing from one bank safety deposit box to another, he was exhausted. The inquiry from the FDIC about his safety deposit box at Broad Street National Bank had scared him to death. Gerald Folsom was correct in telling him to clear out all of his boxes.

He looked at his watch as he drove through Mt. Airy toward Chestnut Hill: 2:45. The safety deposit vault at First Savings Bank always closed at 3.

He'd had a safety deposit box in the Chestnut Hill bank there for twenty-two years, from the first bank deal he and Folsom had done together. He considered it his base. Every time Folsom paid him for putting together a loan pool purchase or a bank takeover, Matson would visit all of his safety deposit boxes. He was smart enough to know spending too much would raise questions at work. He'd pull a few thousand out of one or another of the boxes every few months. But he couldn't stop the adrenaline surge he got from opening his boxes and seeing, touching, and counting his money.

Matson drove into the First Savings Bank's parking lot and took out one of the two valises in the car trunk. He ran up the bank's front steps and, into the building, and speed- walked down the marble steps to the safety deposit vault. The receptionist had worked for the bank for at least as long as Matson had had a box.

"Hello, Mr. Matson," she said. She glanced at the wall clock and added, "You just made it. We'll be closing the vault in a couple minutes."

"Story of my life," he said. "It seems I'm always rushing around. Anyway, I need to get into my box, Alice. And I'm going to close out my account. I've decided to move all my records to a bank closer to my house."

Alice rose from her chair behind her desk and gave him a sad look. "I'm sorry to hear that, Mr. Matson. You've been a customer forever. I hope we haven't done anything to disappoint you."

"On the contrary, Alice. I'll miss doing business with you."

She asked him to sign into a log and then preceded him into the vault, where she inserted and turned a key in a locking door; Matson inserted his key into the second lock and turned it. Alice opened the locking door and slid out the box from inside the space, handed it to Matson, and pointed toward a private cubicle. "Of course, you know where our privacy booths are."

"Thank you, Alice. I'll only be a minute."

She walked out of the vault, leaving Matson alone. He moved to one of the cubicles, closed the door behind him, and placed the valise and the deposit box on the shelf in the cubicle. After raising the box lid, he removed two slightly yellowed and wrinkled 3" x 5" cards that sat on top of the cash.

Trained as an accountant, Matson was precise about record keeping. He drove his wife crazy with his list-making and with his criticism of her checkbook. This tendency applied to his cash "bonuses" from Gerald Folsom as well, noting every payment from Folsom on one card, regardless of where the cash was kept. Each notation included a date, a dollar amount, and a running total currently standing at $2.6 million. The second card showed the date and dollar amount of every withdrawal Matson had taken from any of his boxes. The notations on this card were so tiny Matson now needed glasses to read or make entries. This card showed he had withdrawn $435,000 from his boxes over the last twenty-two years.

Matson dropped the cards into the valise so they slid down between the piles of cash and the side of the valise before stacking the cash from the box on top of the cash already in the bag.

Folsom called Donald Matson's office from his car only to hear Matson's assistant tell him her boss had taken the afternoon off. He asked her to transfer him to Matson's cell phone.

"You playing golf?" Folsom asked when Matson answered his phone.

"When have you known me to play golf during the week? I've been closing out all my safety deposit boxes."

"All of them?"

"Emptied them all. Closed the last one this afternoon."

"Good boy, Donald. One less thing for us to worry about. Hope you don't have the cash in your car. " Folsom laughed.

Matson's silence told Folsom the cash was in fact in his car. "Really?"

"I don't know where else to put it." He sounded at the end of his rope.

"It's four o'clock. Can you come by my place?"

"Sure. Why?"

"I'm going to do you a favor. Bring the cash to my house. I'll put it in my vault. Then I'll start converting the cash to gold coins and jewels. They'll be less bulky, easier to hide but it'll probably take me a month to invest all of it for you. You should get a safe at your home to hold the gold and jewels."

Matson exhaled a huge sigh. "That'd be great. I'll be there in an hour. You're a life saver."

"We've been friends for a long time, Donald. Where are you?"

"Willow Grove."

"What are you doing there?"

"Just driving around, trying to figure out what to do with the money."

"Well, we've got that solved. See you in a little while."

After hanging up, Folsom drove to a full service gas station. While the attendant filled his gas tank, Folsom asked if he could use the station's telephone. "Forgot to charge my damn cell phone," he lied.

"Sure, go ahead," the attendant said. "It's a local call, right?"

"Absolutely."

He called Toothpick Jefferson. "The target is on his way to my place," he told him. "He should arrive in about forty-five minutes and shouldn't be here more than fifteen minutes, so he'll be on the road to his home about an hour from now."

"Perfect. I've already got my best man on the job."

"Well, tell your best man that part of what I owe you will be in a paper bag in the guy's car."

"I love a client who pays on time."

"I'll get information to you about the other person in the next day or two."

Matson arrived at Folsom's home at 4:40. He was about to push the buzzer on the intercom box by the front gate when he had a thought. He walked to the back of his car and opened the trunk. He opened his briefcase, taking out two new 3" x 5" cards and writing on each one: *7/21/10. Placed the following amount of cash in this valise for safe keeping with Gerald Folsom.* He then entered a dollar amount on each card: $1 million on one and $1,065,000 on the other. He thought about having Folsom sign a receipt for the money, but figured that would piss off Folsom. The cards would at least substantiate how much he had left with Folsom, in case there was a disagreement in the future. He popped the trunk lid, got out of the car, opened the valises, and dropped the cards into the appropriate ones. After closing the valises and the car trunk, he pressed the intercom buzzer and got into his car. The gate opened and he drove through to the house.

Folsom helped Matson unload the two valises and carry them upstairs to the third level to Folsom's home office and walk-in vault. The vault held a rack of rifles and shotguns, drawers with trays holding his collections of gold and silver coins, gem stones, and several unlabeled boxes. When Matson entered the vault, he whistled.

"Keep this to yourself," Folsom said. "I don't need word on the street about all of this. How much cash in the valises?"

"Two million, sixty-five thousand dollars."

Folsom opened one of the valises and counted out five packs of one hundred dollar bills. Each pack was wrapped in a band that read $2,000. He put the currency in a paper bag and handed the bag to Matson. "You might need some spending money."

Matson shook Folsom's hand. "Thanks, Jerry."

"You'd better get on your way home," Folsom said. "And don't get stopped for speeding. You don't want a cop wondering what's in the bag."

# CHAPTER THIRTY-ONE

Toothpick Jefferson's man, Michael Toney, sat in his black 2009 Audi A-8 and watched for a silver 2011 Lincoln MKZ sedan. He'd surveilled the streets around Matson's home and knew exactly where he would make the hit: The three-block stretch of heavily-wooded park bracketing the street leading to Matson's driveway. The driveway was little better than a one-lane, dirt track extending two hundred serpentined yards through dense woods and dead-ending at the Matson property.

He straightened his tie and smoothed down his dress shirt, flicking away a stray piece of lint on a pant leg. Toney always dressed for work as though he was an executive, with tailored Hickey Freeman suits, custom-made white dress shirts, silk, hand-made ties, ColeHaan shoes. A cop was less likely to stop a black man dressed like a banker than one dressed like a rap star. Especially one driving a $100,000 Audi.

Toney had parked off to the side of the top of the driveway, hidden from sight of any of the neighborhood houses, and opened the hood. On the lookout for joggers or dog-walkers, he waited for Matson to arrive. He checked his watch: 6 p.m. Dinner time. Less chance there would be anyone around. When he spotted Matson's Lincoln turn onto the street and head toward the driveway, Toney bent over his left front fender and pretended to look under the hood.

As Toney had anticipated, Matson stopped. He lowered the passenger side window of the Lincoln and called out, "Everything all right?"

Toney turned to face Matson. "Damned imported cars. You need a PhD to figure out what's wrong."

"You call for help?"

"I was just about to." Toney said as he half-squatted and rested his forearms on the Lincoln's passenger side door. He reached down with his right hand and pulled a .22 Magnum revolver from an ankle rig. He poked the weapon through the open window and pulled the trigger. The bullet pierced Matson's right eye, throwing his head back against the driver side window. Toney liked the little .22. The light weight round was ideal for taking out a target from close range. The bullet would fragment and rattle around inside the target's head, tearing up the brain, leaving little chance of survival, and very little mess. He reached through the window, across the front seat and put a second round in Matson's temple for good measure.

The job done, Toney looked at the passenger seat at the paper bag resting on a suit jacket. The man's wallet stuck out an inch from the inside jacket pocket. A bonus, Toney thought. He grabbed the wallet and the paper bag, closed the hood on his car, got behind the wheel, and drove away. By the time he'd reached the end of the street, he'd opened the paper bag and found stacks of cash. He searched in the wallet and extracted five one hundred dollar bills. Pulling over to the curb, he wiped off the wallet with his handkerchief, quickly exited the car, tossed the wallet away in a trash can, and just as quickly returned to his car. Cranking up the stereo, he listened to a rhythm and blues station play Wes Montgomery's *California Dreamin'*.

# THURSDAY
# JULY 21, 2011

# CHAPTER THIRTY-TWO

First thing Thursday morning, Paul Sanders telephoned his contact, Gail Moskowitz, at the D.C. offices of the Federal Deposit Insurance Corporation to enlist her support with his client's problems with Broad Street National Bank. She sympathized with Paul, agreeing that the bank's treatment of his client was unfair, but she told him what the bank was doing wasn't illegal. It sounded to her as though the bank was merely trying to live up to the letter of the guidance the FDIC was giving all banks: Reduce your exposure to commercial real estate loans.

"Come on, Gail. If every bank in the country reacted to the agency's guidance in this way, the economy wouldn't just be in recession; it would be in free fall."

"I'm sorry, Paul, but there's nothing I can do."

"Can you at least call the FDIC supervisor in Philadelphia and ask him or her to look into this? Maybe the supervisor can suggest the bank ameliorate its position."

Gail didn't respond right off. But, after a few seconds hesitation, she said, "All right, Paul. That's a fair request. I'll call the area supervisor."

Paul gave Moskowitz his cell phone number and asked her to call him as soon as she heard something. After hanging up, he drove to Katherine's house to meet Sylvia Young, Wendy Folsom's criminal attorney, there at 10 a.m.

Paul was last to arrive. Katherine served him a cup of coffee as he sat down with the others at the dining room table.

Sylvia handed Paul a folder. "The documents I prepared are in there," she said. "The restraining order, a divorce petition, and a criminal complaint against Gerald Folsom for assault and battery and attempted murder. I called Anthony Castiglia, the head of Violent Crimes at the Philadelphia P.D. He's an old friend of mine and he's expecting us downtown at 3 this afternoon. Once he sees the photographs in the file, I am confident he'll get the D.A. to issue an arrest warrant for Folsom.

"Unfortunately, I have to tell you I've handled a lot of cases like this. A man that abuses his wife as badly as Folsom has abused Wendy cannot be trusted. I would bet all my savings he'll blow like Vesuvius when the charges are filed against him. Wendy needs to be somewhere safe until we're sure her husband is locked up."

"She can stay with me," Katherine said immediately.

Sylvia smiled at Katherine. "That's very kind of you, but that might jeopardize your safety as well as Wendy's. No, we need to find a better place."

"How about the convent at St. Francis College?" Katherine asked. "We've made large contributions to the school over the last few years. I'm sure they'd be willing to grant me a favor."

"Sounds perfect," Sylvia said, looking at Wendy. "But you've got to promise you will not leave the convent except for court appearances and the like. I'll have a guard pick you up and take you back as necessary."

"Aren't you being overly protective?" Wendy asked. "I mean, I know Gerald is a monster, but he wouldn't dare come after me once charges are filed. The police would suspect him first if anything happened to me."

"Suspecting him is not the same as proving he harmed you. I'm not being overly protective; I'm being overly cautious."

When she saw Wendy had nothing else to add, Sylvia suggested, "Paul, let's go over the documents. I know criminal law isn't your expertise, but I always like to have a second set of eyes look over anything I file with the court or the police."

"I'll call the college while you work on the documents," Katherine said and walked toward the kitchen.

Sylvia passed a set of documents to Wendy. "You should review these with Paul and me," Sylvia said.


Two hours passed before they finished. Sylvia edited the documents as necessary on her laptop and emailed the revised documents to her office. "We'll pick up the final documents on the way downtown," she advised. "I suggest we go out and get some lunch, then work our way downtown via my office."

"Any luck with the college?" Paul asked Katherine.

"The Mother Superior is going to call me back this afternoon. But I think I'll drive out there and talk to her. It's always harder to turn someone down when you have to look them in the eye."

"You're not going downtown with me?" Wendy asked, a tremble sounding in her voice.

Katherine walked behind Wendy seated at the dining table. She rested her hands on her shoulders and said, "This is the time for lawyers. I would just be in the way. But I'll see you tonight."

Wendy placed a hand on one of Katherine's hands.

Paul, Sylvia, and Wendy walked outside to Paul's Cadillac. Paul's cell phone rang as he opened the driver's door. The women got into the car.

"Hello?" Paul said.

"Paul, it's Gail Moskowitz. I've got bad news."

"I didn't expect the area supervisor to cooperate, but thanks for the effort."

"No, you don't understand. The area supervisor's name was Donald Matson. He was murdered last night, almost right in front of his home. Two shots to the head at close range. At first the police thought it might be a robbery because his wallet was missing. They found it in a nearby trash can. But what's strange is that Matson still had on a very expensive watch and ring. At this point the police aren't certain about motive."

"Holy . . . . What the hell!"

"Everyone's kind of shell-shocked around here."

"I can imagine," Paul said. "I'm sorry. Thanks for calling."

"Good luck, Paul. I hope things work out for your client."

Paul got into his car. He needed to call Edward and tell him what had happened as soon as possible, so that he wouldn't harbor unrealistic hopes for a solution from that quarter. But he didn't want to have that conversation while Wendy was in the car. Hearing about a murder, even if it had nothing to do with her, might unnerve her. He waited until they arrived at the police headquarters. It was 2:45 p.m.

"I need to place a call," Paul told Sylvia. "I'll be right up."

Paul dialed Edward's office number and the receptionist transferred the call to Edward's cell. "Can you talk?" Paul asked.

"I'm at the *Journal*. I've got an appointment with the business editor in five minutes. Why?"

"I got a call from my contact at the FDIC; I asked her to check with the Philadelphia area supervisor about interceding at Broad Street National Bank about your loan. But she never had the chance to talk to him. He was shot and killed last night in front of his home. Fellow named Donald Matson."

"My God! Do they know who did it?"

"No, not yet. They thought it might be a robbery gone wrong, but now they're not so sure."

"Strange."

"It's a big city, Eddie. Murders happen every day. Sorry to bring you bad news. I really hoped the local FDIC supervisor would get involved."

"About par for the course lately."

# CHAPTER THIRTY-THREE

Edward sat down with Kelly Loughridge at *The Philadelphia Journal* newspaper offices. Loughridge, a heavy-set woman with long, thick auburn hair and glasses, wore khaki slacks, a peasant blouse, and Birkenstocks. Her only accessories were a turquoise and silver etched Zuni bracelet and a pencil stuck behind an ear. It was obvious from the woman's body language and skeptical expression she wasn't happy about spending time with Edward. He thought she probably agreed to see him only because of the business Winter Enterprises had done with the paper.

"Thanks for your time, Ms. Loughridge," he said. "I'll make this quick."

Edward handed her a summary of what was happening to his company at the hands of Broad Street National Bank and what bankers had told him about the demands of the regulators.

"If you'll read this over, you should wonder what the heck is going on. Think about what they're doing to us and imagine the impact of this sort of behavior on the overall community."

Loughridge tapped her computer keyboard and then swiveled the screen so Edward could see it. "You know we've done a series of articles on the regulators taking over area banks?"

"Yes, I've read them. But all those articles approached the situation from the bankers' viewpoint. You interviewed the former owners of banks taken over by the government and the new owners the regulators brought in. But you've never done any stories from the perspective of bank customers, business owners."

She considered Edward's comment. "Interesting. That might have some appeal to our readers."

She fiddled with her keyboard again and pulled up a story headlined: FEDS TAKE OVER BROAD STREET NATIONAL.

Edward remembered the article from last Sunday's edition. "Not a happy day for me."

"Any suggestions of who we should talk with?" Loughridge asked.

"I included a list of names on the last page of the write-up I gave you."

"Thanks. We'll consider doing something."

Edward stood and shook her hand. He started turning to leave when he glanced at Loughridge's computer screen. Something caught his attention. He leaned in closer. In the first paragraph of the story, the writer had quoted Donald Matson.

"I just heard that Matson, the FDIC guy, was shot and killed last night."

Loughridge looked at the screen. "I heard someone got shot out off Ridge Pike yesterday, but I didn't make the connection. Interesting."

"Anyway, let me know if I can be of assistance," Edward said and walked out.

Kelly Loughridge had been a newspaper woman for twenty years. Naturally curious and suspicious, she didn't believe in innocent coincidences. She plugged Donald Matson's name into the newspaper's database, skimming the string of references his name popped up on her screen. After discarding the citations that were obviously not the FDIC's Matson, she collected the balance of fifteen and sent them to the printer. An instinct told her there might be something to Winter's story, but there might be more to the Matson story. She'd wasted a lot of time over her career chasing wild geese, but a few of those geese had yielded great stories. She stacked the printed articles and shoved them into her briefcase. "A loaf of bread, a glass of wine and thou," she muttered, although "thou" was more often home work rather than human companionship.

# CHAPTER THIRTY-FOUR

Detective Anthony Castiglia had gone through Wendy Folsom's file without saying a word or showing any emotion, not changing his expression when he picked up the photographs of Wendy. When he finished reading the documents, he closed the file, looked at Wendy, finally reacting. "I gave a heads up to the D.A. that I might need one of his people. I think there's plenty of cause here to have them send an assistant D.A. to meet with us."

Sylvia Young exhaled in relief. "That's what I hoped you'd say."

Castiglia chuckled and said, "You've never brought me a bum case, Sylvia." Then Castiglia turned to Wendy. "I'll recommend to the D.A. that he issue an arrest warrant for your husband; I'll serve that warrant as soon as I get it. After looking at these photographs, I'm going to enjoy throwing Mr. Folsom into jail. But I don't want to waste our time here.

"With Folsom's wealth, after I arrest him, I doubt he'll be held more than overnight. He'll probably be lawyered up in ten minutes.

I suspect the last thing Folsom wants is the negative publicity that would follow his arrest. His lawyers will offer you a settlement to drop the charges and to make a public statement that you and your husband had a misunderstanding. And if that doesn't work, he'll bring charges against you that'll make *you* look like Jack the Ripper and Mata Hari, all wrapped into one.

"I need to know, Mrs. Folsom, if you're committed to the long haul on this case. If you want to work out a settlement with your husband, and are using the police department as a negotiating tool, then we're done here."

Wendy said, "I suspect Gerald abused his previous wives, and that he would keep on abusing women. I can't let that happen. And one other thing: I'm tired of being a victim."

"Do you have a prenuptial agreement with your husband?" Castiglia asked.

Wendy blushed and nodded. "I get $5 million, no questions asked, if we get divorced."

Castiglia whistled. "And what's your husband worth?" he said.

"I don't know for sure, but a newspaper story about his business a couple years ago estimated his net worth at several hundred million dollars."

"Why don't you take the $5 million and run? Avoid the aggravation."

Wendy narrowed her eyes and glared at Castiglia. "You're beginning to piss me off."

Castiglia blurted a laugh. "That's what I wanted to hear. So you're in this until the end?"

"Absolutely."

Castiglia stood and thanked them. "I'll get on this right away."

After Paul, Sylvia, and Wendy left, Castiglia picked up his phone and dialed D.A. Lincoln Marx's number. "Lincoln, it's time to send over that Assistant D.A."

Marx asked, "Is the case good?"

"Oh yeah, Lincoln. It's got power, money, sex, violence, intrigue. Best seller material. In fact, you might want to try this one yourself. The media's going to be all over it."

# CHAPTER THIRTY-FIVE

Gerald Folsom was so frustrated he couldn't focus. It was 6 p.m. and he'd been drinking for an hour, fuming. He couldn't find Wendy, and as long as she was walking around she was a threat. Jefferson had come through with the hit on Matson, eliminating that potential liability. Folsom chuckled. It cost him ten grand to have Matson hit, and he had Matson's two million plus dollars sitting in his vault. Not a bad investment. Folsom knew with Matson out of the picture he might not get future special treatment from the Feds. But he'd made a fortune off his relationship with them and he'd performed well. He wasn't worried about competing for future deals; he'd get his share.

But he was worried about Wendy. His previous wives both jumped ship when he began roughing them up. Folsom had to admit, however, that neither of them had been treated as badly as Wendy. She had been turned on by rough sex in the beginning, which stimulated even more violence. When he beat her, he'd always show remorse afterward, and she always forgave him. Another sucker, Folsom thought, just like Frank Winter and Winter's kid. But he'd never beaten any woman like he'd beaten Wendy last weekend.

He knew he'd screwed up. He should have locked her up in one of the rooms in the attic until her injuries had healed. Then he remembered that the night Donald Matson had called about the damn safety deposit box, Folsom had intended to work Wendy over again. He suspected that if he had not been called away, he would have killed her. The thought gave him a sick thrill.

He poured himself another scotch. If he couldn't focus, at least he could get drunk. Maybe the booze would help him sleep through the night. Downing the drink in one gulp, he reached for the bottle again. But the gate bell rang, interrupting him. Lurching to his feet and swaying slightly, Folsom walked to the intercom speaker in the bar and, pushing a button, shouted, "We don't want any. Go the fuck away."

"Gerald Folsom?" a man demanded.

"Who wants to know?"

"The Philadelphia Police Department wants to know. Open the gate; we need to talk."

"What's this about?" Folsom asked, momentarily worried that the cops had somehow tied him to Matson's murder. He told himself that was impossible. Even if Toothpick Jefferson tried to implicate him, there was no proof of his involvement.

"Open the gate, Mr. Folsom. Now!"

"Hold on."

Folsom pressed a button that opened the front gate. He realized he was still holding the scotch bottle and returned it to the liquor cabinet before opening the front door and waiting for the police in the entryway. He tried to come up with a reason why the cops were here. A sudden thought hit him. Maybe Toothpick had found Wendy on his own and the cops were here to inform him of his wife's death. He started laughing, but quickly composed himself, remembering that the cop's tone hadn't sounded too sympathetic. And he noticed there were two cars coming up the driveway—one patrol vehicle and an unmarked.

Two uniformed officers got out of the first car, one white, the other black. They both looked like weight lifters, with muscles stretching their tailored uniform shirts. Two men in suits got out of the second one. One of them was a short, slightly overweight black man of about fifty years of age. The other was twenty years younger, tall, rail-thin, and white. The older detective presented his identification and said, "My name is Detective Simon Carruthers. My partner here is Detective Bobby Duncan. Step down into the driveway, Mr. Folsom."

Folsom was getting worried now. He walked down the three steps to the driveway. "What's going on?" he asked, truly confused.

The two officers circled behind Folsom as the detective announced, "Gerald Folsom, you're under arrest for the assault and battery and attempted murder of Wendy Folsom."

Folsom felt the cops grab his arms and pull them behind him and cuffs snapped on his wrists. Detective Carruthers read Folsom his rights.

"I want to call my lawyer," Folsom cried.

"You'll have the chance to do that once you're downtown." Then he told Folsom, "We have a search warrant which we're going to execute now. "Bobby," Detective Carruthers said to the other detective, "why don't you start the search on the top floor? I'll start on the ground level. We're looking for anything with blood on it."

# CHAPTER THIRTY-SIX

Edward had had a difficult and disappointing day. Two newspaper editors, two television station producers, and a radio station producer had treated him respectfully, but he'd felt patronized all the same. He decided he needed to be around people he loved, and who loved him. At 6 p.m., he called his wife and mother as he drove back from his last media appointment, and suggested they go out for a good meal. He told them he'd pick them up around seven o'clock.

He didn't want to think or talk about banks or regulators or even Winter Enterprises at dinner; all he wanted was to enjoy his wife and mother's company.

On the drive to his house, against his will, Edward's mind wandered back to the company. Paul Sanders had told him that legal maneuvering could delay any action the bank might take. But, to Edward, that was just postponing the inevitable. He was quickly becoming fatalistic about his company. No, he wasn't going to stop fighting, but he sure as hell wasn't going to be unrealistic.

Shaking his head, he told himself over and over again, "No business talk tonight. No business talk tonight. No business talk tonight."

After picking up Betsy, he drove to his mother's home and from there they drove to a local Italian restaurant. "Gee, I thought we'd eat at one of our Hot N' Chili restaurants," Katherine said after they'd been seated. "You said you'd take us out for a good meal."

Betsy laughed. "Yeah, little Eddie needs to get used to eating spicy food."

Edward gave his wife a strange look. "'Little Eddie'? Since when do you call me Little Eddie?"

"I wasn't referring to you, dummy. I was talking about our son."

"Son? Since when?"

"Since this afternoon when I had the ultrasound."

"Oh my God, Betsy. I'm so sorry, I forgot all about it."

Betsy reached out and patted his hand. "You've got a lot on your mind."

"Dammit! That's no excuse, I—"

Katherine interrupted, saying, "This is wonderful news. I am so happy we can celebrate together." She shot a mischievous smile at Betsy and added, "I can't wait to see how you make my son pay for missing the doctor's appointment today."

"Hey now," Edward protested jokingly, "You're my mother. You're supposed to support me."

Katherine jabbed a finger at her son. "Listen, Buster, once Betsy gives me my first grandchild, you'll be lucky to get a hello from me."

Edward smiled at his mother and took his wife's hand. "I'm going to order a bottle of champagne to help us celebrate."

"Boy, you're on a winning streak," Betsy said. "You know I can't drink while I'm pregnant."

Edward playfully slapped his cheek before raising his hand and signaling their waiter. When the man came over, Edward said, "Three orange juices, please."

While waiting for their drinks, Katherine said, "I have more good news. Carrie's coming home on leave next week. I've known about this for a few days and never seem to have the chance to tell you."

"I've been so preoccupied," Edward said, feeling guilty.

"Oh, come on, son. We understand. You need to keep on doing what you're doing. Something good will come out of all of this. Remember that good things come in threes. We learned tonight you're having a son, Carrie's coming home, and . . . ." She spread her arms. "I'm confident the third good thing is just around the corner."

# CHAPTER THIRTY-SEVEN

Kelly Loughridge tucked her feet underneath her and stared at the wine glass in her hand. It was already 8:15 p.m. and she was fighting an internal struggle: Finish the wine and go to bed, or finish the wine and read the articles she'd copied and brought home. It wasn't much of a struggle. Work always came first with her.

She retrieved her briefcase, took out the copies she'd made before leaving the office along with a pen and notepad, and returned to the couch. She methodically went through the fifteen articles that mentioned Donald Matson. The first two articles dealt with speeches he had given at conferences over the past fifteen years ago. The third article quoted Matson at a press conference in 1996 where he'd announced the federal government's successful sale of $200 million of secured notes from banks the Feds had closed. He'd declined to release the sale price in response to a reporter's question.

Loughridge flipped to the next article: Another loan sale two years later.

An article from 2000 covered the sale of a bank in Long Beach Island, New Jersey, the FDIC had taken over: $1 billion in assets. This time the buyer was announced: Folsom Financial Corporation. Loughridge knew that name well. Her paper had printed several articles about the Feds turning over Broad Street National Bank to Folsom Financial Corporation. The reporter on the story had tried to interview Gerald Folsom, but had been stonewalled.

The sixth article, from 2005, mentioned that Matson had been promoted to the head of the FDIC's regional office in Philadelphia.

The next two articles were fluff pieces about local charities; Matson sat on the  boards of directors. Loughridge tossed those on the floor.

Then another four articles between 2006 and 2008 about loan pool sales with face values of $300 million, $1 billion, $1.2 billion, and $800 million, respectively. Again, no mention of the sale price of the pools or who bought them.

Finally, the last three articles dealt with banks the federal government had taken over and sold to investors. In 2009, the first bank, a community bank in Edina, Minnesota, was sold to a bank located in Anoka, Minnesota. The other two articles were about a bank takeover in Atlanta, Georgia, in 2009 and the Broad Street National takeover in Philadelphia this year. The buyer of the last two banks was Folsom Financial Corporation.

Loughridge went back through the articles and made notes. She drew a diagram with Matson's name at the top of a legal pad and Folsom Financial written at the bottom. In between, she wrote in the names of the banks Folsom Financial had purchased from the federal government and the dates of each of those events. She circled each one. Three sales to Folsom between 2000 and 2011 in New Jersey, Georgia, and Pennsylvania. She turned to the next page in her notebook and wrote a series of questions and things she needed to do:

Were there other banks sold to Folsom Financial? Check database for Folsom references.

Find contact at FDIC. Ask about its relationship with Folsom.

Did Matson & Folsom have a personal relationship? Assign staff reporter to check.

Talk to crime beat reporter covering Matson murder.

She nearly closed her notebook when another two thoughts hit her. She added:

Who were the investors on the loan pool sales mentioned in the articles? Ask FDIC contact.

Call Edward Winter.

# FRIDAY
# JULY 22, 2011

# CHAPTER THIRTY-EIGHT

Attorney Jeffrey Rose didn't normally chauffeur his clients around, except for the occasional really big fish. Gerald Folsom was one of those really big fish. Plus, the charges against Folsom had already fomented a media storm that Rose knew he would benefit from. Rose shifted excitedly, dressed in his trademark blue suit, blue and gold striped tie, and black Santoni tasseled loafers. His brilliantly white teeth set off his perpetual tan.

Rose drove to police headquarters and parked in an official police space. He didn't care about parking tickets; he'd just get them fixed. Besides, no cop would ticket a $400,000 Maybach sedan.

By the time Rose bailed Folsom out of jail at 10 a.m., his client was fuming and barely coherent.

"Those bastards kept me locked up all night with a bunch of perverts," Folsom complained.

Rose pulled him aside, away from others' hearing. "Listen carefully, Gerald. There are a dozen reporters out on the front steps.

Fucking sharks smelling blood in the water. They want to turn this into a feeding frenzy, with you being the food. You need to let me handle the media; don't say a word out there. No whining about the police, no comments about your wife, no nothin'. I know how to deal with those guys. You understand?"

"I'm going to sue the fuckin'—"

Rose stopped Folsom with a raised hand. "We'll do the suing later. Right now, you need to calm down."

Folsom's face went beet-red, but he finally nodded and said, "I got it. Let's get this over with."

Rose preceded Folsom outside. The reporters started lobbing questions at them, sounding like a class full of five-year-olds.

Rose raised a hand for silence. When the noise subsided, he said, "I've got a statement to make. Neither my client nor I will answer any questions, so take good notes." He smiled his best bullshit smile and made eye contact with the reporters.

"I have represented thousands of clients over the past thirty years. Both the innocent and the guilty." He smiled widely again and then continued. "But never in my long career have I ever seen a greater abuse of the U.S. justice system than the charges brought against Mr. Folsom. My client is innocent, a kind and loving husband who has been generous to a fault to his wife. My client brought a penniless young woman into his life and treated her like a queen. But I guess the $20,000 a month he gives her isn't enough. So she brings scurrilous charges against him in a desperate attempt to extort money out of a successful man, and I am surprised the District Attorney would be a party to such a travesty. I will have more to say on a later date. Thank you."

Rose turned, took Folsom's arm, and led him away to his car.

A couple reporters ran after them, but Rose wheeled on them and pointed his hand as though it was a gun. "Get lost," he shouted.

Rose and Folsom fast-walked to the Maybach.

"Nice wheels," Folsom said, a bitter twist to his mouth. "I got a feeling you'll be able to buy a new one by the time I finish paying you."

"Maybe more than one," Rose said. He pulled out of the parking lot and headed out of downtown, toward Folsom's home. After they were on the expressway, Rose asked, "Tell me the truth. Do you beat your wife?"

"What difference does that make? You not gonna represent me if I say yes?"

"Of course I will. But if you're guilty of the charges they've filed against you, then we don't want to go to trial. And we need to get this story out of the media as soon as possible. If you're guilty and your wife is determined to make you pay, the longer the battle and the bigger the press' feeding frenzy. And your wife's attorney, Sylvia Young, is sharp. If your wife had any visible injuries when she talked to Sylvia, then I guarantee you Sylvia now has photos. That would be very bad."

"I might have pushed her around a bit."

"Uh huh. So you kicked the shit out of her. Regularly or just recently?"

Folsom stayed quiet for a moment and then said, "I have no interest in going to court. I'm a businessman who does large deals with the federal government. These charges could jeopardize all of that and a conviction would be devastating. The government would never do another deal with me."

"Gerald, the federal government would be the least of your

worries if you're convicted. You could be spending the next few years in a cell with a 300 pound guy named Tyrone."

"I'll agree to a divorce. I've already got a pre-nup with Wendy that requires me to pay her $5 million if we divorce."

"Your wife knows this, I presume."

"Sure."

"Then why is she bringing these charges against you? Why doesn't she just file for divorce and take the $5 million?"

"Maybe she wants more money."

"Gerald, I want the truth. Did you just hit your wife a few times, or was it worse than that?"

Folsom looked out the passenger side window for a beat. When he turned back to look at Rose, he said, "I nearly killed her."

"I got a bad feeling about this. I don't think this is about money—your wife could be on a crusade. If that's the case, then my job isn't getting you off; it's minimizing the pain. Is there any chance she would talk with you?"

"I don't think so. Besides, I don't even know where she is."

"What did the search of Folsom's house turn up?" District Attorney Lincoln Marx asked Detective Anthony Castiglia.

"Our detectives found blood on a sheet and a pillow case on Wendy Folsom's bed. There was also a blood-stained bathrobe in her closet. And we took pictures of Folsom's hands. His knuckles were bruised and cracked open. Of course, there are the photographs of Mrs. Folsom taken within about twenty-four hours of the assault. She looks like her whole body's been tattooed."

"Any other evidence?"

"There's a vault in the house. Folsom gave us some trouble about opening it, but he agreed to do so when one of the detectives told him he'd get a locksmith to drill it open. They made him watch as they inventoried the items there. They found a shitload of gold and silver coins, jewels, and two valises with a ton of cash. There was nothing there tying the cash to the assault case, but we inventoried the stuff as best we could and then locked the vault."

"How much cash?" Marx asked.

"Hell, Lincoln, I don't know. Could have been hundreds of thousands of dollars, maybe even a million or more. We just showed two valises of cash on our inventory list. Why?"

"No reason. Just wondering why he keeps that much cash around."

"It's not against the law," Castiglia said. "That's why we didn't count it. That would have taken hours."

# CHAPTER THIRTY-NINE

The Mother Superior of the St. Francis Convent had given permission for Wendy Folsom to stay with the nuns. At 11 a.m., she and Wendy drove up Germantown Pike, past the Morris Arboretum and high-end homes to the St. Francis College campus.

"This ought to be interesting," Wendy said. "Living with a bunch of virgins."

Katherine laughed. "You'll have to be on your best behavior."

"In all seriousness, a quiet, safe place is awfully attractive right now. Not that I didn't feel safe at your home, Katherine, I just think I've imposed enough on you."

"Don't you ever worry about imposing on me. I've enjoyed your company; I'm just sorry we had to meet under these circumstances."

"I hope your son is able to solve his problems. I don't know exactly what's going on, but I heard enough to know things must be rough."

"I didn't tell you this before, but the bank that's causing

our problems is the one your husband now owns. They refuse to renew the company's loan when it matures on July 29. The banking environment is so bad in this recession that refinancing a commercial real estate loan at another bank is nearly impossible. You remember that day Paul and I showed up at your house?"

"I don't recall much from that day. Is that how I got Paul's card?"

"Paul and I were there to talk with your husband. I had this misguided thought I could reason with him about our loan at the bank. Paul didn't want me to go there, but he went along to protect me."

"So Broad Street National Bank is treating your son's company badly?"

"Very badly."

Wendy shook her head. "Gerald is such an asshole." Then a thought came to her and her expression changed as she made an "O" with her mouth.

"What is it?" Katherine asked.

Wendy felt her face flush. "Nothing."

"Come on, Wendy, I can tell something's bothering you."

"It's just that . . . you're helping me . . . and your son's company, and all."

Katherine nodded her head, as though in sudden understanding. "I'd be lying to you if I said I didn't want to hurt your husband. But if I wanted to use you to help my son with his bank problem, I would have asked Paul to use you as a bargaining chip with Folsom. We would have threatened Folsom with assault charges in return for relieving the pressure the bank has put on my son, not recommended that you actually bring charges against him. And I assure you that, as much as Paul Sanders cares about my family, he will always do what's right. In this case, what's right is protecting you and making your abusive husband pay for what he's done to you."

Wendy bowed her head. "I apologize for even thinking what I was thinking. You've been—"

Katherine rubbed Wendy's arm and said, "It's okay, honey."

After Katherine left the convent, Wendy contemplated what Katherine had said. That lovely woman and her son were going through a very difficult time because of Gerald. She'd caught snippets of conversations between Katherine and Edward and between Paul and Edward at Katherine's house, all sounding as though the family was at risk of losing its business. She didn't understand any of it, but she did understand that Gerald was in a position to harm the Winters.

She owed Katherine so much. At the same time, she felt awful about what she was about to do. She would be breaking her promise to Detective Castiglia.

There was no telephone in her room, so she wandered down the hall until she found an office. A young woman dressed in a St. Francis College tee-shirt and jeans sat at one of the two desks.

"Hi," Wendy said. "Would it be okay to use the telephone to make a local call?"

"Sure," the young woman said. "Will you watch the office until I get back? I need to go to the ladies room."

"Happy to," Wendy said.

As soon as the young woman left, Wendy quickly dialed Gerald's cell number.

"What!" he barked.

"Gerald, it's me."

"Jesus, Wendy, where are you?"

"I'm not going to tell you that."

Folsom didn't immediately respond. Then he said, "What were you thinking, going to the cops? Are you nuts?"

"You coulda killed me, Gerald. I should have walked out on you months ago."

"How much do you want? Ten million?"

"Screw you, Gerald. This isn't about money. You think money's the only thing that motivates people."

"You married me for my money, Wendy. Don't insult me by telling me it was true love."

"Gerald, I thought you were a knight in shining armor. You were worldly, gracious and handsome; little did I know you were also a monster."

"What do you want, Wendy?"

"A favor."

"You go to the cops and get me thrown in jail, and now you want a favor. What's it going to cost me?"

"Not a penny. You can help some friends of mine. You do that and I'll drop the complaint."

"What friends?"

"The family's name is Winter. Edward Winter has a loan at your bank. If you take care of Edward's problem at the bank, I'll withdraw my complaint and issue a statement that it was all a misunderstanding."

"How the hell do you know the Winters?"

"Not important."

Folsom was silent for a few seconds, and then he said, "You've got a deal."

"When I find out from Edward Winter you solved his problem at the bank, I'll complete my end of the deal. Goodbye, Gerald. Do something good for a change."

Folsom had already read and jotted down the telephone number showing on his cell phone's display by the time he hung up with Wendy, writing the number on the top edge of today's newspaper, right above the headline that screamed, *BANK EXECUTIVE ARRESTED FOR SPOUSE ABUSE.* He ripped the number from the front page and stuck it in his shirt pocket. He flung the rest of the newspaper across the room, snatched his jacket from a chair, and rushed to the garage. After jumping into his Mercedes, he pressed the garage door opener, and scraped the car roof against the bottom of the partially retracted garage door in his hurry to leave. He finally cleared the garage and looked back at the door. It had been knocked off its track. He cursed and roared away.

At the first convenience store he saw, he parked in front of a pay phone, got out of the car, and dialed the number Wendy had called him from. A woman answered, "St. Francis College." Folsom hung up without saying anything. Clever girl, he thought, hiding out at the Catholic women's college. He then dialed Toothpick Jefferson's number.

"Who's calling?" Toothpick asked.

"You did nice work on the first job."

"You got the information I need to finish the assignment?"

He told Toothpick where Wendy had called him from.

"Shit! That's going to complicate things."

"I think the fee I agreed to pay you should cover a few complications."

"Plus the bonus."

"Yeah, yeah. Plus the bonus."

"Anything else?"

"It needs to look like an accident. A violent death will only bring heat on me."

# CHAPTER FORTY

Kelly Loughridge was feeling vibes that only came when she felt a good story was in the making. She'd had a busy morning and was now working through the lunch hour. She'd asked the reporter working the Broad Street National Bank takeover if he had a contact at the FDIC.

"Not anymore," the guy told her. "It was Donald Matson until he got murdered the other night."

She called the area FDIC office, but the place was apparently in turmoil as a result of Matson's death. All she got were recorded messages.

Finally, she called Washington, D.C. and left a message. She had a suspicion she'd never get a call back.

The last item on her TO DO list was a reminder to call Edward Winter.

She got past the receptionist at Winter Enterprises and was put though to Edward.

"Ms. Loughridge, I'm pleased to hear from you."

"Hello, Mr. Winter. I wanted to update you."

"Yes?"

"I checked past news items that mentioned Donald Matson's name and came up with a few interesting things. You remember Matson was the man who was the FDIC supervisor here in Philadelphia and was murdered a couple nights ago? Some of the articles led me to suspect Matson and Gerald Folsom knew each other. Perhaps more than professionally."

"That doesn't seem particularly strange considering Folsom has done more than one deal with the FDIC."

"Maybe not. But the articles did mention three bank deals that had gone to Folsom's company. In each one, Matson played a role. There were also mentions of loan pool sales to investors, but not who the investors were. I ran Gerald Folsom's name through our database, but didn't come up with anything substantive on the subject. I've been trying to talk to someone at the FDIC with no luck so far."

"You suspect there might have been hanky-panky going on between Folsom and Matson?"

"I don't suspect anything. I'm an unbiased, objective member of the media. But I sure do have a funny feeling."

"Not quite the story I wanted you to write about," Edward said.

"You never know where a story might lead. Now, if I can only get someone from the FDIC to call me."

"I might be able to help you there. Paul Sanders, my attorney, knows someone at that agency. How about if I have Mr. Sanders call you?"

"That'd be great."

"Keep me informed, Ms. Loughridge. I'm running on fumes here. I need a shot of good news, something that will get Broad Street National Bank off my butt."

"I'll be in touch."



Paul was reading a draft of a restraining order he'd prepared – he was going to try to get a judge to delay Broad Street National's impending foreclosure action on the Winter Enterprises' loan – when he got a call from Edward. After Edward briefed him on what Kelly Loughridge had told him and given him her number, Paul called the newspaper editor.

Loughridge picked up his call on the second ring and seemed thrilled to hear from him. "I hear you might be able to help me get through to the right person at the FDIC."

"I can try," Paul answered. "But on one condition. I want to be kept informed of anything you learn and are going to write about."

"You know I can't do that," she said.

"Ms. Loughridge, I'm trying to save the business of a very fine man, one who has done everything right. His business and his financial survival are being threatened by a very bad man. You can help me save a very good man."

"I'm a journalist, not a social worker, Mr.—"

"*Quid pro quo.* You share with me and I'll share with you any information I get about Gerald Folsom, Ms. Loughridge. Also anything I learn about the FDIC or anyone else involved in this matter."

Loughridge didn't respond right away. After a while, she said, "Okay, Mr. Sanders. What's our next step?"

"I'll call my friend at the FDIC and see if she'll talk with you."


Paul called Gail Moskowitz at the FDIC's Washington, D.C. offices.

"I need your help again. I just talked with a newspaper editor here in Philadelphia. She's got a question about the deals Gerald Folsom has closed with your agency and wants to talk to someone at the FDIC."

"Paul, you're a friend, but you're pushing our friendship. I talk to a reporter and my career will be over."

"Gail, if there's something rotten in the agency, don't you want to expose it?"

"Last time I looked I didn't have a bull's-eye on my back and I sure as hell don't have a martyr complex. I'm not going to participate in a witch hunt based on the suspicions of some newspaper editor."

"Okay, Gail, then just do this. Check your files and see how many deals Gerald Folsom and/or Folsom Financial Corporation have done with the agency. And then cross-check those deals against Donald Matson's name. If you find something strange, then call me. If not, forget we had this conversation."

"I'll think about it," she said and hung up.

# CHAPTER FORTY-ONE

Toothpick Jefferson ordered one of his men to drive by the college. The guy called him back an hour-and-a-half later.

"You recruiting street talent from colleges now, Toothpick?"

"Stop talking bullshit. What d'ya see?"

"It's pretty quiet out there, being summertime and all. Got a security guard old as Methuselah driving 'round in a golf cart. You want me to hang around, do somethin' for you?"

"Nah," Toothpick said. "I need finesse for this job."

"I got finesse," his man said, sounding put out.

"You got as much finesse as an elephant in heat." He hung up and then thought about Philippa Gonzalez, a forty-year-old woman he used sparingly for more sophisticated work. Philippa was a dark-haired knockout of medium height, 120 pounds, hourglass figure and long raven-colored hair. She had a college degree in education and spoke three languages in addition to being a skillful boxer and a black belt in karate. The hundred grand Toothpick paid her annually for tough jobs was more than she could make in two-and-a-half years as a school teacher. And she liked the challenge. He dialed her number.

"Hey, Sugar," Philippa said.

"Girl, you got some time to meet me?"

"Would this be a social call or business?"

"Business, Sweetie. What else would it be?"

"I'll see you in an hour."

"Wear something maternal."

An hour later, Toothpick briefed Philippa about the job, the target, and the target's location. They agreed on a $5,000 fee upon completion of the assignment before laying out a strategy. First, reconnaissance. She would enter the college campus, pretending to have a teenage daughter considering applying for admission. Philippa would claim she was in Philadelphia on business and was taking the opportunity to visit the campus and to possibly get a tour.

At 4:25 p.m., Philippa patted her hair one last time and checked her makeup in her car's rearview mirror. Satisfied, she got out and walked to the reception building on the St. Francis College campus. She wore a gray suit with a white blouse with a conservative gold necklace, small gold earrings, and a wedding ring. The young woman who greeted her listened to her story and then made a telephone call. Within a few minutes, a woman about Philippa's age joined them in the lobby. She was tall and thin, and wore a blue blazer over a white blouse and gray slacks. Her brown hair was piled onto her head, high over her intelligent, alert brown eyes.

"Hello," the woman said. "My name is Helen Davis. I understand you have a daughter who is considering our school."

Philippa beamed at Helen Davis and introduced herself as Lourdes Sanchez. "Yes, my daughter, Emilia, wants to go to school near a large city." Philippa chuckled and added, "Anything to get out of Akron."

"When does your daughter graduate from high school?"

"She'll be a senior this coming year, so she'll graduate in May next year. Her father and I are nervous about her going away to college, but we've agreed to allow it as long as she goes some place where she will be safe."

Ms. Davis smiled at Philippa. "We find that girls who come from caring families like yours adjust to being away from home the best. As to the safety issue, we have twenty-four hour security patrols on campus and do not allow our freshman students to be off campus during the week and students have a midnight curfew on weekends. And, as you probably noticed, this area is mostly residential and upscale."

Philippa nodded her approval. "Is there a chance someone could give me a tour of the campus?"

"It would be my pleasure," Davis said. "I can't give you a complete tour as I have a meeting in a little over an hour, but I can at least give you enough of a tour to provide an appreciation for our school."

"That would be wonderful."


Helen Davis's tour was comprehensive yet efficient. She took Philippa through a classroom building, the library, the sports facilities, and a dormitory. The last place they toured was the grotto with its fountain and the chapel.

"Do you have summer classes going on right now?" Philippa asked.

"No, all the students are off campus except for a couple who have summer jobs here. That's why it was so hot in the dormitory; we shut off the air conditioning to keep our utility bills down."

"Good idea."

"We're a small institution that depends on the generosity of our alumni and friends. We don't have a large endowment like the Ivy League schools do."

"I noticed a few other buildings on campus, away from the school buildings."

"Yes, we are more than just a college. We also have a church and convent on site." Davis pointed at a parcel of high ground. "That's the Mother Superior's residence. The convent is off to the right about one hundred yards."

"Beautiful buildings."

"Thank you. By the way, a lot of our students come from out-of-state. When their parents visit here we make rooms available to them at a small charge." Davis laughed deprecatingly. "The rooms are not luxurious, so you might prefer one of the area hotels."

"Where do these visitors stay?"

"In a wing of the convent." Davis pointed at the far right side of the convent building. "Can't have fathers wandering around the main part of the building."

Philippa chuckled. "I can understand that. It might have been fun to stay there during this visit. I haven't spent a night in a convent since I was a little girl at summer camp."

Davis smiled and said, "We would love to have had you stay with us. Right now there's only one visitor, a woman."

"You've been very kind," Philippa told her. "I'm sure my daughter will apply to your school. It's so beautiful here; I wish I was the one about to go to college."

"We hear that a lot."

Philippa said goodbye and walked back to her car. She drove out to Germantown Pike and turned right. At the next intersection, a corner of the campus property, she took another right. A couple hundred feet down the street, she pulled off to the side, peeked over the stone wall bordering the property, and eyeballed the convent. The visitors' wing was the part of the building closest to the street. She could easily climb over the wall – there didn't appear to be any security devices, like cameras or electronic alarm wiring on the wall. Ten second run to the visitors' wing. No windows showing in the convent building, except on the front entrance side. She smiled. Wouldn't do to have peeping Toms looking in on the nuns.

She'd have to find a place to park that wouldn't attract attention. There was an entrance to Fairmount Park on the other side of Germantown Pike. She could pretend to be out jogging; although that might come across lame if a cop stopped her. This was an after-dark job. Most people in their right minds didn't jog at that hour.

# CHAPTER FORTY-TWO

Katherine was thinking about Carrie. The letter she'd received from her daughter had said that she would be released from a hospital in about a week. Considering the time that had passed since Carrie wrote the letter, she figured Carrie should be home already. But Katherine knew she was always doing something mysterious and her schedule was likely to change at a moment's notice. The telephone rang, breaking into her thoughts. The display showed it was Edward.

"Hi, son," she said.

"Hey, Mom. How are you doing?"

"Good. How about you?"

"Some reason for hope; nothing definite. But I didn't call to talk about work; I've got something else we need to discuss. I was just checking to see if you were home. I'll be there in a few minutes, if that's okay."

"Of course," she said.

Edward sounded mysterious. Katherine hoped there wasn't more bad news. She quickly shucked out of her dress and pulled on jeans and a work shirt. She opened a bottle of California Chardonnay, a 2007 Londer, and was halfway through her first glass when the doorbell rang. She went to the door, swung it open, and shouted, "Carrie!"

A grinning Edward stood behind Carrie, holding her travel bag.

Katherine moved to embrace her daughter, but Carrie took the wine glass from her mother, downed the contents, and tossed the glass over her shoulder onto the lawn.

"Now I'll take that hug," she said.

Mother and daughter squealed and danced around, all the while wrapped around one another. Edward squeezed around them and set Carrie's bag inside the front door. Katherine and Carrie finally followed him inside.

"You look great," Katherine told Carrie. "After I read your last letter, I was afraid you'd look like your brother did when he returned from Iraq."

Carrie smiled at Edward and said, "I've always been tougher than Eddie. Actually, I'm feeling great. And I'll feel even better after I have another glass of that fantastic chardonnay and you tell me where we're having dinner tonight."

"What do you feel like eating?" Katherine asked.

"Steak, steak, and more steak. I've had so much lamb, flat bread, and grape leaves, I'm starting to turn into an Afghani."

"Is that where you've been, Afghanistan?" Edward said.

She waggled her hand in front of her and laughed. "Let's just say where I've been is the armpit of the universe and I never want to return there ever again."

"Okay, steak it is. How does Paisano's sound?"

"Great!"

Edward hugged and kissed his mother. "I'll go get Betsy and meet you there. Say, in an hour." He turned to Carrie and hugged her as well. "Are you sure you're up to this? I mean, you just flew more than halfway around the world."

"Still looking out for me, big brother?"

"Absolutely."

Carrie kissed Edward on the cheek and hugged him tightly. "Go get Betsy. I'm fine. Well, besides being starving."

"What's going on with Edward?" Carrie asked after she and her mother sat down in the kitchen. "Something's bothering him."

Katherine shook her head. "It's a long story, but the essence is the federal government has overreacted to the banking and capital markets crises. The bank regulators are taking over banks all over the country and forcing most of them to stop making commercial real estate loans. Edward's loan is coming due at the end of this month and the bank told him they won't renew it. He's tried to get it refinanced at another bank, but most of them aren't in the market for new commercial real estate paper. The one bank that wants his business isn't large enough to take the whole loan.

"Edward's been working like crazy trying to get his bank to change its position, but without success. His bank was taken over by the Feds and then sold to an investor who . . ." Katherine paused.

"What is it, Mom?"

"The new owner of the bank is Gerald Folsom, the same man who put your father into those real estate deals more than twenty years ago. The same guy who wound up owning your father's bank and all his real estate after he died."

Katherine saw a change come over Carrie, a dark and vengeful force that invaded her being. Her eyes narrowed.

"So, what happens at the end of the month?" Carrie asked.

"The bank can foreclose on the collateral behind the loan. That's all of the restaurant locations, which would, in effect, put an end to the company. I assume the bank would close down the restaurants and sell the buildings and land. I doubt they want to be in the restaurant business. There's so much equity in the property the bank should easily come out ahead."

"And Edward gets the shaft."

"Edward and Betsy and you and me. All shareholders. And the hundreds of employees who helped us build the company."

Carrie was quiet for a while and then said, "I'd better go change." She smiled, the dark and evil spirit apparently gone. "I really am starving."

"I think I'm ready to crash," Carrie said after they'd finished coffees and cannoli's.

"Oh, thank goodness, me too," Betsy responded. "I had no idea being pregnant could be so tiring."

Katherine chuckled and said, "Wait until the baby is born. You don't even know what tired is."

"Oh, great," Betsy said, smiling.

Edward and Betsy drove off while the valet retrieved Katherine's car. While Carrie and Katherine waited, Katherine pulled her cell phone out of her purse and punched in a number.

"Hello, Wendy, it's Katherine. Just checking to see how you're doing."

"Thanks for calling. I'm okay." Wendy's voice wobbled, then she broke down, crying.

"What's wrong?" Katherine said, alarmed.

"We need to talk. You're not going to be happy with me, but I think it was the right thing to do."

"What?"

"Let's wait until we get together. How does tomorrow morning at 9 work for you?"

"Honey, I'm no more than ten minutes away from you. I'm coming over there now. By the way, my daughter is with me." Katherine closed her cell phone.

"Who was that?" Carrie asked.

"I know you're tired, but this is important. Can you stay awake for a story?"

"Go ahead and start. If I fall asleep, you can continue tomorrow."

"Once I start this tale, there's no chance you'll fall asleep."

Katherine drove to the convent as she started her story in 1988 with Frank's death and then segued to the current problems in the banking industry, explaining how the politicians and the regulators and the banks and the investment banks and the rating agencies and greedy borrowers created a toxic economic environment that was now threatening Winter Enterprises. She then told Carrie how she met Wendy Folsom and what had transpired since then.

Ten minutes later, they checked in at the administration building at St. Francis College and told the young woman there where they were going.

"I can't let you go anywhere on campus after hours without first announcing you and then having a security guard escort you."

"Fine. Please call Mrs. Folsom."

The woman blushed. "There are no phones in the visitors' rooms."

Katherine gave her Wendy's cell number. "Try this."

The woman got through to Wendy and then called a security guard.

Katherine guided Carrie to a corner of the massive reception area and filled her in on some details about Wendy. When she described the way Folsom had beaten Wendy, Katherine saw Carrie's darkness reemerge, something visceral and vengeful and dangerous.

"Have you met this guy, Folsom?" Carrie asked.

"A long, long time ago."

"Tell me what you know about him."

"Wendy's his third wife. All of them were young, blonde, and blue-eyed. All from good families. He seems to have a thing for preppie girls. Apparently he treated Wendy well in the beginning, but became more violent as the months went by and she thinks he would have killed her if she'd stayed with him, and that he wouldn't have cared. The only thing that's important to him is money, she said. He's manic about it. "

"And now this bastard's bank is trying to ruin Edward."

"Seems that way," Katherine said.

A seriously overweight, sixtyish man wearing a wrinkled gray uniform arrived ten minutes later. His hair looked tousled and his eyes were puffy. Katherine thought he looked as though he'd been sleeping. In fact, he looked like an unmade bed. The young woman at the reception desk asked the guard to take Katherine and Carrie to the visitors' wing of the convent. They all loaded into an extended golf cart and rode up to the convent.

After thanking the guard, the women entered the building and found Wendy waiting for them in the hall. Her eyes were wet. Katherine noticed Carrie's eyes narrow when she looked at Wendy, whose face was still swollen and bruised. Katherine introduced Carrie to Wendy.

"Let's go down the hall," Wendy said. "There's a break room we can use."

Philippa Gonzalez found an empty lot across from the college, next to a small, darkened building with a sign out front that said a paving contractor occupied the building. It was almost 10 p.m. and dark. She ran across the street and scaled the rock wall onto the college grounds. After a quick run, using trees and bushes to cover her approach, she entered the convent's visitors' wing. She padded softly down the hall to an intersecting hallway, and peered left and then right. A light shone twenty yards away, on the right. She was about to turn the corner but stopped when she heard female voices.

"It's good to finally meet you," Wendy told Carrie after they were seated in a small room with a two-seater couch, two arm chairs, and a coffee table. "Your mother talks about you a lot."

Carrie smiled. "Don't believe half of what a mother says about her children."

"Wendy, what's going on?" Katherine interrupted.

Wendy lowered her gaze to her hands in her lap. "I called Gerald today."

"Why, Wendy? Both Paul and Sylvia Young told you to have no contact with him."

"I made him a proposal. He's agreed to do something for me in return for my dropping the charges against him."

"Is this about money? Did you demand more money from him?"

Wendy's head came up and met Katherine's eyes angrily. "No, it's not about money. I would never make a deal with him so I could get more money out of him."

"Then *what*?"

Wendy dropped her gaze again.

"Come on, Wendy," Katherine implored. "What is it?"

She looked at Katherine and said, "I told him I'd drop the charges if he made the bank stop harassing Edward."

Katherine was dumbstruck. She sat on her side of the couch without any idea how to respond. Finally, she leaned forward, elbows on her knees and said, "Wendy, Edward wouldn't want you to do anything to jeopardize your safety, nobody does. I truly appreciate your desire to help us out with the bank, but negotiating with Gerald Folsom is like negotiating with the devil. Maybe worse"

"But it's a win-win situation for everyone," she protested.

"Only if your husband holds up his end of the deal."

Carrie cleared her throat and said, "I hope you don't mind my butting in here, but how did you call your husband?"

Wendy considered the question for a few seconds and said, "I used the phone in the office around the corner."

"So, Folsom could have captured the phone number and figured out where you are?"

Wendy's face went pale; her eyes widened.

"Wendy, my mother explained about your husband's abuse. Do you believe he's capable of doing you more harm?"

Wendy nodded slowly.

"Do you believe he's capable of killing you?"

Wendy hesitated a second before nodding again and saying, "Yes."

Philippa heard one of the women speak the name Wendy and she heard a reference to Gerald Folsom and the threat he posed to this Wendy. Philippa put two and two together and guessed the hit on Wendy Folsom had been commissioned by her husband through Toothpick Jefferson. It made no difference to her.

Katherine's stomach cramped. "You're coming home with Carrie and me," she said, standing, moving toward Wendy, and extending her hand. "Let's go. Now."

They didn't take time to pack any of Wendy's things. Katherine and Carrie escorted her from the convent, fast-walking down toward the parking lot.

Philippa heard one of the women say they were going to leave the building. The woman said, 'You're coming home with Carrie and me.' Philippa backtracked and went outside, hiding behind a corner of the building. She saw three women hustle toward an SUV parked in a lot fifty yards down the hill. Sprinting back to the campus perimeter, Philippa climbed over the wall and ran to her car. She backed out onto the street and gunned the engine. At the intersection with Germantown Pike, she edged the nose of her vehicle forward until she could watch the college's parking lot exit. When the SUV pulled out, she turned left, ignoring the red light, and followed.

# CHAPTER FORTY-THREE

Hanging back far enough to avoid detection, Philippa trailed the SUV for fifteen minutes. After it turned into a rural residential area, where there were no street lights and houses appeared to be on one-acre lots, she allowed even more distance. Even when she lost sight of the other vehicle, she could still see the occasional flash of its headlights. But three blocks into the subdivision, she lost sight of the vehicle and no longer saw its lights. She came to an intersection and slammed the steering wheel with her hand in frustration. Opting to turn left, Philippa drove for half-a-block and suddenly spotted three women bailing out of the SUV she'd been following. She cruised past the driveway, which meandered for about thirty yards to a one-story house bordered by enormous oak and pine trees.

Philippa decided to wait until the women retired for the evening. She'd been paid to eliminate one target; she would prefer not to have to take out three for the price of one. Although she would do so if necessary. Besides, one woman or three women would pose no obstacle for her.

The last of the house lights went out at 11:20. Philippa waited another fifteen minutes and then slipped out of her car and circled the property on foot, keeping to the densest part of the tree growth. Wearing all black, including a watch cap and skin tight gloves, she broke through the tree line and carefully approached the back of the house, watching for fallen branches or anything that might trip her up. An air conditioner unit sat on a concrete pad near the left corner of the house. It was running and making enough covering noise to mask the sound of her approach.

The windows on the rear of the house indicated there were three large rooms there, separated by smaller rooms Philippa assumed were bathrooms. The room on the left had a sliding glass door opening onto the back patio. The other two rooms had large windows, but no doors. Assuming the women were in the bedrooms, the best course of action would be to attempt entry on the front side of the house. She walked around the house and peered inside the sidelight window by the front door. There was no alarm pad visible on the entry wall and no signs of a dog – no water bowls, no dog houses in the yard.

She tried the front door handle. Locked, with a deadbolt. Moving to the right front corner of the house, she eyed the driveway where it curved around to the garage. There was a door that accessed the back of the garage. It, too, was locked. But this lock was a simple device inset in the door knob. Philippa pulled a plastic card the size of a credit card and slipped it between the door jamb and the lock. Jiggling the card, she inserted it past the tongue of the lock and pulled on the door handle. The door opened smoothly, and silently. She propped the door open with a handy bucket partially filled with potting soil in case she had to make a quick exit. Entering the garage, she took six steps to an interior door. She didn't need to use the plastic card this time; the door was unlocked.

Now inside the house, Philippa removed a switchblade knife from her fanny pack. She tip-toed down a short hallway terminating at another hallway that lead to the rooms at the back of the house.

The first room she came to was the one with the sliding glass door opening onto the patio. The door to that room was open, and Philippa saw a woman lying in bed, facing her. The woman appeared to be in her fifties and was snoring lightly.

Philippa passed an open bathroom door, arriving next at a closed door. She grasped the lever door handle and began to press down on it when an almost indiscernible, muffled noise caused her to recoil from the door, looking up and down the hall. But there was no one else in the hallway. Maybe the wind had moved the garage door she had propped open. She had barely heard anything herself and doubted any of the pampered suburbanites would have been roused by it. Despite that thought, she had a momentary impulse to abandon the job, at least for tonight. But the $5,000 fee she would earn swamped that impulse.

Placing her hand back on the door lever, she slowly applied just enough pressure to crack open the door. The movement of the door was almost soundless—just a slight brushing of the door bottom against carpet. The sleep-bound woman in this room was lying with her back to the door. A nightlight in the connecting bathroom shined just enough light on the bedroom to allow Philippa to see the woman's long blonde hair. That was part of the description of the target Toothpick had provided her. The third woman she'd seen at the college had also been a blonde, but that woman's hair had been very short.

Philippa opened the door enough to allow her to glide into the room. She moved the door to an inch of closing and rapidly moved to the bed. She was one step from the side of the bed when she stopped, the hair standing up on the back of her neck. It wasn't a sound or a smell or something she saw. Something else in the room had changed, almost like an electrical charge in the air. She had almost convinced herself that she was imagining things as she looked back over her shoulder. Then her stomach clenched and her breath caught in her chest.

Philippa spun around, raising her left arm in a defensive move and thrusting out with her knife hand, confident her strike would finish the woman standing in front of her. But the woman ducked her thrust. Philippa pulled her arm back, altered her stance, and shifted the knife to her left hand. She struck out again, but hit nothing but air. About to wade in closer to the woman, Philippa was suddenly disoriented and in excruciating pain, collapsing to the floor. She gasped as though she would never take another breath.

Wendy jerked upright in bed, screaming. She had been dreaming that Gerald was beating her, but this was no dream. Someone she couldn't see was making pained, animal-like noises and another person stood near the footboard, framed in the doorway. She retreated against the headboard, then scrambled off the far side of the bed, moving toward the bathroom. She ignored the pain that quick movement caused.

"Wendy, calm down," someone said.

Wendy fled into the bathroom before she realized the voice was Carrie's. She came back into the room and walked over to Carrie, trembling as she looked at someone writhing on the floor. Before she could say anything, the hallway light came on and Katherine, holding a fireplace poker, rushed into the room. She flipped the bedroom light switch, bathing the room in bright light and momentarily blinding the occupants.

"What happened?" Katherine demanded. She pointed the poker at the figure on the floor. "Who's that?"

Carrie bent down, picked up the knife the intruder had dropped, and knelt down next to her. The intruder appeared to be breathing easier now. Carrie summarily searched the woman, finding a revolver in her jacket. She handed the pistol to Katherine. Knife in hand, she shook the woman with her free hand.

The intruder's eyes darted around; her face was beet red.

"You get one chance to tell me the truth," Carrie said to the woman. "If you do the right thing, I'll let you go."

The woman looked around at the women in the room. "You'll really let me go?" she asked hoarsely.

"You've got my word," Carrie said. "But if I ever see you again I'll kill you."

Wendy saw the woman's eyes widen for just a split second.

"You tell me who sent you and you get a break. You take the stupid route and I'll call the police."

The woman looked at Carrie. Her breathing had eased a lot and she no longer looked as panicked.

"Three seconds," Carrie said.

"Okay, okay," the woman croaked. "Guy named Jefferson. Toothpick Jefferson."

"Got a number for this Jefferson?" Carrie asked.

The woman recited ten digits.

"Now describe him to me."

SATURDAY
JULY 23, 2011

# SATURDAY
# JULY 23, 2011

# CHAPTER FORTY-FOUR

Gail Moskowitz knew she had something that smelled really bad. Nearly every time Donald Matson had been in charge of an agency transaction, Gerald Folsom and Folsom Financial Corporation's names had popped up. But she had found absolutely nothing indicating anything illegal had occurred, even if there was no question Matson had violated FDIC policies and guidelines for asset disposal. He had sold assets the agency accumulated from bank closures on a sole-source basis to Folsom, instead of sales based on competitive bids. And Folsom had purchased assets from the FDIC at the low end of the range of such sales to other investors.

Folsom had purchased sixteen secured loan pools averaging $87 million in loan face value per pool over the past twenty years. The price he'd paid was an average of twenty-three and a half percent of the face value of the loans. That meant Folsom had paid only slightly more than $327 million for about $1.4 billion in loans. The last time Gail had checked, the average investor in loan pools recovered fifty-eight percent of the face value of loans, plus accrued interest. Before interest, she figured Folsom recovered at least $807 million on an investment of $327 million. Not a bad return.

But Donald Matson had a reputation in the agency as a guy who got things done. Did she want to destroy Matson's reputation now that the man was dead? Especially since she had no proof anything had gone on between Matson and Folsom, other than a relationship that had benefitted the agency.

At the same time, she was conflicted over what Edward Winter told her about the problems in the banking industry and the impact those problems were having on the business community. She also remembered Paul Sanders' comment about trying to save a good man's business.

Gail agonized over what to do. At 8 Saturday morning, she pulled up Google and typed in Folsom's name, trying to find a photograph of the man. She wondered what he looked like. Maybe, if he looked evil, she'd know better what to do. But there was no photo available. She was about to shut down her computer when she saw a link: *Bank Executive Released on Bail*. She clicked on the URL and, skimming the article, learned Gerald Folsom had been charged with assault and battery against his wife. Picture or no picture, Gail made a decision. She called Paul Sanders' cell phone number.

"Paul Sanders."

"Paul, it's Gail Moskowitz. We need to talk."

"I'm over at Katherine Winter's house, Gail, Edward Winter's mother. Can I call you back?"

Hearing something different in Paul's voice, Gail asked, "Is something wrong?"

"A hired killer broke into Mrs. Winter's home to kill Wendy Folsom."

"Kill . . . Folsom? Wendy Folsom? Gerald Folsom's wife? Is she okay?"

"She's fine."

"I'm confused. What was Gerald Folsom's wife doing with Edward Winter's mother?"

"It's a long story. I'll call you back in an hour."

After hanging up, Gail pondered this new development. Who would benefit from Wendy Folsom's murder? If the answer to that question was Gerald Folsom, then there was even more reason to be concerned about the FDIC's reputation. Was Donald Matson funneling sweetheart deals to Folsom? If so, that could be embarrassing to the agency. If Folsom had solicited the murder of his wife, that news would be devastating. Then another thought hit her: What if Folsom had something to do with Donald Matson's death?

When Paul returned to the living room where the Winters and Wendy Folsom were gathered, he found an argument going on.

"I think we made a mistake," Katherine said to Carrie. "This attempt on Wendy's life is police business."

"Mom," Carrie said, "that woman was hired by a broker. She only knows who hired *her*. Let's say we told the police she was here to kill Wendy and gave them the number she provided for Toothpick Jefferson, what will the police do?"

"They'll go talk to Jefferson; make him tell them who hired him."

"First, Jefferson will deny knowing the woman. Second, even if the police can prove Jefferson and the woman know one another, Jefferson will just deny any involvement. And would the person who paid Jefferson to kill Wendy be stupid enough to write him a personal check? Would the person behind this have called Jefferson from a home or business phone, so the police can find a trail of their conversations? And how long would it take the police to dig up anything meaningful, if they could even find anything?"

"What's the alternative?" Edward asked. "If there's someone out there who wants Wendy killed, whoever it is, is probably not going to stop. If the police knew she was a target for murder, at least they could protect her."

"For how long?" Carrie asked. "A couple weeks, maybe. Then they'll pull the guards."

"So, I'll return to my question: What's the alternative?"

Carrie shrugged.

"By the way," Paul interjected into the silence, "that call I got a few minutes ago was from my friend at the FDIC. I had asked her to check to see if there might be a special relationship between Folsom and the FDIC's area supervisor. I told her I'd call her back in an hour. Why don't I do that now?"

"God, I hope she has some helpful news," Katherine said.

"That would be a welcome change," Edward said.

Paul called Gail Moskowitz and told her in more detail what had happened at Katherine's house the night before.

"Do you have any idea who hired the killer?"

"No facts; just suspicions."

"Do you suspect Gerald Folsom?" Gail asked.

"Top of the list," Paul answered. "But we have no way of proving it."

"Why would Folsom want his wife killed?"

"She accused him of assault and battery and attempted murder. The D.A. has filed charges and Folsom actually spent a night in jail before his attorney convinced a judge to grant bail."

"I just saw that on the internet. But do you think he's capable of soliciting murder?" she asked.

"He was capable of beating his wife to a pulp."

There was silence on Gail's end of the line. Paul filled the void. "Anyway. You called me earlier."

"Paul, your suspicions were correct. Matson and Folsom had more than just an arms-length relationship. Folsom has made hundreds of millions of dollars from FDIC deals. And the structure of those deals was generous to say the least. I have no way of knowing why Matson was so good to Folsom, but these deals raise all sorts of red flags."

"Will you talk to a reporter at the *Journal*?" Paul asked. "Tell her what you told me?"

"There is no way I'm talking to the press."

"Come on, Gail. She can't use any of this if it comes from me."

"Paul, I'm not committing career suicide. But I will do one thing for you: I'll provide you with a summary of the transactions Folsom executed with the agency and will give you enough information so you can compare Folsom's deals against other similar transactions. But you can't use my name."

"Okay, Gail. I understand. Thank you. How are you going to get the information to me?"

"I'll send you a fax from the local Kinko's. It will be at your office by noon today."


After Paul ended the call with Gail Moskowitz, he brought everyone up to date.

"What can we do with this information?" Edward asked, confused. "How is it going to help us?"

"I think it will convince Kelly Loughridge at the *Journal* to do a story on this. It won't be the explosive story it would have been if Folsom and Matson could be shown to be corrupt. But it surely will raise questions. And, I suspect Folsom has seen his last FDIC deal."

"Paul, something just crossed my mind," Edward said. He looked at Wendy and asked, "You told your husband you would drop the criminal charges against him if he agreed to renew my loan?"

"Right."

Edward looked back at Paul. "So, it would be interesting to learn if Folsom called the bank and gave any instructions about our loan."

Paul said, "And, if he didn't, that could mean he didn't think he would need to, because Wendy was supposed to be dead. No Wendy, no threat, no deal."

"Exactly."

Edward pulled his cell phone from his pants pocket and dialed Stanley Burns' cell.

"Burns."

"Stan, it's Edward Winter."

No response from Burns.

"Stan, I need to ask you a question. That's all. I'm not calling to ask for your help with our loan. Just one question."

"I hope I can answer it," Burns said.

Edward thought Burns sounded as depressed as anyone he'd ever known. He almost felt sorry for him.

"Did Gerald Folsom or one of his cronies recently order you to renew my loan?"

He scoffed. "Why would Folsom do that?"

"So, your answer to my question is no."

"That's right. Folsom is almost giddy about putting you out of business. I don't understand it, Edward. I'm really sorry about everything. I—"

"Thanks for answering my question, Stan."

Edward closed his phone and said to the others, "No order came from Folsom about our loan."

"That bastard!" Wendy blurted. "That evil bastard!"

# CHAPTER FORTY-FIVE

Carrie announced she was going to get some fresh air and went outside. When she was out of sight of the house, she used her cell phone to call a friend who had served with her in Iraq and Afghanistan. A Special Ops officer, Darren Noury had been wounded in an IED explosion and decided to put in his separation papers after spending six months in rehabilitation at Landstuhl Army Hospital in Germany. Carrie knew Darren now worked in a software firm headquartered in Willow Grove, a community outside Philadelphia.

"This better be good," Darren said. He sounded groggy, hungover.

"Hello, Darren. You been partying?"

"Who the hell is this?"

"It's the woman who saved your ass in Fallujah."

"Carrie! Where the hell are you? Last I heard, you were wearing a chador and sneaking around Azerbaijan."

"That was supposed to be top secret. Who told you that?"

"Once a spook, always a spook. But where are you?"

"Chestnut Hill at my mother's house. I'm home on leave."

"Damn, we gotta get together."

"Sooner than you think. I have a problem, Darren. I need someone to cover my back."

"Action? Are you talking about action? Hot damn. Just you and me?"

"I could use another man, too."

"I know just the guy," Darren said. "Mike Perico. He was a Force Recon Marine in the first Gulf War and then joined the Company for a few years. Very dependable guy. Selling drugs now."

"What!"

Darren laughed. "No, no, he's a pharmaceutical rep."

"Big change from the agency," she said. "You available tomorrow morning?"

"Sure."

"Check with Mike and see if he can meet with us at 6:45. Use this number to call me back. If the time works, I'll meet you at Maria's Bakery on Bethlehem Pike in Chestnut Hill."

"Do I need to bring any equipment?"

"Nothing too heavy."

"Gotcha!"

Carrie walked around the block three times before Darren called her back.

"The time works," Darren said.

"Thanks, Darren. See you."

She ended the call and returned to the house.

"You okay, honey?" Katherine asked as Carrie walked in. Worry showed on her knitted brow and in her frightened eyes.

Carrie looked around. "Where is everybody?"

"Wendy's in her room. The others went home."

"I'm going to get some rest. It was a long night."

"Carrie," Katherine said, "I hope you're not planning something stupid."

"Mom, I need you to understand something. I'm not the person you knew before I joined the service. I've learned a special set of skills that are very effective against bad people. And I've put them to use on dozens of occasions. When I look at the photographs of me you've got scattered around your house, I don't recognize that person anymore."

"I see something in you that's foreign to me, that scares me," Katherine said. "But I know you're the same good person inside."

"I hope you're right, Mom; I just can't be sure. But that's irrelevant. That woman who snuck in here last night could have murdered all of us. What you're doing for Wendy is a good thing. But as long as she's here, you're in danger too. I know you won't send her away, so we've got to figure out a way to eliminate the danger."

"How?"

"First, I think you should check into a hotel for a few days. That assassin could have told any number of people where Wendy is now. And you and Wendy need to be very careful about who you talk to. Keep telephone calls limited to emergencies only. Talk to Paul Sanders or Wendy's attorney, or our family members, but no one else. Second, I'm going to bring on a couple security people to watch over you, twenty-four hours."

Carrie hugged Katherine. "And don't worry; I won't do anything stupid." She then went to her room, closed the door, and used her cell phone to call Toothpick Jefferson's number.

"Yeah," a man answered.

"We need to meet."

"Who the hell is this?"

"The person who took down your hired killer. She gave me your number."

"What you talkin' about?"

"Don't go into jive mode on me, asshole. I know you sent the woman and I know why."

"What do you want?"

"I want to meet, have a short conversation, and then I'll go my way and you'll go yours. Pretty simple, huh?"

"How do I know this isn't some kind of setup?"

"You don't. But you can't afford to ignore me. That I guarantee you."

"When?"

"Tomorrow at 8 a.m. Pastorius Park in Chestnut Hill."

"Where the hell is Pastorius Park?"

"Figure it out. Look it up on the internet. And come alone."

# CHAPTER FORTY-SIX

Paul left Katherine's home and drove to his office to finish the Injunction Order he would need to file if nothing good happened at the bank for Winter Enterprises between now and next Friday.

Good to her word, Gail Moskowitz's fax arrived just before noon. Paul read the lengthy document and realized why Gail was nervous about tying her name to the information. Compared to the typical FDIC asset sale, the deals Donald Matson gave Gerald Folsom were "special." As Gail had said, there was nothing showing what Matson might have got out of giving Folsom sweet deals—if anything—but there sure as hell was plenty of reason to raise the ugly suspicion of extortion or bribery. At a minimum, the FDIC needed to investigate the relationship between the two men.

Paul called Kelly Loughridge's office at the *Journal* and left an urgent message for her before going back to reading Gail Moskowitz's fax. He'd gotten through it a second time when Kelly Loughridge called back.

"I've got some very interesting information from the FDIC."

"How about a summary?" Kelly said.

"Donald Matson was giving Gerald Folsom extremely preferential treatment on asset sales. Over the past decade, Folsom made hundreds of millions of dollars or more from buying loan pools and banks at prices even below the normally ridiculous sale prices offered to other investors. I've got dates and prices of all the deals Folsom made with the agency. When you compare the prices he paid against the appraised value of the assets themselves, you have to come to the conclusion Folsom was someone's best buddy."

"What was Matson getting in return?" Kelly asked.

"I don't know. I'm going to leave that to you to discover. After all, you need to do a little work on this story."

"Very funny, Paul. I'll have you know my staff and I have been turning over every rock we can find."

"I've got something else to tell you, but you can't disclose it to anyone until I give you permission to do so. I'm giving it to you for background only. This is off the record, you understand?"

"You've got more conditions than a federal government contract. Yeah, I understand."

"A hired killer tried to murder Gerald Folsom's wife last night."

"You've got to be kidding me. What happened? Is she okay?"

"Yes, she's fine. But there's a reason why I can't tell you anything more right now. I'll explain later."

"Paul, I know you're hoping any story I publish will help your client, but that could be a pipe dream. I might not even be able to gather enough information to put together a story we can print."

"Jesus, Kelly. Sweetheart deals are being made between a federal government agency and a private investor, the banking industry is paying for the huge losses the FDIC is taking as a result of these special deals through huge deposit insurance assessments, a top FDIC executive has been murdered, the private investor receiving these sweetheart deals is arrested and charged with assault and battery and the attempted murder of his wife, and a hired killer tries to take out the investor's wife. What more do you need?"

"You're one royal pain in the ass."

"There's a story you can write. A lawyer who's a pain in the ass."

"Cute, Paul. I'll be talking to you."

Kelly hung up. Paul sent an email to his assistant instructing her to finalize the Injunction Order and to have it ready as soon as possible Monday morning. He then called Katherine at home and offered to take Wendy, Carrie, and her out to dinner.

"Carrie thinks we should check into a hotel until this blows over," Katherine said. "Even wants to hire security guards. I think she's correct about going to a hotel. We're going to the Marriott. I don't think it's a good idea for us to go out to eat, but we can eat in. Come by the hotel at 7."

# CHAPTER FORTY-SEVEN

Katherine, followed by Wendy and Carrie, led the way through the packed Marriott Hotel lobby at 5 p.m. Each of them pulled a wheeled suitcase and carried a shoulder bag. They ignored an offer of assistance from a bellman, checked in at the front desk, and rode an elevator to their floor.

As soon as they unpacked in their suite, Carrie told them she needed to check on something.

Borrowing Katherine's SUV, Carrie drove to Pastorius Park at Hartwell Lane and Abington Avenue in Chestnut Hill. The small park was situated in a residential area and had a slightly rolling landscape with scattered pockets of bushes and trees. The terrain drained toward a small pond in the center of the park.

After parking the SUV on the street, Carrie surveilled the area. The park hadn't changed since her mother brought her here when she was a little girl. She would scoop up tadpoles with a kitchen ladle and take them home in a fish bowl. When the tadpoles grew into baby frogs, they brought them back to the park and released them. In winter, she ice skated on the pond.

There were a dozen dog-walkers roaming the park, a few joggers, and a lone man reading on a bench. She hoped the park would be less crowded at 8 a.m. tomorrow, Sunday morning.

Carrie walked until she found a spot where she could sit down with Jefferson—a weathered bench set in a slight depression against a backdrop of dogwood trees. Darren Nouri would cover the area behind the trees; she would station Mike Perico over by the pond, where he would have a clear one-hundred-yard line of sight to the bench. Although she'd told Toothpick Jefferson to come alone, there was zero chance, she guessed, that he would follow her instructions.

She returned to the car and drove back to the Marriott Hotel. As she entered the lobby, she spotted Paul Sanders waiting for an elevator. She caught up with him and he asked, "Out sight-seeing?"

"Sort of."

They entered the elevator. When it began to ascend, Paul asked, "Do me a favor. When you find out who hired that woman to kill Wendy, call the police. Let them deal with it. Don't do something stupid."

Carrie smiled back at Paul innocently. "I don't know what you're talking about, Paul."

They walked out of the elevator and down the hall to the suite without another word. In the suite, Katherine took everyone's order and called room service. It took almost an hour for the food to arrive. They were finished eating by 8:45.

Wendy retired first; Carrie followed shortly thereafter. Paul and Katherine sat on the couch with their glasses of wine.

"How do you think this is all going to end?" Katherine asked.

Paul reached over and placed his hand on Katherine's. He was surprised when she didn't remove her hand after a few seconds. "I wish I could tell you everything would end happily ever after," he said, "but I don't have any idea. There is one thing I *can* tell you. I have a sense that events are tying together."

"That's good?" she said.

He raised his shoulders. "Who knows? The way the bank is treating Winter Enterprises isn't illegal. Unethical, but not illegal."

"The spirit of the law versus the letter of the law?"

" 'No man has ever yet been hanged for breaking the spirit of the law.' Grover Cleveland."

"What if it's the federal government breaking the spirit of the law?" Katherine asked.

"Louis Brandeis wrote, 'Crime is contagious. If the federal government becomes a lawbreaker, it breeds contempt for the law.' I contend this goes with breaking the spirit of the law as well."

"You spend a lot of time reading, don't you?"

He looked at her and tried to keep the sadness he suddenly felt from his face. "It's what you do when you're waiting for a woman to pay attention to you."

Katherine shivered as though she was chilled. She withdrew her hand from Paul's and placed her wine glass on the coffee table in front of them. She moved closer to him and kissed his lips. "I think I should start paying more attention to you."

" 'Thou art to me a delicious torment.' "

"Ralph Waldo Emerson," she said. "Now shut up, Paul."

# SUNDAY
# JULY 24, 2011

# CHAPTER FORTY-EIGHT

Edward had always been more than a big brother to Carrie; he'd been her best friend. Despite their seven year age difference, they had always had a connection beyond being siblings. Even though she'd followed him around as much as she could, Edward never resented her hanging around. Since his father died, he'd felt responsible for Carrie.

But Edward realized Carrie was no longer a dependent little sister. She was a confident woman who obviously had developed skills beyond the average Army officer. The way she handled the killer who broke into Katherine's home was evidence enough. He also realized Carrie was up to something. He could always tell.

He'd called Carrie's cell the night before and asked whether she might want to get together for an early morning run and then breakfast. She'd answered, "Sorry, but I'm getting together with a couple old friends. How about dinner tomorrow?"

Edward sensed something sinister behind his sister's seemingly innocent words. He knew Carrie was aware of what he meant by an "early morning run." They used to take these runs together at 6:30 a.m. Why would she be meeting with friends that early in the morning? He got up at 6, leaving Betsy dozing and wrote her a note, saying he needed to go out for a few hours and would call her later. He drove his Corvette to the Marriott Hotel and circled the parking lot finding where his mother's SUV was still parked. He found a secluded spot under a willow tree, behind a huge RV, and parked. And waited.

At 6:30, Carrie exited the hotel. She fast-walked to the SUV, got in, and drove off. Edward followed at an eight-car distance, keeping at least two cars between Carrie and him. Carrie drove to Chestnut Hill, to Bethlehem Pike, and then followed it northwest for a few blocks to a bakery shop. She parked in front of the shop and walked inside. It was now 6:40 a.m.

A couple minutes later, two men arrived and entered the shop. They were medium height and wore their hair short. Edward thought they looked military, with solid, athletic builds and a way of walking that exuded confidence and readiness for action. They both wore light-weight jackets despite the warm summer temperature.

Edward sat in the car for thirty-five minutes, until Carrie and the two men exited together. She went to the SUV with one of the men and drove off. The second man got into a late-model Pontiac and followed the SUV.

Trailing the Pontiac, Edward drove through Chestnut Hill to Germantown Avenue, down to Hartwell Lane, and then over to Pastorius Park. Carrie parked the SUV on one side of the park; the man in the Pontiac found a space one hundred yards away on the same side. Carrie carried a couple magazines as she and the two men walked into the park and leisurely strolled around the perimeter. But Edward could tell the three were doing more than taking a Sunday stroll. They seemed to be checking the grounds, performing reconnaissance.

The three returned to where they had started fifteen minutes earlier. It was now 7:45 p.m. Carrie handed one of the men a magazine and then walked away. She went to a bench, another magazine in hand, and sat down. One of the men skirted a slight rise behind the bench and disappeared behind a copse of trees. The man with the magazine walked toward the pond, passed it, and sat on a bench there.

From the way the men had positioned themselves, with Carrie in between, it appeared to Edward they were providing security.

There were few parking spaces on the streets fronting the park as the residents in the area parked on the street. Driveways and garages were few and far between in this neighborhood. There were a few parking spaces available in a parking lot on the southeast side of the park. Edward drove his Corvette in that direction. He pulled into a space and remained behind the wheel. A few people came and went—mostly morning walkers and joggers—but the park was generally empty.

At a couple minutes past 8, a black Cadillac sedan with tinted windows pulled into the parking lot two spaces from Edward. Three African-American men got out of the vehicle with a fourth man remaining behind the wheel. One of the men was huge, grossly obese. Just as the assassin had described him. He moved away from the car, stopped at the edge of the park, and looked around, focusing in Carrie's direction. Edward saw her raise a hand and then the man walked across the grass toward her. The two other men followed but, after twenty yards, separated, one circling left in the direction of the trees behind where Carrie was seated; the other moving right to a spot about fifty yards away from Carrie. The fourth man from the Cadillac got out, leaned against the car's left front fender, and lit a cigarette.

The obese man was slowly approaching Carrie. The other three men were alert, seemingly on edge, expecting trouble. Carrie's man on the bench between her and the parking lot was leafing through the magazine on his lap and, at the same time, keying in on the stranger off to his right. Carrie's other man, along with the man from the Cadillac who had circled the park toward the trees, were out of sight.

The fat man arrived at Carrie's bench and sat down.

Toothpick Jefferson eyed Carrie. "You're one gutsy broad," he said.

Carrie smiled at the man. "How gutsy do I have to be to meet a man who's so out of shape he's wheezing like he's got emphysema?"

Jefferson laughed. "You got a point."

"I've got another point to make. I told you to come alone. So far, I've seen three men with you."

"Can't be too careful. What happened to Philippa Gonzalez?"

"Who?"

"The woman you say I hired to kill someone."

"I subdued her."

"What's that mean?"

"Exactly what it sounds like. She was in the wrong place at the wrong time. She paid for her arrogance."

"I've been trying to reach her on her cell phone since you called me. She's not answering the phone. She's disappeared."

Carrie shrugged. "I don't give a rat's ass what she does, as long as she stays away from people I care about."

"So, what can I do for you?"

"I've got one question," Carrie said. "You answer my question; you get to go on your way. You don't and I'll hurt you."

Jefferson's eyes widened as he laughed uproariously. The laugh devolved into a phlegm-rattling cough from deep in his lungs.

"Smoking's bad for you," Carrie said.

Jefferson finally stopped his coughing and said, "Little bitty thing like you? *You're* going to hurt *me*?"

Carrie shot him an angelic smile and shrugged.

"You think I'm stupid?" Jefferson asked.

Carrie continued beaming. "I don't think anything about you, Mr. Jefferson, other than you're a low-life scumbag who'll do anything for a buck, including paying an assassin to murder Wendy Folsom. Now, I think I know who paid you. I just need you to confirm my suspicion."

"That kind of information is worth a lot of money, Missy."

"Maybe in your world, but not in mine. No more fooling around. One name; that's all I want."

Toothpick ignored her words. "I came here to find out who you are, see what you look like. I've done that. Now I'm going to leave and you should go someplace far away from here. Because, if I ever see you again, I'll turn you into one of my bitches and have you working the streets as a $50 hooker."

Carrie smiled and leaned closer to Jefferson as he tried to heft his enormous bulk off the bench, placing her left arm on his right shoulder and, the fingers of her right hand acting like pinchers, grabbing his sternocleidomastoid muscle on the right side of his neck. She squeezed the muscle with incredible force, at the same time pressing against the man's carotid artery. She knew what would happen to Jefferson: Inability to flex his neck, his head frozen in place, dizziness. Jefferson sagged back against the bench and moaned.

Edward saw Carrie's move against the man. Carrie's man by the pond immediately came off his bench, dropped his magazine, and moved toward Carrie. But Edward noticed he wasn't moving with any apparent urgency.

Edward anticipated the reactions from the men who had arrived in the Cadillac. The guy in the park off to the right, his hand under his jacket, had apparently seen that the large man was in distress and ran towards Carrie. Her man from the bench began moving more quickly, but it suddenly became apparent to Edward the guy was intercepting the on-rushing African-American man. Moving in an unthreatening manner, the man from the bench tripped up the other man, taking him down to the ground with almost no sound or fuss. The man lay still on the ground. Carrie's man reached under the other man's jacket, pulled something away, and pocketed it.

Movement to Edward's right caught his attention. The driver had dropped his cigarette and was now moving toward Carrie. Carrie's man from the bench was preoccupied with the man he'd taken down to the ground and didn't appear to see the driver coming. Edward knew he couldn't exit his car and catch up to the man in time. He started the Corvette and threw it into DRIVE, gunning the motor. The car leaped forward, spewing gravel behind it, and rode over a two inch high concrete lip between the parking lot and the grass. The car slued on the grass before the tires bit into the soft grassy loam of the park and raced forward like a hungry predator.

The Cadillac's driver must have heard the roar of the engine and looked back while still running towards Carrie. Edward saw the terror on the man's face as he tried to veer away, but he lost his footing and almost fell just as the nose of the Corvette clipped the man's legs, cartwheeling him into the air. The guy landed on the ground with a thud and a shout. Edward stopped the car and climbed out. He kicked the scrambling man's gun hand, sending his pistol flying before leaping on him to pummel his face until he felt the man sag beneath him. He retrieved the man's weapon, pocketed it, and ran over to where Carrie's man from the bench was standing next to the man he had subdued. The man was wary, reaching inside his jacket at his approach. Edward threw up his hands, showing his palms.

"I'm Carrie's brother Edward Winter." He pointed at the driver from the Cadillac. "I'd keep an eye on that one. He'll be coming around soon."

Edward sprinted to Carrie, who looked at him with a mixture of amusement and surprise. She was still squeezing the fat man's neck. He was in obvious pain, moaning, his head tilted to his left as though permanently set that way. Edward glanced around and for the first time noticed that the few visitors to the park were doing one of two things: Running away as though their lives depended on it, or frozen in place, watching the action. But then he noted a couple of people talking on cell phones.

"I think it would be a good idea if you got out of here," Edward said. "Someone's probably already called the police."

"Get that Corvette off the lawn before someone takes down your license plate number," Carrie said. "I'll be along in a second."

Carrie turned to look at Toothpick Jefferson. She shifted her grip from the side of his neck to his throat. She dug her fingers around the man's windpipe and slightly pulled on it. Jefferson's eyes bulged.

"One name, asshole. You have one chance."

He tentatively nodded his head, groaning with the effort.

She released her hold on his windpipe and waited while he swallowed once, then twice. Finally, he mouthed something, but the words came out as a squeak. He tried again. This time his throat muscles and his voice box worked, although he sounded more like a crow than a man.

"Fuck you!"

Carrie shook her head slowly from side to side. "I didn't want to have to hurt you," she said.

Jefferson's eyes bulged. He opened his mouth as though to say something more, but Carrie struck him full force with her fist against his right temple. He sagged like an empty sack and collapsed sideways onto the bench.

Carrie looked over her shoulder and whistled.

Darren quickly emerged from between the trees on the knoll behind her.

"Everything okay?" she asked.

"There's a guy sleeping in the trees. He's going to have a real bad headache."

# CHAPTER FORTY-NINE

Gerald Folsom, having been up all night, watched the sun come up through his living room window. His mind was whirling like a pinwheel. He hadn't heard a thing about Wendy, no call from either the police or Toothpick Jefferson. Nothing. He'd agreed to pay the man an extra $10,000 if he took care of business within a week. That week wasn't up yet, but Folsom assumed Jefferson would work as quickly as possible. He didn't care about the money; he cared about getting rid of that bitch, and soon. He would have paid almost anything to eliminate her.

He walked outside and looked at the expansive lawn, punctuated by shrubs and trees, flowing from the house down to the front gate, thrilled by the view. He walked down to the entrance and collected the Sunday paper. Removing the rubber band, he opened it, his stomach tense, expecting to see his name blasted across the top of the front page. He was relieved to find nothing above the fold about his arrest. But, turning the paper over, he found an article headlined

*Spousal Abuse: A Growing Problem.* He read the introduction to the article quickly. There was no mention of him on the front page, but he suspected his name would come up in the continuation of the article. He dropped the rest of the paper and searched for the continuation page. Scanning down the article, he found his name, immediately followed by a paragraph where a psychiatrist detailed the personality traits and psychological make-up of men who abused women. Folsom's eyes grasped words at random: misogynist, low self-esteem, inferiority complex, insecure, family history of abuse. The words were like blasts from stereo speakers and he seemed to hear them more than see them. Folsom ripped the paper to shreds and threw the pieces on the ground, screaming his anger to the heavens.

He raced back to the house and climbed the stairs to his third floor office, trying to imagine all of the alternative events that could have occurred. Was Wendy hiding where Jefferson couldn't find her? Had she been killed? Had she been wounded and somehow escaped? Folsom knew none of the realistic alternatives were good for him. The only event that would free him of the assault and battery charges was Wendy's death, and if that had occurred, someone would have called him by now.

Folsom roared like a wounded grizzly bear, echoing his anger and fear through the cavernous rooms and halls of his mansion. "Where are you, bitch?" he screamed.

By 9 a.m., he went down to the living room on the first floor and was calm enough to think critically about every person his wife knew well enough to go to for help. Her parents were old and decrepit, and living in New Hampshire. He didn't think she'd take her problems to them. She used to have a couple tennis friends. But, as far as he knew, she hadn't seen them in a couple years. She'd been at the college in Chestnut Hill, but he'd called and they'd told him she'd left. That woman lawyer who represented her; Wendy might be staying with her. He was trying to expand the list of Wendy's contacts when his telephone rang.

"Hello," he snapped.

"Gerald, it's Sanford. I haven't heard from you since you were arrested. I'm just checking to see how you're doing."

"Not worth a shit, Sandy. As you can imagine, being arrested and thrown in jail is no fun. Especially when the charges are based on lies."

"Is there anything I can do?"

"No, but thanks. If you keep handling things at the bank, it takes a lot of pressure off me."

"You can count on me, Boss."

"I know that, Sandy. Any matters I need to be aware of?"

"We could have problems with Winter Enterprises. The attorney is an asshole. He's not going to give up easily."

"Is he with one of the large Philadelphia law firms?"

"No, he's got his own practice. Apparently, he's worked for the Winter family for years. Guy named Paul Sanders."

The name seemed to tickle Folsom's memory.

"Well, stay on top of things. I'll call you tomorrow."

"Hang in there, Boss."

After Folsom hung up, he tried to recall where he had heard Paul Sander's name. It took a couple minutes, but he finally remembered his attorney, Jeffrey Rose, mentioning Sanders' name in connection with the complaint filed by Wendy. Sanders had somehow been involved before Sylvia Young signed on to represent her.

But the name Paul Sanders rang another bell with Folsom, one he couldn't place. He racked his brain to come up with another connection. But nothing came to him.

He was beat. He lay down on the living room couch, thinking maybe a nap would help. It took him only a few minutes to fall asleep and he was soon dreaming about his "Wendy problem" and Paul Sanders. At some point, his mind working overtime, he jerked awake, making the connection. Paul Sanders not only represented Edward Winter, he'd represented Frank Winter. Sanders had called him after Frank Winter died, trying to negotiate a favorable financial arrangement for Frank's widow and children. He recalled laughing at Sanders at that time, asking him if he thought he was the United Way. "This is business, Sanders," Folsom had said. "It's not personal." Sanders had responded, "It's personal to me, Mr. Folsom."

# CHAPTER FIFTY

Kelly Loughridge felt as though there was a little bird on her shoulder that kept whispering, "You've got to help Edward Winter, you've got to help Edward Winter." She knew it had nothing to do with being a journalist, but she couldn't keep the thought out of her head. She had come to the conclusion Winter was the victim of a political system and a federal government bureaucracy run amok. Even without corruption, the damage the federal government had done to the economy and people's lives was gargantuan. Maybe it was stupidity and ignorance, rather than intentionally corrupt behavior. Or maybe it was arrogance. What was it that Einstein had said? 'The only thing worse than ignorance is arrogance.' Plenty of both in D.C.

She outlined the article she wanted to write and decided to start with how decisions made in D.C. created the economic problems. How the Federal Reserve kept interest rates low in 2003. How congressional committees headed by Senator Chris Dodd and

Representative Barney Frank pushed Fannie Mae and Freddie Mac to invest in sub-prime loans, which ultimately went bad, undermining the capital markets. How one thing led to another, and how good citizens lost their jobs, lost their homes, lost their businesses, lost their investments, lost their dreams.

Then the story would segue to Broad Street National Bank and how Sol Levin, a popular and well respected man, lost his job and his bank. How the FDIC took over the bank, condemning Levin's and hundreds of other shareholders' ownership interests. Then how the FDIC sold the bank to Folsom Financial Corporation, which was owned by a man with an unusual relationship with a senior officer at the agency who just happened to be murdered last week. And how Gerald Folsom was charged with beating his wife. And then there was the hired killer she wasn't supposed to know about. She needed to talk again with Paul Sanders about that piece of information.

Kelly had doled out targets for interviews to three reporters: One would go to Broad Street National Bank, another to the FDIC in Washington, D.C., and the third would interview Edward Winter and Paul Sanders. She also had an intern digging up information on Folsom. Then she would try to get an interview with Folsom.

She'd told her staff she wanted to go to press on the story by no later than Thursday. That was the little bird's influence.

# CHAPTER FIFTY-ONE

While Katherine was visiting with Edward and Betsy at their home, Carrie sat down with Wendy in the hotel suite. They shared a fruit platter ordered from room service and tried to watch a Phillies game. But neither of them seemed very interested.

"You mind if I shut this off?" Wendy asked.

"Not at all," Carrie replied.

Wendy lay back on the couch and stared out the window.

"How long have you been married to Folsom?"

"Too long."

"Tell me about your husband," Carrie said.

"Why?"

"Just curious. If you don't want to talk about him . . . ." she trailed off.

Wendy looked back at the window. "Gerald is a good looking guy. Tall, dark hair, keeps himself in good shape. He was so damned attentive when we met. Treating me like a princess, sweeping me off my feet. Trips to Paris, San Francisco, Hawaii. Dinners at the best restaurants. Expensive gifts. I knew he'd been married twice before. Like me, they were much younger than Gerald. I would see them, once in a while, at the club or around the city." She chuckled.

"What's funny?"

"They looked like they could be my sisters. About the same height. Blonde, blue-eyed."

"All men have a preferred type of woman."

"It's different with Gerald. It's not just a preferred type with him; it's an obsession. He likes blonde, blue-eyed women from families with long histories and good names, but no money. It was as if he preyed on that type." She paused and said, "You'd be a perfect candidate to be his next wife. You've got the look."

"Did he abuse his other wives?"

"I can only guess that he did. He mentioned once he had sent each of his wives on her way with $5 million. Gerald made me sign a prenuptial agreement that gives me $5 million as long as I kept my mouth shut about anything personal between us. I thought that was strange wording, but I wasn't thinking about abuse when I signed it. Anyway, the $5 million pre-nup kept us from going to a lawyer. At least until he beat me so badly."

"When he got rough with you, did it follow anything in particular? Like an argument?"

"He tended to be a bit rougher, even in the beginning, after he'd been drinking. But, over the last few months, he got more and more violent, with or without booze."

"How rich is he?"

"Hugely. Money is all he really cares about. And he never has enough. One of the reasons I brought a complaint against him is to damage his reputation, and make it more difficult for him to do business, to make money. But, even if he never does another deal, he's got enough money for one hundred lifetimes."

"He have any other interests besides money and spousal abuse?"

"Not really. Oh, he likes to hang out at a steak place named The Towne House. It has a bar separate from the restaurant. He knows the owner. Apparently, they're from the same neighborhood. Grew up together. That's where we met. He told me he'd go to this place between wives. Almost every night."

They sat in silence for five minutes or so.

"You know things are going to work out, Wendy."

"I wish I could be as certain as you."

"They teach us that in the Army. You can't very well take on a mission without feeling confident."

"I'll never feel that level of confidence until Gerald is locked up."

"Or dead." Carrie said.

# CHAPTER FIFTY-TWO

Katherine was asleep in her hotel suite bedroom at 8:30; Wendy retired to her bedroom at 9. Carrie waited until they turned off the lights in their rooms and then went to her room, changed into a pair of jeans, a white blouse, a blue blazer, and black cowboy boots. She closed the door to her bedroom, found her mother's keys to the SUV, and went down to the lobby. She asked the concierge for directions to The Towne House Restaurant and then went to the parking lot and drove away.

At The Towne House, she took a stool at one end of the bar and ordered a shot of scotch and a glass of water. She sipped at the water and hardly touched the liquor. She shooed away a couple young guys who tried to cozy up to her. One of them was persistent and ignored Carrie's put downs.

"Come on, baby, you don't want to sit here drinking by yourself."

"Listen, asshole, that's exactly what I want to do. And if I wanted company, I'd find someone with some class and balls. Now get lost."

The guy wandered away, muttering, "Bitch!"

She had downed three glasses of water and barely any of the scotch after an hour, and was about to abandon her place at the bar. Besides, she was getting tired of the bartender's nasty looks. She dropped $20 on the bar and swiveled around on her stool, preparing to leave, when she spied a fifty-something man enter the bar through the restaurant. He resembled the description Wendy had given her of her husband. Instead of dropping off the stool, Carrie swiveled back to face the bar.

The man took a stool in the middle of the bar, four places away from Carrie. The bartender brought him a beer and a shot of whiskey, without the man saying a word. Obviously a regular.

"How ya doin', Mr. Folsom?" the bartender said to the man.

"Okay. You know."

"I don't mean no disrespect," the bartender said, "but I hope your wife pays for what she's doin' to ya."

"Thanks, Marty. Is the boss in tonight?"

"He went home a coupla hours ago. Sunday nights are usually pretty slow."

The man took a moment to look around the bar. There were two men at both tables. He then eyed Carrie sitting at the end of the bar. He stared at his whiskey and then downed the shot, after which he took a pull on his beer. Then he looked up and eyed Carrie some more.

"Any chance of me buying you a drink?" he asked.

She shot him a warm smile, raised her scotch glass, and said, "Thanks, but I've already got one."

The man moved two stools closer to Carrie. "Haven't seen you around here before."

"First time," she said.

"Where you from?"

"Here, originally. I just came down for a visit with my folks." She smiled. "I had to get away from them for a while. My parents treat me like I'm fifteen." She hunched her shoulders and spread her hands. "I understand how they feel, I suppose. Only child leaves home and they're rolling around a house the size of a small hotel. They're just lonely, but I can stand just so much hovering."

"My name's Jerry; what's yours?"

"Tammy Bryan."

He raised his glass as though to toast her. "Well, welcome to The Towne House, where a lot of people come to escape all variety of things."

Carrie smiled again. "What are you escaping from, Jerry?"

"I'll have to get to know you better before I start spilling all my secrets."

"Ah, the private type."

He shrugged.

"What's the matter, bitch; you can't handle a man your own age?" It was the younger guy who had tried to pick her up earlier.

Folsom slipped off his stool and moved between Carrie and the man. "Apologize to the lady, and then go sit down and behave yourself."

The guy looked twenty pounds lighter than Folsom, but was the same height and at least twenty-five years younger. He wheeled on Folsom, gave him a mad-dog look, and said, "You sure you don't want to get back on *your* stool, Pops?"

Folsom half-turned as though he was returning to his stool, but then whipped back around and shot a straight right jab into the man's nose, knocking him to the floor. Blood spurted from his nose as he struggled to get to his feet. A second man, shaking his head, came over from the table where the first man had been sitting and hefted him to his feet before leading him back to the table they had come from. The bartender brought a towel to the bleeding man and told him to get out.

Folsom returned to his stool and tapped the bar, signaling another round.

"I think I should buy *you* a drink for coming to my rescue," Carrie said.

"It's a deal," Folsom said. "But only if you let me buy you dinner tomorrow night."

"Seems like I get the better end of that deal," she said.

"Not even close to being accurate, Tammy. Being seen with a woman as gorgeous as you will improve my reputation immensely."

She giggled, play-acting a bit ditzy. "Dinner sounds great. What time?"

"How about 7?"

"Sounds good," she said.

The bartender delivered the new round of drinks. Carrie watched Folsom finish his shot and beer, while she barely sipped her drink. Then she slid off her stool, leaving a second $20 bill on the bar, waggled her fingers at Folsom, said, "I'll see you here tomorrow at 7," and walked out.

Carrie went to the SUV and drove toward the Marriott Hotel. She reflected that she had gotten lucky with Folsom showing up. She hadn't enjoyed being so close to him or role playing with a man she despised so much, but things had gone as well as she could have hoped. Even the young guy who had gotten drunk and approached her had helped things move along. Folsom was as charming as Wendy had told her he was when she first met him. Either charming or full of shit. Now she would let nature take its course.

# MONDAY
# JULY 25, 2011

# CHAPTER FIFTY-THREE

Nick Scarfatti and Edward sat in Edward's office—Edward in a chair and Nick on the couch behind the coffee table. Nick briefed Edward on the state of the company's bank account at Third Community Bank, where they had been depositing business receipts since Monday the 19th.

"There's now $452,313 in the account. We've deposited $2.23 million in receipts. The difference has gone out in accounts payables, salaries, and wages."

"Sales are up nicely," Edward said.

"Yeah, we're bucking the downtrend most restaurants are experiencing."

"Have you heard anything more from Broad Street National about our deposits in Third Community Bank?" Edward asked.

"Not a thing. I don't think they want to push that. Besides, between our real estate and our frozen money in Broad Street Bank, their loan to Winter Enterprises is more than secure."

Nick sat in silence.

"What's on your mind, Nick?" Edward asked.

"My job, Eddie. How the hell is this going to wind up?"

"Listen, my friend, you and I have been together a long time. Worse comes to worst and we have to start all over again, then that's what we'll do. You may have to be the bookkeeper for a while, instead of the CFO, and I'll have to flip tortillas instead of being CEO, but we know how to grow a business. We won't make the same mistakes we did the first time."

Nick sighed. "If that happens, I'm going to have to tighten my belt. You won't be able to pay me enough to cover my current bills."

Edward cringed inwardly. "I'm sorry, Nick. I shouldn't have assumed you would want to start all over again. With your education and experience, you could get a good job with another company."

"Forget it," Nick said. "I know what we're capable of doing. Besides, this ain't a job to me. I'm a shareholder here. We'll make do until things turn around. You're stuck with me."

"Thanks, Nick. The thought of going forward without you by my side is not something I want to consider."

"Hell, maybe the bank will come to its senses and extend our loan."

"Probably not a healthy thing to hang your hopes on."

"Yeah, I know. But it's better than obsessing about the alternative."

"You know there is one thing we haven't tried," Edward said. "I've always been my own boss. The thought of working for someone else makes me nauseous. But if I can save the business, and our employees' jobs, then I could learn to live with it.

"Hot N' Chili's got a franchisee in Florida with fifty-seven restaurants, one of their most successful operators. I'll check with

Pete Mora about how the guy's doing and then call him in Florida."

"Not much time left. Four-and-a-half days to find $20 million."

"It's worth a try."

Gerald Folsom looked across his desk at Sanford Cunningham. "Go over the numbers with me."

"Winter Enterprises has the rights to the Hot N' Chili franchise for the entire state of Pennsylvania. It has twenty-four restaurants today and was just about to expand to the western side of the state. Sales last year were $58 million. Net profit before interest expense, taxes, depreciation, and amortization, $8.2 million. They've plowed their earnings into new store locations. Even at today's depressed real estate prices, the company has at least $30 million in equity in their land and buildings."

"So, when they don't pay off the loan this Thursday, what happens?"

"We foreclose on the collateral behind the loan. The money they have in their bank accounts will offset nearly $3 million of the loan amount, which will leave a $17 million balance. The value of the franchise in this market is *de minimis*. The value of the real estate is significantly more than $17 million, assuming we could find another restaurant operator who would want the locations."

"What about the FF&E?" Folsom asked.

"The furniture, fixtures, and equipment cost about $200 thousand per location. We'd be lucky to get ten grand for that stuff per location if we liquidate the business."

"What's the written-down value of the loan on the bank's books?"

"Before we took it over, the Feds forced the bank to write down all of its real estate loans; this loan was written down from $20 million to $12 million. Under our Loss Share Agreement with the FDIC, the Feds would cover eighty percent of any sale difference between $20 million and whatever we sold the company's assets for. For example, if we got $12 million, the Feds would write us a check for $6.4 million."

"In other words, I could buy the $20 million note from the bank for $12 million without raising any eyebrows at the FDIC?"

"Or even less than that. They're making sweetheart deals in order to get commercial real estate loans off bank balance sheets." Cunningham frowned and added, "But why would you do that? I gotta tell you Jerry, paying $12 million of closed down restaurants and a bunch of furniture, fixtures, and equipment doesn't make any sense."

"Sandy, you're thinking like a passive investor, not an entrepreneur. You're thinking about our collateral as something to liquidate. Surely someone in the restaurant business would want Winter Enterprises on a going concern basis. You said Winter Enterprises made $8.2 million last year. Keeping the business open means an $8.2 million return per year on a $12 million investment. We could probably easily sell the business with the real estate for five times earnings. That's $41 million. I pay $12 million to the bank and then turn around and sell the business for $41 million. Now that's what I call a deal."

# CHAPTER FIFTY-FOUR

Carrie timed her arrival at The Towne House's restaurant to make an entrance that would get Gerald Folsom's attention, wearing a short black halter dress showing enough cleavage to be interesting, two-inch black heels, diamond stud earrings, and a diamond pendant necklace—all borrowed from her mother's closet at her home, without her mother's knowledge.

She saw Folsom seated in a booth toward the back. There were about ten tables and fifteen booths in the place—all occupied. She saw the appreciative look on Folsom's face as she approached him. She suppressed a smile. Folsom stood and took her hand, helping her into the booth.

"I've been thinking about you all day," he said, entering the other side of the booth. "You sure are worth waiting for."

"Why, thank you, sir."

They made small talk for a few minutes. Then Folsom asked, "What kind of work do you do?"

Carrie fed him a line about working in the investment department for a bank in New York City. She'd done her homework on the internet, so she was able to dump just enough facts about a real bank in New York City to sound credible.

Folsom then told her about his business, how he bought loan pools and banks from the federal government.

"I could sure use a pretty gal like you in one of my banks," he told her.

"We should discuss that some time," she answered. The, she said, "I assume buying loan pools and banks is a game the little guy can't play in."

He shook his head. "That's right. The loan pools are often $100 million. Banks aren't cheap either."

"So, how many banks do you own?"

"Three right now. What I usually do is liquidate the assets of the banks I buy."

"You don't hold them long term?"

"Not usually since I have no interest in doing business with depositors and borrowers. I just want to buy the assets at a discount from the federal government, sell them at a profit, and then go on to the next deal."

"Why does the federal government sell a bank to you if all you're going to do is sell off the assets? Why does the federal government need you? You know, they could just cut out the middle man."

Folsom winked at her. "You're not just a pretty face, are you? Damn good question. The federal government doesn't have the staff to do what I do. And it has no idea how to sell anything at market value. The government forces a bank to write down its loans and securities to a fraction of what the real value is, reducing the bank's capital below regulatory requirements. If the bank can't raise the required additional capital, the federal government takes over the bank and brings in someone like me."

"Sounds like a bad deal for the original owners of the bank."

"You could say that." He beamed and added, "But a great deal for me."

Carrie watched Folsom's alcohol consumption. He was drinking scotch on the rocks and had finished three by the time their salads were served. She had ordered chardonnay and was still on her first glass. Folsom ordered a bottle of cabernet sauvignon with dinner – he ordered a T-bone steak, while Carrie had the petit filet mignon. He polished off most of the bottle of wine. She limited herself to one glass, making sure to  drink at least twice as much water as wine.

After dinner, Carrie had a cup of coffee; Folsom ordered a *Vin Santo*.

By the time the check came, Folsom was slurring his words and his face had turned florid.

"How'd you like to join me for a drink at my place?" he asked after giving the waiter his credit card.

"I don't know, Jerry," Carrie said. "That's not my style."

He raised his hands, showing her his palms. "Hey, done get me wrong now; is jus coffee. I enjoy your compney."

She laughed and said, "On one condition. I drive."

"Was tha matter? You think I had too mush to drink?"

"What do you think, Jerry?" she asked.

He scowled and then seemed to force a smile. "Okay, mebbe I had a lot to drink." The waiter came back with the credit card receipt. Folsom signed and stuffed his credit card in his shirt pocket. He stood and wavered while waiting for her to stand. Then they walked arm-in-arm to the restaurant's front door and out to the valet stand.

Carrie handed her valet ticket to one of the young men waiting by the valet stand and cringed inwardly as Folsom wrapped an arm around her shoulders, pulling her to him roughly. The blast of breath he blew in her face smelled like a distillery. She shrugged off his arm and chuckled, saying, "Take it easy, big boy."

Folsom mumbled something unintelligible.

After they got in the SUV and Carrie drove away, Folsom gave her directions to his place. On the way he said, "Sexy gal like you should be driving a Ferrari, not a truck."

"I've heard that line many times before, but no one has put up the dough."

"I could change all tha."

"Promises, promises," she said, laughing.

She stopped the car in front of the gate to Folsom's estate and said, "Now what?"

"Aw, shit," he swore. "My gate opener's in my car back at the restaurant."

"It's getting late, anyway," Carrie said.

He pointed past her and laughed. "I don give up tha easy. Pull up next to tha metal arm'n open your window."

She did as he had instructed, punching in the four-digit code he gave her.

"Jeez, Jerry," Carrie said, as the gate slid open and she drove onto the property, "What is this place?"

"Jus my humble abode."

"Humble, huh?"

He directed her to the front door where she parked.

"Is this your house, or a museum?"

He laughed boisterously. "Maybe a little of both."

Pulling out a set of keys from his pocket, he fiddled with the front door lock for ten seconds until he finally inserted the key and opened the door. He waved Carrie into the house with a flourish and closed the door behind her.

She wanted to play the dazzled young woman, but actually didn't have to put on much of an act. The interior was spectacular, with a five-tiered leaded crystal chandelier that hung from three levels above. A staircase started from each side of the huge entry and wound its way upward for three stories. The rooms off the entry—a living room, a den, and a dining room—were each large enough to seat thirty people.

Folsom gave her a "follow me" wave and opened a closed door leading to an enormous kitchen with a black granite countertopped island at least twenty-five feet by twelve feet. The appliances would have been right at home in a first-class restaurant kitchen.

"You do much entertaining?" Carrie asked.

"Nah. I gave my architect a free hand in designin this place. I really only use four rooms in the place: The kitchen, my office, the bathroom, and the bedroom." He leered at her when he mentioned the bedroom.

"How about that cup of coffee?" she said.

Folsom punched a button on a coffee maker, which started to make whirring sounds. Coffee began pouring into a glass pot after a couple minutes. After the coffee had brewed, Folsom poured them each a cup, managing not to spill. "Wanna tour of the place?"

She smiled. "That would take a couple hours. I think I'll pass."

"Oh come on. At least my office'n bedroom suite?"

Carrie fully intended to see as much of Folsom's house as she could. The more she knew about the guy and this place, the more likely she'd discover something she could use to her benefit. But she wasn't about to make it easy for the guy, and she sure as hell didn't want him getting the wrong idea.

She feigned looking at her wrist watch and then gazed at Folsom. "Ten minutes, Jerry, and then I've got to go. I don't want my parents worrying."

He sloppily crossed his heart and said, "I promise. Ten minutes."

Coffee cups in hand, they marched upstairs, past the second level to the third. "How much help do you need to maintain this place?" she asked.

"Coupla gardeners' n a full-time maid." He shot her the same leer he'd shown her before. "But no one's here at night."

She followed him into a room half the size of a basketball court. Big game trophies were mounted all over the walls. Two stuffed bears stood on their hind legs in opposite corners of one side of the room, their front paws outstretched, their mouths open menacingly.

"Jeez," Carrie exclaimed. "This is a scary room."

Folsom put an arm around her, caressing her back. "Don't worry, babe, I'll protect you."

She slipped away from his arm, walked to a sedan-sized mahogany desk, and perched on the edge. Crossing her legs for full effect, she smiled at Folsom and said, "I'm impressed, Jerry. This is a real man cave."

"No man cave is complete until it includes a beautiful woman. This room has never looked better."

"Thank you. What's next?"

"I've got an idea," he said. He walked over to her and took her hand, pulling her off the desk. He led her to a four-seat couch and asked her to sit. "I'll be right back."

She looked around the room and marveled at the man's ego. A fleeting thought crossed her mind: The tent she'd lived in while hiking through Azerbaijan on her last assignment. Quite a difference between that and this place.

Folsom returned after a couple minutes, carrying a valise. He hefted the valise onto the coffee table in front of the couch and said, "This is to show you I don't bullshit, that I'm a man of my word." He opened the valise and took from it a handful of wrapped one hundred dollar bills and placed them on the couch next to Carrie. He repeated this five times and, when the pile of currency was eight inches high, he said, "That oughta be enough."

Carrie looked at Folsom and replied, "Enough for what?"

"For your Ferrari."

"I know bullshit when I hear it. That may be enough money to buy a Ferrari, but not me. I'm out of here." She pushed off the couch to stand, but Folsom placed a hand against her shoulder and shoved her back.

"If that's not enough, how about this?" He lifted the valise and upended it on the couch, creating a pile over eighteen inches high. It teetered and then collapsed onto Carrie's lap.

She knew the situation was quickly deteriorating. Folsom was a man used to getting his own way, and Wendy had told her he tended to get violent when he'd been drinking.

"I've had a nice evening, Jerry," she said. "Up to now. I think it's time for me to go." She stood up and skirted the coffee table.

Folsom moved to cut off her escape. "I don't think so." He grabbed her left wrist in his right hand and yanked her toward him. "You need—"

Before he could finish, she spun under his right arm, breaking his grip on her wrist, and twisting his arm behind him, putting torque on his shoulder until he shouted, "What the fuck!"

But instead of backing off after she released him, he smiled and said, "Now you're really turning me on." He stepped forward and reached for her throat.

Carrie used his forward momentum to her advantage. She struck out with the heel of her right hand, striking Folsom over the heart with slightly less than maximum force. She didn't really want to kill the guy since too many people had seen her leave the restaurant with him. But she did want to disable him temporarily.

Folsom went down to the floor as though he'd been pole-axed. He moaned and clutched his chest. Rolling back and forth on the floor, he gasped, "Oh, God."

She bent down and held his chin so he would look right at her face. "You need to learn how to treat a lady, Jerry. Not everybody is into money like you are." Carrie grabbed two handfuls of the one hundred dollar bills from the couch and dropped them on Folsom's chest. "Sleep with these tonight." She went back to the couch to grab her handbag when she saw a 3" x 5" card resting on one side of the bills. She bent down to read the hand-written words on it: *7/21/10. Placed the following amount of cash in this valise for safe keeping with Gerald Folsom: $1,000,000.* It was signed Donald Matson. Carrie recalled that a Donald Matson had worked for the FDIC and had been murdered over a week ago. Her mind was spinning. Where had Matson got $1,000,000 and why was the money in Folsom's home? She glanced at Folsom, still writhing in pain. She knew he'd be incapacitated for at least ten minutes. She picked up the card by its edges, holding it between her thumb and index finger, and dropped the card into the empty valise.

Folsom had gone out of the room to get the valise. She walked in the direction he'd gone and stopped in the hall outside the room. There were three closed doors on the opposite side of the hall. The middle door opened into a full bath. The door on the left was a file room. She went to the door on the right and walked into a vault. A dozen rifles and shotguns in a rack lined the left side; the right side had built-in drawers. She took a tissue from a Kleenex box on top of the drawers and wrapped it around her fingers. She then opened one of the drawers and found trays of gold coins, each in a plastic protective sleeve. The next drawer to the right held silver coins. She opened four more drawers and found more of the same. Then she opened another drawer that held what she estimated must be at least one hundred and fifty loose gem stones. Lots of valuable stuff, but nothing that appeared to be helpful in her quest to assist her brother . . . unless. For a moment, she wondered what a handful of jewels might be worth, but quickly put the thought out of her mind.

She turned to leave the vault, when she spied a valise on the floor by the door. It was identical to the one Folsom had just carried into his office. There was a tag on the handle with the logo of the Philadelphia Police Department. She'd noticed a similar tag on the case Folsom had brought into his office. Written on the tag were a date and a statement that a Detective Carruthers had opened it in the presence of Gerald Folsom, had not counted the cash, and had closed and tagged the valise.

Again ensuring that her fingers were covered by the tissue, Carrie popped the clasps on this valise and opened it. Like the other one, it was stuffed with bundles of hundred dollar bills. She wondered if there was a similar card in this valise and lifted out stacks of cash until she saw a white 3" x 5" card resting against the side of the case. This one had the same wording on it as was on the other card, except for the total amount of cash. This valise held $1,065,000, according to the card. It was also signed by Donald Matson and dated 7/21/10.

$2,065,000 in cash consigned to Folsom by Matson. Where would a federal government bureaucrat get that kind of cash, and why would he "place" the cash "for safekeeping," as the cards read, with Folsom?

She started to replace the card in the valise when she noticed something else white on the bottom of the valise. She removed the stacks of cash and found two other cards on the bottom. These cards showed dates and amounts—one recorded inflows of cash, the other listed withdrawals. She studied the cards for a minute, memorizing the first ten dates on the first card. Then she replaced the cards on the bottom of the case, repiled the bundles of cash on top, closed the valise, and left the vault. She returned to Folsom's office and found him sitting up against the side of a plush chair holding his arms against his chest, still moaning. Ignoring him, Carrie moved to the couch, carefully held the cash bundles by their edges, and stacked them on top of the card in the valise on the coffee table.

"What are you doing with my money?" Folsom whined when she stepped to the side so he could see the valise.

"I'm thinking about taking it with me. Reparations for treating me so badly."

"That's robbery. I'll call the police."

"Gee, what about my Ferrari?"

"Fuck you and fuck your Ferrari," he groaned.

She pointed at the valise on the coffee table and said, "There's your godforsaken money. You'd better lock it up before I change my mind and take it with me."

# TUESDAY
# JULY 26, 2011

# CHAPTER FIFTY-FIVE

Folsom felt as though he was having a heart attack. That bitch last night had hit him so hard that his chest now felt as though an elephant was sitting on it. It still hurt to breathe. He had never met a woman like her before. He would have loved to go a couple rounds in the sack with her. But then he thought that might not be a good idea, after all. She might kill him.

He was frustrated, angry, and in pain. He wanted to hurt someone. Folsom called Sanford Cunningham at 9 a.m. and asked him for the name and telephone number of the Hot N' Chili franchiser.

"Mr. Mora please," Folsom said into his telephone.

"Senior or Junior?" a woman asked.

"Whichever one is in charge of franchise operations."

"That would be Peter Mora, Junior. I'll connect you."

After a few seconds, a man said, "Peter Mora."

"Mr. Mora, this is Gerald Folsom, President of Folsom Financial Corporation. My company owns Broad Street National Bank in Philadelphia."

"Yes, Mr. Folsom, what can I do for you?"

"You may not be aware that one of your franchisees financed his restaurant locations with my bank. I—"

"I'm very familiar with your bank's relationship with our Pennsylvania franchisee, Edward Winter. Our franchisees advise us any time they use our franchise agreement as collateral on a loan. We approved that transaction."

"Well, as of this Thursday, if Winter Enterprises does not pay off its loan in full with my bank, we will be forced to foreclose, taking possession of the company's real estate, its deposits here at our bank, and the franchise agreement. We obviously are not looking forward to taking this action."

"And why are you calling me?" Mora asked.

"Just to put you on notice of the bank's intentions and to give you a heads up that you will need to work with us on the future of the Hot N' Chili business in Pennsylvania."

"I have to say, Mr. Folsom, that your calling me is very irregular."

"Just a friendly heads up, Mr. Mora."


After Peter Mora hung up with Folsom, he immediately telephoned Edward Winter and told him about the call. "I find it absolutely unethical that a bank would call me in anticipation of a foreclosure event. It's as if this guy Folsom is looking for trouble."

"I think it's something else entirely," Edward said. "I think the guy suspected you would call me. He's rubbing salt in the wound."

"My God, Eddie, what did you ever do to this guy?"

"Nothing, Pete. Absolutely nothing. Gerald Folsom is a sociopath who enjoys inflicting pain on people."

"How are things going with Raul Morales down in Miami?"

"Thanks, by the way, for putting me in touch with him. He's got a hell of a business down there. But he's got the same problem with banks that I do. Al least his real estate loans don't come due for another two years. Maybe, by then, the economy will have recovered and the Feds will have lightened up on the banks. In the meantime, he can't do a thing for us. He was sick about it, too."

"Anything else in the works?"

"My CFO has contacted a private equity firm in New York City. I haven't heard anything yet, but I'm not optimistic. Sixty days notice wouldn't have been enough time for the average private equity firm to make an investment decision."

"Jesus, Eddie, you've got to pull a rabbit out of a hat between now and Thursday."

"Listen, Pete. By Friday of this week, I'll have about $800,000 in cash the bank can't touch without a huge legal battle. That would just put what they're doing to me in the media. I don't think they want that. This guy Folsom tends to stay below the radar. I know you have some open franchise territories. Would you consider selling one of them to me if the bank takes over our Pennsylvania assets?"

"In a minute," Mora said. "In a damned New York minute. In fact, actually, New York State is available."

# CHAPTER FIFTY-SIX

Carrie called Paul Sanders and asked him to have lunch with her.

"It would be my pleasure," Paul said. "How about noon at the country club?"

"Sounds good. I'll see you there."

"You want to give me a hint about why we're meeting?"

"Sure. The subject is Gerald Folsom. I have a few questions."

They met at the Chestnut Hill Cricket Club at a table on the porch overlooking the grass tennis courts.

"How about a glass of wine?"

"Between eating all these big meals and drinking wine at lunch and dinner, I'm going to fall out of shape real fast. This leave I'm on is for a little more than three weeks, then I have to go back to Army food and no alcohol during the work day."

"Is that a yes or no to my question?" Paul asked with a smile.

"Yes, of course. A glass of chardonnay would be wonderful."

Paul raised a hand to the waitress and, when she came over, ordered two glasses of wine.

Carrie gazed out on the rows of grass courts that extended to Willow Grove Avenue. "I can remember taking tennis lessons on these courts before Dad died. After he was gone, my days of country club life ended. Sometimes I think I'm better for having grown up without the privileges of private schools and country clubs."

"A life of privilege can make a person soft, but privilege and softness don't have to go hand-in-hand. Knowing your father and mother, I doubt any level of privilege would have undermined the toughness they both have imparted to you and Edward."

Paul looked off into the distance and then returned his gaze to Carrie. "I think your father would have found your career unnerving, but he would have been extremely proud of you."

"Sometimes, I have trouble remembering what he looked like."

"You were pretty young when he passed."

The waitress came over, served their wine, and took their orders for two chicken Caesar salads.

"What do you want to know about Folsom?" Paul asked.

"I think I already know more than I want to about that psycho. What I want to ask you are a few questions about issues ancillary to Folsom."

"Go right ahead."

"I remember when we all gathered at Mom's house, after that woman broke in and tried to kill Wendy, a lot of the conversation revolved around Folsom and his relationship with a man named Donald Matson. If I recall correctly, Matson was shot near his home one evening last week. Do the police have any suspects?"

"Not that I've heard. I stay in touch with Sylvia Young, Wendy's lawyer, on a daily basis and she's pretty close to the police. She hasn't mentioned anything to me."

"Do you remember on what day he was killed?"

Paul looked up at the porch ceiling and, dropping his gaze, finally said, "It was the day I went to your mother's home with Sylvia. I think that was the twenty-first."

That was the same date on the 3" x 5" cards in the valises in Folsom's place, Wendy remembered.

She knew the police had found the valises with cash in Folsom's house because of the evidence tags she had seen on the valise handles, but she couldn't admit to Paul she had been in Folsom's place. "What would the police do if they found over $2,000,000 in cash in Folsom's house?"

"Probably nothing," Paul answered. "It's not against the law to have a lot of cash."

"What if there was proof the money had been given to Folsom by Matson?"

Paul thought about that for ten seconds and then said, "That could raise some questions, like where a federal government employee would get that much cash and why he would give it to Folsom."

"What if Matson gave it to Folsom for safekeeping?"

"So what?"

"I'm just fishing here, Paul. But what if there was a list of dates and dollar amounts going back twenty-two years with the cash?"

Paul's expression registered surprise.

"What?" she asked after he didn't say anything.

"Probably nothing, but it was twenty-two years ago that your father died and Folsom took over his bank."

They sat in silence when the waitress brought their salads.

"What's this all about, Carrie?"

"I can't really explain why I'm asking these questions, but," she reached into the pocket of her blouse and extracted a piece of paper, handing it to Paul, "the dates I wrote down match up to dollar amounts. I suspect the dates have some significance. I just don't know what it is."

"Where did you get this information?"

"Don't ask. But suffice it to say, I have reason to believe the police already know Gerald Folsom has two valises full of cash in his home, and that, according to the evidence tags on the valises, the police did not count the cash, just noted it was a large amount. Also in those valises, but not included on the evidence tags, are notes on 3" x 5" cards written and signed by Donald Matson, claiming he put $2,065,000 in cash on July 21 for safekeeping with Gerald Folsom. There are also cards in one of the cases listing dates of cash inflows and outflows. Some of those inflow dates are written on the piece of paper I just gave you. It appears the two valises were given to Folsom on the same day Matson was murdered. And, finally, I think Folsom is unaware of the presence of the cards in the two cases. But sooner or later he's going to find them and destroy them."

# CHAPTER FIFTY-SEVEN

Paul went straight from the country club to his office. Sitting at his desk, he stared at the dates on the paper Carrie had given him. Most ranged from 1988 to 1996, but there were two others: 1/15/10 and 7/15/11. Carrie had told him there were also a dozen or more dates running from 1996 to 2011 on the card in the valise at Folsom's, but she didn't have those specific dates.

Some of the dates seemed familiar, but he couldn't figure out why. He looked at his desk calendar and saw July 16 was a Friday. He paged back to January and noted the 15th was also a Friday. However, neither date rang any bells for him.

Taking the dates from Carrie's list, he Googled them one at a time, but there didn't seem to be any recurring events on the dates.

Trying to come up with a common theme matching all the dates was giving him a headache. He decided to focus on something else and would then get back to Carrie's list later. He buzzed his secretary on the intercom and asked her to bring in his telephone message slips. He shuffled through the slips, found one for Kelly Loughridge at the *Journal* and called her first.

"I hope you have something good to tell me," he said.

"Nothing yet. I've got all kinds of circumstantial evidence Donald Matson and Gerald Folsom had an unusual relationship, but nothing really concrete. I still can't figure out what was in it for Matson."

Paul thought about what Carrie had told him at lunch. "What if Folsom was bribing Matson?"

"What if the Easter Bunny's real?" Kelly asked. "Come on, Paul, get serious. If that's true, show me some proof."

"Did you get anything more out of the list I sent you? The one with the dates of the deals Folsom did with the agency?"

"No. I don't—"

"Holy sh—!" Paul blurted. "Hold on a second." He leaped out of his chair and threw open his office door, yelling to his secretary, "Maxine, get me the Winter Enterprises file. Now!" He hurried back to his chair and fell back into it.

"Kelly, do you have the list of deals between Folsom and the FDIC at hand?"

"Yeah. Why?"

Paul's secretary came in and placed three large files in front of him. He opened the third folder and found the tab labeled FDIC. He flipped open the file and found the list Gail Moskowitz at the FDIC had faxed to him. He laid Carrie's list of dates next to Gail's list and felt a chill go up his spine.

"Kelly, I have a list of dates in front of me I got from a confidential source. This source claims there are valises in Folsom's house loaded with cash. And in those valises are cards signed by Donald Matson on which he wrote that he had given over $2 million to Folsom for safekeeping. The cards were dated July 21 of this year, the day Matson was murdered." He paused to let Kelly absorb what he had told her, and then continued. "My source also claims there is a written record of cash payments received and cash withdrawals in one of the cases. I am now comparing the dates from my confidential source against the dates in the fax I got from my friend at the FDIC. They're identical, at least from 1988 to 1996, plus two dates in 2011. Those are the only dates my source provided."

"Wait a minute. Are you telling me someone has seen this cash and a list of dates showing cash received by Matson?"

"The police actually saw the valises when they searched Folsom's house, but they apparently didn't inventory the contents beyond noting they were filled with cash. I don't know how my source got this information."

"Does it say anything about Folsom making payments to Matson?"

"No."

"But the cash is now sitting in Folsom's house; put there in safekeeping by Matson on July 21? And then Matson took a couple bullets to the head?"

"Yep."

"Why hasn't Folsom destroyed the information your source claims is in the valises?"

"I don't know. But, if I had to guess, I'd say he doesn't know they're there."

"Is your contact at the FDIC aware of this information?"

"No."

"Call your contact and pass this on. Maybe they'll agree to come out of hiding if you can convince them that Matson was dirty."

# WEDNESDAY
# JULY 27, 2011

# CHAPTER FIFTY-EIGHT

Sanford Cunningham walked into Stanley Burns' office at Broad Street National Bank. Burns had been promoted to president of the bank because of his "sterling commitment to creating profits for Folsom Financial." That was how Folsom had put it when he broke the news of the promotion to Burns.

"How are things?" Cunningham asked, dropping into a chair in front of Burns' desk.

Burns swallowed the distaste he had for Folsom's right-hand man. "Everything's going great. We've reduced the bank's commercial real estate exposure from sixty percent to fifty-one percent, mostly through not renewing maturing loans. But we've also had loans that borrowers couldn't pay off when they came due, so we're beginning the foreclosure process on the real estate collateral behind those loans. The real estate department manager estimates we'll come out way ahead on the sale of these properties."

Cunningham nodded his approval. "What happens with Winter

Enterprises' loan when it matures this Thursday?"

"Well, if they can't pay off the loan, we'll start foreclosure action against them."

"I don't want any delay in that happening. Have our attorneys draw up the papers now."

"What's the rush?" Burns asked.

Cunningham's lips compressed into a straight line and the frown lines in his forehead became furrows. "You got this job because you did what needed to be done since Folsom Financial took over this bank; are you beginning to have second thoughts?"

Burns felt his face go hot. "Of course not. It would just be nice to know why I am asked to do something."

"Let's get something straight. I'm not *asking* you; I'm *ordering*. And, although you don't need to know why I've ordered you to streamline foreclosure against Winter, I'm going to tell you anyway because you need to understand that Gerald Folsom is a very generous guy. You make money for him; he'll share the profits with you. I want foreclosure completed ASAP on the Winter loan because we want to own the business."

"You mean the restaurant locations?"

"Not just the real estate; the restaurant business, too. Part of our collateral on the loan is the franchise agreement with Hot N' Chili. Winter's franchise in Pennsylvania is a fuckin' cash cow. We're going to buy the loan from the bank and then take over the franchise."

"I see," Burns said slowly.

"I assume you're okay with this."

Burns hesitated for a beat and then nodded.

After Cunningham left his office, Burns took out his handkerchief and mopped his sweating brow. He felt sick, as though he'd been hit by the flu. This wasn't what banking was supposed to be about. When Sol Levin ran the bank, Broad Street National focused on helping its loan customers grow their businesses and contributing to the Philadelphia community. Now, Burns felt like a vulture picking over carrion. Worse, like a murderer, killing businesses and people's dreams.

Burns stared at the picture of his wife, Becky, and their two daughters on the credenza beside his desk. His job at the bank had given them a good life and his promotion to president included a thirty percent increase in his pay, plus a performance bonus. Becky had been so proud of him when he called to tell her about the promotion, but she had no idea how bad the working conditions were at the bank, or what he was being ordered to do to the customers.

He exhaled loudly and pressed the intercom button for his assistant to ask for the Winter Enterprises' loan file. "And," he added, "call Franklin Means at the Walker Law Firm. I need to see him right away."


Edward Winter called Paul Sanders at his office and asked him if he had any news.

"No, nothing, Edward. I'm sorry."

"What will our response be to the bank filing foreclosure proceedings?"

"We will respond to the foreclosure complaint and ask the court to enjoin the bank from proceeding with the foreclosure. At least we should be able to delay things, assuming a judge will grant the injunction. Even without it, though, the foreclosure will take months. But the bank could close the businesses in the meantime."

"That would be a disaster."

"I understand, Edward. I'll do everything possible."

"I know you will. I can't understand what's happening. It truly feels like I've fallen into a black hole. Common sense seems to have been suspended."

"Hang in there," Paul said. "You never know how things will turn out."

After hanging up, Paul came to a decision about something he had been contemplating for several days. He called Gail Moskowitz's number in D.C. Her assistant answered.

"Is Ms. Moskowitz in today?"

"Yes, Mr. Sanders, but she's out to lunch. She will be back here around 1:30. Would you like her to call you?"

"No, that's all right. I'll call back."

Paul called to his secretary while he packed the Winter Enterprise files in his briefcase. "Cancel the rest of my appointments for today."

"Where are you going?" she asked.

"Washington, D.C. Call and find out when the next train to D.C. leaves. And I want a car to pick me up at Union Station to take me to the FDIC's offices."

"When are you coming back?"

"Hopefully, tonight, assuming I accomplish my mission."

# CHAPTER FIFTY-NINE

Paul made notes on a legal pad during the train ride to D.C., racking his brain to come up with every argument, legal and emotional, that he could throw at Gail Moskowitz. The information Carrie gave him about the cards in Folsom's valises was incriminating, but not legal proof of anything criminal. Even so, he had come to the conclusion that the money had been given to Donald Matson by Folsom for "services rendered." The information Gail provided appeared to show that Matson had helped Folsom get favorable deals from the FDIC. But, again, the deals weren't unlawful, unless Folsom had bribed Matson. That brought him back again to the money in Folsom's house, put there by Matson for safekeeping.

He was beginning to realize his argument was more emotional than legal. Gail would think he was an idiot trying to get her to do something to save Edward Winter's business based on nothing but emotion. And, even if something illegal had gone on, could Gail take action? She was a staff attorney at the FDIC, not a member of executive management.

Gerald Folsom took a deep breath, wincing at the pain. That blonde he'd brought home had humiliated him, and every time he took a breath, the pain in his chest reminded him of that humiliation. His friend, Leon Naxos, the owner of The Towne House Restaurant, had asked around, but no one he talked to had ever seen the woman at the restaurant or around town before, and she hadn't been around since.

Folsom began jerking his head around every time he drove past a tall, good looking blonde, hoping he'd run into that bitch. He'd follow her; find out where she lived and then call Toothpick Jefferson for another assignment. But he would sure like to spend a night in bed with her before she was eliminated.

Get a grip, he told himself. No woman is worth obsessing over. But then he saw another blonde standing at a bus stop and his heart rate accelerated.

He pulled into Broad Street National Bank's parking lot and walked toward the entrance. At the front door, his cell phone rang.

"Yeah," he said.

"Jerry, it's Leon."

"Hey, Leon. What's up?"

"You wanted to know about that blonde you brought to the restaurant the other night? I've been asking around. There was a guy here in the restaurant that night who saw you two together. He came in again today for lunch and asked about you, wondering who the gal was with you that night. One of my waiters brought it to my attention. Apparently, the customer knew the girl from high school. Her name is Carrie Winter."

Folsom snapped his phone shut. He felt like screaming. What the hell was going on?

He pulled himself together and entered the bank. He went straight to Sanford Cunningham's office and closed the door behind him.

"Anything new on the Winter loan?" he demanded, pacing the office.

"Jerry, you've got to relax. If Winter pays off the loan on Thursday, so be it. If not, you'll be in the restaurant business. I don't think you—"

"I want that guy dead!" Folsom yelled.

Cunningham's mouth dropped open. "Jerry, what are you saying?"

Folsom rubbed his hands over his face. Dropping them, he collapsed into a chair. "I mean . . . I want his business. I've got to have that business."

"What's your obsession with Winter?" Cunningham asked.

Folsom leaped out of his chair and lunged toward Cunningham, who pushed back away from his desk, his eyes suddenly wide and fearful.

Folsom stopped abruptly and stared at his outstretched hands. He dropped them to his sides, turned on his heels, and left the office without a word.

# CHAPTER SIXTY

Paul sat in the reception area at the FDIC's legal department for twenty minutes, and was beginning to wonder if Gail Moskowitz was even going to see him. He was second-guessing his decision to come to D.C. when Gail walked out of her office and waved him over curtly, glaring at him as he passed her and entered the office. She closed the door behind him and walked to the chair behind her desk. After sitting down, she continued to glare at him, not saying a word. Moskowitz was a slender, attractive woman who downplayed her good looks—minimal jewelry and makeup, her auburn hair swept back in a pony tail. An understated, conservative blue suit and white blouse completed the look.

"Gail," Paul said, "I apologize for just showing up like this, but we really need to talk."

"About what?"

"About Gerald Folsom, Donald Matson, and Edward Winter."

"I'm getting damned tired of hearing about this. I already gave you all the information I'm going to provide." She stood and barked, "Now get out. You've pushed our friendship too far already."

Paul didn't move. He put steel in his voice and said, "I need five minutes. That's it. Then I'll leave and never talk to you again, if that's the way you want it."

She dropped back into her chair, an exasperated look on her face. "Five minutes. Go."

Paul told her about the cards signed by Donald Matson, with deposit and withdrawal information in Folsom's house. He added his suspicions about where the money, over $2 million, had come from, tying his suspicions to the information Gail had given him about the sweetheart deals. Then he repeated what he had told Gail before, about the killer who had gone after Wendy Folsom. He talked about Donald Matson's murder. Finally, he briefed her on what was going on between Edward Winter and Broad Street National Bank.

"There's too much here to ignore, Gail. You've got to bring this to the attention of someone with authority around here, someone who will make things right."

"Your five minutes are up," she said. "Don't come back."

Paul was shocked at the way Gail dismissed him. He slowly stood, gathered his briefcase, and walked out. He felt drained, and barely had the energy to walk out of the building. After finding his hired car, he told the driver to take him to the train station. As the driver pulled away from the curb, Paul thought about having to wait in the station for the next train and then the long ride back to Philadelphia.

"How much to take me to Philadelphia?" he asked.

The driver looked at him in his rearview mirror. "You serious?"

"Absolutely."

The guy thought about it for a minute and then said, "$800."

Paul told him where he wanted to go. "Wake me when we get there."

# CHAPTER SIXTY-ONE

"What's the latest?" Edward asked Nick Scarfatti. They were seated in Edward's office.

"I heard back from the private equity firm in New York City. They're very interested in making an investment and will put up $30 million to pay off the debt at Broad Street Bank and cover the cost of building new sites in Pittsburgh."

"That's great news," Edward said, "but the look on your face tells me that's not all you have to say on the subject."

"Three things. One, they want the option to convert their $30 million loan to forty percent of the company's stock. Two, the interest rate on the loan would be ten percent. Three, it'll take them two months to perform their due diligence and to close the deal."

"The interest rate's onerous, but we can afford to pay it, and giving up forty percent ownership is better than losing one hundred percent of our company to the bank, but the two months are a deal killer."

"Unless Paul Sanders can use some tactics to delay the foreclosure or convince a judge to grant an injunction against the bank," Nick offered hopefully. "That could give us a few months of breathing room."

"But even with an injunction, or with normal foreclosure procedures, if the bank changes the locks or shuts down the business, as they have the right to do according to our loan agreement, there will be nothing to sell sixty days from now."

"Paul's going to file a motion requesting the injunction on Friday or the following Monday, assuming the bank gives us a formal foreclosure notice at the end of the day tomorrow. Our future will then be in the hands of the court. Forgive me for being pessimistic, but, at this point, I've lost confidence in the fairness of the system."

Nick nodded his agreement.

"Let's call an all-hands meeting for our restaurant managers and department heads for Saturday morning at 9. If the bank pulls the plug tomorrow, I want to inform our people and tell them what our options are."

"Some of the employees are going to start looking for jobs as soon as they hear about this."

Edward shrugged. "That's their right."

# THURSDAY
# JULY 28, 2011

# CHAPTER SIXTY-TWO

Stanley Burns' head was spinning as though he'd had way too much to drink, but alcohol wasn't his problem. Rather, his and his family's futures were on his mind. He'd gone home last night and felt distant from his wife and children all evening. After the children were put to bed, Burns' wife, Yolanda, brought him a cup of tea, sat down next to him on the couch, and leaned her head on his shoulder. They'd sat like that for ten minutes, neither saying a word.

Finally, Burns whispered, "I don't know what to do, Yolanda."

"What's bothering you, Stanley? You haven't been happy for a couple weeks."

He looked at her, surprised. "You didn't say anything."

"I thought, sooner or later, you would tell me about whatever was troubling you. But you were so cold tonight I couldn't let this go on. Besides," she said, smiling wryly, "we haven't made love for two weeks."

He explained how he hated going to work every morning and

how he felt he was violating his principles working there. He'd told her about his conversation with Sanford Cunningham about the Winter Enterprises' loan and what the bank was doing to Winter. And he told her he felt dirty participating in what the bank was doing to Edward Winter, a man with whom he'd had a long-standing relationship and for whom he had high regard. "

"You remember that speech you gave to the Temple University business ethics class a couple years ago?" Yolanda asked. "You told me after you came home that day that one of the students had asked you to list the most important traits of a leader. You told her three of the most important qualities of a leader were education, experience, and character. But if you could only pick one trait, it would be character."

He'd hugged Yolanda and later that evening they'd made love. Before he fell asleep, he thanked God for giving him such a wonderful wife.

He now sat at his desk in the bank, where he'd been since 6:30 that morning, and stared at the tiny article on the last page of the front section of that morning's *Journal*. The stories about the charges against Gerald Folsom for spousal abuse had dwindled down to almost nothing. He had decided last night he was going to do something, but he hadn't yet decided what that would be. This article finally made up his mind for him.

He logged onto his computer and accessed the bank's financial files. Selecting information about the bank's capital accounts, loan delinquency information, and appraisal data on loan collateral, he ran off copies. Then he looked up the number for the *Journal* and called. He asked to be put through to the reporter covering Gerald Folsom. The operator put him through, but he got voicemail suggesting he leave a name and number, or dial a four-digit number to transfer to the business editor. Burns punched in the four numbers and listened to the rings. He almost bailed on the call after five rings when a woman finally answered.

"Kelly Loughridge."

"Ms. Loughridge, my name is Stanley Burns. I'm president of Broad Street National Bank. I'd like to talk to someone about the bank and its new ownership."

"Listen, Mr. Burns, if you've got a problem with one of our articles about the bank, you need to have your attorney call our legal department, and—"

"I have information for you, Ms. Loughridge, about practices here at the bank that I believe are unethical and illegal. I suggest you should talk with me."

The woman muttered something that sounded to Burns like, "Thank God Almighty," but Burns couldn't be certain.

"I'm sorry, what did you say?"

"Uh, nothing, Mr. Burns. When would you like to meet?"

"How about right now? I'm downtown; I could be at your offices in ten minutes."

"That would be perfect."

When Stanley Burns arrived at the *Journal*'s offices, Kelly Loughridge and a staff reporter named Russell Morgan were waiting for him in a conference room.

"Can I get you something to drink, Mr. Burns?" Kelly asked.

"Water would be good."

Kelly went to a small refrigerator in a corner of the room and took out three bottles of water and passed them around. She watched Burns take a long pull on his bottle and then set it on the table.

"You said you wanted to talk about Broad Street National Bank," she began.

"Ms. Loughridge, I want to talk about a whole lot more than that."

Kelly felt a chill run down her spine. "Do you mind if we record this meeting?"

A sudden look of uncertainty crossed Burns' face, but he finally said, "Go right ahead."

She nodded at Morgan, who pressed a switch on a recorder in the middle of the table. She noted the time and date and the people in attendance and then asked, "Would you like to make a statement, Mr. Burns? And is this for the record?"

"Yes, to both of your questions." He took a deep breath and rattled it out slowly. "I've been employed at Broad Street National Bank for sixteen years. I started as a credit analyst, moved to a commercial loan officer position, ultimately became Senior Credit Officer, and am now President. Until about two weeks ago, I worked for Sol Levin, the founder and a significant owner of the bank. But on July 16, Mr. Levin was fired by the board, at the insistence of federal regulators. That night, the FDIC took over the bank. They had already worked out a deal to sell the bank to Gerald Folsom and his Folsom Financial Corporation. I would like to bring a few things to your attention, which I believe you will find interesting. Actually, every citizen of this country should be interested in what I am about to tell you.

"First, it makes no sense why the Feds took over Broad Street National. Sure we had some loan problems, but our capital base was well above statutory requirements, and ninety-eight percent of our loans were current. Yet the regulators decided the collateral on our loans was worth only sixty percent of the value determined by appraisals, and they also decided many of our borrowers would begin to renege on their loans. The regulators came into the bank with a mindset that the Philadelphia and Pennsylvania economies were going to go down the drain and that commercial real estate borrowers were going to default in droves, even though there was no evidence to back that up. With that mindset, there isn't a bank in the country safe from being taken over by the federal government. They came into Broad Street National Bank, wiped out Sol Levin and the other stockholders, and handed the bank to a guy who cares about nothing but making the biggest bang for his buck."

"Isn't that what banks are all about, Mr. Burns?" Morgan asked.

Burns looked at Morgan with a sour set to his mouth. "I'm not here to have a discussion about philosophy and capitalism, Mr. Morgan. But your question displays a complete lack of understanding about the banking business. Banks, especially community banks like Broad Street National, have to apply for a charter. They have to establish that they are providing a service to the community. So, no, they're not in it for the biggest bang for the buck. In fact, even if a bank's management was in it for profit alone, the regulators would fine them for not giving back sufficiently to the community. "

Kelly glared at Morgan and said, "Perhaps we can let Mr. Burns complete his statement without further interruptions."

Morgan looked down at the table top. His face was flushed and he looked sufficiently chastised.

Burns pointed at his briefcase resting on the table beside him. "I brought detailed data about the bank's loan portfolio and capital positions to back up what I just said.

"The second point I want to make is that the arrangement between Gerald Folsom and the federal government represents an abuse of the trust Americans have placed in their federal government. The deal Folsom received is unconscionable. An uneducated person with a 50 IQ could make money off a deal like the Feds gave Folsom—and not just a little. A fortune. I'll also provide you with information about the terms of that deal.

"Finally, I think Folsom is using the bank to rob bank customers of their assets and, in some cases, their businesses. All with, at the very least, the passive assistance of the federal government. I don't believe the government knows exactly what Folsom is doing, but that, in effect, means the government is not properly supervising the people they are handing these banks over to. I've got some examples of what Folsom is doing to take over bank customers' businesses."

"Would one of the examples be Winter Enterprises?" Kelly asked.

Burns showed shock. "How could you know that?"

"Lucky guess. I've talked with the attorney for the company. He is hopping mad about the way your bank has dealt with his client."

"As he should be," Burns said. "Winter Enterprises is the poster child for Folsom's perfidy."

Burns opened his briefcase and took out an inch-thick file. He slid the file across the table to Kelly.

"We'll need some time to digest all of this," Kelly said. "Where can we contact you?"

"I'm going back to the bank to submit my resignation. Then I'll be at home." He gave them his home and cell phone numbers. "Oh, if you want to know about everything Folsom is doing, you should call Sanford Cunningham. He's Folsom's right-hand-man. I doubt he'll talk to you, but you can always try."

"How does this headline sound: Bank President Resigns, Claims New Owner Is Stealing Customer Assets?"

"Just about right," Burns said, smiling.

After he left, Kelly said to Morgan, "I'm going to read Burns' file. I want you to try to meet with this guy Sanford Cunningham. Ask him about Burns' allegations. Then call Folsom and try to get an interview. Tell him we're going to run an article about corruption at the bank. Remind him that declining to comment will not look good."

Morgan got up to leave, but Kelly stopped him and added, "Try not to ask any stupid questions."

Kelly Loughridge spent two hours going over the file from Stanley Burns before calling Paul Sanders.

"Someone finally grew a conscience," Paul said.

"Paul, I need to get a statement from someone at the FDIC. I think it's time you gave me your contact's name there."

Paul didn't have to think about Kelly's request for more than a second. He provided Gail Moskowitz's name and number. "Good luck. I went to D.C. yesterday to try to talk her into cooperating with your investigation. She gave me the boot."

"She'd better not try that with me. With the information I just got from Stanley Burns, I'm going to embarrass the hell out of the FDIC."

"And don't forget about the cash and 3" x 5" cards in the valises in Folsom's house. I can't prove Matson was on the take, but just the threat of you asking how an FDIC official accumulated over $2 million that he then placed with an FDIC investment partner for safekeeping ought to shake her up."

"Did you already tell her about the money?" Kelly asked.

"Oh yeah. But at the time we didn't know you were about to run an article about Broad Street National Bank, Gerald Folsom, and the FDIC."

"It'd be great if we had those valises in our hands. I'd love to print pictures of all that cash and of the cards."

Paul considered that for a minute and then said, "Let me see if I can make it happen."

# CHAPTER SIXTY-THREE

"Sylvia, how much pull do you have with Detective Castiglia?" Paul asked, facing the Lawyer across her desk.

Sylvia Young looked at Paul as though he were an alien from outer space. "Paul, how long have we known one another? Maybe twenty years?"

"A little longer, I think."

"And in all that time you've never just dropped by my office. Yet, here you are, seemingly asking me a favor. So, I assume you've got something very important and urgent on your mind."

"Important, urgent, and a bit diabolical."

She smiled. "That sounds like fun. To answer your question, I have a very good relationship with Castiglia. Why do you ask?"

"I have information that on the day Donald Matson, the local FDIC supervisor, was murdered, he put $2.065 million in a vault at Gerald Folsom's home."

"And there's proof this happened?"

"There are two valises with money and signed, hand-written cards from Matson in Folsom's vault. I'd say $2 million is a pretty good motive for murder. Even for a multi-millionaire."

"So would I," Sylvia said. "But are you sure the cards are still there?"

"I'm not one hundred percent certain, but my source doesn't think Folsom knows the cards even exist."

"Your source is going to have to talk to the police. There's no way they're going to be able to get another search warrant for Folsom's home on second- or third-hand information."

"I'll call my source. You call Castiglia and get us an appointment. Today."

What's the rush?"

"Two things. First, I don't want Folsom to find the cards and destroy them. Second, I'm trying to put as much pressure on a government agency as possible so I can save a client from losing his business. Don't ask me how, but there is a connection here. All roads go through Gerald Folsom."


Paul called Carrie's cell.

"What's up?" Carrie asked."

"We may have caught a break. The president of Broad Street National Bank is talking to the *Journal*. Carrie, are you prepared to tell me how you learned about the money and note cards in Folsom's home?"

"Depends on why you need to know."

"The Broad Street National Bank president is talking to the press. I just received a call from Kelly Loughridge at the *Journal*.

She's putting together a story, but most of what she has isn't necessarily criminal. I mean, Gerald Folsom may be screwing customers like your brother, and it may be unethical and bad for the bank's image if it gets into the media, but it isn't against the law. But what if a connection can be made between Donald Matson's death and Folsom? Those note cards signed by Matson could establish a motive for Folsom to commit murder."

"Paul, I know $2 million is a lot of money, but it's chicken feed to Folsom. Why would he kill Matson for that amount of money?"

"If he did kill Matson, or hire someone to do so—which is more likely—the reason was probably something other than money. But anything we can do to pile suspicion onto Folsom will, hopefully, bring about an investigation of his relationship with Matson and the government, and of his business practices."

"I understand," Carrie said. "I'll do whatever I can if it helps Edward. Or, hurts Folsom."

"Good. Then tell me how you learned about the cases of money and the cards."

After a slight pause, Carrie said, "I saw them with my own eyes."

"Jesus, Mary, and Joseph, Carrie. How did that happen?"

"I went out on a date with Gerald Folsom and then afterwards went with him to his home."

"Carrie, you've got to be kidding me."

"Nope. That's exactly what happened."

"That guy's a monster. He likely is the one who contracted to have Wendy killed. You knew about the beatings he gave her. Why would you take a chance like that?"

"You know why: I was looking for information that might help my brother."

"What if he had gotten violent?"

"He did. I kicked his ass. So, what do you want me to do?"

"Talk to the police about what you saw at Folsom's."

# CHAPTER SIXTY-FOUR

Wendy's cell phone rang. She looked at the incoming number and saw it was Gerald. She breathed out slowly, trying to relax, and then answered the call.

"Wendy, where are you?" he asked.

"Oh, like I'm going to tell you that! You tried to have me killed. How stupid do you think I am?"

"Wendy, what are you talking about?"

"Go to hell, Gerald."

"Wait, listen. I'm calling to tell you I just gave the order to renew Winter Enterprise's loan at the bank. The paper work's being prepared as we speak. It will be ready to sign on Monday. I wanted you to know so you can drop your claim of abuse."

For a moment, Wendy thought he might be telling her the truth. But then she thought about what Carrie had just told her about Paul Sanders' call. "It's too late for that," she said. "Besides, I don't believe a word you say. You're going down, Gerald, and I'm damn happy I'll have a hand in making it happen." She hung up on him.

Folsom stared at his phone and then slammed it down. He shouted at the top of his lungs, cursing Wendy until his voice became hoarse. He then decided what he needed to do, once and for all. Taking out the Philadelphia telephone book, he looked up the listing for Katherine Winter. Her number was listed, but when he called there was no answer. He jotted down the woman's address.

He went down to his car and, with a clear sense of purpose, drove for twenty minutes. Disappointed, but not surprised, he found no vehicles in the driveway of Katherine's house. Through a window in the garage door, he saw the garage was empty. Several days of newspapers were scattered on the front lawn.

Back in his car, he called Sanford Cunningham.

"I need some information," he barked.

"Sure, Boss. What is it?"

"Check to see if Winter Enterprises or any of the Winter family have credit cards with the bank."

"Is there a problem?" Cunningham asked.

"I just want to make sure they're not racking up credit card charges in anticipation of taking bankruptcy."

"Knowing what I know about them, it doesn't seem likely, but I'll check."

"And if they have cards with us, let me know what the last few charges have been. Call me when you have the information."

"Why don't you just hang on? I've already pulled up a list of their accounts. There's a company credit card account, but there's only a $2,200 balance. We have a card in Edward's name, but he hardly ever uses it. It's zero-balanced at the moment. Ah, here's another one in Katherine Winter's name. She owes a little over $3,000."

"What are her more recent charges?" Folsom asked.

"Hmm, that's funny."

"What?"

"Several charges at the Marriott Hotel on the northwest side of the city. I don't know why she'd be in a hotel if she has a home in the same area. Maybe she's having repairs done."

"Yeah, maybe," Folsom said, trying to hold in his glee. "Thanks."

He drove to the Marriott Hotel and pulled up to the front door. The parking valet came over, waited for him to lower his window, and asked if he was checking in.

"No," Folsom said, "I'm checking whether a friend of mine is here yet."

"You can go inside and talk with someone at the reception desk. They'll be able to tell you."

"How about you finding out for me?"

"That's against hotel policy, sir."

Folsom stuck a one hundred dollar bill through the open window. "You find out if my friend is here and what room she's in and you get another hundred."

The kid looked around, making sure no one was paying attention, and then pocketed the bill. "Ok. What's your friend's name?"

"Katherine Winter."

"Yeah, she's here. Been around for a few days. There are three of them staying in a suite." The kid smiled. "All good-looking women. I've taken meals up to them a couple times."

"And the room number?" Folsom prompted.

"1045."

Folsom slipped him another hundred and peeled away.


Folsom stopped at a convenience store and used the pay phone outside to call Toothpick Jefferson.

Jefferson answered the call, but before he could even say hello, Folsom blurted, "Toothpick, it's Jerry. We need to talk."

"I don't think so," Jefferson said. "You're cursed, Jerry. First, my best damn agent gets beat up and disappears trying to do your dirty work and then I get a concussion and a lump the size of a tennis ball from someone trying to find you. I don't need this kind of attention."

"What do you mean, concussion?"

"I don't want to talk about it. Just get out of my life."

"Whoa, just a second, Toothpick. Tell me what happened."

"None of your damned business."

Jefferson's tone sounded more embarrassed than angry. But embarrassed about what? And then a thought came to him. Maybe a woman injured him.

"You got beat up by a woman, didn't you?"

"Fuck off!"

"Listen, Toothpick. If I'm right, the woman who attacked you also attacked me. And I'm pretty certain I know where she's at. I think we need to pay her a visit."

"You know who the bitch is?"

"Oh yeah. Tall, short blonde hair, blue eyes. Drop dead gorgeous."

"Yeah, that's her."

"You want to get even?"

"Damn straight! What you got in mind?"

"Take a couple guys with you to the Northwest Marriott Hotel at 10 tomorrow night. Go to the east emergency exit. I'll open the door for you. And make sure you're all armed."

Jefferson was silent for a few seconds and then said, "On one condition. I get to spend an hour with her, one-on-one."

Folsom could imagine what Jefferson had in mind. The thought of him naked, having his way with Carrie Winter was laughable and abhorrent. "You can spend as much time with her as you like, Toothpick, as long as she's no longer a problem when you're done."

"You can count on that, my man. See you at 10 tomorrow."

# CHAPTER SIXTY-FIVE

"This is Kelly Loughridge from *The Philadelphia Journal* calling for Gail Moskowitz."

"Please hold, Ms. Loughridge," the receptionist said.

Kelly remained on hold for over a minute. Then the woman came back on the line.

"Ms. Moskowitz cannot speak to the press, Ms. Loughridge. She instructed me to forward your call to our Public Affairs office."

Using her sweetest voice, Kelly said, "Please tell Ms. Moskowitz I am going to go to press in one hour with a story about corruption at the FDIC. The article will mention the following names: Gerald Folsom, Donald Matson," she paused for effect, "and Gail Moskowitz. Ms. Moskowitz's name will be mentioned in the context of obstruction of justice. Also, please tell Ms. Moskowitz I could care less if she calls me back or not, but it would really be better for her and your agency if she talked to me." Kelly left her telephone number and hung up. By the time she leisurely walked to the break room, got a cup of coffee, and returned to her desk, her phone rang. It was 3:35 p.m.

"Loughridge!" she barked into the phone.

"Ms. Loughridge, this is Gail Moskowitz. I am a staff attorney for the Federal Deposit Insurance Corporation. I understand you want to discuss something with me."

Might as well go for the kill, Kelly thought. "I understand an attorney here in Philadelphia has had several conversations with you about the dire situation his client has been put into by a bank the FDIC recently took over."

"You'll have to be more specific, Ms. Loughridge."

"Broad Street National Bank is the bank in question. I believe your agency took over that bank two weeks ago and handed it over to one of your *preferred* investors almost immediately after the FDIC threw out the previous owners."

"I object to your characterization of events, Ms. Loughridge. The FDIC has no preferred investors, and we don't *throw out previous owners*, as you so indelicately stated."

"I'm terribly sorry if I offended you, Ms. Moskowitz," Loughridge said, her voice oozing sarcasm. "We can discuss that in a minute. Will you admit to having had conversations with a Mr. Paul Sanders?"

"I admit to nothing."

"I see. Do you admit Mr. Sanders told you about evidence in Gerald Folsom's home implicating one of your employees, Donald Matson, in a possible bribery scheme?"

A long pause occurred before Moskowitz said, "I'm listening."

"How about we stop dancing around, Ms. Moskowitz, and get down to the basics? We're going to run the first of three articles tomorrow about Broad Street National Bank, Gerald Folsom, and the FDIC. Whether you cooperate or stonewall, the article's running. Your decision in the next half-minute will determine whether the FDIC comes across as a conspirator or a well-intentioned, public-spirited organization that was the innocent victim of two corrupt individuals: Gerald Folsom and Donald Matson."

Kelly sat silently and watched the hand on her desk clock count down the seconds. Time was almost up when Gail Moskowitz said, "I need to confer with my superior."

"Good idea. To show my good faith, Ms. Moskowitz, I promise I will not disclose you as the source of the fax listing the dates and deal terms of the transactions Gerald Folsom executed with your organization. I will live up to that promise if I receive a call from you or someone with serious authority within the next half hour."

# CHAPTER SIXTY-SIX

Detective Anthony Castiglia called Jeffrey Rose, Gerald Folsom's criminal attorney, at 3:40 p.m. to advise him that a team of detectives and uniformed officers were going to search Gerald Folsom's home. He told him he was making a courtesy call so Rose could call his client and have him admit the police, rather than them having to break down the door.

"This is pure harassment, Castiglia," Rose said.

"Tell it to the judge, counselor."

Rose immediately called Gerald Folsom and informed him of Castiglia's call.

"What the hell are the cops looking for?" Folsom asked. "They went all over my place last time and found nothing."

"Is there anything new in your house that wasn't there when the last search was done?"

"Nothing important."

"Jerry, they've got to have something or they wouldn't be searching your place again. Did your wife leave anything there that might be incriminating?"

"Not a damned thing," Folsom responded.

"What about weapons?"

"Yeah, but they're all registered with the state."

"Okay," Rose said. "Just stay calm and let them do their thing. Call me after they leave."

The police arrived fifteen minutes after Jeffrey Rose's call. Folsom was steaming mad about them being there and, despite Rose's warning, shouted at the police, "Why don't you guys go out and bust some criminals for a change, instead of bothering law-abiding citizens?"

The lead detective, Simon Carruthers—the same one who had arrested him—slapped a copy of the search warrant into Folsom's hand before walking past Folsom into the house.

"I want you to open your vault," Carruthers said.

"What the hell for?" Folsom shouted.

"Is that aggression I hear in your voice, Mr. Folsom? I'm getting the impression you might become physical." Carruthers crooked a finger at one of the uniformed officers and told him to keep an eye on Folsom and put him in handcuffs if he started acting up.

Carruthers smiled mockingly at Folsom, which only made him angrier. "Let's go upstairs, Mr. Folsom. I'd like to get out of here at a reasonable hour."

Folsom surged up the stairs to the third level, muttering all the way there. He dialed in the safe combination and opened it. "You were in here the last time. Nothing's changed, so what are you looking for?"

Carruthers didn't hesitate before going to where the two valises sat on the floor. He pointed at them and said, "My men are going to remove these two valises from your vault and take them to whichever room you direct us to. We're going to open them in front of you and inventory everything inside. We're going to count the cash in front of you and then you're going to sign an affidavit as to the correct count."

"What, is it against the law to have cash in your house now?"

"Of course not, Mr. Folsom. Law abiding citizens can have as much cash as they want in their homes." He smirked at Folsom and added, "By the way, where did all this cash come from?"

Folsom hesitated for a beat and then said, "I saved it up over the last thirty years."

"You don't trust banks?"

Folsom glared at Carruthers. "I'm not answering any more of your smartass questions."

Carruthers pointed at one of his men and said, "Please write down in your notebook that Mr. Folsom informed us the cash in his vault represents money he has saved over the past thirty years."

Turning back to Folsom, Carruthers asked, "Where can we inventory the contents of these bags?"

"Dining room," Folsom responded petulantly. "You can use the table there."

In the dining room, Carruthers instructed his men to carefully remove the contents from one valise and to place them on the table. The second valise was placed in a corner to await its turn.

Two policemen, wearing rubber gloves, unloaded the first valise and stacked the cash on the table. One of the police officers said, "Detective Carruthers, there are a couple cards at the bottom of this case."

"What cards?" Folsom demanded, moving between the officers and trying to look inside the valise. They grabbed Folsom's arms and jerked him away from the table.

Carruthers ignored Folsom, walked around the table and looked down into the valise. He pulled on a pair of rubber gloves, extracted the cards one at a time and placed each into a separate plastic evidence bag. He looked back into the case to make sure it was now empty, moved it to the corner where the other valise was resting, and announced, "Let's get the cash counted. Don't break the bank wrappers. Mr. Folsom, you will stand where you are and observe the counting."

"I want to see those cards," Folsom demanded.

"All in good time," Carruthers answered, smiling.

# CHAPTER SIXTY-SEVEN

It was a bit after 4:05 p.m. when Gail Moskowitz called Kelly Loughridge back. She had a man named Henry Rentz on the line with her.

"Ms. Loughridge," Moskowitz said, "Mr. Rentz is the Division Superintendent for Asset Acquisitions in the Middle Atlantic Region, which Pennsylvania is part of. I've briefed him on our earlier conversation and on the conversations I've had with Paul Sanders."

"Thank you for taking time to talk with me, Mr. Rentz. I'm sure, with all of the bank acquisitions the FDIC is making, you're a very busy man."

"It's a difficult economic environment, Ms. Loughridge. We're doing what we can to stabilize the economy."

"How does putting bank clients out of business help stabilize the economy?"

"What are you talking about, Ms. Loughridge?"

"Your investor of choice in the Philadelphia area, to whom you handed Broad Street National Bank on a platter, is intentionally putting unnecessary pressure on companies like BGT Automotive, Robin Healthcare, Swisstack Foods, and Winter Enterprises and driving them out of business. I can name another dozen companies getting the same treatment at Broad Street National Bank.

"This is despite the fact not one of these businesses has ever missed a loan payment; every one of them has at least forty percent equity in the real estate they put up as collateral, even at today's reduced values; and every one of them has ten percent or more of their loan balance in cash deposits at Broad Street National Bank. The bank has either started or threatened to start foreclosure action against every one of these companies, and has frozen or offset the companies' deposits against the loans, in effect starving these businesses to death."

Rentz laughed. "I think you've either received bad information or are exaggerating the situation, Ms. Loughridge. Neither the FDIC nor our investor partners would ever treat our good bank customers in such a manner."

"So, you agree that, if my information is correct, treating bank customers as I described would be wrong?"

"*If* your information is accurate, then I would say such treatment would be more than wrong. It would be a violation of the agreement we have with our investors, and would be a violation of the public trust."

"Okay, then let's move on to Gerald Folsom, the investor who bought Broad Street National Bank from the FDIC. Are you aware he has been charged with beating his wife?"

Rentz cleared his throat. "Yes, but the last time I looked we were still a nation that believes in innocent until proven guilty."

"That's terribly high-minded of you," Loughridge said. "Perhaps you'd think differently if you saw the photographs of his battered wife. I've seen those photos and they are not pleasant. But that's another matter. Have you had the opportunity to review the transactions Folsom has done with the FDIC?"

"Yes, Ms. Moskowitz showed the list to me before we made this call."

Playing dumb to honor her promise to Gail Moskowitz, Kelly asked, "Is it an extensive list?"

"Where is this going?" Rentz said.

"As to the transactions I *am* aware of, Mr. Rentz, I understand Donald Matson, your former Philadelphia Area Supervisor, managed every deal made with Gerald Folsom and his firm, Folsom Financial Corporation."

"That isn't surprising. That was Mr. Matson's job."

"Have you reviewed the terms of the deals Folsom Financial Corporation received versus the terms of other deals Matson managed?"

"No, why?"

"Ms. Moskowitz, would you care to characterize any difference between Folsom's deals and those of other investors?"

Moskowitz coughed. Her voice squeaked a bit as she started to talk. "I would have to say that Folsom Financial Corporation received dramatically more favorable terms than any other investor with whom Donald Matson worked, and than any other investor in transactions I am aware of in other regions."

"And what happened to all of the banks Folsom took over from the FDIC?" Loughridge asked.

"I don't have that information," Rentz answered.

"Ms. Moskowitz?" Kelly asked.

"Most of them were liquidated within four years of Folsom taking them over."

"In other words, those are no longer operating as banks?" Kelly said. "Folsom bled the assets and then closed down the banks?"

"Other than the ones he bought in the past three years," Moskowitz offered.

"Give Folsom time," Kelly said.

"Where is this going?" Mr. Rentz demanded.

"Let me put it this way, Mr. Rentz. I believe there is sufficient evidence that Gerald Folsom and Donald Matson were operating against the best interests of the FDIC, bank shareholders, bank customers, and the general public. The story we are writing will focus on just that."

"You've raised a lot of points here, Ms. Loughridge," Rentz said. "I would like to assign a committee from my staff to investigate these matters. I assure you if they find anything criminal has occurred, I will take immediate and appropriate action."

"Mr. Rentz, is there a manual in Washington, D.C. that tells you people how to speak. I've heard that bullshit phrase so many times I've got it memorized."

"I resent that, Ms. Moskowitz. You're way off—"

"One more question, Mr. Rentz. Are you aware an informant has told the Philadelphia Police Department that there are two valises in a vault in Gerald Folsom's home that hold somewhere just over $2 million, and that these valises also hold notes signed by Donald Matson? Two of these notes indicate Matson put the money with Folsom for safekeeping. Another note lists dates and amounts when

Matson received and spent cash."

"I don't get the point, Ms. Loughridge."

"The point, Mr. Rentz, is every one of the dates I have from the cards matched dates on which the FDIC and Gerald Folsom executed a transaction."

Rentz gasped audibly.

"Oh, one other thing, before you get back to *stabilizing* the American economy. You earlier questioned the soundness of my information about customers of Broad Street National Bank, and you questioned my integrity by raising the possibility of exaggeration. Let me put to rest any doubts you might have: I have a recording of a conversation I had with a Broad Street National Bank senior officer, and I have a signed statement from that same officer, giving names, dates, dollar amounts, and so forth, concerning a long list of bank clients Folsom Financial Corporation is robbing blind. If you like, I would be happy to provide you with a copy of the first article before it hits the street tomorrow."

"Hold on," Rentz said, with more than a hint of panic in his voice. "Perhaps I should send some of my people to Philadelphia to look into this situation."

"Perhaps? You think? When my series of articles runs about the FDIC, Folsom, and Broad Street National Bank, you're going to be inundated with calls and letters from other members of the media, elected officials, attorneys of former shareholders of the banks your agency took over, attorneys for bank customers who have been damaged, and irate citizens who are already up in arms about an overbearing federal government. *Perhaps*, you should also give the other regional directors a heads-up."

After terminating the call to Kelly Loughridge, Rentz stared at Gail Moskowitz in shock. "What the hell!"

"This can turn into a huge scandal. The last thing we need now is more problems at the agency."

"Gail, I appreciate you trying to protect the FDIC, but don't forget we work for the American people. If we have a rogue partner taking advantage of bank clients who deserve fair treatment, then we have a severe problem."

"Yes, sir."

"But something else concerns me. The FDIC steps in when a bank is in trouble, but it's the Office of the Comptroller of the Currency that examines nationally-chartered banks and brings problems to our attention. The OCC would have examined Broad Street National Bank. The OCC would have determined loan collateral values and then required the bank to write down loans when applicable. When our agency came into Broad Street National Bank, our determination of the bank's value was, in part, based on those write-downs."

"What are you suggesting?"

"I think you should check to see who the head of the OCC bank examination crew was at each of the banks Folsom purchased."

The OCC examination crews have guidelines they're supposed to follow."

Rentz snorted. "You know damn well that examination crews are like mini-Gestapo teams. They can pretty well do whatever they want to do."

Moskowitz said, "You realize if the same person was in charge of the examinations at each of Folsom's banks, we've got a big red flag that could implicate the OCC too."

"Especially if we can establish a relationship between Matson and the OCC examiner, or between Folsom and the examiner.."

"You sure you want to go down this road?"

"I thought I already made my position clear."

"Just checking."

Rentz stood and turned to leave Moskowitz's office. He suddenly stopped and looked back at her. "One other thing. See if you can discover what is written on those cards Kelly Loughridge mentioned."

# CHAPTER SIXTY-EIGHT

Folsom fumed as the police counted the cash bundles. It took the police an hour and a half. Detective Carruthers marked down $1 million on an Evidence Affidavit, signed it, and then had Folsom countersign the document. He taped a copy of the affidavit to the valise, handed Folsom a second copy, and put the original in a folio. Folsom tried to see what was on 3" x 5" cards that had been pulled from the valise, but Carruthers replaced the note cards, safe in evidence envelopes, into the valise and closed it, sealing the handles with a plastic tie.

Counting the second valise took almost the same amount of time, but this time the count came to $1,055,000. Folsom knew there had been $10,000 more, but he knew where the missing $10,000 had gone: Matson, and ultimately to Toothpick Jefferson's man. There was another card in the second valise, but, again, Carruthers didn't allow Folsom to see what was written there. Carruthers documented and safeguarded the second valise in the same manner as the first one.

"Sign the Evidence Affidavit," Carruthers ordered Folsom, who did as he was told.

"You said you saved this money, is that right, Mr. Folsom?"

Folsom felt a sour taste in his mouth. He'd told the police he'd saved the cash. But what if there was something on those 3" x 5" cards that proved otherwise? "I'm not saying anything else unless my lawyer says it's okay."

"I see," Carruthers said. "We're taking these cases down to headquarters. I'm sure you'll hear from the D.A."

Without another word, Carruthers and his crew of police officers took the valises and departed.

Folsom called his attorney, Jeffrey Rose, and told him what had happened as soon as the cops left.

"What was written on the cards they found?" Rose asked.

"I have no idea," Folsom said. "The cops wouldn't let me see them."

"The cards were in your valises with over $2 million?"

"Yeah."

"Well, why don't you know what's on the cards?"

"I didn't put them there," Folsom answered.

"Jerry, this is like pulling teeth with you. I'm your lawyer; how about telling me who put the cards in the valises and where the valises came from?"

Folsom blew out a long breath and said, "The money belonged to Donald Matson, so I assume he put the cards in the valises."

"Remind me who Donald Matson is."

"He *was* the area supervisor for the FDIC. We worked together on a lot of bank and loan pool deals."

"Why don't you call him up and ask him what was on the cards?"

"That's not possible; he was murdered recently."

"Murdered?"

"Yeah."

"The police arrest anyone for the murder?" Rose asked.

"Nope. Not yet."

"Why don't you explain to me how a government bureaucrat got hold of so much money?"

"I don't have a clue."

"Why did he leave the money with you?"

"He was a friend. He showed up here a little over a week ago, asked me to put the money in my vault, and then took off."

Rose didn't respond right away. He finally said, "That's a good answer, Jerry. I suggest you stick with it when the police ask you the same question."

"Uh, well," Folsom said. "I originally told the police I'd saved the money."

"Wonderful," Rose exclaimed. "Fuckin' wonderful."

# CHAPTER SIXTY-NINE

Katherine and Carrie left Wendy in the Marriott suite and drove to Winter Enterprise's offices for a summit conference at 7 p.m. Edward, Betsy, Nick, and Paul were already there when the women arrived.

"Well, we missed the deadline today, so the bank can start foreclosure action tomorrow," Edward said. "The only chance we have is if Paul gets a judge to issue an injunction against the bank."

"I'll do my best," Paul said, "but I have to tell you, it's not probable. The courts are not prone to interfere in matters like this since we're asking the court to abrogate the bank's rights under the loan security agreement and promissory note you signed."

"We're asking the court to intervene because, in part, actions directed by a sociopath are impacting our company," Katherine interjected.

Paul nodded. "In my opinion, Gerald Folsom *is* a sociopath, but we can't prove he's done anything illegal."

"What specific actions can the bank take tomorrow?" Carrie asked Paul.

"It will formally notify you you're in default on the loan and demand payment within the grace period provided for in the loan documents, which is fifteen days. They could, theoretically, immediately change the locks on all the doors at the restaurants and offset the money in your bank account at Broad Street National Bank against the loan balance."

"That would ruin our business," Nick said. "Even if the bank changed its mind later, or we raised the money to pay off the loan, we'd probably never recover."

"And our employees would be out of jobs," Edward said. "We've got great people. They'll be able to get jobs pretty quickly at other restaurants. Even if we were able to re-open the restaurants later, we'd have to begin with new crews. That would take months."

"When are you going to tell the employees what's going on?" Katherine asked.

"We've scheduled a 9 a.m. meeting on Saturday with all our managers. Assuming the restaurants are still open, the employees will still work their shifts until further notice. The managers will speak to each of their teams."

Edward's desk phone rang. After looking at the console screen, he saw it was Broad Street National Bank. He looked at Paul and said, "It's the bank. Should I take it?"

Paul shrugged. "Sure, why not? Maybe we'll learn something."

"Winter Enterprises," Edward said into the receiver.

"Mr. Winter, it's Sanford Cunningham at Broad Street National Bank. I'm glad we connected. There's something we need to discuss."

"I'm putting you on speaker, Mr. Cunningham. My partners

and our attorney are here with me."

Cunningham voiced no objection.

"What can we do for you, Mr. Cunningham?" Edward said.

"I am calling as the bank owner's representative. You are aware you were officially in violation of your loan agreement with the bank at 5 p.m. today?"

"Of course we're aware of that," Edward said.

"Mr. Folsom has decided to make you an offer he hopes you will find attractive."

Edward made eye contact with Paul, who looked surprised.

"We're listening." Edward asked, suspicious.

"The bank has the right to close down your operations in the instance of non-payment of your loan. We realize closing down your business locations will not be good for the real estate, the business operations, or the employees. Mr. Folsom's proposal is as follows: If you agree to sign over all your rights to the business and assets, including the franchise agreements with Hot N' Chili, Inc., the bank will immediately agree to forgive your bank debt."

"And if my client refuses to accept your offer?" Paul asked.

"Then the bank will exercise its right to change the locks on all of your properties, close the restaurants, and fire the employees. But there's one other part of the offer I need to bring to your attention. If you agree to our terms, Folsom Financial will sign a management contract with Winter Enterprises to manage the restaurant business for the next two years, with renewal options thereafter."

"How long is your offer open, Mr. Cunningham?" Paul asked.

"Until 5 tomorrow evening."

"What about the cash balances?" Paul asked.

"They would be part of the assets you sign over to the bank."

"So, let me get this straight," Paul said. "You want Winter Enterprises to sign over $50 million in real estate, over $3 million in cash, and franchise rights worth millions, in return for forgiveness of $20 million in debt."

"And no exposure to a deficiency judgment should the ultimate sale of the company's assets yield less than the total debt and related legal costs," Cunningham added.

"Anyone have any questions?" Edward asked. When no one asked anything, he said, "We'll be in touch."

No one spoke after Edward hung up—it was as though all the oxygen had been sucked from the room—Edward looked at his mother and saw she was crying. He stood, walked around his desk, sat next to her on the couch, and put an arm around her.

"It's better than the alternatives we had just a few minutes ago," he said.

"Is it?" Katherine said. "You'd be working for that sonofabitch, Folsom. He stole your father's bank and now he's taking the business you've built."

Edward kissed his mother on the cheek and stood. "Mom, I will never work for a man who has visited so much evil on this family." He turned to look at Nick. "How do you feel about running Winter Enterprises?"

Nick's head came up and he looked suddenly ghostly pale. "I thought we agreed if we lost the business we would start all over again. As a team."

"Think about it, Nick. Without either of us there's no Winter Enterprises and Folsom's deal would collapse. All of our employees would be out on the street. Although most of them will find other jobs, in this economy, some will still be unemployed after their severance pay runs out. If you stay on, they keep their jobs and, at the end of two years, if you want to, you can walk away from Folsom and join me. But at least you'll have an executive job in the interim."

Nick looked around at the group and shook his head. "This is emotional blackmail," he said.

Edward smiled. "It's also the right thing to do."

"Let's see what happens with my request for an injunction," Paul said.

"Does anyone think Folsom's offer is beyond surprising?" Carrie asked.

"Yes," Edward said. "But it makes sense on two levels. One, he knows no one can run this business better than we can, which means he'll make more money with Winter Enterprises and its employees at the helm than without."

"And the second level?" Carrie said.

"I can answer that," Katherine said bitterly. "Nothing would give that bastard more pleasure than having Frank Winter's son taking orders from him."

"Oh, my God!" Betsy suddenly cried. She wrapped her arms around her stomach and leaned forward as though she were in terrible pain.

Stunned silence struck the room and no one moved.

"The baby!" Betsy shrieked.

# CHAPTER SEVENTY

Betsy Winter's obstetrician walked exhaustedly from the hospital operating room to the waiting room, her head down and her hands in the pockets of her green surgical scrubs.

"How is she?" Edward asked, his face drawn with stress and fear.

The doctor looked up at Edward, as members of his family and friends gathered around him. "Betsy's fine." The doctor smiled. "And so's the baby. You have a healthy son."

Edward moved back a step as though he'd been struck. "The baby? Betsy wasn't due for another six weeks."

"All indications were this pregnancy would go full term. Everything was fine, Mr. Winter; I don't understand why the baby came prematurely. Has Betsy been under any undue stress lately?"

Edward thought about the strain they had all been under, but it hit him that he had not considered Betsy's pregnancy might be impacted by troubles at work. He had not considered Betsy at all. The business had occupied all his thoughts and time. He felt sick with guilt.

"Can I see her, Doctor?"

"Of course. Come with me."

Edward followed the doctor to the recovery room and spied Betsy in a gurney bed in the middle of the room. She looked pale and tired, strands of wet hair plastered to her forehead. He rushed to her, took her hand, and kissed her lips.

"I'm so sorry, honey."

"About what? We have a beautiful son."

"About not thinking about you. About being so focused on the business. Nothing is more important to me than you, but that's not the way I've acted lately."

Betsy patted his cheek and squeezed his hand. "Everything's going to be all right, Eddie. I just know it."

"Everything is just right," he said. "You're okay and we have a son."

A nurse interrupted and told them she had to get Mrs. Winter up to her room.

"Why don't you go take a look at your son," Betsy suggested. "By the way, I've been considering names. I know we've talked about it, but I've made up my mind. Franklin Edward Winter, after your father."

Edward found the maternity ward and located the bassinette with "Baby Winter" on the end. He hadn't thought about what the premature baby would look like, but was shocked to see how small his son was compared to the half-dozen other infants in the room.

"It's amazing how big he is considering he came six weeks early."

Edward looked at his mother. "I didn't hear you come up. He looks so tiny."

"Five pounds, six ounces isn't that tiny. My God, if he had gone full term he could have been a twelve pounder."

"Where are the others?" Edward asked.

"Waiting for you to tell them it's okay to join us."

"All things considered," Edward said, "I'm pretty lucky. Great family and great friends, and now a son."

"Yes, son, you're a very lucky man. Have you named the baby yet?"

"Betsy has. She named him after Dad. Franklin Edward Winter."

Katherine stepped into her son's arms and hugged him. It took several minutes before she stopped crying.

# FRIDAY
# JULY 29, 2011

# CHAPTER SEVENTY-ONE

Carrie called her old Army compatriot, Darren Noury, at 7 a.m. and asked him to meet her.

"Everything okay?"

"I've still got concerns."

"I'll bring Mike with me," he said, referring to Mike Perico who had helped out in Pastorius Park.

"I'm at the Northwest Marriott Hotel. In the coffee shop."

"We'll be there in thirty minutes."

"You sure Mike's available on such short notice?"

"Naturally. He's always ready for action." He laughed and hung up.


Darren called Mike Perico on his cell phone. Mike, a pharmaceutical rep for one of the big drug companies, usually started his days at 7 a.m. and finished at around 3 p.m.

"What are you doing?" Darren asked.

"Meeting with a bunch of interns at a hospital. I brought in donuts. I'm about to tell them what a great drug we have, then I'll give them a bunch of pens and note pads."

"That stuff really gets them to prescribe your products?"

"Mostly the donuts."

"Carrie called. She needs to see us."

"Gee, I don't know if I can break away right now. I've got eight interns hanging on my every word. Besides, I'll have to report to my boss about this meeting. I can't very well tell him I paid for donuts and then walked out."

"I think we're talking about bad guys here."

"Action?"

"Carrie attracts action like sugar attracts ants."

"Where and when?"

"Northwest Marriott Hotel coffee shop at 7:30."

Carrie was seated in a corner booth when Darren and Mike arrived. She thanked the men for coming on such short notice.

"What's up?" Mike asked, his bright blue eyes sparkling with excitement.

Carrie looked at Mike and then at Darren. They were both calm, but she sensed the adrenaline running through their veins. Two good looking guys—recruiter poster perfect—ready to take on trouble whenever a friend called. She understood once again why she loved being an officer in the U.S. military.

"As I explained before we did that thing in the park, my mother befriended a woman named Wendy Folsom who was badly abused by her husband. An assassin was hired to kill Wendy. The assassin entered my mother's home and would have completed the job if I hadn't interrupted her."

"Interrupted?" Darren said, a smile creasing his face.

"I got her to tell me who hired her by agreeing to let her go. I didn't see any point in telling the police what her real purpose was; I figured whoever hired her was a middle man anyway. The police would never have been able to pin anything on the client unless the guy who brokered the hit rolled over. And as I learned during my meeting in Pastorius Park, the broker wasn't willing to disclose who hired him."

"The middle man was the guy in the park?" Darren asked.

"Yeah. But as I said, he clammed up. So I never did find out who paid him to murder Wendy."

"But you think you know who hired him, don't you?" Mike said.

"I'm pretty sure it was her husband, Gerald Folsom. And I don't think the guy's going to stop trying to take her out."

"What else?" Darren asked.

"What do you mean, what else?" Carrie said.

"It can't be that simple."

"Why not?"

"Because I know you, Carrie. Come on, what else?"

"Well, I might have cold-cocked the husband when he tried to get fresh with me."

"He touched you?" Mike asked, his eyes now slits.

"He tried to," Carrie answered, wondering at Mike's reaction.

"I'm going to rip his balls off."

A woman at a table several feet away scowled at Carrie and covered the ears of a little girl seated next to her. The little girl was laughing hysterically.

Carrie put a finger to her lips, telling Mike to keep his voice down.

"Okay, here's the deal. My mother, Wendy Folsom, and I are staying here in room 1045. We'll be here until tomorrow morning. I want you two to watch the hotel once it gets dark until we leave in the morning, and then follow us to my mother's place. Then I'm going to move Mrs. Folsom down to Cape May to a bungalow there. As long as she doesn't use her credit cards or her cell phone, her husband shouldn't be able to find her. Hopefully, they'll throw his ass in jail and she can go somewhere where she can make a new life for herself. Once we get her to Cape May, your job will be done."

"You call it a job. Does that mean we're going to be compensated?" Darren asked, smiling.

"Of course," she said. "You'll receive the most valuable compensation there is: My undying gratitude and eternal respect."

"Thank goodness," he said. "I thought we might be working for nothing."

Then Darren told her to come outside with them. At his car, he popped the trunk, removed a satchel, and handed it to her. "Just in case," he said.

# CHAPTER SEVENTY-TWO

At 10 a.m., Paul Sanders met with Byron LaMotte, the most respected district judge in the Philadelphia area. The judge gave Paul the opportunity to brief him on background information behind the reason for his injunction request. This was more leeway than the judge would have granted most attorneys, but Paul was an old friend and a respected colleague.

After Paul had finished his presentation, Judge LaMotte said, "I think you knew what I would say when you walked in here. I agree there is plenty of circumstantial evidence showing that your client has been, at a minimum, taken advantage of, and at worst, cheated out of the ownership of his company. But there isn't evidence a crime has been committed. In the absence of such evidence, I am not about to set a precedent that would undermine the contractual rights of lending institutions. I'm sorry, Paul, but you're going to have to come up with something more definitive for me to take action."

Paul was dejected, but not surprised. "I appreciate your time, Judge. You're right. I anticipated you would rule as you have, but I had to try anyway. I have never seen a more inequitable situation."

Paul left the courthouse and called Edward's cell. As the phone rang he considered that he might have misspoken to Judge LaMotte. He had seen a situation at least as inequitable as what was happening to Edward. It was when Frank Winter, Edward's father, had died and Gerald Folsom took over Winter's bank and real estate assets, stealing Frank Winter's legacy to his wife and children.

"Hello."

"Edward, it's Paul. I just left Judge LaMotte's chambers. He declined my request for an injunction against the bank."

"Thanks for trying, Paul. It was a long shot. You said so yourself last night."

"How's Betsy?"

"She's doing great. The hospital will be discharging her on Saturday afternoon."

"Have you decided about Folsom's offer?"

"I decided last night," Edward said. "I was just waiting to see what happened with the judge this morning. I don't have a choice. It's the only way my people will keep their jobs.

"I do need your help on something, though. Cunningham said on the call last night that Folsom wanted Winter Enterprises to manage the restaurants. I want to hold a special board meeting. The only items on the agenda will be my resignation from the company and Nick Scarfatti's promotion to CEO. We'll hold the meeting after we sign the documents with Folsom. He won't like it, my being gone, but after the deal is executed, there's nothing he can do about it."

"What are you going to do, Edward?"

"I'm going to start again in New York. Pete Mora at Hot N' Chili folks already said they will work with me. The money in the company's account at Third Community Bank should be more than enough to open a couple stores and cover working capital until the stores are cash flowing. I should be in good enough condition within two years to bring Nick over, assuming he'll want to."

"The cash sitting in your account at Third Community Bank is an asset of the corporation. Cunningham said the deal was for all corporate assets."

Edward's jaw clenched and he took in a great breath. "Paul, without that cash, I might as well fight Folsom and let the bank go through the whole foreclosure process. I don't think he wants that. Make sure the agreement excludes those monies."

"Okay, I'll get on it."

"By the way," Edward said, "did you see this morning's paper?"

"No, I didn't get the chance. Why?"

"The *Journal* had a front-page article about Folsom and Broad Street National Bank. It had a lot of innuendo wrapped around some interesting facts and figures. The bottom line is it makes Folsom look like the asshole he is." Edward laughed. "He's got to be fuming."

# CHAPTER SEVENTY-THREE

Folsom hadn't been able to sleep most of the night. He'd finally dropped off at 5 a.m. and woke at 10:30 a.m. when he heard the cleaning lady moving around.

"Sonofabitch!" he groaned as he sat on the side of his bed and used his hands to brush his hair off his forehead. He showered and shaved and then went downstairs, where he knew Esmeralda would have coffee and the morning paper waiting for him.

"Good morning, Meester Fullsome," Esmeralda greeted him.

"*Fullsome*, my ass," he muttered under his breath.

"You want *café*?" she asked.

"Yes, Esmeralda."

"The paper ees on the table."

Folsom moved to the kitchen table and sat down, slipping the rubber band off the paper and spreading it out in front of him as Esmeralda placed a cup to the side of the newspaper. He lifted the cup, but stopped halfway to his mouth as his gaze froze on the headline: BROAD STREET NATIONAL BANK AND THE FDIC. Under the banner headline, in smaller print, was: COMPLAINTS AND CHARGES OF CORRUPTION.

If that headline wasn't enough to ruin his day, the first paragraph of the article guaranteed it:

*From a complex collection of information gathered by this newspaper, including statements provided by the former president of Broad Street National Bank and documents submitted by the Federal Deposit Insurance Corporation, it has become apparent that activities of Broad Street National Bank's new owner, Folsom Financial Corporation, are destroying perfectly viable businesses in the Philadelphia area. Additionally, it appears the bank's actions are personally benefitting Folsom Financial Corporation's owner, Gerald Folsom, at the expense of the bank's customers.*

Folsom threw the cup at the wall, shattering it and splashing coffee on the wall paper and the floor.

Esmeralda screamed.

"Bastards!" Folsom shouted, "Goddam bastards!"

He stood and stormed around the kitchen. "Clean this shit up," he yelled at Esmeralda.

Esmeralda snatched her purse from the kitchen counter and marched out of the room toward the front door without a backwards look, cursing under her breath, *"Pendejo! Hijo de puta!"*

Folsom momentarily froze, surprised at his maid's sudden backbone. He watched her leave and then cursed her and all women. He then ran to the telephone and called Jeffrey Rose.

"Have you seen the newspaper?" Folsom shouted into the

receiver.

"Sure," Rose answered.

Folsom thought his lawyer sounded shockingly calm.

"We'd better meet. A lot of damage control needs to be done. You need to hire a public relations expert, Jerry; this is a mess. Can you be at my office by noon?"

Folsom agreed and hung up. He didn't know what to do with himself and this vulnerable feeling. Things had started to unravel after he took over Broad Street National Bank and the bank calling the Winter Enterprises loan.

"Those fucking Winters!"

The telephone rang.

"What!"

"Jerry, it's Sandy. We've got a problem down here. The newspaper story this morning has caused a run on the bank and we've got depositors lined up around the block wanting to close their accounts. Also, I got a call a couple minutes ago from a Henry Rentz at the FDIC in D.C. He'll be here this afternoon at 3 and he wants you here."

"Fuck him!" Folsom screamed. "No two-bit government bureaucrat is going to give me orders."

"This isn't a two-bit bureaucrat, Jerry. This guy is one of the top people at the agency. You don't want to screw with him."

"Whose side are you on, Sandy?"

"That's twice you've questioned my loyalty in the past few days. I know you're under a lot of pressure. But, if you question my commitment again, I'll walk and you can deal with the bank and regulators by yourself."

Folsom was just about to tell Cunningham to take a walk, and what he could do during that walk, but stopped himself at the last instant.

"I apologize, Sandy. I'll see you at 3. In the meantime, make sure there's enough cash in the vault to give the depositors their money. But close the doors at 3 sharp. This should blow over during the weekend."

"I don't know, Jerry. The newspaper's going to run two more articles over the next two days. We might be inundated on Monday morning with more people wanting to take out their money."

"We'll talk about that after the FDIC guy leaves."

"By the way, Edward Winter called. He's agreed to take your offer and will sign over all of his rights in return for you keeping the business open. And he's agreed to have Winter Enterprises continue to manage the restaurants. We'll have to agree to compensation, so let me know what you have in mind."

"Let's discuss that later, too."

Folsom replaced the receiver and commended himself on his restraint on not telling Cunningham to go screw himself. Cunningham would be the perfect fall guy. All of his orders about bank customers had been made through Cunningham, and they had all been delivered to Cunningham verbally. Nothing was in writing. He could claim Cunningham let the power of his position go to his head. That he was operating independently and not keeping Folsom informed of his actions.

# CHAPTER SEVENTY-FOUR

"Eddie, it's Carrie."

"Hey, Sis. Everything all right?"

"Yeah, fine. Betsy doing okay?"

"Great. They're keeping her in the hospital for another night. She'll be home tomorrow."

"I'll stop by and see her today," Carrie said. "The reason I called is to tell you we're moving out of the hotel tomorrow morning. Wendy's going down to the Cape. She'll stay there until things settle down."

"Tell her to stay off the phone."

Carrie laughed. "I think she's learned that lesson. *You* okay?"

"I'm pissed and I'm frustrated, but I'm okay. I remember Dad telling me life isn't fair, but I never believed it could be this unfair. Maybe someone will pay Folsom back one day, but I'm not optimistic. Guys like Folsom always seem to come out smelling like roses."

"Don't be too sure about that, brother. Between Wendy's complaint against him and the newspaper articles, maybe things are starting to fall apart for him.

"One other thing, those two men who helped me at Pastorius Park are going to watch the hotel tonight."

"You expecting trouble?"

"Just being cautious. I'm certain Folsom was behind the last attempt on Wendy's life. With all the pressure on him, he could go off the deep end."


Katherine sat in a chair next to Betsy's hospital bed while Betsy nursed the baby.

"He's going to grow fast if he keeps eating like that," Katherine said, marveling at the hungry baby.

"He's just like his father, passionate about everything, even his food."

Katherine laughed. "Eddie has always been able to eat anything and everything and has never had a weight problem. Lucky. I gain weight if I even look at food."

The two women sat quietly for a while, and then Betsy said, "I've only known Eddie for a little less than three years. Can you tell me how losing his company will affect him?"

Katherine thought about the question. "Both of my children are tough and resilient. They're survivors. The loss of the restaurants will be difficult for Eddie to take, but not difficult for him to live with. He'll recover emotionally and financially. That's not what I'm worried about. Eddie and Carrie have an almost unnatural sense of right and wrong. When they see someone being wronged, they want to make things right. To nurture the wronged party and to punish the abuser. Gerald Folsom has done so much wrong in his life—a lot to this family. I just hope they don't try to make him pay."

"Well," Betsy said, "someone has to make that man pay for the wrongs he has done."

"That's what the law's for, Betsy."

"The law has done nothing to stop Folsom."

# CHAPTER SEVENTY-FIVE

"Jeffrey, this article in *The Philadelphia Journal* is a disaster," Folsom complained to his attorney. "It's caused a run on the bank. I'm portrayed as a monster."

Jeffrey Rose rested his elbow on the arm of his desk chair and spread his hand over his mouth and chin. "I won't lie to you, Jerry; this *is* a mess. I've seen things like this happen before. One problem piles onto another and pretty soon the client collapses under the weight of it all. We need to remove some of that weight."

"Like how?"

"Like settling with your wife, getting her to drop the complaint against you. Like telling your damn bank officers to stop forcing customers to go out of business, rather than renewing good borrowers' loans. This is a PR nightmare."

Folsom nodded his head, as though he agreed with Rose. "Some bigwig at the FDIC is coming into the bank today for a meeting at 3. Maybe you should be there."

"No shit, Jerry. You think I ought to represent you when you meet with a bureaucrat from a government agency that could not only put you out of business but throw your ass in jail? Jesus, what are you thinking?"

"I just found out a little while ago."

Rose's jaws clenched. "I haven't heard anything from the police or the D.A. about those valises of cash they took out of your home. Or about those cards that were in with the money. Is there anything there I should be concerned about?"

"I can't imagine what. Of course, I don't know what was written on the cards."

"What the hell could be written on anything that would implicate you in a crime?"

"Nothing, Jeffrey. I swear."

"Okay. What's the FDIC guy want?"

"I assume he's reacting to that damn newspaper article. By making me look bad, the newspaper has damaged the FDIC's reputation. After all, it was the FDIC that brought me in to buy the bank."

"What are we going to tell the guy at 3?"

"If what the paper wrote is true about the way borrowers are being treated at the bank, then my right-hand man has abused his position. He's taken too much authority on himself and has made decisions without clearing them through me. I think I should fire Sanford Cunningham on the spot at that meeting and promise to clean things up."

"That's good," Rose said. "We can issue a press release—no, better yet, you're going to hold a press conference at 5 this evening. It'll make the 6 o'clock news. You'll announce Cunningham's firing.

And you'll say you're going to investigate everything he has done and make restitution to all customers who have been mistreated."

"Is that necessary? Can't we—"

Rose interrupted Folsom. "Are you kidding me? Your fucking livelihood, your future are on the line here, and you want to quibble about spending money to save your ass. Besides, you're saying that you're going to make restitution; you don't have to actually do it. After a few weeks, the heat will be off."

"I like that, Jeffrey."

"So Cunningham is the one who has been making the decisions at the bank?"

"That's right."

"Then fire his ass this afternoon and announce it to the world at 5."

"The paper quoted a Stanley Burns, who was appointed president of the bank after you took over. What's his story?"

"He was senior lending officer. He was promoted based on Cunningham's recommendation. I've never really had any contact with the guy. He reported to Cunningham."

"Good."

"Anything else?"

"I'm still worried about the cash and cards the police took from your place," Rose said. "But we'll have to deal with that when we find out what's on them. And between now and 3, try to contact your wife and offer to pay her whatever she wants to withdraw her complaint."

"Will do, Jeffrey," Folsom lied, knowing he wouldn't have to pay that bitch a dime, not even the $5 million he'd written into their pre-nup agreement. She would be dead tonight, along with Carrie

Winter, and anyone else with them.

# CHAPTER SEVENTY-SIX

Jeffrey Rose had a bad feeling about his client. He knew when he was being lied to because he had a lot of experience dealing with sociopaths and psychopaths. He wasn't certain about what part of Folsom's story had been true and what had been false, but he knew it wasn't all true.

He didn't like paying for information. It wasn't the cost—his clients ultimately paid. Rather, he didn't like the risk and the implied favor he would now owe someone. But he found the number he was looking for in his electronic Rolodex and dialed it anyway.

"Sergeant Rhoades."

"Hey, Gil. How ya doin?"

There was a brief silence on the other end of the line until the man apparently finally recognized Rose's voice.

"Hey. It's been a while."

"Yeah, Gil. I need your help."

"Depends on what it is."

"Always does, my friend. The department served a search warrant on the home of Gerald Folsom yesterday. All the detectives took out of the house were two cases of cash and a few note cards."

"Gerald Folsom?"

"Yeah. Assault and battery charge."

"There's a real buzz going on around here about that search warrant. But it's not about the assault and battery charge. In fact, I heard the cash and cards have been passed on to the White Collar Crimes Division. I also heard the Feds have been brought in."

"You still in charge of the evidence room?"

"Yep."

"I need to know what's written on the cards that are in those cases."

"Word gets out I released that information, my job and pension will be down the drain. No thanks; you're asking too much this time."

"Twenty grand, Gil."

"Holy shit! Fine, I'll call you back."


"Kelly, your article made quite a splash."

"Hey, Paul, good to hear from you. I've been meaning to call; I haven't thanked you and Edward Winter yet for bringing this to my attention."

"At least you listened, Kelly."

"I think you'll like the next two articles. Today's article mentioned that Folsom and Matson worked together on a lot of deals and that Broad Street National Bank is putting a lot of pressure on some of its customers, forcing them out of business to foreclose on them. In tomorrow's story, we're going to give dates of each deal Folsom did with the FDIC and how much he paid. Thanks to the information you got from Gail Moskowitz, we can show a lot of detail, including how the prices Folsom paid were better than the prices paid by any other investor made with the FDIC."

"I heard a rumor you might find interesting," Paul said. "I hear the PPD executed a search warrant on Folsom's house and now has certain information in its possession."

"And why would I be interested in that?"

"Because written on cards taken from Folsom's home are dollar amounts and dates coinciding with the dates of the transactions Folsom did with the Feds."

"What would these amounts and dates tell me?" Loughridge asked.

"That Donald Matson received large amounts of cash on the same dates Folsom closed deals with the FDIC."

"Are you telling me Folsom bribed Matson?"

"Now, now, Kelly, don't you think you should do a little leg work of your own? The next thing you'll want me to do is write your articles."

# CHAPTER SEVENTY-SEVEN

The instant all of the attendees were in their seats, Henry Rentz took charge of the 3 p.m. meeting at Broad Street National Bank. Seated at the head of the table, Rentz was professorial-looking in his brown horn-rimmed glasses, thick snow-white hair, bow tie, white shirt, and brown suit. He pointed at the stenographer and said, "I am Henry Rentz, Regional Superintendant of the Federal Deposit Insurance Corporation for the Mid-Atlantic Region. I am advising everyone in this room that we are now on the record and everything in this meeting is being recorded. I would appreciate it if each of you would introduce yourself, stating your position and affiliation. Let's start with Ms. Moskowitz at my left."

"Gail Moskowitz, Staff Attorney with the FDIC at the Washington, D.C. headquarters."

"Bruce Couples, Area Supervisor for the Office of the Comptroller of the Currency." Couples sat in the middle of one side of the table, between Moskowitz and Sanford Cunningham.

A fifty-something, rotund little man with a walrus mustache and wire-rimmed glasses, Couples wore a perpetual frown and seemed humorless. His suit was gray; his tie striped red and blue.

"Sanford Cunningham, Folsom Financial Corporation's Chief Financial Officer and representative at Broad Street National Bank."

"Gerald Folsom, President of Folsom Financial Corporation, which owns Broad Street National Bank." Folsom sat on the other side of the table, across from Bruce Couples, to the right of Jeffrey Rose.

"Jeffrey Rose, attorney for Mr. Folsom." As usual, he wore his blue suit, blue and yellow striped tie, and black Ferragamo tasseled loafers. With his year-round tan, he looked healthier than the others in the room.

"All right, ladies and gentlemen," Rentz said, "let's get started. I assume you've all read today's *Philadelphia Journal* article about Broad Street National Bank." He looked around the room and noted that each person nodded or murmured that they had read the article.

"We have a public relations problem here that can go well beyond just Broad Street National-specific issues. The newspaper is claiming Broad Street National Bank has aggressively damaged some of its customers by refusing to renew perfectly good loans, and then foreclosing or threatening to foreclose on the collateral behind these loans. Perhaps this is stating the obvious, but when an investor takes over a bank from the FDIC, it does so at a discounted price. In other words, Mr. Folsom here was able to buy Broad Street National Bank at a significant discount to the bank's book value. The FDIC allows this to happen because we recognize the investor assumes a risk in taking over a troubled financial institution.

Everybody with me so far?"

Again he waited for some sort of response from the people in the room. Then he continued.

"In fact, we construct a lot of these bank transactions under a loss-share arrangement, whereby the FDIC, in effect, indemnifies the investor from a substantial part of any loss that might occur. But it should be immediately apparent to all of you that there is room for significant abuse in this type of situation.

"For instance," he picked up a file and raised it, "let's take the bank's loan to Winter Enterprises." He now looked directly at Gerald Folsom. "You familiar with Winter Enterprises?"

"The name's familiar, but I can't say I really know anything about it," Folsom said.

Rentz caught the surprised look on Cunningham's face, but didn't acknowledge it.

"Well, since you're not familiar with the details of the Winter Enterprises loan, how about if I bring you up to date?"

Folsom shrugged, seemingly indifferent.

"Winter Enterprises owes the bank $20 million, secured with real estate originally appraised at $67 million, and recently appraised at $50 million. The loan is also collateralized by the company's franchise agreement. The original loan to value was even lower than the current LTV of forty percent. The company is amazingly profitable and is growing at a time when the economy is contracting.

"What do you think, Mr. Folsom, is this a loan you would like to keep on the bank's books?"

"Sounds like it," Folsom said. "I guess I'd want to know what other business the customer would bring to the bank, like deposits and credit card transactions."

"So, $2 to $3 million in average collected balances in the bank and $20 plus million in credit card transactions annually would get your attention?"

"Absolutely."

"Then explain, Mr. Folsom, why your bank is unwilling to renew Winter Enterprises' loan? Every number I just gave you describes your bank's relationship with this borrower. I thought you said this is the sort of relationship Broad Street National Bank would like to have."

"I have no idea, Mr. Rentz. It seems to me we should be doing business with this company."

"Who would know the answer to my question?" Rentz asked.

Folsom looked across the table at Cunningham. He had thought about taking Jeffrey Rose's advice about firing Cunningham before this meeting, but decided terminating Cunningham in front of all these people would be much more fun. He'd make the bastard pay for raising his voice at him during their last telephone conversation. "Sandy, you handle the day-to-day dealings of the bank; perhaps you should answer Mr. Rentz's question."

Rentz, along with everyone else in the room, looked at Cunningham, who appeared to be confused. Cunningham's face had turned crimson-red and his eyes were boring into Folsom like laser beams.

"I am quite familiar with the Winter Enterprises relationship," Cunningham said finally. "Before Folsom Financial took over Broad Street National, the bank had already made the decision to not renew their loan because of the bank's commercial real estate exposure. The Office of the Comptroller of the Currency criticized Broad Street's previous ownership and management for its high concentration of commercial real estate loans. When we took over the bank, we merely tried to comply with the OCC's direction."

Cunningham glared next at Bruce Couples, the OCC man. "Your agency forced the previous owners of Broad Street National Bank to write down its commercial real estate loans to levels deeply discounted from real market values. I was shocked at the write downs. Candidly, that's the main reason I recommended to Mr. Folsom that he invest in the bank. The deep discounts created a very profitable opportunity for us."

Cunningham then turned to look at Rentz. "What do you think would have happened if we started making real estate loans after the OCC and the FDIC criticized the former owners for doing the same thing?"

"But, Mr. Cunningham, the OCC never told the previous bank owners or Folsom Financial Corporation to not extend credit to Winter Enterprises, did they?"

"No, not that I'm aware of."

"I can understand why the previous owners would have decided to eliminate as much of their commercial real estate debt as possible. They were trying to survive. They needed to raise capital to prevent the FDIC from taking over the bank. But what's your excuse? You don't have that sort of pressure on you. Why would you destroy a sound, profitable business?"

Cunningham's face flushed red again. He looked at Folsom, as though searching for a life line, but none was forthcoming. He muttered something under his breath and then looked back at Rentz.

"Because, Mr. Rentz, Gerald Folsom told me to take down Edward Winter and his company."

Jeffrey Rose jerked forward in his chair and shouted, "That's preposterous. Mr. Cunningham is trying to place blame on my client, who has had nothing to do with the daily workings of the bank. He trusted Mr. Cunningham to manage the bank's affairs in a legal and ethical, but profitable manner. Obviously, he has failed to do so."

"Calm down, Mr. Rose," Rentz said.

"Just a minute, Mr. Rentz," Rose said. "I have a question to ask Mr. Cunningham." Without waiting for approval from Rentz, Rose pointed at Cunningham and said, "Do you have anything in writing—a memorandum, a letter, an email—from Mr. Folsom directing you to do anything untoward, including *taking down Edward Winter*?"

Cunningham's tough demeanor had dissolved. "Mr. Folsom always gave me direction by telephone or in face-to-face meetings."

"How convenient!" Rose said, leaning back in his chair.

Rentz looked at Folsom. "So you have had nothing to do with the day-to-day bank operations and you never told anyone to *take down* Winter Enterprises."

"I resent you asking that question," Rose interjected.

Rentz ignored Rose and said to Folsom, "Answer the question."

"Of course not."

"What was your relationship with Donald Matson?"

"Mr. Matson and I had a professional relationship. We worked effectively in saving failing banks, and he managed several loan pool transactions I purchased from the FDIC."

"Uh huh," Rentz said. "Did you ever give Mr. Matson gifts?"

Folsom half-rose from his chair. "That's insulting; that would have been illegal."

"You're right about that, Mr. Folsom. So, please explain these."

Rentz opened a file in front of him and extracted several sheets of paper. He passed copies to Folsom and Rose.

"Those are copies of note cards found in two valises holding $2.055 million in cash. Those valises were removed from your home, Mr. Folsom, by the Philadelphia Police Department. We've verified the signatures on two of the cards as being Donald Matson's. Would you explain why Mr. Matson would have entrusted that amount of cash to you? And maybe you can tell us where he got that much money."

"Oh come on, Rentz," Rose said, after cursing in his mind his cop friend in the PPD's Evidence Room for not getting back to him before this meeting. "This is ridiculous. I could give you a half-dozen explanations."

Rentz looked at Rose as though he were staring at a cow paddy. "I'm sure you could, Mr. Rose, but I'm interested in the truth." He looked back at Folsom and said, "Do you know what the annotations on the third card represent?"

"Not a clue," Folsom said, showing an innocent, toothy smile.

"Dates," Rentz continued, "identical to the dates of every transaction you closed with the FDIC and which Donald Matson managed. In case you haven't had the time to add up the numbers next to those dates that cover a twenty-two year period, the total comes to $2.5 million. That's a lot of money. I wonder how Matson accumulated that kind of nest egg."

"I'm sure I don't have any idea," Folsom said, looking bored.

Rentz looked back at Rose. The lawyer looked as though he was about to grab his client and bolt out of the room. Rentz realized he needed to bring the meeting to a climax before Rose did just that.

"Mr. Folsom, are you surprised that Mr. Couples with the OCC is here?"

"What's one more government bureaucrat?" Folsom said.

"Well, let me tell you. Ms. Moskowitz called Mr. Couples and asked him to give her the names of the heads of the examination teams that examined each bank you and your company have purchased from the FDIC. We were very surprised to learn that the same crew chief was in charge of every bank examination. In other words, Abigail Makris headed up the crew that performed the examinations on banks that were shortly thereafter declared under-capitalized and were taken over by the FDIC. In each of those bank takeovers, the former owners filed formal complaints with the OCC, claiming the examinations had been improper and had come to inaccurate conclusions. Needless to say, the complaints were essentially ignored and the examinations formed the basis for the government's takeover of those banks."

"I hope you have a point here, Mr. Rentz," Rose said.

Rentz couldn't help himself. He allowed a small smile to cross his face. "What do you think Ms. Makris told Mr. Couples when he confronted her with the amazing coincidences he had discovered?"

Folsom's face suddenly went pale.

"No idea, Mr. Folsom? Ms. Makris was relieved to finally disclose what she had done and how she had violated her principles and her oath to the agency. All for money, Mr. Folsom. $300,000. Cheap at ten times the price, wouldn't you say?"

"We're out of here," Rose growled, shoving his chair back against the wall and standing up.

Rentz watched the lawyer move toward the door. Folsom followed Rose. Rentz waited until Rose's hand was on the door knob and then said, "Don't you want to hear what comes next?"

"We've already heard enough," Rose said.

"It's your client's money."

Folsom whipped around and glared at Rentz.

"Here's what's going to happen, Mr. Folsom. The FDIC is going to rescind your purchase of Broad Street National Bank. It's going to manage the bank until Mr. Couples can complete an investigation into what role his examination crew chief played. If we find that the examination crew chief forced the demise of Broad Street National Bank, then we will make restitution to the former owners."

Rentz shook his head. "I can't even imagine what we'll do with the other banks you bought from the FDIC, but in any case, we're going to hold in escrow the investment you made in Broad Street National Bank and use it to pay claims that will surely arise once all of this gets out."

"You can't do that," Folsom shouted. "I put $500 million in this bank."

"Oh, but I can. You know what else I can do? What I've already done? I've put a hold on $150 million in cash and securities you have deposited in various other banks, to be used to reimburse the Broad Street National Bank clients you have damaged."

"I'll sue your ass for breach of contract and—"

"Please do, Mr. Folsom," Rentz said cheerfully. "I can't wait to meet you in court."

Folsom pushed Rose out of the way and barged out of the room.

Rentz waited until Rose had left as well and then turned to Cunningham, who had his elbows on the table, his head in his hands.

"I don't know whether you did anything illegal, Mr. Cunningham, but I am convinced you acted unethically. Here's the deal I'm going to offer you. I think you can shine a lot of light on Folsom's operations. You cooperate with us and I'll protect you as much as possible. I want you to continue to work here at the bank to remediate the problems you created for bank borrowers. I'm going to ask Sol Levin to come back to the bank and resume his role as president. You will report to him if he accepts. What's your answer?"

"Thank you, sir, yes. I'll do everything I can."

"Good."

"Ms. Moskowitz, I want you to work out of our Philadelphia office and collaborate with Mr. Couples until his investigation is completed. I'm going back to D.C. to make the director aware of what's been going on." That ought to be fun, he thought.

"What about Folsom?" Moskowitz asked. "You're not going to just let him walk away?"

"As soon as you and Bruce here are finished with your investigation, I'm going to turn over everything to the U.S. Attorney in Philadelphia. I don't think Folsom will be walking much of anywhere, except maybe in a prison exercise yard."

Rentz got up to leave.

Cunningham stood with him. "Can I make a suggestion, Mr. Rentz?"

"That's part of your job, Mr. Cunningham."

"I'd like to call each of the customers whose loans Folsom ordered not to be renewed and let them know we've rescinded that decision."

"Excellent idea," Rentz said.

# CHAPTER SEVENTY-EIGHT

The telephone rang on Edward's desk. The screen on the console displayed that the call was from Broad Street National Bank's main telephone number. Edward looked across his desk at Nick and Paul, his stomach tensing.. They were preparing an agenda for the Saturday morning meeting with their restaurant managers.

"It's the bank. They're probably calling about executing the documents turning the business over to Folsom."

Edward paused, then punched the speaker button with more force than necessary. "Winter," he barked.

"Mr. Winter, it's Sanford Cunningham. I—"

"Where do you want me to sign the papers, Mr. Cunningham? I'd like to get it over with."

"Actually, that's not why I'm calling. We've had a big turn of events here at the bank. Mr. Folsom is no longer associated with Broad Street National Bank and I have been authorized by the FDIC to inform you that the bank will be renewing your loan according to the terms of your original note. And the hold on your deposit accounts will be removed."

"This isn't a joke?" Edward asked, suspicious about the sudden change.

"No, sir. Uh, I want to apologize to you for the way you have been treated. I don't expect you to forgive me, but I promise I will do all I can to make amends."

Edward's eyes were saucers when he looked at Nick and Paul. "I think you've gone a long way toward making amends, Mr. Cunningham. What happened to Folsom?"

"He's in big trouble. The Feds are going after him for bribing government officials, among other things."

A sudden picture of his father flashed in Edward's brain. It's payback time, he thought.

"I'll have a letter in the mail Monday morning confirming the loan renewal," Cunningham said. "Please call me if you have any questions or need anything."

"Thank you," Edward said.

After the call, Edward spread his arms in disbelief. "What the hell just happened?"

"I'm not sure," Paul answered, "but I sure am going to find out. And if that bank thinks they're going to get off by just renewing your loan, they're nuts. They're going to pay a big price for what they put you through."

"Let's put off thoughts of legal action for a while," Edward suggested. "Until we figure out what's going on at the bank."

Nick laughed. "Does this mean I don't get to work for Folsom?"

Edward and Paul laughed with Nick. "Are you complaining?" Paul asked between chuckles.

"Well, I *was* going to be president of Winter Enterprises," Nick said, still laughing.

"You're still going to be president," Edward said. "You've earned it. I'll continue to be chairman of the board, but you're going to run the company's day-to-day operations. I think the plan to expand to New York is still a good one. I'll assist you in getting things started there."

"Jeez, Eddie, this is sure a day of surprises," Nick said, smiling.

"I assume you're accepting the promotion?" Edward said.

"Yes, yes, yes. Thank you. I'm thrilled."

"Let's finish up here. Nick, you're going to run the meeting tomorrow. I'm going to sleep in, pick up Betsy from the hospital, and spend the day with her and our son. Paul, have you drawn up Nick's employment agreement?"

"I'll have it done next week," Paul said. "But we should celebrate tonight."

Edward noticed Nick's smile fall from his face. "What's wrong?"

"I promised Annie and the kids we'd go out to dinner tonight."

"Then that's what you're going to do. Paul and I will join Katherine, Carrie, and Wendy at the hotel. Paul, does that sound okay to you?"

"You bet!"

The three of them worked for another hour. Edward told Paul he'd meet him at the Marriott at 9; he wanted to visit Betsy and the baby at the hospital before going to the hotel. Then he walked out of the building with Nick; their cars were parked next to one another's in the lot.

"Say hello to Annie," Edward said. "Oh, and tell her your new position includes a fifty percent pay raise and stock options for another five percent of the company. And, one other thing, Nick. Take that Hawaiian vacation before you take over as president of the company."

Edward got into his car before Nick responded. He felt as relieved and relaxed as he had in a long time. He dialed the number for Betsy's hospital room and gave his wife the good news.

"I told you everything was going to be all right, didn't I?"

"You sure did, Honey. But, candidly, I thought you were nuts."

"You'd better start listening to me, Eddie. Mothers always know best."

# CHAPTER SEVENTY-NINE

Folsom was so bitterly angry, he felt nauseous. Everything he had worked for was going down the drain. This morning, he was just a few million dollars short of being a billionaire; now that dream was shot.

"Shit! Shit! Shit!" he screamed, his words bouncing off the walls of his vault. "I should have killed that OCC bitch, Abigail Makris, too. She took my money and now she's got a guilty conscience. What a fuckin' hypocrite!"

Folsom placed a canvas gym bag on a table and unzipped it. He yanked one of the drawers out of the cabinet and poured the gem stones from the drawer into the bag. Then he did the same with the drawers holding the gold coins. He ignored the drawers with the silver coins; there were some valuable pieces in those drawers, but the total value of the silver was maybe $150,000 and not enough to justify carrying the additional weight. The fire sale value of the jewels and the gold coins was probably $3 million.

He moved to the opposite wall and pulled on the left side of the gun rack, swinging the rack away from the wall and exposing a built-in safe. Thank God the cops hadn't found it during their search. Dialing in the safe's combination, he cranked the handle and opened it. There were five things there he would need: An unregistered .45 caliber pistol, with two extra magazines; a U.S. passport in his own name and a Panamanian passport issued to a George Domenico that had cost him $10,000 paid to a politician in Panama; ID and credit cards in Domenico's name; $200,000 in cash; and $50 million in Swiss government bearer bonds.

Folsom stuck the pistol and the false ID in pockets of his casual zippered jacket. The rest of the items from the safe went into the canvas bag. With the bag packed to the brim, he zipped it, closed the safe, and secured the gun rack. After closing the vault door, he walked downstairs to his bedroom and picked up the black leather suitcase he'd packed earlier with a couple changes of clothes before loading the bags in his trunk and driving away.

After clearing the front gate, he called his pilot and told him to have the Gulfstream V ready to go at 1 a.m. Then he drove twenty minutes to the Northwest Marriott Hotel. He carried both bags into the hotel at 7:30 p.m. and used the Domenico credit card and ID to check in. He asked for a room on the tenth floor and was assigned to 1027.

Edward finally left the hospital at 8:45 p.m. when the maternity nurse chased him out. He called Carrie's cell to let her know he was on his way.

"It's getting awfully late," Carrie told him. "Mom looks like she's about to crash."

"Don't let her go to bed. I've got some news I want to tell her."

"I hope it's good news. She's so stressed out she's only been getting four or five hours sleep a night. Or less."

Edward chuckled. "I think you'll all like it."

"What is it, Eddie? What's going on?"

"You'll find out in a few minutes. Be patient."

"You're a bastard, you know it?"

"I love you, too."

Edward hung up and felt a chill go down his spine. He couldn't wait to see his mother's face when he told her the good news. He probably should have called her but the news was so important he wanted to share his happiness with her. Especially considering the Winter family's history with Gerald Folsom. He felt like a parent on Christmas Eve, setting up for his family's joy.

At 9, he parked outside the hotel, went inside, and took the elevator to the tenth floor. Carrie let him into the suite where his mother and Wendy were seated on the living room couch in muted light.

"Do you mind if I turn up the lights?" Edward asked. "I want to see your faces when I give you my news."

"This better be good," Katherine said, smiling. "I can barely keep my eyes open."

Edward turned up the lights and looked at Katherine. "I got a call from the bank. They're renewing our loan. Everything's going to be okay."

Katherine propelled herself off the couch and ran to Edward. She hugged him and cried out, "Thank you, Lord. Oh thank you, thank you, thank you." She then went to Carrie and hugged her too.

"Did Gerald finally do the right thing?" Wendy asked, looking incredulous.

"No, Wendy," Edward said. "The FDIC apparently forced the bank to make this move. I don't know anything else, but I do know Folsom's going down for breaking the law and bribing government officials. They took Broad Street National Bank back from him and he could go to prison for a very long time."

Wendy laughed, and then her laughter became almost hysterical before dissolving into tears. "Perfect," she said. "It's absolutely perfect."

A knock on the door quieted the group.

"That's probably Paul," Edward said.

Katherine went to the door and opened it. She threw herself against Paul and shouted, "Isn't the news wonderful?"

"Not as wonderful as my reception," he said.

Edward's and Carrie's eyes met and they smiled at one another.

Katherine backed away from Paul, turning red. He raised a bottle in the air and announced, "I have here a vintage bottle of Dom Perrignon I've been saving for an important occasion. I think this qualifies."

Wendy went to the kitchen and found wine glasses. She placed them on the coffee table while Paul popped the cork on the champagne. When the glasses were filled, Edward raised his and toasted, "To a bright future for all of us."

They each sipped their champagne. Then Wendy said, "And good riddance to Gerald Folsom. I hope none of us ever see his face again."

"Here, here," Katherine said.

Carrie's cell phone rang.

"Hello?" she said.

"It's Darren. Just wanted to let you know we're here. Mike's in his car watching the back; I've got the front."

# CHAPTER EIGHTY

Folsom checked his watch. It was 9:50 p.m.

He took the .45 caliber pistol from his jacket and switched off the safety. He figured it would take him no more than two minutes to go down the emergency exit stairs to the first floor, so he'd leave the room at 9:58 to meet Toothpick Jefferson. He'd scoped out the floor layout earlier. The staircase to the east emergency exit door was to the right when he exited his room, past Room 1045, after a slight curve in the hallway.

He shoved the pistol into the back of his waistband and pulled his jacket down to cover it, putting on a baseball cap to hide his face. At 9:58, after downing a scotch—his third since checking in—straight from a miniature from the minibar, he left the room. When he reconnoitered the hallway earlier, he'd discovered security cameras in three locations on the floor: one each by the emergency doors at opposite ends of the hallway, and one by the elevator. Because of the curve in the hallway, the only camera that had line of sight to his room and Room 1045 was the one at the east end of the corridor, by the exit he would take to meet Jefferson. He lowered his head, gazing down at the carpet, pulled a wad of chewing gum from his mouth and tore off a piece. He pressed the gum on the camera lens at the east exit before entering the stairwell there and walking down ten floors. At the bottom of the staircase, he opened the emergency exit door and felt a wave of humid air rush over him. Crossing the lawn toward him from the parking lot to the building was Toothpick Jefferson, followed by two men. Folsom could hear Jefferson's labored breathing already. A fleeting thought crossed Folsom's mind: How the hell is the fat slob going to climb up ten stories? And then have the energy to fuck the blonde bitch?

Edward and Paul had finished their champagne and were saying their goodbyes when Carrie's cell phone rang again.

"Yeah," Carrie said.

"You got company," Darren said. "They just entered the east emergency staircase."

"Who are they?"

"Three black guys. Another guy let them in."

"How do you know they're here for us?" Carrie asked.

"The fat guy from the park is with them."

"Aw, Jesus. We're in Room 1045. I'm going to get everyone out of here. Can you follow them up the staircase?"

"Probably not. The door's more than likely locked from the inside."

"Hold on," she told him.

"Everybody listen," Carrie called out with authority. The room went silent. "We've got bad guys coming up the emergency stairwell just down the hall to the right of our room. Let's get out in the hall. NOW!"

Edward led them out of the room and into the hall as Carrie spoke again into her cell phone.

"Darren, go to the west side of the building. We'll come down the staircase there and meet you.

"Go," Carrie told Edward. "I've got to get something from the room. Go left down the hall. Take everyone down the staircase there."

Edward started to move back to the room, but Carrie shouted at him, "I'll be right along. My two friends from the park will be waiting outside the door at the bottom. Take care of Mom."

They ran to the end of the hall and Edward pounded the locking bar on the emergency exit door, throwing it open, crashing it into the wall. He held the door open as Wendy, then Katherine and Paul ran into the stairwell and began descending the stairs as fast as they could. Edward looked back down the hallway, but Carrie wasn't in sight. He looked over the railing and saw the others were already two floors down.

"Keep going," he shouted. "There are two of Carrie's friends waiting for you at the bottom."

Edward watched the others for a second and then turned around and ran back down the corridor toward Carrie. He was back in Room 1045 within a few moments and found the door open, the suite empty. He stepped back into the corridor and looked left and right.

"Dammit, Carrie. Where are you?"

Suddenly, someone grabbed the neck of his jacket and yanked him backwards.

"What the—"

"Keep quiet," Carrie whispered as she closed the door to the linen storage room across from 1045.

"Why the hell didn't you come with the rest of us?" he demanded.

"Because I'm tired of reacting to Folsom. It's time I took charge."

"How do you know these guys are connected to Folsom?"

"I don't, but who the hell else would be behind this?"

She removed a .9 mm automatic pistol from a satchel and handed it to him. "It's loaded and the safety's on. Here's another magazine."

Edward's eyebrows went up, but he accepted the weapon and pocketed the magazine without a word. Carrie smiled at him when he ejected the magazine, checked the load, and racked the magazine back into the pistol.

By the time they reached the seventh floor landing, Toothpick Jefferson was breathing like a rutting rhinoceros and sweating buckets.

Folsom looked back at Jefferson and thought the man might croak on the spot. All four men were now taking baby steps in their climb to the tenth floor since he had to pause every third or fourth step.

"Listen, Toothpick, why don't you stay here and cover our backs? I'll take your men with me."

"No way. I got plans for that blonde up there. I ain't missin' out on that."

Folsom figured that whatever Jefferson's plans for Carrie Winter were, the man wouldn't have the energy to perform, but he kept his thoughts to himself.

They trudged up the last three flights and waited on the landing on the tenth floor while Jefferson caught his breath and wiped his face with an already soaked handkerchief.

"Okay, I'm ready," Jefferson gasped.

"Follow me," Folsom said. "The room's on the left, four doors down." He looked at the larger of Jefferson's two men and said, "You kick in the door. We'll follow you."

The big man grunted in affirmation.

"It's a suite, so there are probably bedrooms left and right of the entry." He pointed at the big guy. "You go left." He told the other man to go right. "There are three women staying in the room."

"Don't . . . get . . . trigger . . . happy," Jefferson wheezed. "We gonna . . . have . . . some . . . fun . . . first."

"Okay, Boss," the big man said.

"Ready?" Folsom asked. He checked to make sure the other three men had their pistols out.

The others nodded.

Folsom cracked open the door and stared down the hall's length; no one was there. He pushed the door all the way open and quickly marched toward the suite.

"Hold it," he whispered to the big man, placing a hand on his chest. "The door's open."

"What's happening here, Jerry?" Jefferson demanded. "Is this another one of your clusterfucks?"

"Shh," Folsom said as he peeked into the room. The suite was dark, the drapes closed. "Go on in," he said quietly. "You left, you right."

Jefferson's two men entered the suite, while Folsom and Jefferson waited a few steps inside the entry, Jefferson in front of Folsom.

"If this is another screw-up, Jerry, I'm going to have your ass," Jefferson said.

Folsom ignored Jefferson. He was getting a bad feeling. Jefferson's two men returned to the sitting area. The smaller of the two said, "Clothes are still in the closet; stuff is in the bathroom."

"Same with the other rooms," the big guy said.

Folsom was beginning to fear for his life. Jefferson was a stone-cold killer, and now he was mad. He took a step backwards, toward the hall, preparing to bolt. But Jefferson must have heard him move, because the fat man turned. Folsom met Jefferson's gaze and was ready to shoot the gangster when Jefferson's eyes bulged and his mouth gaped open. At that same instant, something slammed into Folsom's back, propelling him against Jefferson. His momentum carried him into the room, knocking Jefferson to the floor. Folsom fell on top of him and then rolled off the gangster and looked back through the open door at the lighted hallway. There was no one there.

"Get him!" Jefferson shouted.

"Get who, Boss?" one of his men asked.

"In the hall, you dummy."

But before either of the men reached the entry, an arm briefly showed on the side of the doorway and something was tossed into the room. Two seconds passed and then a tremendous explosion ripped through the space, with bright light illuminating the room for a brief time. Then all was darkness, smoke, and pain.

Folsom knew he was screaming, but he couldn't hear anything. He gained his feet with effort and staggered to the light switch by the door. He flipped the switch on and looked down at the other men in the room. They were in obvious agony, holding their hands over their ears; screaming tormentedly. Folsom knew he looked the same. He'd dropped his pistol somewhere, but didn't bother to try to find it. Hands over his ears, he staggered into the hallway.

He knew he needed to get out of there. The explosion must have roused everyone on this floor and on at least the floors immediately above and below the tenth. He stopped dead in his tracks when Carrie Winter stepped forward from the right side of the hall, the pistol in her hand pointed at Folsom. A movement to the left drew his attention away for a moment.

Carrie Winter shouted something, but all he could make out was, "Brother Edward."

A man, also with a pistol, ran into the suite and collected the dropped weapons.

The woman shouted again, but Folsom couldn't hear her. When he hesitated, she hit him on the forehead with the butt of her pistol and, with her other hand, shoved him backwards. He fell onto the floor before scrambling to a sitting position against a chair.

Jefferson and his men were no longer screaming, but they groaned as though pain permeated every cell of their bodies.


Carrie dug her cell phone out of a back pocket of her jeans and dialed Darren Noury's number.

"Yo," Darren answered.

"Everybody okay?"

"I have Mrs. Folsom in my car. The man and your mom are with Mike in his truck. How's things there?"

"Good. Please take Wendy, Paul, and my mom to her house. Wait for us there. I'm going to call the police. I don't want them anywhere near here when the police arrive."

"Will do," Darren said, and hung up.

Carrie noticed hotel guests were beginning to peek out of their rooms. A couple people were standing in the hall.

"Get back in your rooms and lock your doors," she shouted. "Everything's okay." To the woman peeking out at her from her cracked-open door, she calmly said, "Call the police, please."

"Are you nuts?" the woman yelled as she moved back into her room. "I already did that."

Carrie moved to go back into the room when a rent-a-cop came into view in the hallway. He had a pistol extended in front of him.

"Drop your weapon," he shouted at her, his voice quavering.

"Put that damned thing away before you shoot yourself," she calmly said. "The action's all over. The best thing you can do is go down to the lobby and wait for the police. Show them up here."

To Carrie's surprise, the rent-a-cop didn't argue with her. He said, "Yes, ma'am," and ran back the way he had come.

Carrie entered the room, leaving the door open behind her. She and Edward watched the four men and waited for the police. Sirens could be heard in the distance.

"Carrie, why don't you do something smart?" Folsom shouted, his hearing obviously still impaired.

"Shut up, Folsom!" Edward barked.

"I've got $2 million in bearer bonds down the hall you can have if you let me go. The cops are going to be here any minute now.

Why blow a chance of a lifetime?"

"And what about your friends here?" Carrie asked.

"Fuck them. The cops will be thrilled to finally take down Jefferson."

"You asshole," Jefferson yelled.

"Will you guys shut up?" Edward yelled. "You're making my head hurt."

"Think about it, Carrie. Think what you could do with $2 million."

"Stand up!" Carrie ordered Folsom.

Folsom stood and smiled, as though he'd found an ally.

"Let's go," she told him. "What room?"

"1027."

"Carrie, what are you doing?" Edward said.

"It'll be all right," she told her brother.

Folsom took a step toward the door when a gunshot sounded in the room. He spun around like a top and dropped to the floor on his back. Blood oozed from his right eye.

Edward fired his pistol at Jefferson, hitting the gangster in the chest. Jefferson collapsed on his side and started laughing as Edward wrenched the small pistol from Jefferson's hand.

"You sonofabitch!" Edward growled.

"Shoulda checked me for an ankle rig," Jefferson said. Then the man laughed again and twice gasped for breath. He convulsed and was dead in ten seconds.

Carrie moved to Folsom and felt his pulse. Nothing.

"Crap," she groaned.

Edward moved next to her, all the while watching the other two men. "What were you going to do with Folsom?" he asked, his voice full of accusation.

She gave him an anguished look. "Do you really believe I would have taken his money for myself?"

"I'm sorry, Carrie," Edward said, chastised. "Of course not."

"I was going to take Folsom's cash and then bring him back here. The money was for Wendy. After what's happened with the bank, there may be nothing left for her. There's no way I would ever do a deal with that bastard."

The sirens were now so loud it was obvious the police had arrived outside the hotel.

"Why don't you follow up on your first instinct?" Edward told Carrie in a low voice so Jefferson's men didn't hear him, assuming they were getting their hearing back.

"What do you mean?" Carrie asked in a whisper.

"Get his room key out of his pocket and go find the bonds."

"Great idea, Eddie. But let's change roles. You go get the cash and get out of here."

"No way, Sis."

"Don't play hero with me. You've finally got the bank off your back and Betsy's just given you a son. You don't need this hanging over the company or your family." She knelt down and rummaged through Folsom's pockets until she found his room card key. She handed it to Edward and said, "Remember, it's Room 1027. Give the money to Wendy, assuming you get out of here before the police come up. Go! You wait any longer and the police will impound the cash and Wendy may not get any."

Edward nodded as though he saw the sense in Carrie's suggestion. But he asked, "What if these guys tell the police I was here?"

Carrie chuckled. "These two aren't going to say a word. They're professional hoodlums and probably learned a long time ago that nothing good comes from talking to the authorities. And if they do say something, I'll claim they're lying."

Edward walked to the door, but Carrie stopped him. "Give me that gun. And take that satchel out of the linen storage room, take it to Folsom's room, and leave it there."

"What's in it?"

"Don't ask."

# SATURDAY
# JULY 30, 2011

# CHAPTER EIGHTY-ONE

Having gone through an Army course in Duress Interrogation, Carrie found the interrogation conducted by the Philadelphia Police detectives mild by comparison. By pretending to be upset over the events of the night, the police treated her with kid gloves. The only part of the interview process that was getting to her was having to answer the same questions over and over and over again. She was now on the fourth iteration of the story; all she wanted to do was get to her mother's home and make sure everyone there was okay.

"Tell us what happened, again from the top," Detective Anthony Castiglia said.

Carrie wagged her head as though from frustration. "How many times do I have to go over this with you, Detective? It's 3 in the morning."

"Come on, Ms. Winter. You had two dead men in your hotel room. Don't you think that requires us to be diligent?" Castiglia said.

"Oh, all right. As I said before, my mother, Wendy Folsom, and I decided to stay at the Marriott Hotel as a precaution. After the beating Mrs. Folsom's husband had given her, we felt that moving out of the house made sense. We'd been in the Marriott since last Saturday."

"But you were checking out?" Castiglia asked.

"Yes. I was going to drive Mrs. Folsom down to Cape May this morning and drop her off at our home down there. I was going to come back to my mother's place after dropping off Mrs. Folsom. Now that her husband is dead, I guess there's no need to take her to the shore."

"You mentioned Gerald Folsom beating his wife. Do you have some reason to believe he was planning more violence against his wife?"

Carrie wasn't about to disclose what she knew about an assassin breaking into her mother's place. "Not really," she said. "I mean, I think the man was capable of hiring someone to harm his wife."

"So, you were still there in the room when Folsom and the other men broke in?"

"I was about to pack up our things and leave. My brother drove Mrs. Folsom, Paul Sanders, our family attorney, and my mother to her house. And, to be accurate, the men didn't break in. My brother must have left the door ajar when he left."

"And then what happened?"

"I heard this enormous explosion and saw a flash of light. Thank God I was in the bedroom. I looked into the living room and there were four men rolling around on the floor, screaming. I saw a pistol on the floor next to the man closest to me, so I grabbed it and ran to the front door of the suite to get away. But I tripped on the man nearest to the door, Gerald Folsom. He got to his feet and came after me, and was about to grab me when I heard a gunshot and," she feigned a shudder here, "blood spurted out of his eye. I think one of the other men tried to shoot me and hit him instead. I pointed the pistol I had picked up off the floor at the man who shot Folsom and fired at him.

"I ran into the hall and saw people gathering. I screamed at them to get back into their rooms; one woman said she had called the police. A hotel security guard appeared in the hall and I told him to go downstairs and show the police to my room."

"How do you explain the explosion and the flash of light?" Castiglia asked.

"As you know, Detective, I'm in the Army. I've heard and seen flash bang grenades go off before. I can only assume Folsom or one of the other men brought one along to disable us."

"But they disabled themselves, Ms. Winter."

"Is that a question?" Carrie asked.

Castiglia smiled. "Just wondering if you have an opinion as to what happened."

"Let's say it was a flash bang grenade that went off. Maybe whoever was holding it didn't toss it into the room early enough. Maybe it was old ordnance and was defective. Whatever happened, Detective Castiglia, was to my benefit and not theirs."

"Pretty good shot you made. Do you know anything about the man you killed?"

"Nothing," she lied. "But he was so large, it was pretty hard to miss him."

"You ever been to Pastorius Park?"

Carrie shot the detective a surprised look. "Dozens of times when I was a kid. Why?"

"Recently?"

"I haven't been a kid for years, Detective. Why do you ask?"

"Oh, we had multiple reports of an incident in the park last Sunday. Witnesses reported seeing a tall young woman with short blonde hair assault a very fat black man. Could have been the same guy you shot tonight."

"And?" Carrie said.

"Sounds like it could have been you, Ms. Winter."

"Lots of tall blondes with short hair running around Philadelphia, Detective."

Castiglia nodded. "We also received reports of a Corvette running down another man there. Doesn't your brother drive a Corvette?"

"Lots of Corvettes in Philly, too."

"Yeah, you're probably right." He paused for about ten seconds and then said, "I suppose I should be thanking you for shooting Eli "Toothpick" Jefferson. The guy has been an organized crime fixture around the city for decades."

"Can I ask you a couple questions?" Carrie said.

"Sure."

"What was Folsom doing hanging around an organized crime figure?"

Castiglia hunched his shoulders. "Hopefully, that will come out in our investigation."

"I noticed security cameras in the hall at the hotel. Why didn't the presence of armed men outside our room send up red flags with the hotel security people? And how did Folsom and his men even get past the lobby?"

"Someone tampered with the camera at that end of the hall. Besides, hotel security is not usually highly efficient. As far as Folsom getting past the lobby, he checked into the hotel under a false identity and waltzed right to his room on the tenth floor. The security guard recognized Folsom as the man who checked in under the name Domenico, in Room 1027. When we searched it, we found an overnight bag there along with a leather bag with two pistols, three flash bang grenades, one regular grenade and two serrated Special Forces killing knives. We assume when he left his room, he then went down one of the emergency staircases and let the other men in that way."

'Flash bang grenades?" Carrie asked. "Huh."

"Yeah. Looks like Folsom was the one who brought that grenade to your room."

Carrie shook her head as though to indicate she was surprised by all of this.

"I think you can go now, Ms. Winter," Castiglia said. "But don't leave town without checking with me."

"Detective, I'm only home on leave; I have to report to my unit by August 15."

"What sort of work do you do in the Army?" Castiglia asked.

Carrie stood and laughed. "Nothing very exciting. Administrative work."

# CHAPTER EIGHTY-TWO

One of Castiglia's men drove Carrie back to the Marriott, where she gathered all of the clothing and belongings they'd left there. A bellman loaded the suitcases into Katherine's SUV while Carrie stopped at the front desk and learned Katherine had already covered the bill. Carrie rolled her eyes at no one in particular. So like Mom.

She went to the SUV and drove to her mother's house. Darren and Mike were in their vehicles, parked on the street in front of the house.

Darren got out of his car when Carrie approached him in the SUV and walked over to the driver's side. Rolling down her window, she told him to collect Mike and come inside, but Darren wanted to know if the danger had passed.

"Folsom and Jefferson are dead. Jefferson's two men are in jail. So, it looks as though the threat is gone. Why don't you guys come in and sack out here. We'll talk about everything after we all get some rest."

"Nah," Darren said. "You need to be with family now. Maybe Mike and I can come over later. When I drove Mrs. Folsom and your mom over here, Mrs. Folsom talked about going down to Cape May. She sounded like she wanted to get away from the city. Maybe I can drive her down there; keep an eye on her for a while."

Carrie gave Darren a sideways look and asked, "Just playing Good Samaritan?"

"Something like that," he said, winking.

"Okay, why don't you guys come back at 10? By that time I will have caught four or five hours of sleep and we can sort this all out."

"Sounds like a plan," Darren said. He waved to Mike, got back in his car, and drove away. Mike followed.

When Carrie pulled the SUV into the driveway, she saw Paul's sedan and Edward's Corvette parked there. She used her key to enter the house and found Katherine, Wendy, Edward, and Paul seated in the living room, surrounded by the remnants of coffee and sandwiches on the coffee and end tables. Everyone stood and rushed her when she walked into the room.

"What happened?" Katherine asked. "Where have you been?"

"I had to tell the police my story over and over again. I think they finally believed me."

"Why wouldn't they believe you?" Katherine asked.

Carrie glanced at Edward. He winked at her. "You know the police. They suspect everybody." She turned back to Edward and said, "The police found grenades, guns, and knives in Folsom's hotel room. That stuff seemed to seal the deal as far as the cops are concerned."

Edward smiled.

"I think it's time for sleep," Katherine said.

"Wonderful idea," Paul responded.

"I told Darren and Mike to come back at 10. I think we should ensure our stories all match; I wouldn't want the police to get the wrong idea."

Katherine gave her daughter a cock-eyed look, but Carrie purposefully ignored her. "Let's all meet here at 10."

Edward hugged Carrie, then his mother, and walked out, with Paul following close behind. Carrie was about to go to her bedroom when an errant thought crossed her mind. She hurried outside and stopped Edward before he got into his car.

"Did you give Wendy the bonds?"

Edward slapped the side of his head, making an annoyed grunt. "I kept putting it off because I wanted to give them to her when no one else was around. I figured the fewer people who know about the money, the better. Then I dozed off for a while and forgot all about it."

"We really need to let Wendy know she can make a new life for herself."

"Oh, she'll be able to make a new life for herself, all right," Edward said, looking mischievous.

Carrie found her brother's comment and tone odd, but she was too tired to question him. "Maybe we can meet with her before the others show up. Say 9:30."

"Sounds good."


Edward returned to Katherine's house promptly at 9:30 that morning, lugging Folsom's canvas bag into the house. Carrie was in the kitchen.

"Where's Mom?" he asked, dropping the heavy bag on the floor.

"Paul showed up about an hour ago and took her out to breakfast. Wendy's in her room."

"Let's do this then."

Edward hefted the bag from the floor, following Carrie to Wendy's bedroom. After Carrie knocked, Wendy said, "Come in."

They entered the room and Edward placed the bag at the bottom of the bed.

"We have something for you," Carrie said.

"What is it?" Wendy asked, a child-like birthday smile on her face.

"Your husband—"

Wendy interrupted Carrie, "My former husband."

"Right. Your former husband tried to bribe Eddie and me to let him go, offering us $2 million in bonds. After the shooting last night, Eddie took the bonds. They're in there; we thought you could use it to make a new start. Especially with the Feds tying up all of Folsom's other assets."

Wendy looked shocked. Her mouth hung open until she realized she looked like a hooked fish and she snapped her mouth closed. "Does the Winter family ever stop coming to my assistance?" she cried, tears running from her eyes.

Wendy leapt up, hugging Carrie and then Edward. "$2 million. I wonder what that much money looks like."

"Why don't you open the bag and see?" Edward said, a huge smile on his face.

Wendy moved to the bottom of the bed and pulled the zipper on the bag. She looked first at the contents and then looked back at Carrie and Edward. "That's a lot."

She giggled and dug her hands into the bag, pulling out stacks of hundred dollar bills. She tossed them onto the bed and did the same thing twice more. "This is fun," she said, falling back and laying on the money before bouncing back up.

Carrie looked at Edward, who hunched his shoulders. She was certain Folsom had mentioned bonds, not cash.

Wendy stared back down at the bag and said, "What's this?" She dug deeper inside the bag and extracted a stack of paper.

"Bearer bonds," Edward said. "$50 million worth. Plus jewels and gold coins in the bottom of the bag."

Wendy half-sat, half-collapsed on the bed. Edward looked at Carrie standing in the middle of the room, her mouth open, at a loss for words, and laughed.

"Can I keep this? I mean, is this mine?"

"Folsom was your husband," Edward answered. "I assume you're his only heir. But you should ask Paul for a legal opinion."

# WEDNESDAY
# AUGUST 3, 2011

# EPILOGUE

"So, things are going well, Nick?"

"Yeah, Eddie. Since the managers' meeting last Saturday morning, now that the rumors about our pending demise have stopped, the staff are back to being positive again."

Edward parked the Corvette in Broad Street National Bank's parking lot and waved at Paul Sanders as he pulled in behind him. Edward and Nick waited for Paul to join them.

Paul tapped the file under his arm and said, "No surprises in any of these loan documents the bank sent me. They were good to their word."

"I have to admit," Edward said, "I expected some last minute change. After the way they treated us, I thought they'd drop a surprise bomb."

Paul placed a hand on Edward's back and said, "I understand, but it's a new regime at the bank. I don't know if you heard, but the FDIC brought Sol Levin back to run the bank, and they're in negotiations to reinstate the previous ownership." Paul laughed. "Whatever money Folsom put into the bank has been appropriated by the Feds and placed into the bank's capital account. There's no question now about the bank's stability. Not that the bank's real condition was ever that bad."

"I wonder if we'll ever know how many banks were taken down because of corrupt investors and regulators," Nick said.

"I think it's tempting to take this one instance and use it as the foundation for a nationwide conspiracy theory," Edward said. "But I suspect the truth is there have only been a few cases like Broad Street National Bank. The bigger issue is that the regulators are probably honest, well-intentioned people who have overreacted due to political pressure to clean things up. They start with the premise that all bankers are stupid, greedy bastards, and then act accordingly."

They stopped outside the bank entrance. Edward looked up at the building that had been a fixture of Philadelphia's downtown since the early 1900s. "The shame here is, assuming the bank really needed capital, the government could have put a fraction of the money they used to subsidize Folsom into Broad Street's capital base, taken an ownership piece of the bank, and given the old owners a few years to pay the government back. Essentially, that's what they did for the big banks. Instead, the Feds brought in a vulture investor and wiped out the stockholders, many of whom did nothing more than invest in a bank that had served them and their community for years."

"That's the Feds for you," Paul said. "Save the big boys and screw the little guys."

Once inside, Edward led the familiar way to the executive

offices on the mezzanine level. Sanford Cunningham met them at the elevator and took them to a conference room. After they were seated, Edward asked, "Who's our account officer going to be now that Stan Burns is gone?"

"I'm your primary contact, but Francis McNamara, one of our senior commercial lenders, will back me up."

"By the way, whatever happened with Stan Burns?" Nick asked.

"I just heard he was offered a job as President of a bank in West Chester. Apparently, the FDIC recommended him." Cunningham's face went red and he looked ashamed. "Stan did the right thing; I didn't. He deserves whatever good comes his way."

"Well anyway, let's sign the papers," Paul said.

Cunningham looked confused. "I was surprised you all showed up here for your appointment. I—"

"What are you talking about?" Paul blurted, suddenly angry. "What are you trying to pull?"

Cunningham raised his hands in defense. "No, no, you misunderstand. I just assumed when the wire paid off the balance on your loan, you had taken your business elsewhere."

"What wire?" Edward barked.

"We received a wire at 11 this morning for just over $20.3 million, covering principal and accrued interest."

Edward looked at Nick. "You know something about this?" he asked, but he could tell from the confused expression on Nick's face that they were both equally confused.

"There was no payer name on the wire and the only identification on it was that it came from a bank in Zurich. The instructions were to apply the amount to the Winter Enterprises loan balance at Broad Street National Bank."

Cunningham looked from Edward to Paul to Nick, and then back to Edward. "I don't understand. You didn't know about this?"

Edward was stunned. He just shook his head in response to Cunningham's question; no words would come out.

"Even though the loan is zero-balanced now, the bank would still like to do business with you and Winter Enterprises," Cunningham said. "I assume you'll want to continue to grow the company. We would like to finance that growth."

"You'll need to discuss that with Mr. Scarfatti," Edward said.

Nick said, "I saw that the loan papers you sent us to review included a $30 million line of credit secured by all of our real estate; that is more than enough to finance our growth for ten years. But now that our loan balance is zero, I see no point in tying up all our real estate here at Broad Street National Bank. You'll remember, when things were . . . up in the air over the last few weeks, that we talked with Ernest Deakyne at Philadelphia Savings & Trust. He offered us an $11 million credit facility."

Nick paused. Edward watched Cunningham go pale and swallow nervously.

"Here's what I propose," Nick continued. "We'll accept an $11 million credit line from you and will secure it with half of the new restaurant locations we're financing at a sixty percent loan to value ratio. We'll commit to put at least forty percent equity in all our new locations. We'll establish an identical $11 million facility with Philadelphia Bank & Trust on the same terms. And we'll split our deposit business equally between the two banks."

"That seems reasonable," Cunningham said, although he didn't look happy about sharing business with another lender.

"There's something else," Nick said. "I want a twenty-year

amortization and maturity on the loan. The bank can adjust the interest rate every five years at prime rate, but the bank can't call the loan before twenty years."

"Twenty years?" Cunningham said. "That's really not bank policy. I'll have to talk to the senior loan committee."

"You do that, Mr. Cunningham. I'd like an answer by Friday, so we know how to proceed. We're a fast-growing company and we don't want to miss out on opportunities while the bank dallies."

Nick nodded at Edward. "I think we've finished here," he said.

Edward and Nick stood, but Paul remained seated. They looked at Paul and Edward asked, "Was there something else?"

"I think it would be a great idea, Mr. Cunningham," Paul said, "if the bank released the hold on Winter Enterprises' bank account. As the company no longer owes you anything, maintaining a hold on its account is not only a bad faith action but a breach of the loan agreement."

Cunningham went beet red. "I'm terribly sorry; I completely forgot about that." He picked up the telephone receiver, hastily punched in a number, and ordered someone on the other end to remove the hold on the company's account.

Paul then stood, thanked Cunningham, and said, "That should do it for now."

Once outside the bank, Edward started chuckling. By the time they reached their vehicles, all three men were laughing uproariously.

"That was mean, but it felt so damned good," Nick said. "That sonofabitch took five years off my life in these past three weeks. He deserved that."

Edward put on a stern look and said, "All you Mediterranean

types care about is revenge. I'm laughing because I've never felt so relieved in my life."

"So there was no feeling of payback in there for you? None at all?" Nick asked.

Edward kept the stern look on his face as long as he could, but cracked and began laughing again. He held up his hand, his thumb and index finger almost touching. "Oh, maybe just a little." A few peaceful moments passed. "When are you going to meet with Ernest Deakyne?" Edward asked. "That guy was the only one who stepped up to help us when we felt the end was near."

Nick smiled. "I've got an appointment with him first thing in the morning."

Edward thanked Paul and walked toward his car with Nick. But Paul called out to him and asked, "Can I have a minute?"

"Of course," Edward answered. He tossed his car keys over to Nick and said, "I'll be right with you. What's up?"

"I'm having dinner with your mother tonight. I wanted you to know I'm planning on spending as much time with her as she will allow. If that's a problem for you, I will resign from being your lawyer because as much as I value your business and our friendship, I value my relationship with your mother even more."

Edward was a bit surprised at Paul's frankness. He thought for a second about how to respond, and finally said, "I couldn't think of anyone I would rather see my mother with than you, Paul. You've been a stalwart friend and counselor to all of us for a long time. You and Mom deserve one another, and happiness."

Wendy drove across the Swiss border into Italy and marveled at the green expanse of valley that extended southward from the mountain pass. She sighed contentedly, as though she didn't have a care in the world. Switzerland had been interesting, but the people were too reserved for her taste. Besides, she'd always wanted to see Florence and Rome.

She looked down at her cell phone resting on the passenger seat and thought momentarily about calling Darren Noury. She'd liked the man; he was kind and considerate, and made her feel safe. But she wasn't ready for a relationship right now.

She brushed a stray tear away when she thought about how long it had been since a man had done something compassionate or affectionate—before all this happened.

Wendy recalled her last conversation with Darren before he dropped her off at the Philadelphia Airport. "What would you do if you had all the money in the world?" she'd asked.

He thought about that for a minute before answering, "The same thing I do now. I like to work, and I like the adrenaline rush I get from security. Plus, it feels good making people feel safe." He laughed and added, "Besides I need to work, since I don't have 'all the money in the world.' I don't even have a miniscule percentage of all the money in the world."

"Thank you, Darren," Wendy said abruptly.

"For what?"

"For making *me* feel safe."

"You know, this isn't a job to me, Wendy," he'd said.


Carrie Winter had used up less than a week of her one-month leave, but she made a calculated decision to report early to her new assignment at the Pentagon. Philadelphia Police Detective Castiglia had told her he would like her to come in to Police Headquarters to answer some questions. She knew the guy was on a fishing expedition because he was suspicious about some of the reports he'd received about a blonde woman in Pastorius Park, and about her role in Folsom's death. She was half-tempted to match wits with Castiglia but, in the end, decided that was a no-win tactic. Besides, Eddie and Betsy were busy with their newborn son and the New York franchise, and Mom was busy with Paul. She had begun to feel like a fifth wheel. Her assignment to the Pentagon would be for two years. There would always be weekends with the family in Cape May, once the heat from Castiglia subsided.

Carrie hugged her mother and, before saying goodbye, asked her to do her a favor: "If the Philadelphia police ask you for a contact number for me, just tell them I went back to Afghanistan. Tell them to call information for Helmand Province."

In response to her mother's confused look, she hugged Katherine again.

"How would you like me to make dinner tomorrow night at my place?" Katherine asked, smiling at Paul across the small restaurant table.

"Isn't that a bit forward coming from a woman of your generation and gentility?" Paul teased.

"The last time I calculated the years that passed since Frank died, I came up with twenty-two. That's twenty-two years of you being a friend and supporter who I've taken for granted and, most of the time, ignored. You want gentile and reserved for another twenty-two years, or do you want aggressive?"

Paul rubbed his chin as though considering his options.

Katherine feigned anger and said, "Okay, forget it; I'll find someone who wants to spend time with me."

Paul shot her a Cheshire cat grin and said, "That sounds aggressive, all right."

"I guess it did. Is that too aggressive for you?"

"Damn," he said. "I always wanted to be dominated by a woman. But I want you to pretend I'm in charge every once in a while. Like maybe Mondays and Thursdays."

"As long as it's not more than two days a week." She smiled and added, "Remember what Dorothy Sayers said: 'Time and trouble will tame an advanced young woman. But an advanced old woman is uncontrollable by any force.' "

She placed her hand softly on his and said, "I think we need to order another bottle of wine."

"A woman drove me to drink, and I never had the courtesy to thank her."

Katherine smiled. "Now you're quoting W. C. Fields?"

"I always fall back on W. C. Fields when I run out of other material."

"I think I won that round," she said.

# ABOUT THE AUTHOR

Joseph Badal's thirty-eight years in the banking and financial services industries provide a solid foundation for the storyline in "Shell Game," a thriller that uses the financial meltdown that began in 2007 as a backdrop for murder, greed, corruption, and mayhem. His roles as a financial consultant and as a senior executive in banking and mortgage organizations give him unusual insight into the capital markets meltdown that continues to impact economies and markets to this day.

Prior to his finance career, Joe served as an officer in the U.S. Army in critical, highly classified positions in the U.S. and overseas, including tours of duty in Greece and Vietnam. He earned numerous military decorations.

Joe's first suspense novel, "The Pythagorean Solution," was released in April, 2003. His next release, "Terror Cell" (#2 in the Bob Danforth series), was published in July 2004. The paperback version of "The Pythagorean Solution" was released in 2005. His books "The Nostradamus Secret" (#3 in the Bob Danforth series) and "Evil Deeds" (#1 in the Bob Danforth series) were released in 2011. All of his books are available in paper and digital formats.

He was recognized in 2011 as "One of The 50 Best Writers You Should Be Reading." His short story *Fire & Ice* will be included in the anthology Uncommon Assassins," which will be released in Fall 2012.

To learn more, visit Joe's website at www.josephbadalbooks.com. You can see Joe's blog at http://www.josephbadal.wordpress.com.

Made in the USA
San Bernardino, CA
03 April 2015